PENGUIN  CLASSICS

THE KREUTZER SONATA
AND OTHER STORIES

COUNT LEO TOLSTOY was born in 1828 at Yasnaya Polyana in central Russia, and educated privately. He studied Oriental languages and law (unsuccessfully) at the University of Kazan, then led a life of dissipation until 1851, when he joined an artillery regiment in the Caucasus. He took part in the Crimean War, and on the basis of this experience wrote *Sevastopol Stories* (1855–6), which confirmed his tenuous reputation as a writer. After a period in St Petersburg and abroad, where he studied educational methods for use in his school for peasant children at Yasnaya Polyana, he married Sofya (Sonya) Behrs in 1862. The next fifteen years was a period of great happiness. The couple had thirteen children; Tolstoy managed his estates, one in the Volga steppeland, continued his educational projects, cared for his peasants and wrote *War and Peace* (1869) and *Anna Karenina* (1877). *A Confession* (1879–81) marked a spiritual crisis in his life; he became an extreme moralist and in a series of pamphlets after 1880 expressed his rejection of state and church, indictment of the weaknesses of the flesh and denunciation of private property. His last novel, *Resurrection* (1899), was written to earn money for the pacifist Dukhobor sect. His teaching earned him many followers at home and abroad, but also much opposition, and in 1901 he was excommunicated by the Russian Orthodox Church. He died in 1910, in the course of a dramatic flight from home, at the small railway station of Astapovo.

DONNA TUSSING ORWIN, who teaches Russian Literature at the University of Toronto, was editor of *Tolstoy Studies Journal* from 1997 to 2004, and is now President of the North American Tolstoy Society. She is the author of *Tolstoy's Art and Thought, 1847–1880* (Cambridge University Press, 1993; in Russian by Akademicheskii Proekt, St Petersburg, 2006) and *Consequences of Consciousness: Turgenev, Dostoevsky, and Tolstoy* (Stanford University Press, 2007). She is also editor of *The Cambridge Companion to Tolstoy* (2002) and is currently editing a collection of newly commissioned essays about Tolstoy to be published in Russia in 2010 by the Russian Academy of Sciences.

DAVID MCDUFF was born in 1945 and was educated at the University of Edinburgh. His publications comprise a large number of translations of foreign verse and prose, including twentieth-century Russian and Scandinavian work. He has translated a number of nineteenth-century Russian prose works for the Penguin Classics series. These include Dostoyevsky's *The Brothers Karamazov*, *The House of the Dead*, *Poor Folk and Other Stories* and *The Idiot* (2004), Tolstoy's *The Cossacks*, and Nikolay Leskov's *Lady Macbeth of Mtsensk*. He has also translated Babel's *Collected Stories* and Bely's *Petersburg* for Penguin.

PAUL FOOTE was, until his retirement, a University Lecturer in Russian and Fellow of The Queen's College, Oxford. His publications include translations of Lermontov's *A Hero of Our Time* (Penguin Classics) and Saltykov-Shchedrin's *The History of a Town* and *The Golovlevs*.

LEO TOLSTOY

The Kreutzer Sonata and Other Stories

Translated with notes by
DAVID MCDUFF *and* PAUL FOOTE
With an introduction by DONNA TUSSING ORWIN

PENGUIN BOOKS

PENGUIN CLASSICS

Published by the Penguin Group
Penguin Books Ltd, 80 Strand, London WC2R 0RL, England
Penguin Group (USA) Inc., 375 Hudson Street, New York, New York 10014, USA
Penguin Group (Canada), 90 Eglinton Avenue East, Suite 700, Toronto, Ontario, Canada M4P 2Y3
(a division of Pearson Penguin Canada Inc.)
Penguin Ireland, 25 St Stephen's Green, Dublin 2, Ireland
(a division of Penguin Books Ltd)
Penguin Group (Australia), 250 Camberwell Road, Camberwell, Victoria 3124, Australia
(a division of Pearson Australia Group Pty Ltd)
Penguin Books India Pvt Ltd, 11 Community Centre, Panchsheel Park, New Delhi – 110 017, India
Penguin Group (NZ), 67 Apollo Drive, Rosedale, North Shore 0632, New Zealand
(a division of Pearson New Zealand Ltd)
Penguin Books (South Africa) (Pty) Ltd, 24 Sturdee Avenue, Rosebank, Johannesburg 2196, South Africa

Penguin Books Ltd, Registered Offices: 80 Strand, London WC2R 0RL, England

www.penguin.com

This collection first published in Penguin Classics 2008

007

Introduction and Further Reading copyright © Donna Orwin, 2008
Family Happiness new translation and notes copyright © David McDuff, 2008
The Kreutzer Sonata and The Devil translation and notes copyright © David McDuff, 1983
Father Sergius translated by Paul Foote, previously published 1977
Father Sergius translation and notes copyright © Penguin Books, 1977, 2008
All rights reserved

The moral right of the translators and introducer has been asserted

Set in 10.25/12.25 pt PostScript Adobe Sabon
Typeset by Rowland Phototypesetting Ltd, Bury St Edmunds, Suffolk
Printed in England by Clays Ltd, St Ives plc

ISBN: 978-0-140-44960-0

www.greenpenguin.co.uk

Contents

Contents

Chronology

1724 Pyotr Tolstoy (great-great-great grandfather) given hereditary title of Count by Tsar Peter the Great

1821 Death of Prince Nikolay Volkonsky, Tolstoy's grandfather, at Yasnaya Polyana, Tula Province, 130 miles southwest of Moscow

1822 Marriage of Count Nikolay Tolstoy and Princess Marya Volkonskaya

1828 28 August (Old Style). Birth of fourth son, Leo Nikolayevich Tolstoy, at Yasnaya Polyana

1830 Death of mother

1832 The eldest, Nikolay, informs his brothers that the secret of earthly happiness is inscribed on a green stick, buried at Yasnaya Polyana (Tolstoy later buried there)

1836 Nikolay Gogol's *The Government Inspector*

1837 Death of Alexandr Pushkin in duel
    Death of father

1840 Mikhail Lermontov's *A Hero of Our Time*

1841 Death of Lermontov in duel
    Death of first guardian Alexandra Osten-Saken, an aunt. The Tolstoy children move to Kazan to live with another aunt, Pelageya Yushkova

1842 Gogol's *Dead Souls*

1844 Enters Kazan University, reads Oriental languages

1845 Transfers to Law after failing examinations. Dissolute lifestyle: drinking, visits to prostitutes

1846 Fyodor Dostoyevsky's 'Poor Folk'

1847 Inherits estate of Yasnaya Polyana. Recovering from gonorrhoea, draws up scheme for self-perfection. Leaves

university without completing studies 'on grounds of ill
health and domestic circumstances'

1848–50 In Moscow and St Petersburg, debauchery and
gambling, large debts. Studies music

1850 Ivan Turgenev's *A Month in the Country*

1851 Travels to the Caucasus with Nikolay, who is serving in
the army there. Reads Laurence Sterne: starts translating his
Sentimental Journey (not completed). Writes 'A History of
Yesterday' (unfinished, first evidence of his powers of psycho-
logical analysis). Begins writing *Childhood*

1852 Death of Gogol. Turgenev's *Sketches from a Hunter's
Album*

Enters the army as a cadet (*Junker*); based mainly in the
Cossack station of Starogladkovskaya. Sees action against
the Chechens, and narrowly escapes capture
Childhood

1853 Turkey declares war on Russia
'The Raid'

1854 France and England declare war on Russia. Crimean War
starts

Commissioned, serves on Danube front. November: transferred at own request to Sevastopol, then under siege by
allied forces
Boyhood

1855 Death of Nicholas I; accession of Alexander II

In action until the fall of Sevastopol in August. Gains
celebrity with 'Sevastopol in December' and further sketches,
'Sevastopol in May', 'Sevastopol in August 1855' (1856),
'Memoirs of a Billiard Marker', 'The Woodfelling'

1856 Peace signed between Russia, Turkey, France and England
Turgenev's *Rudin*

In St Petersburg, moves in literary circles; associates with
Turgenev, Ivan Goncharov, Nikolay Nekrasov, Afanasy Fet
and others. Leaves the army. Death of brother Dmitry
'The Snowstorm', 'Two Hussars', 'A Landowner's Morning'

1857 February–August. First trip abroad, to Paris (lasting
impression of witnessing an execution by guillotine), Geneva
and Baden-Baden

Youth, 'Lucerne'

1858 Long-term relationship with peasant woman on estate, Aksinya Bazykina, begins
'Albert'

1859 Goncharov's Oblomov; Turgenev's The Home of the Gentry
Founds primary school at Yasnaya Polyana
'Three Deaths', Family Happiness

1860 Death of his brother Nikolay from tuberculosis
Dostoyevsky's Notes from the House of the Dead (1860–61). Turgenev's On the Eve

1860–61 Emancipation of serfs (1861). Other reforms follow: Elective District Councils (zemstvos) set up (1864); judicial reform (1865). Formation of revolutionary Land and Liberty movement. Commencement of intensive industrialization; spread of railways
Serves as Arbiter of the Peace, dealing with post-Emancipation land settlements. Quarrels with Turgenev and challenges him (no duel). Travels in France, Germany, Italy and England. Loses great deal of money through gambling. Meets Proudhon in Brussels

1862 Turgenev's Fathers and Sons
Starts a magazine at Yasnaya Polyana on education for the peasants; abandoned after less than a year. Police raid on Yasnaya Polyana. Considers emigrating to England and writes protest to the Tsar. Marries Sofya Andreyevna Behrs (b. 1844)

1863 Polish rebellion
Birth of first child, Sergey (Tolstoy and his wife were to have thirteen children – nine boys and four girls – of whom five died in childhood). Begins work on a novel 'The Decembrists', which was later abandoned, but developed into War and Peace
'Polikushka', The Cossacks

1865 Nikolay Leskov's 'Lady Macbeth of Mtsensk'
First part of War and Peace (titled 1805)

1866 Attempted assassination of Tsar Alexander II
Dostoyevsky's Crime and Punishment

1867 Turgenev's *Smoke*

Visits Borodino in search of material for battle scene in *War and Peace*

1868 Dostoyevsky's *The Idiot*

1869 Publication of *War and Peace* completed

1870–71 Franco-Prussian War. Municipal Government reform Dostoyevsky's *Devils*

Studies ancient Greek. Illness; convalesces in Samara (Bashkiriya). Begins work on primer for children. First mention of *Anna Karenina*. Reads Arthur Schopenhauer and other philosophers. Starts work on novel about Peter the Great (later abandoned)

1872 'God Sees the Truth But Waits', 'A Prisoner of the Caucasus'

1873 Begins *Anna Karenina*. Raises funds during famine in Bashkiriya, where he has bought an estate. Growing obsession with problems of death and religion; temptation to commit suicide

1874 Much occupied with educational theory

1875 Beginning of active revolutionary movement

1875–7 Instalments of *Anna Karenina* published

1877 Turgenev's *Virgin Soil*

Journal publication of *Anna Karenina* completed (published in book form in 1878)

1877–8 Russo-Turkish War

1878 Reconciliation with Turgenev, who visits him at Yasnaya Polyana. Works on 'The Decembrists' and again abandons it. Works on *Confession* (completed 1882, but banned by the religious censor and published in Geneva in 1884)

1879 Dostoyevsky's *The Brothers Karamazov*

1880 Works on *A Critique of Dogmatic Theology*

1881 Assassination of Tsar Alexander II. With accession of Alexander III, the government returns to reactionary policies Death of Dostoyevsky

Writes to Tsar Alexander III asking him to pardon his father's assassins

1882 Student riots in St Petersburg and Kazan Universities. Jewish pogroms and repressive measures against minorities

Religious works, including new translation of the Gospels. Begins 'The Death of Ivan Ilyich' and *What Then Must We Do?*. Studies Hebrew

1883 Deathbed letter from Turgenev urging Tolstoy not to abandon his art

1884 Family relations strained, first attempt to leave home. 'What I Believe' banned.
   Collected works published by his wife

1885 Tension with his wife over new beliefs. Works closely with Vladimir Chertkov, with whom (and others) he founds a publishing house, The Intermediary, to produce edifying literature for the common folk. Many popular stories written 1885–6, including 'What Men Live By', 'Where Love Is, God Is', 'Strider'

1886 Walks from Moscow to Yasnaya Polyana in five days.
   Works on land during the summer. Denounced as a heretic by Archbishop of Kherson
   'The Death of Ivan Ilyich', 'How Much Land Does a Man Need?', *What Then Must We Do?*

1887 Meets Leskov
   'On Life'

1888 Chekhov's *The Steppe*
   Renounces meat, alcohol and tobacco. Growing friction between his wife and Chertkov. *The Power of Darkness*, banned in 1886, performed in Paris

1889 Finishes 'Kreutzer Sonata'. Begins *Resurrection* (works on it for ten years)

1890 'Kreutzer Sonata' banned, though on appeal by his wife to the Tsar publication was permitted in Collected Works

1891 Convinced that personal profits from writing are immoral, renounces copyright on all works published after 1881 and all future works. His family thus suffers financially, though his wife retains copyright in all the earlier works. Helps to organize famine relief in Ryazah Province. Attacks smoking and alcohol in 'Why Do Men Stupefy Themselves?'

1892 Organizes famine relief: *The Fruits of Enlightenment* (published 1891) produced in Maly Theatre, Moscow

1893 Finishes 'The Kingdom of God Is Within You'

1894 Accession of Tsar Nicholas II. Strikes in St Petersburg
   Writes preface to Maupassant collection of stories. Criticizes *Crime and Punishment*
1895 Meets Chekhov. *The Power of Darkness* produced in Maly Theatre, Moscow
   'Master and Man'
1896 Chekhov's *The Seagull*
   Sees production of *Hamlet* and *King Lear* at Hermitage Theatre, severely critical of Shakespeare
1897 Appeals to authorities on behalf of Dukhobors, a pacifist religious sect, to whom permission is granted to emigrate to Canada
   What is Art?
1898 Formation of Social Democratic Party. Dreyfus Affair in France
   Works for famine relief
1899 Widespread student riots
   Serial publication of *Resurrection* (in book form in 1900)
1900 Meets Maxim Gorky, whom he calls a 'real man of the people'
1901 Foundation of Socialist Revolutionary Party
   Excommunicated from Orthodox Church for writing works 'repugnant to Christ and the Church'. Seriously ill, convalesces in Crimea; visitors include Chekhov and Gorky
1902 Finishes 'What is Religion?'. Writes to Tsar Nicholas II on evils of autocracy and ownership of property
1903 Protests against Jewish pogroms in Kishinev
   'After the Ball'
1904 Russo-Japanese War. Russian fleet destroyed in Tsushima Straits. Assassination of V. K. Plehve, Minister of the Interior
   Death of Chekhov
   Death of second-eldest brother Sergey. Pamphlet on Russo-Japanese war published in England
   'Shakespeare and the Drama'
1905 Attempted revolution in Russia (attacks all sides involved). *Potemkin* mutiny. S. Yu. Witte becomes Prime Minister
   Anarchical publicist pamphlets
   Introduction to Chekhov's 'Darling'

1908 Tolstoy's secretary N. N. Gusev exiled
   'I Cannot Be Silent', a protest against capital punishment
1909 Increased animosity between his wife and Chertkov, she
   threatens suicide
1910 Corresponds with Mahatma Gandhi concerning the doctrine of non-violent resistance to evil. His wife threatens
   suicide; demands all Tolstoy's diaries for past ten years, but
   Tolstoy puts them in bank vault. Final breakdown of relationship with her. 28 October: leaves home. 7 November:
   dies at Astapovo railway station. Buried at Yasnaya Polyana
1911 'The Devil', 'Father Sergius', *Hadji Murat*, 'The Forged
   Coupon'

Introduction

*New readers are advised that this Introduction makes
details of the plots explicit*

Marriage has many pains, but celibacy has no pleasures.

Samuel Johnson

The four stories in this volume are all about love, but they take
such different attitudes towards it that it is hard at first to
believe they were written by the same person. Their author,
Count Leo Tolstoy, wanted to believe when he was young that
people could be both sexually virtuous and happy. Virtuous
happiness meant marriage and fidelity for him, and in *Family
Happiness* (1859), his first love story, he attempts to domesti-
cate sexuality. In his later life, when he was writing the other
three stories in the volume – *The Devil, The Kreutzer Sonata*
and *Father Sergius* – he no longer believed this to be possible.

At the time he wrote *Family Happiness* Tolstoy had limited
experience of family life: he had lost his mother before he
was two, and his father at eight, after which he and his four
siblings were raised mostly together by benevolent relatives.
He did not yet have a wife and children of his own, leaving
him free to dream up a perfect family life without memories
or experience to contradict it. *Family Happiness* was a dress
rehearsal for courtships depicted in the great novels *War and
Peace* (1865-9) and *Anna Karenina* (1875-8). He wrote both
of these during the first twenty, happy years of his marriage to
Sofya Andreyevna Behrs. Tolstoy's most detailed sympathetic
description of marriage itself, as opposed to courtship, is in
Anna Karenina, which also describes both open infidelity and
married bliss and many states in between. In this novel, Kitty
and Konstantin Levin get to have their wedding cake and eat it

too, but Anna is not so lucky. She has to choose either love or virtue, and pays the price for her choice.

After *Anna Karenina* Tolstoy mentioned happy marriages from time to time, but never again made one a major subject in his fiction. In the 1880s, he and his wife began to quarrel seriously about the radical simplification of their lives that Tolstoy believed necessary for moral reasons. Although Tolstoy was a titled member of the landed gentry, he wanted the family to live like the peasants around them who, as he saw it, so unjustly supported their idleness and luxury. By now the mother of a large family, Sofya Andreyevna defended its interests against her husband's utopian dreams. There was another, related source of tension as well, one which resonates ironically with *Family Happiness*. Early in the 1880s, the Tolstoy family began to winter in Moscow for the sake of the older children. For the first time, Sofya Andreyevna was able to lead the society life of which she had been deprived when her husband had brought her, in 1862, as an eighteen-year-old bride to his country estate, Yasnaya Polyana. Tolstoy was very dependent on his wife, and disliked the socializing that took her away from her role as wife, mother and, not incidentally, his helpmate. Like Sofya Andreyevna, moreover, he suffered from extreme jealousy.[1] These tensions and Sofya Andreyevna's resolute opposition to Tolstoy's preferred way of life undermined his earlier hope of happiness and virtue within marriage. The three late stories in this volume – written around the same time (1886–91) – are all connected to one another, and to this struggle: they are modern morality tales intended to shock with their brutal realism about sex.

Tolstoy's definition of love, once formed, did not change substantially over his lifetime. As is typical of him, even as he was debunking clichés about love in his early writings he was replacing them with a new, complex definition crafted out of personal experience and his reading of the few but great writers who were his primary mentors on this and many other subjects in his youth. These included his Russian predecessors Alexandr Pushkin and Mikhail Lermontov, as well as Jean-Jacques Rousseau (*Emile* and *Julie, ou La Nouvelle Héloise*), Laurence

Sterne (*A Sentimental Journey Through France and Italy*), Johann Wolfgang von Goethe (*The Sorrows of Young Werther*) and Plato (the *Symposium*). Like Sergey in *Family Happiness*, Tolstoy loved women but wanted to manage their extraordinary power over him. He was ashamed of his own sensuality and feared the loss of self that occurred in sex. At the same time, he craved an intimacy so complete that two selves might dissolve into one, and he found a model for this in the idea of eros expounded in the *Symposium*. As a social critic and moralist, Tolstoy also understood from his own case that sexual desire, as the most potent passion, had to be restrained if the needs of the individual were to be subordinated to those of society. As long as he thought this was possible, he was one of the great poets of love and married life. When he ceased to believe that sexual love could be tamed enough to make it serve virtue, he turned against sex and even marriage itself.

It is clear from diaries and letters as well as fiction that Tolstoy believed that the psyche contained several 'voices'. Among these were the body, the mind, the conscience and the will, which may speak for any of the other three. In his opinion, what we call love was a product of those several voices, and at times he simply broke it down into its constituent parts. On 19 October 1852, for instance, he declared in his diary that 'there is no such thing as love. Instead there is the physical desire for intercourse and the demand of reason for a life partner.'[2] When separate, physical desire corresponds to lust and the rational demand for a partner to friendship–love, which Tolstoy later associated with Christian *agape*.[3] But when he depicted it in fiction, Tolstoy almost never defined love out of existence by simply equating it with one of its parts. For better or for worse, for the major characters in his stories it usually involves *both* body and mind, and perhaps the conscience as well. What he could not decide upon was the relation between body and mind, between lust and *agape*, whether one should be sacrificed for the other, whether this was even possible, or whether there was some way that the two might work together harmoniously. This last alternative was the most desirable, and, starting with *Family Happiness*, Tolstoy tried to depict it.

The story has autobiographical roots. In 1856 the twenty-eight-year-old Tolstoy began a brief courtship of Valeriya Arsenieva, who was seventeen. We know about the relationship from correspondence in which Tolstoy preaches to her about everything from her dress to her vocation as a woman. In the story, Tolstoy debunks romantic stereotypes, replacing them with the virtuous love that he advocates in his letters to Arsenieva. The story also offers a polemic response by the young writer to the love stories of his rival and more famous contemporary Ivan Turgenev. These never describe married life in any detail, and Tolstoy now claimed this subject for himself. *Family Happiness* went unnoticed by the literary critics, and Tolstoy himself turned against it so quickly that he tried to prevent the publication of its second part. Yet just three years after its publication, in 1862, contemporary critic Apollon Grigoriev recognized Tolstoy's subtle handling of its subject matter and praised it as a forgotten gem, which successfully depicted 'the transition from the feeling of passion into another feeling'.[4]

Family Happiness is partly an idyll of a love animated but not corrupted by sensuality, and partly the tale of its inevitable unravelling. In the love affair between Sergey and Masha, sexual desire is sublimated so as to serve the higher aims of eros. As lovers, each character wants to give himself or herself entirely to the other, and each fears to do so. Sergey appears first as Masha's guardian and a friend to her late father. He struggles to maintain that role, but he is the first to fall in love, and she is seduced by her power over him. Over the summer Sergey visits frequently and treats her as a 'young and favoured companion', so that friendship comes *before* sex. At this stage though, Masha still feels that he has not admitted her to his 'entire alien world', and this tantalizes her. She knows that he loves her – in what way she is not yet sure – but she wants to please him so she pretends to be better than she is, and while practising this pretence she *becomes* better. In the process she studies him so closely that she is finally able to anticipate his moral advice. For Tolstoy, this is a crucial moment of bonding for both man and woman, because Sergey, like Rousseau's Emile, has projected his moral self into the beloved woman, who now can act out the impulses of this self better than he can. In this Rousseau-inspired version of Platonic eros as described in the *Symposium*, love makes two incomplete souls whole and one.

The moral lesson that Masha absorbs during the courtship – crucial for the merger of virtue and happiness – is that one should live for others. While in love, one painlessly and spontaneously gives oneself to another. This state of soul will not last, but through the memory of it it will have an enduring influence on the psyche. Meanwhile, the peak of 'wild delight' (*dikii vostorg*), Tolstoy's code for sexual energy, precedes actual consummation, and is unselfconscious, at least for Masha. The two lovers, Sergey as well as Masha, are repeatedly compared to children at this stage in the courtship, the 'wildness' of eros having been thoroughly tamed in the ideal romance that Tolstoy is constructing.

Masha stands at the apex of her power in the episode in the walled garden. When Sergey goes to get the cherries, she clandestinely follows him and hears his murmured endearments. Angry that she has breached his last defences, Sergey attacks the very notion of romantic love in a rearguard and unsuccessful attempt to re-establish distance between himself and Masha, who recognizes that he continues to love her.

Later, when Masha aggressively pushes Sergey towards a declaration of love, he hides behind narrative – the story of A. and B. – but Masha breaks out of the storyline to declare her love for him. Even once they are engaged, the couple are ambivalent about giving themselves up completely to their feelings for one another: Sergey seems afraid 'to give in to the enormous, harmful tenderness that was in him', and Masha has similar misgivings. At one point, Sergey looks at her with his 'attentive, magnetic gaze'.

I made no reply and *involuntarily* looked into his eyes. Suddenly something strange happened to me: first I stopped seeing what was around me, then his face disappeared before me, and only his eyes shone, it seemed, facing my own, then it seemed to me that these eyes were inside me; everything grew dark, I could see

nothing and had to screw up my eyes in order to tear myself
away from *the sense of pleasure and fear* which that gaze was
producing in me ... [emphasis mine].

The subsequent night walk in the garden, with its magical
contrasts of light and shade, is emblematic of their romantic
love as both pleasurable and frightening. Tolstoy's lovers wish
for this perfect union, but they also want to preserve their
individuality, and this tension persists even beyond their marriage. The wedding day coincides with the first frost, and the
bride feels fear rather than passion as Sergey hands her into his
carriage at the end of Part One of the story. Part Two begins
with the two-month honeymoon, a decline from the heights of
happiness before the wedding as Tolstoy charts the transition
away from romantic love. The pre-marital merger of self-
sacrifice, duty and erotic love gives way now to 'merely a selfish
feeling of love for each other, a desire to be loved, a constant
gaiety that had no apparent cause, and a forgetting of everything in the world'.

The rest of the story illustrates the fact that being in love
cannot survive habituation and must yield to other feelings.
Having won Sergey, Masha begins to feel enslaved by him
because they are too close. Realizing that she is bored, Sergey
takes her to Petersburg, where she sets out to conquer society.
In a series of subtly described moments, she pushes Sergey away
until he closes the door to his heart, never again fully to open
it to her. As this happens, Sergey begins to parody the language
of love: he speaks bitterly of Masha's 'sacrifice' in giving up the
Prince's praise to go home to the country with her husband,
and, most cruel for Masha, he uses the term 'family happiness'
ironically.[5]

In *Family Happiness* lust is tamed by friendship so that the
two co-exist at least temporarily, and furthermore sexual desire
encourages self-sacrifice, at least during the courtship. (True,
Masha's attraction to the sexy Marquis suggests something
lacking in her relationship with her husband, and only coinci-
dence – the summons from her friend – saves her from disaster.)
The 'family happiness' that the couple supposedly achieve at

the end of the story seems too rational to be a satisfying substitution for the romantic love that precedes it, and therefore the title retains an ambiguity that its author surely did not intend. This is especially true because Tolstoy did not yet fully understand the powerful and even erotic bond between mother and child that could keep a woman interested in family life, and that he depicts so magnificently in *Anna Karenina*. The two babies in *Family Happiness* are merely stage props.

Tolstoy may have turned against this story because he sensed something forced about his heroine's retreat from her quest for sexual satisfaction. While spinning his own male fantasy about the perfect wife, perhaps he had given short shrift to *her* needs. And it is possible that Tolstoy realized this shortcoming in his characterization because, in the midst of writing the work, he himself fell truly in love for the first time. Embarrassingly for the young theoretician, his beloved was a married woman, Aksinya Bazykina, a local peasant whose husband worked in the city. The affair lasted for four years, until his marriage in 1862, and in 1860 he wrote in his diary about Aksinya that 'it's no longer the feelings of a stag, but those of a husband for a wife'. When his young bride Sofya found these lines and others in the diary that her bridegroom insisted she read, she became very jealous of Aksinya, who occasionally worked as a cleaner in the house. Many years later, the love affair with Aksinya and his wife's reaction to it provided autobiographical material for *The Devil*.

The Devil has alternate endings (see Appendix 2) because it is unfinished: it appeared only posthumously in 1912. Tolstoy concealed its existence from his family, probably because he knew that his wife would recognize Aksinya Bazykina in Stepanida, though of course Stepanida and Liza are not intended as exact equivalents to Aksinya and Sofya Tolstaya: Tolstoy's works are never crudely autobiographical in this way. The actual plot of the story is based on the real-life murder by a man called N. N. Frederikhs of his married peasant lover Stepanida Munitsina, whom he shot three months after his marriage while she was at work threshing grain in a barn. Irtenev, the hero's last name in *The Devil* (though not his first one), is a variant form of the protagonist's name in Tolstoy's early trilogy *Childhood–Boyhood–Youth*. In notes and letters, Tolstoy referred to the story variously as 'The Story of Frederikhs' or 'Irtenev', and named it *The Devil* only on a fair copy of the manuscript produced after he had written the story in 1889. The change in titles indicates the process by which Tolstoy transforms raw material from life into a story shaped by artistic and moral considerations.

Tolstoy was struggling to control his own sexual appetites when he wrote *The Devil* in November 1889. The hero of the story loves two different women, one for her body and the other for her mind. Stepanida's bedroom eyes radiate the energy that animates her whole body. She is not ashamed of her sexual appetite, which she also indulges with other lovers, and there is no suggestion that she has any other reason for coupling with Irtenev than lust. In turn, he imagines her through his various bodily senses, freely mixing his memory of her with that of the places in which they have had sex. The spiritual, but angular and rather sickly Liza is represented mostly by her 'clear, gentle and artless' eyes, and her love for her husband is said to give her an ability 'to see into his innermost thoughts'. Readers of *War and Peace* will recognize her as a rewriting of Marya Bolkonskaya, without Marya's strength of soul.[6]

In *The Devil*, in a pale echo of the Platonism of *Family Happiness*, both Irtenev's love for his wife and his lust for Stepanida are presented as legitimate and natural needs of the human soul. Perhaps if Tolstoy had continued to work on the story he would have depicted his hero as more corrupted by his milieu. In any case, Irtenev's friendship–love for Liza does not satisfy him sexually, because he finds himself desiring his former mistress even though he imagines that it is not he, but 'someone else' (*kto-to*), who lusts after Stepanida. The depiction of lust as irresistible may reflect the influence of the philosopher Arthur Schopenhauer, whom Tolstoy began reading in the later 1860s and who equated sex with the amoral and overwhelming life force from which one could free oneself only by suicide. The moral goal in *The Devil* is freedom rather than the perfect intimacy of love. This is also consistent with Tolstoy's new-found devotion to the philosophy of Immanuel Kant, according to which the truly human is the rational, and freedom *from* passion is the primary desire of the reason.[7] In the story sexuality and spirituality are seen as separate, and reason must cage desire rather than harness it.

Tolstoy had interrupted his work on the final drafts of *The Kreutzer Sonata*, which he had started in 1887, to write *The Devil*. *The Kreutzer Sonata* was banned in 1890 for its explicit sexual content until his wife received special permission from the Tsar to include it in the collected works that she edited (and that provided the principal income for the family). The so-called frame narrative, in which the hero Pozdnyshev tells his story to another narrator, repeats the structure of several of Turgenev's love stories, such as *First Love* (1861) and *Spring Torrents* (1871). In these stories Turgenev depicts failed romantic love and opportunities that his narrators usually lacked the courage to pursue. By contrast, *The Kreutzer Sonata* attacks romantic love, and even associates it with murder. The opening is a modern version of the *Symposium*, in which characters, rather than gathering at a feast as in Plato, meet as strangers on a train. They discuss the nature of love, but none of them provides a satisfactory definition of it. The old merchant defends the old-fashioned double standard according to which women stayed faithful and men strayed. Meanwhile, the modern woman and her lawyer companion argue in favour of free love. For Pozdnyshev such 'love' is nothing but physical attraction, and therefore cannot be the basis of marriage, because it cannot last.

Pozdnyshev, following Rousseau, blames excessive lust on the effects of civilization on man, and he then illustrates his arguments by recounting his own courtship and marriage. Before he gets to this reminiscence, he puts forward a series of outrageous propositions. Too much rich food and too little physical labour inflame sexual desire among the upper classes. The main sin in our society is the possibility of physical relations without moral ones; men just pay women off, thereby avoiding human interaction. With a concentration exclusively on bodies and bodily satisfaction, 'brotherly' relations between the sexes are impossible after childhood; in fact there is no real difference between prostitutes and married women, who are just prostitutes paid for the long haul. Like Jews, women take revenge on men for the injustices done them. They use male sensuality to capture men, and their demands for luxury are a source of the great injustices and inequalities of society. Pozdnyshev then advances his most shocking claim, that the human race should end, because if celibacy became universal the goal of human life would be achieved, and there would be no reason for life to go on.

Tolstoy's contemporaries were scandalized by Pozdnyshev's advocacy of total celibacy, and many could not believe that Tolstoy would take such a position himself. In response, in 1889, even before he had finished *The Kreutzer Sonata*, Tolstoy wrote a Postface (see Appendix 1) to it in which he declared that he agreed with Pozdnyshev. Tolstoy had borrowed some of his ideas about chastity from American Shakers and the American gynaecologist Alice B. Stockham (1833–1912), whose book, *Tokology*, which Tolstoy had read in 1888, recommended sexual continence (intercourse no more than once a month, and never during pregnancy or menstruation) in marriage.[8] He did make a subtle distinction between himself and his hero, however. Pozdnyshev calls for celibacy now, while in the Postface Tolstoy presents it as an ideal, rather than a realizable goal. At one point in the text itself, the frame narrator offers a counter-argument to Pozdnyshev's perverse idealism by saying that the purpose of life can only be life itself, rather than, as Pozdnyshev maintains, the pursuit of a goal, no matter how lofty. And Tolstoy was aware that though his argument has merit, Pozdnyshev's extreme position is counterintuitive, and unnatural for a healthy man. Hence it is adopted by a character who, having committed murder, has lost the will to live.

Pozdnyshev's discussion of music in Chapter XXIII is clearly related to his concerns about the dangers of romantic love. As the purest form of art, music is the most 'infectious', to use the term by which Tolstoy described art's effect in his book *What is Art?* Pozdnyshev argues that, since music induces such a receptive mood, it should always be placed within a moral setting; otherwise, it arouses listeners without guiding their conduct. The actual performance of Beethoven's Kreutzer Sonata by his wife and the violinist Trukhachevsky at the home concert makes Pozdnyshev feel joyful and conciliatory. The murder itself, however, with its ominous rhythms – 'the laws of fury' – and its 'crescendo', is described using musical terminology, as if later the memory of the sonata focuses Pozdnyshev's later rage.

Tolstoy himself passionately loved music, and often wept when he heard it. He seems to have chosen Beethoven's Kreutzer Sonata as the catalyst to the murder because he regarded it as especially infectious and therefore dangerous. He may have experienced the relationship between the violin and the piano, especially in the presto, as sexual; in any case, for the later Tolstoy morality requires that we stay in touch with ourselves, so vulnerability to the influence of others in love or art can be risky.[9] Yet both remain immensely attractive, even to Pozdnyshev and surely to his creator. Pozdnyshev's murderous rage must be stoked by the unity that he observes between his wife and Trukhachevsky as they perform the sonata. He must recognize that while he rules his wife by intimidation, his rival conquers her with music-making. In reacting so violently to the harmony of their performance, even the hero of *The Kreutzer Sonata* does not simply lust after women. Just as in *Family Happiness* and other positive accounts of love, he yearns for intimacy that is more than physical.

Of the four stories in this volume, *Father Sergius* is the only one that is not primarily about love, but all three crises in the life of its hero involve sex. Tolstoy at first associated the story with *The Devil*, but in 1891 he wrote about it to his friend Chertkov that '[t]he battle with lust is an episode or rather, one step, the main battle is with something else, with human glory'.[10] The chief vice of Stepan Kasatsky, who as a monk takes the name Sergius, is ambition or vainglory (*tshcheslavie*), and he also possesses to a very high degree the life force that fuels sexual desire. He is enormously tall with gleaming eyes, charismatic and volatile: at military school his perfect behaviour is spoiled by 'animal' fits of temper. Like Irtenev in *The Devil*, he tries to control his passions, with imperfect results. Having become a monk, he is tempted by ambition as his reputation as a holy man and healer spreads. Eventually he also succumbs to lust. Although the story's narrator does not address this theme, it is worth asking why Sergius is so ambitious: it indicates pride, of course, but also a need for the love and praise of others. When Sergius was twelve, his father died, and Tolstoy, perhaps drawing on his own experience, may see this as one source of Sergius's vulnerability. It has a more universal cause as well, which may underlie love and ambition alike. Tutored by Plato in this respect, Tolstoy believed that both love and ambition are reactions to our knowledge of our own mortality and the resultant sense of incompleteness and insecurity. Recurrences of 'fleshly desire' in Father Sergius are invariably paired with religious doubt: Tolstoy seems to suggest that belief in God will heal the wound of mortality and thereby curb desire. Tolstoy underscores the connection between erotic love and vainglory by having Stepan Kasatsky fall in love with both Tsar Nicholas I, closeness to whom is the ultimate goal of his ambition, and Countess Korotkova. The discovery that Korotkova has been the mistress of Nicholas discredits both passions at once because Kasatsky ceases to love both figures, but the passions resurface in Sergius's later religious life. Eventually Sergius learns that the only way to control them is to avoid temptation. This is one reason why he eventually chooses to become a wandering beggar among the peasant masses where, it may be, he can leave behind his imperfect mortal self by truly living for others anonymously, without personal reward or recognition.

By the time Tolstoy wrote *Father Sergius* he knew the Russian hagiographic tradition well, and his story borrows motifs from medieval lives and legends. Like *The Devil*, however, it is written from the perspective of an ethical Christianity that rejects mysticism and assimilates the language of saints and demons to ethical concerns. Sergius's final choice of a beggar's life signifies a rejection by Tolstoy of the life of hermit saints and those who perform spectacular acts of self-abasement such as chopping off a finger. According to Tolstoy, a saintly man practises charity and commits no miracles other than the reform of his own sinful life.

Father Sergius's flight can also be understood as a projection of Tolstoy's own desire to flee his family as he argued with his wife about their luxurious way of life. (Eventually, of course, in 1910, he did leave home to live among the people, only to die of pneumonia a few days later at the Astapovo railway station.) The depiction of Sergius's struggle with the consequences of fame may also reflect Tolstoy's desire to resist the temptations of fame as his own mounting literary reputation in the later 1880s and especially the 1890s brought him admirers and disciples from all over the world. In Chapter VII, Sergius has come to think of himself as a 'burning light' (goriashchii svetil'nik), and this metaphor links the holy man to the poet in Tolstoy's conception: both have an inner intensity that comes from their connection to transcendental truth and that is the source of their charisma. Fame, however, dampens the intensity, and, as happens to Sergius, prophets of truth lose their connection to the Divine when they become proud. Psychologically, holy man and poet share the same dilemma in Tolstoy's poetics. Their authenticity and power depend upon their freedom from the need for fame.

As I have tried to demonstrate in this introduction, Tolstoy's fiction is both confessional *and* didactic, and if it were one without the other it would be much less profound. He tells all, leaving out nothing he has felt or understood, but moral considerations shape the telling. All four controversial stories in this volume balance these two imperatives. In *Family Happiness*, Tolstoy celebrates healthy sexuality within moral boundaries and makes the complete though temporary spiritual union of lovers psychologically convincing. And yet this happiness – and the success of the story – is precarious and ultimately unconvincing because it does not take full account of the problem of female sexual desire. For related reasons, the structure of the work is not entirely successful: although Masha narrates the work, Sergey seems closer to the author's point of view because he, unlike the naive heroine, understands what is happening to the two of them. The later tales are grimmer than *Family Happiness*. Even in old age Tolstoy cannot honestly depict pleasure in total abstinence, so he provides instead a chilling account of the pains of surfeit. He nudges his readers towards virtue by frightening and disgusting them with the consequences of vice. What the later stories lack is the sympathetic account in *Family Happiness* and other earlier works of love between men and women. In them the tender battle of the sexes has turned into all-out war without a winner.

At the same time, these later stories do not fence sexual desire within a domestic and marital relationship and therefore it ranges with all its natural force and attraction. Contemporary reaction to *The Kreutzer Sonata*, the only one of the three to appear during Tolstoy's lifetime, may be gauged from a letter from the provincial city of Voronezh about responses to readings of the work there:

> 'The Sonata' has had an extraordinary effect on everybody, struck them like the blow of a club. Furious discussions flame up; some are for, some against. Most adherents are *women*. The common reaction to 'The Sonata' is: 'strong stuff, very strong stuff!' [...] Some women have said that they could not sleep the night after they heard it the first time.[11]

Even today Pozdnyshev's description of the murder of his wife is hard to take. By it Tolstoy showed that he could depict sex and violence as well as any Zola (or Scorsese).[12] Tolstoy's rhetorical strategy in his fiction in general depends upon his readers' tacit agreement that he is writing truly about emotional states that they themselves have experienced or imagined. The strategy is tested most seriously when the reader is made to recall the bitter and shameful rather than the sweet. If readers have been in love but fallen out of it; if they have wanted to kill their loved ones; if they have lusted vigorously; or desperately sought the approval and even worship of others: Tolstoy depends upon our own memories to entangle us in his later tragic stories. Since such states can feel enslaving and to that extent shameful, even readers who consider Tolstoy moralistic cannot wholly reject his ambivalence towards them. Violent though the narratives of the later Tolstoy may be, he scandalizes today's readers even more thoroughly with his uncompromising moral stances. These would be rejected out of hand as politically incorrect if they did not emerge with such inevitability from his stories.

Donna Tussing Orwin

NOTES

1. In 1896, for instance, Sofya Andreyevna became infatuated with the pianist and composer S. I. Taneyev, Tchaikovsky's favourite student and twelve years her junior. Taneyev was homosexual and the friendship, which continued over four years, was platonic. Nonetheless, Tolstoy, who was sixty-eight in 1896 and had supposedly renounced sexual love, in his jealous rage more than once contemplated leaving home.

2. *Polnoe sobranie sochinenii* [PSS], vol. 46 (Moscow, 1937) p. 146.

3. The word is a Greek one that in Christian usage came to mean unselfish brotherly love.

4. Apollon Grigoriev, 'Iavleniia sovremennoi literatury, propushch-ennye nashei kritikoi', *Vremia* 1 and 9 (1962). Quoted in *L. N. Tolstoi: Sobranie sochinenii v dvadtsati tomakh*, vol. 3 (Moscow: Gosudarstvennoe izdatel'stvo Khudozhestvennoi literatury, 1961), p. 502.

5. This whole history of the course of the love between Sergey and Masha must be what Grigoriev had in mind when he praised the story.

6. Princess Marya Bolkonskaya is the daughter of old Prince Bolkonsky and the sister of Prince Andrey. In the course of the novel she discovers and satisfies her own need for a husband and family life.

7. In 1887, Tolstoy read Kant's *Critique of Practical Reason* and was so impressed that he started to translate it.

8. The Shakers were founded by Ann Lee in 1772 in Manchester, England, but soon emigrated to America and settled in 1776 in Watervliet, New York. They practised total celibacy, so they depended upon conversions and adoptions to maintain

membership. At its height around 1850, the movement had about six thousand members in communities from Maine to Kentucky.

9.   A presto is a very quick part in a piece of music. Readers might want to listen to the presto in Beethoven's sonata to see if they agree with Tolstoy's judgement of it.

10. 16 February 1891. *PSS*, vol. 87 (Moscow, 1937), p. 71.

11. G. A. Rusanov to Tolstoy, 15 April 1890. Quoted in Peter Ulf Møller, *Postlude to* The Kreutzer Sonata: *Tolstoi and the Debate on Sexual Morality in Russian Literature in the 1890s* (Leiden: E. J. Brill, 1988), p. 99. I have slightly revised Møller's English translation from the Russian.

12. It is no accident that all three of the later stories have been made into excellent films. For a list of film adaptations of works by Tolstoy, see www.tolstoystudies.org.

Further Reading

Bayley, John, *Tolstoy and the Novel* (New York: The Viking Press, 1966).

Benson, Ruth Crego, *Women in Tolstoy: The Ideal and the Erotic* (Urbana, Illinois: University of Illinois Press, 1973).

Berlin, Isaiah, *The Hedgehog and the Fox: An Essay on Tolstoy's View of History*, 1953 reprint (New York: Simon and Schuster, 1970).

Bloom, Harold, ed., *Leo Tolstoy: Modern Critical Views* (New York: Chelsea House, 1986).

Christian, R. F., *Tolstoy: A Critical Introduction* (Cambridge: Cambridge University Press, 1969).

Donskov, Andrew, ed., *Lev Tolstoy and the Concept of Brotherhood* (Ottawa: Legas, 1996).

Egan, David R., and Melinda A. Egan, eds., *Leo Tolstoy: An Annotated Bibliography of English Language Sources to 1978* (Netuchen, New Jersey, and London: The Scarecrow Press Inc., 1979).

——, *Leo Tolstoy: An Annotated Bibliography of English Language Sources from 1978 to 2003* (Lanham, Maryland: The Scarecrow Press Inc., 2005)

Eikhenbaum, Boris, *The Young Tolstoy*, translated and edited by Gary Kern (Ann Arbor, Michigan: Ardis, 1972).

Gifford, Henry, *Leo Tolstoy: A Critical Anthology* (Harmondsworth: Penguin Books, 1971).

Gustafson, Richard F., *Leo Tolstoy, Resident and Stranger: A Study in Fiction and Theology* (Princeton: Princeton University Press, 1986).

Jones, Malcolm, *New Essays on Tolstoy* (Cambridge: Cambridge University Press, 1978).

Knowles, A. V., ed., *Tolstoy: The Critical Heritage* (London and Boston: Routledge & Kegan Paul Ltd, 1978).

Matlaw, Ralph, ed., *Tolstoy: A Collection of Critical Essays* (Englewood Cliffs, New Jersey: Prentice-Hall, 1967).

Maude, Aylmer, *The Life of Tolstoy*, two vols. in one (Oxford: Oxford University Press, 1987).

McLean, Hugh, ed., *In the Shade of the Giant: Essays on Tolstoy* (California Slavic Studies, vol. 13. Berkeley: University of California Press, 1989).

Mjør, Johan Kare, *Desire, Death, and Imitation: Narrative Patterns in the Late Tolstoy* (Slavica Bergensia 4. Bergen: University of Bergen Press, 2002).

Møller, Peter Ulf, *Postlude to* The Kreutzer Sonata: *Tolstoi and the Debate on Sexual Morality in Russian Literature in the 1880s*, translated from the Danish by John Kendal (Leiden: E. J. Brill, 1988).

Orwin, Donna Tussing, *Tolstoy's Art and Thought, 1847–1880* (Princeton: Princeton University Press, 1993).

——, ed., *The Cambridge Companion to Tolstoy* (Cambridge: Cambridge University Press, 2002).

Rancour-Laferriere, Daniel, *Tolstoy on the Couch: Misogyny, Masochism and the Absent Mother* (New York: New York University Press, 1998).

Rowe, William W., *Leo Tolstoy* (Boston: Twayne Publishers, 1986).

Sankovitch, Natasha, *Creating and Recovering Experience: Repetition in Tolstoy* (Stanford: Stanford University Press, 1998).

Shestov, Leo, *Dostoevsky, Tolstoy and Nietzsche* (Athens, Ohio: Ohio University Press, 1969).

Shklovsky, Victor, *Lev Tolstoy* (Moscow: Progress Publishers, 1978).

Silbajoris, Rimvydas, *Tolstoy's Aesthetics and His Art* (Columbus, Ohio: Slavica Publishers, 1990, 1991).

Simmons, E. J., *Leo Tolstoy* (New York: Vintage, 1960).

Sorokin, Boris, *Tolstoy in Pre-Revolutionary Russian Criticism* (Columbus, Ohio: Ohio State University Press, 1979).

Steiner, George, *Tolstoy or Dostoevsky: An Essay in the Old Criticism*, 2nd edition (New Haven: Yale University Press, 1996).

Tolstoy Studies Journal 1988–. In addition to many articles, the journal, published annually, contains an annotated bibliography. For a list of the articles published in *TSJ*, see its website at www.tolstoystudies.org, which also contains many other materials related to Tolstoy, including a list of film versions of his works.

Wasiolek, Edward, *Tolstoy's Major Fiction* (Chicago: University of Chicago Press, 1978).

——, ed., *Critical Essays on Tolstoy* (Boston: G. K. Hall & Co., 1986).

Wilson, A. N., *Tolstoy* (London: Penguin, and New York: W. W. Norton & Co., 1988).

Donna Tussing Orwin

FAMILY HAPPINESS

A NOTE ON THE TEXT

The text used for this translation is that contained in volume 3 of *L. N. Tolstoi, Sobranie sochinenii v 22 tomakh* (Moscow, 1979).

PART ONE

I

We were in mourning for my mother, who had died in the autumn, and all that winter I lived in the country alone with Katya and Sonya.

Katya was an old friend of the household, the governess who had brought us all up, and whom I had remembered and loved ever since I could remember myself. Sonya was my younger sister. We were spending a gloomy and melancholy winter in our old house at Pokrovskoye. The weather was cold and windy, with the result that the snowdrifts piled higher than the windows; the windows were almost always dim and covered in frost, and for almost the whole winter we never walked or rode anywhere. It was seldom that anyone came to visit us; and those who did added no cheer or joy to our house. They all had sad faces, they all spoke quietly, as though afraid of waking someone up, they did not laugh, they sighed and often wept, as they looked at me and especially little Sonya in her black dress. In the house it was as if one could feel death; the sadness and horror of death hung in the air. Mother's room was locked, and I had a sense of terror, and something drew me to peep into that cold and empty room when I passed it on my way to bed.

I was then seventeen, and in the very year she died Mother had wanted to move to the city in order to bring me out. The loss of my mother was a great grief to me, but I must admit that behind that grief there was also a feeling that I was young and pretty, as everyone told me, but that I was wasting a second winter in seclusion on our estate. Before the end of the winter, this feeling of melancholy, loneliness and sheer boredom increased to such an extent that I never left my room, never opened the piano and never took a book in my hands. When Katya tried to persuade me to occupy myself with the one or the other, I would reply: 'I don't feel like it, I don't feel able for it', but in my heart a voice said: 'Why? Why do anything, when the best days of my life are being wasted like this? Why?' And to this *why* there was no reply other than tears.

I was told that during this time I grew thin and lost my looks, but this did not even interest me. Why? For whom? It seemed to me that the whole of my life was bound to pass in this same lonely backwater and hopeless melancholy, from which I myself, alone as I was, had neither the strength nor even the will to escape. Towards the end of the winter, Katya began to fear for me and decided to take me abroad no matter what. But for this, money was needed, and we had very little idea of how much remained to us after Mother's death; with each day that passed we awaited our guardian, who was to come and sort out our affairs.

In March our guardian arrived.

'Well, thank goodness!' Katya said to me one day as I wandered from one part of the room to another like a shadow, without occupation, without thought, without desires. 'Sergey Mikhailych has come, he has sent to inquire about us and wants to come to dinner. You must rouse yourself, my dear Mashechka,' she added, 'or what will he think of you? He loved you all so much.'

Sergey Mikhailych was our near neighbour, and had been a friend of our deceased father, though much younger than him. In addition to the fact that his arrival had altered our plans and gave us the possibility of leaving the estate, I had also grown accustomed to loving and respecting him since I was a child, and Katya, in advising me to rouse myself, had guessed that it would give me the greatest pain to appear before Sergey Mikhailych, of all our acquaintances, in a disadvantageous light. In addition to the fact that I, like everyone else in the house, from Katya to Sonya, his god-daughter, to the last coachman, loved him by habit, he had a special significance for me because of something Mother once said in my presence. She said that he was the kind of husband she would like me to have. At the time this seemed to me strange and even unpleasant; my hero was quite different. My hero was thin, haggard, pale and sad. Sergey Mikhailych, on the other hand, was an older man, tall, thickset and, it seemed to me, always cheerful; in spite of that, however, these words of Mother's stuck in my imagination, and even six years earlier, when I was eleven and he said 'thou' to me, played with me and called me 'the girl like a violet', I would sometimes ask myself, not without fear, what I would do if he were to suddenly want to marry me.

Before dinner, to which Katya added pie with cream, and a spinach sauce, Sergey Mikhailych arrived. I watched through the window as he drove up to the house in a small sleigh, but as soon as he turned the corner I hurried to the drawing-room, wanting to pretend that I wasn't expecting him at all. But when I heard the thud of feet, his loud voice and Katya's footsteps, I could not restrain myself and went to meet him. Holding Katya by the hand, he was talking loudly, and smiling. When he saw me, he stopped and looked at me for a while, without bowing. I felt awkward, and sensed that I was blushing.

'Oh! Is it really you?' he said in his decisive, straightforward manner, spreading his arms and coming up to me. 'Is it possible to change so much? How you've grown! To think I used to call you "violet"! You are a veritable rose now.'

With his own large hand he took mine, pressing it so firmly and honestly that it almost hurt. I thought he was going to kiss it, and was about to lean towards him, but he gave it another press and looked straight into my eyes with his steadfast and cheerful gaze.

I had not seen him for six years. He had changed greatly; grown older and darker, and now wore side-whiskers, which did not suit him at all; but there was no change in his simple manners, his open, honest face with its large features, his clever, brilliant eyes and affectionate, almost childlike, smile.

Five minutes later he had ceased to be a visitor, and had become one of our own for all of us, even for the servants who, as could be seen by their eagerness to oblige, were especially glad of his arrival.

He behaved quite differently from the neighbours who had come to see us after my mother passed away and thought they had to sit with us in plangent silence; he, on the contrary, was talkative, cheerful, and never said a word about our dear mother, to a point where at first this indifference struck me as odd and even improper for a person so close to us. Later, however, I realized that it was not indifference but sincerity, and was grateful for it.

In the evening Katya sat down to pour out the tea in her old place in the drawing-room, as she used to when Mother was alive; Sonya and I sat down beside her; old Grigory sought out one of Father's pipes and brought it to Sergey Mikhailych, who began to pace up and down the room as he had done in the old days.

'What a lot of dreadful changes there have been in this house, when one thinks about it!' he said, coming to a halt.

'Yes,' said Katya with a sigh and, putting the lid on the samovar, looked at him, now on the point of tears.

'I think you remember your father?' he said, turning to me.

'Not very well,' I replied.

'And how nice it would have been for you to be with him now!' he said, quietly and thoughtfully looking at my head above my eyes. 'I loved your father very much!' he added even more quietly, and it seemed to me that his eyes had become more brilliant.

'And now God has taken her, too!' said Katya, softly, and at once she put her napkin on the teapot, got her handkerchief out, and began to cry.

'Yes, there have been terrible changes in this house,' he repeated, turning away. 'Sonya, show me your toys,' he added after a while, and went through to the reception room. With my eyes full of tears I looked at Katya, after he had gone out.

'What a wonderful friend he is!' she said.

And, indeed, I felt a warmth and goodness in the sympathy of this good man who was not a member of our family.

From the drawing-room I could hear him moving about with

Sonya, and her squeals. I sent tea in to him; and then I heard him sit down at the piano and begin to strike the keys with Sonya's little hands.

'Marya Alexandrovna!' his voice called. 'Come here and play something.'

I found it pleasant that he should treat me so straight-forwardly, and with such a tone of friendly command; I got up and approached him.

'Play this,' he said, opening a volume of Beethoven at the adagio of the Sonata quasi una Fantasia.[1] 'Let us see what your playing is like,' he added, and walked away with his glass to a corner of the room.

For some reason I felt it was impossible for me to refuse, or to make preambles about how badly I played; I obediently sat down at the keyboard and began to play as well as I could, though I feared the verdict, knowing that he loved music and knew a great deal about it. The adagio was in keeping with the sense of remembrance that had been evoked by the teatime conversation, and think I played it decently. But when I came to the scherzo, he would not let me finish it. 'No, you're not doing very well with that,' he said, coming over to me. 'Leave that one, but the first movement was not bad. You seem to have an idea of what music is about.' This moderate praise delighted me so much that I even blushed. I found it so novel and pleasant that he, my father's friend and equal, should speak to me seriously, one to one, and not as to a child as he had earlier done. Katya went upstairs to put Sonya to bed, and we were left alone in the reception room.

He told me stories about my father, about how he had come to know him, and the happy times they had spent together, when I was still at my books and toys; and in the stories my father appeared to me for the first time as a simple and charming man, such as I had not known him hitherto. He also asked me about my likes and dislikes, what I read and what I intended to do, and gave me advice. For me he was now no longer the jocular and convivial person who had teased me and made me toys, but a serious, simple and loving man for whom I felt an involuntary respect and sympathy. I found talking to him easy and pleasant, yet at the same time I felt an involuntary tension there. I was fearful about each word I spoke; I so much wanted to deserve his love, which had been granted to me only because I was my father's daughter.

After she had put Sonya to bed, Katya joined us and complained to him about my *apathia*, about which I had said nothing.

'She didn't tell me the most important part!' he said, smiling and shaking his head at me reproachfully.

'What is there to tell?' I said. 'It's very tedious, and it will pass.' (It really did seem to me now that not only would my melancholy pass – it had already passed, and had never existed.)

'It's a bad thing not to be able to endure solitude,' he said. 'Are you really a young lady?'

'Of course I am,' I replied, laughing.

'Well, it's not much of a young lady who's only alive as long as she's being admired, and as soon as she's left alone simply goes to pieces and loses interest in life; she's all just for show, and doesn't have anything in herself to fall back on.'

'What a nice opinion of me you have,' I said, for the sake of saying something.

'No!' he said quietly after a short silence. 'I mean it when I say that you take after your father; there are *many things* in you.' And his kind, attentive gaze again flattered me and delightfully embarrassed me.

Only now did I notice in his face, which at first sight seemed merely cheerful, this gaze that belonged to him alone – at first clear, and then more and more attentive and rather sad.

'You ought not to be bored, nor can you be,' he said. 'You have music, which you understand, books, study, you have your whole life ahead of you, a life for which now is the time to prepare, in order not to have regrets later on. Another year and it will be too late.'

He spoke to me like a father or an uncle, and I felt that he was constantly restraining himself in order to stay on my level. I found it both hurtful that he considered me inferior to him, and pleasant that for me alone he considered it necessary to try to be different.

For the rest of the evening he talked with Katya about business.

'Well, goodbye, dear friends,' he said, getting up, coming over to me and taking me by the hand.

'When shall we see you again?' asked Katya.

'In the spring,' he replied, continuing to hold my hand. 'Now I am going to Danilovka (our other estate); I shall make inquiries there, arrange what I can, take a trip to Moscow – that's on business of my own – and when summer comes we shall meet again.'

'But why does it have to be for so long?' I said, with intense sadness; for, indeed, I had hoped to see him every day, and I suddenly felt deep regret, and fear that my melancholy was going to return again. This must have shown itself in my gaze and tone.

'Yes; occupy yourself with study a bit more, and don't brood,' he said in what seemed to me a tone that was too cold and blunt. 'And in spring I shall give you an exam,' he added, letting go of my hand and not looking at me.

In the hallway, where we stood ready to see him off, he began to hurry as he put on his fur coat, and again avoided my gaze. 'He's trying too hard!' I thought. 'Does he really think I'm so keen for him to look at me? He's a good man, a very good man . . . but that's all.'

That evening, however, Katya and I stayed up late talking, not about him but about how we were going to spend the summer, and where and how we would pass the winter. The terrible question, 'Why?' no longer bothered me. It appeared quite plain and simple to me that one must live in order to be happy, and in the future I saw much happiness. Our gloomy old house at Pokrovskoye suddenly seemed filled with life and light.

II

Meanwhile, spring had arrived. My earlier melancholy had passed and was replaced by a dreamy springtime melancholy of incoherent hopes and desires. Although I did not live as I had done at the start of winter, I occupied myself with Sonya and music and reading, I often went into the garden and wandered along its avenues, or sat on a bench, for a long, long time, thinking, wishing and hoping for Heaven knew what. Sometimes I would spend whole nights, especially moonlit ones, sitting at the window of my room until dawn; sometimes, in secret from Katya, I went out into the garden in nothing but a blouse, and ran through the dew as far as the pond, and once even went as far as the open fields and walked round the whole garden alone at night.

It is hard for me now to remember and understand those dreams that filled my imagination then. Even when I do remember them, I cannot believe that they really were mine. So strange they were, and so remote from life.

At the end of May, as he had promised, Sergey Mikhailych returned from his journey.

On the first occasion, he arrived in the evening, when we were not at all expecting him. We were sitting on the terrace, getting ready to have tea. The garden was already covered in green, and nightingales had taken up residence in the overgrown flowerbeds for the whole of the Feast of Peter and Paul.[2] The curly lilac bushes were sprinkled on top with something white and purple. Those were the flowers, ready to open. The leaves on the trees in the birch avenue were transparent in the setting sun. On the terrace there was cool shade. A heavy evening dew must have been settling on the grass. Outside, beyond the garden, one could hear the last sounds of the day, the noise of cattle being driven home; Nikon, the simpleton, was driving a cart with a barrel along the path in front of the terrace, and the cold stream from the watering rose made dark circles in the freshly dug earth beside the stems of the dahlias and their supports. On our terrace the brightly polished samovar gleamed and hissed on a white tablecloth where there were cream, pretzels and biscuits. Katya was busily washing the cups with her plump hands. I – unable to wait for tea and famished after bathing – was eating bread with thick fresh cream. I wore a gingham blouse with open sleeves, and my wet hair was bound with a kerchief. Katya spotted him first, through the window.

'Ah! Sergey Mikhailych!' she said softly. 'We were just talking about you.'

I got up, and was about to go and change, but he caught me in the doorway.

'Oh, why bother with ceremony in the country?' he said, looking at my head in its kerchief, and smiling. 'After all, you're not ashamed to let Grigory see you like that, and I'm really a sort of Grigory to you.' But it was precisely now that I had a sense that he was looking at me not at all in the way that Grigory would, and I felt uncomfortable.

'I shall be back in a moment,' I said, as I walked away from him.

'What's wrong with what you're wearing?' he shouted after me. 'You look like a fine young peasant girl.'

'How strangely he looked at me,' I thought, as I hurriedly changed upstairs. 'Well, thank goodness he's here, it will make things more cheerful!' And, with a quick look in the mirror, I cheerfully ran downstairs and, not trying to conceal my hurry, emerged on to the terrace, out of breath. He was sitting at the table, telling Katya about our affairs. Glancing at me, he smiled, and continued to talk. According to him, our affairs were in excellent shape. All we needed to do now was spend the summer on the estate, and then go either to St Petersburg, for Sonya's education, or abroad.

'I wish you would come abroad with us,' said Katya, 'for we shall be just like babes in the woods on our own over there.'

'Oh, how I'd love to go round the world with you,' he said, half in jest and half in earnest.

'Very well then,' I said. 'Let us go round the world.'

He smiled and shook his head.

'And what about my mother? And my business affairs?' he said. 'Well, but that's not important just now: tell me, how have you passed the time? You didn't start brooding again, I hope?'

When I told him that I had kept busy in his absence and had not been bored, and Katya confirmed what I had to say, he praised me and caressed me with his words and gaze, as if I were a child, and as if he had a right to do so. It seemed to me that I was obliged to tell him in detail, and above all with frank sincerity, all the good things that I had done, and to admit, as at confession, to all the things that might incur his displeasure. The evening was so fine that we stayed on the terrace after tea was cleared away, and I found the conversation so interesting that I did not notice how, gradually, the sound of human voices died away around us. From everywhere there was a stronger scent of flowers, abundant dew suffused the grass, a nightingale began to trill in a lilac bush close by and fell silent, having heard our voices; the starry sky seemed to lower itself over us.

I only noticed that dusk was falling when a bat suddenly flew without a sound under the canvas covering of the terrace and began to flutter around my white shawl. I pressed myself against the wall and was on the point of screaming, but just as swiftly and silently the bat dived out from under the awning and vanished in the semi-darkness of the garden.

'How I love your Pokrovskoye,' he said, interrupting the conversation. 'I could sit still like this out here on the terrace till the end of my life.'

'Well, do, then,' said Katya.

'Yes, I wish I could,' he said quietly. 'But life doesn't sit still.'

'Why don't you get married?' said Katya. 'You'd be an excellent husband.'

'Because I like to sit,' he laughed. 'No, Katerina Karlovna, it's too late for you and I to marry. Everyone long ago ceased to regard me as a man who might marry. And I myself even more so, and ever since then I have felt much better, truly I have.'

I had the impression that he said this in a way that was somehow unnatural and absorbed.

'There's a fine thing! The man's thirty-six, and he's too old,' said Katya.

'Too old indeed,' he continued. 'All he wants to do is sit. But in order to get married one needs something rather different. Go on, ask her,' he added, nodding in my direction. 'It's ones like her who ought to marry. While you and I can be happy for them.'

His tone betrayed a hidden sadness and a tension that were not lost on me. He was silent for a little; neither Katya nor I said anything.

'Well, imagine,' he continued, turning slightly on his seat, 'if I were suddenly, by some unfortunate chance, to marry a girl of seventeen, like Mash . . . Marya Alexandrovna, for example. That's a splendid example, and I'm very glad it's come out like that . . . it's the very best example there could be.'

I began to laugh, and was quite unable to understand why he was so glad, or what had come out like what . . .

'Well, tell me truly, with your hand on your heart,' he said, addressing me playfully. 'Would it not be a disaster for you to unite your life with an old man, a man whose time is past, who only wants to sit still, while in you goodness only knows what's fermenting, what desires are hatching?'

I felt uncomfortable, and I was silent, not knowing what to say in reply.

'Look, I'm not making you a proposal, you know,' he said laughing, 'but tell me the truth now, I'm not the sort of husband you dream of when you're walking alone along the avenue in the evening, am I? And it would be a disaster, wouldn't it?'

'No, not a disaster . . .' I began.

'Well, not a good thing,' he finished the sentence.

'Yes, but I mean, I may be mistak –'

But again he interrupted me.

'Well, there you are, you see, and she is perfectly right, and I am grateful to her for her sincerity, and very glad that we have had this conversation. And not only that: for me it would be the very greatest disaster,' he added.

'What a strange man you are, you haven't changed at all,' said Katya, leaving the terrace in order to give instructions for supper to be served.

We both stopped talking after Katya's departure, and around

us everything was quiet. Only a nightingale, not in an evening mode now, abrupt and uncertain, but in nocturnal fashion, began to sing, slowly and calmly suffusing the whole garden, while in the dell below, for the first time that evening, another responded to it from afar. The nearer one fell silent, as though listening for a moment, and then once again, even more sharply and intensely, began to emit a spasmodic, resonant trill. And with regal calm did those voices resound in their nocturnal world that is alien to us. The gardener passed by on his way to sleep in the greenhouse, and the sound of his heavy boots echoed along the path, ever receding. Someone whistled piercingly twice at the foot of the hill, and again everything grew quiet. Barely audibly, a leaf began to tremble, the awning of the terrace flapped and, quivering in the air, some fragrant thing floated on to the terrace and bathed it all over. I found it uncomfortable to remain silent after what had been said, but what I should say, I did not know. I looked at him. The brilliant eyes looked round me in the semi-darkness.

'It's wonderful to be alive!' he said softly.

For some reason, I sighed.

'Well?'

'It's wonderful to be alive!' I echoed.

And again we fell silent, and again I felt uncomfortable. It kept occurring to me that I had upset him by agreeing with him that he was old, and I wanted to console him, but did not know how to do that.

'However, I must take my leave of you now,' he said, getting up. 'Mother is expecting me for supper. I've hardly seen her at all today.'

'But I was going to play you a new sonata,' I said.

'Another time,' he said coldly, or so it seemed to me.

'Goodbye.'

I now had an even greater sense that I had upset him, and I was sorry. Katya and I saw him to the front steps and stood outside for a while, looking down the road along which he had vanished. When the sound of his horse's hooves could no longer be heard, I walked round to the terrace and again began to look at the garden, and in the dewy mist where the sounds of the night hung suspended for a long time after I saw and heard all that I wanted to see and hear.

He came a second and a third time, and the awkwardness that proceeded from the strange conversation that had taken place between us completely disappeared and did not return again. Throughout the whole summer he came to see us two or three times a week; and I got so used to him that, when he didn't come for a long time, I felt uncomfortable being on my own, and I was angry with him and felt that he had done me wrong by deserting me. He treated me like a young and favoured companion, asked me questions, provoked me to the most heartfelt frankness, gave me advice, encouraged me, sometimes scolded me and stopped me. But, in spite of all his efforts constantly to remain on my level, I felt that beyond what I understood of him there still lay an entire alien world, into which he did not consider it necessary to admit me, and it was this more than anything else that sustained my respect for him and drew me to him. I knew from Katya and our neighbours that, besides his concerns about his old mother, with whom he lived, besides the management of his estate and our guardianship, he had some kind of manorial business that caused him no end of trouble; but as to the manner in which he viewed all this, the nature of his convictions, his plans and hopes, I was never able to ascertain anything from him. As soon as I brought the conversation round to his affairs, he would frown in that special way of his, as though to say: 'That will do, thank you, what business is that of yours?' – and change the subject. At first this used to offend me, but later I got so used always to talking about things that only affected me that I found it natural.

Something else that at first I did not like, and then later, on the contrary, found pleasant, was his complete indifference and apparent contempt as far as my personal appearance was concerned. Never by a glance or a word did he lead me to think that I was pretty; on the contrary, he would frown and laugh when anyone called me pretty when he was near. He even liked to find defects in my appearance, and teased me about them. The fashionable dresses and hairstyles in which Katya liked to deck me out on special days also merely provoked his mocking remarks, which upset kind-hearted Katya and at first disconcerted me. Katya, who had decided in her mind that he liked me, could not for the life of her understand how a man could fail to want the woman of his fancy to display herself in the most advantageous light. But I soon realized what he wanted. He wanted to believe that there was no coquetry in me. And when I realized this, in my clothes, my hairstyles, my movements there did indeed remain in me not even the shadow of coquetry; it was, however, replaced by a coquetry of ingenuousness, sewn with white threads, while I could not yet be ingenuous. I knew that he loved me – whether as a child or as a woman, I did not yet ask myself; I valued this love and, sensing that he considered me the very best young woman in the world, I could not help wishing this deceiving illusion to remain with him. And deceive him I did, involuntarily. But, in deceiving him, I myself became better. I felt that it was better and more worthy for me to display before him the better aspects of my soul, rather than those of my body. My hair, hands, face, habits, no matter what they were, good or bad, it seemed to me, he had appraised at once and knew so well that, apart from the wish to deceive him, I could add nothing to my external appearance. My soul, on the other hand, he did not know; because he loved it, because at the same time it was growing and developing, and here I could deceive him and did deceive him. And how at ease I became with him, once I clearly understood this! Those groundless embarrassments, those awkward movements completely disappeared from my behaviour. I felt that whether he saw me from in front or from the side, sitting or standing, with my hair up or my hair down – he knew the whole of me and, I fancied, was pleased with me as I was. I think that if, contrary to usual custom, he had suddenly told me, as others did, that I had a pretty face, I would not even have been happy about it. But on the other hand how radiant and joyous did my soul become when, after something I had said, he gave me a fixed look, and said in a voice of emotion, to which he tried to give a joking tone:

'Yes, yes, there are *many things* in you. You are a wonderful girl, I must tell you that.'

And after all, for what did I receive such rewards, which filled my heart with pride and cheerfulness? For saying that I felt for old Grigory in his love for his granddaughter, or for being moved to tears by some poem or novel I had read, or for preferring Mozart to Schulhof.[3] And it was surprising, I thought, with what remarkable sensitivity I was able to guess all the things that were good and worthy of love; though at the time I certainly did not yet know what was good and worthy of love. A large part of my earlier tastes and habits was not to his liking, and it only needed a movement of his eyebrow or a look from him to show that he did not like what I was trying to say, to adopt his special, regretful, slightly scornful expression, for me to feel that I no longer loved the things I used to love. He had only to want to give me some advice, and I would know what he was going to say. He would ask me a question, looking into my eyes, and his gaze would draw from me the thought he wished to hear. All the thoughts, all the feelings I had then were not my own, but were his feelings and thoughts which suddenly became mine, moved across into my life and illuminated it. Quite imperceptibly to myself, I began to look at everything with different eyes: at Katya, at our servants, at Sonya, at myself, and at my studies. Books, which previously I had dipped into merely to avoid boredom, suddenly became one of the chief pleasures of my life; and all just because we talked about books and read them together, and because he brought them to me. Before, the studies with Sonya, the lessons I gave her, had been a heavy obligation for me, one which I forced myself to discharge merely out of a sense of duty; he had only to be present at the lesson, and keeping track of Sonya's progress became a delight for me. Before, learning a whole piece of music by heart had seemed to me impossible; but now, knowing that he would listen and praise, perhaps, I would play the same passage forty times at a stretch, until poor Katya had to stop her ears with cotton wool, and yet I still was not tired of it. Those same old sonatas somehow phrased themselves quite differently now, and sounded quite different, and far better. Even Katya, whom I knew and loved like my own self, even she changed in my eyes. Only now did I understand that she was not at all obliged to be the mother, friend and slave that she was for us. I understood all the self-effacement and devotion of this loving creature, understood all the ways in which I was obliged to her; and began to love her even more. He also it was who taught me to look at our servants, serfs, menials and maids in a completely different way from before. It is ridiculous to say it, but until the age of seventeen I had lived among these people more estranged from them than from people I had never seen; never once did I reflect that these people had loves, desires and regrets, just as I had. Our garden, our groves, our fields, which I had known so long, suddenly became new and beautiful for me. Not for nothing did he say that in life there is only one indubitable happiness – to live for another. At the time this seemed strange to me, and I did not understand it; but this conviction was already unconsciously entering my heart. He opened to me a whole life of joys in the present, without changing anything in my life, without adding anything to each impression except himself. All these things had been silently around me since childhood, and only his arrival was needed in order to make them all begin to speak and go vying among themselves for entrance to my soul, filling it with happiness.

Often that summer I would arrive upstairs in my room and lie down on the bed, and instead of the former spring melancholy of wishes and hopes for the future, I was seized by a turmoil of happiness in the present. I was unable to sleep, got up, sat on Katya's bed and told her that I was perfectly happy, something that, when I recall it now, it was quite superfluous to tell her: she could see it for herself. But she told me that she too lacked for nothing and was also very happy, and kissed me. I believed her, it seemed so necessary and just that everyone should be happy. But Katya was also able to entertain the notion of sleep, sometimes she would angrily chase me away from her bed, and go to sleep; but for a long time yet I continued to go over in my head all the reasons I had for being so happy.

Sometimes I would get up and say my prayers a second time, pray in my own words to thank God for all the happiness he had given me.

And in the little room it was quiet; there was only Katya's even and drowsy breathing, the ticking of the clock beside her bed, as I tossed about and whispered words or crossed myself and kissed the cross around my neck. The door was closed and there were shutters on the windows, in one place a fly or a mosquito buzzed as it hovered to and fro. And I felt that I never wanted to leave that little room, did not want the morning to come, did not want all that mental atmosphere that surrounded me to be dispelled. It seemed to me that my dreams, thoughts and prayers were living creatures, living there in the darkness with me, floating near my bed, standing over me. And every thought was his thought, and every feeling was his feeling. I did not yet know that this was love, I thought that things might be like this for ever, that this feeling was given just so, gratis.

III

One day after dinner, at the time of the corn harvest, Katya, Sonya and I went into the garden, to our favourite bench – in the shade of the lime trees above the dell, beyond which a view of the woods and the field opened out. It was now three days since Sergey Mikhailych had been to see us, and on this day we were expecting him, all the more so as our estate manager said he had promised to come to the field. Just after one o'clock we saw him ride on to the rye field. Katya gave instructions for peaches and cherries, of which he was very fond, to be brought, glanced at me with a smile, then lay down on the bench and began to drowse. I tore off a flat, crooked lime tree branch with sap-filled leaves and sap-filled bark, which wetted my hand, and, as I fanned Katya, continued to read, constantly breaking off and gazing at the road through the field, along which he had to come. Sonya was making a summer house for her dolls by the root of an old lime tree. The day was hot, windless and sultry, the clouds were growing thicker and darker, and a thunderstorm had been gathering all morning. I was anxious, as always before a storm. But in the afternoon the clouds began to part along their edges, the sun came sailing out into a clear sky, and only in one place was there an occasional rumbling, where a heavy thundercloud stood above the horizon, mingling with the dust in the fields, and pale zigzags of lightning cut through to the ground. It was apparent that on this day the weather was going to clear up, for us, at least. Along the road that was now visible in places beyond the garden, in a constant movement now one after the other the tall, creaking wagons slowly trundled with their sheaves, and now swiftly to meet them rattled the empty carts, legs a-shake and shirts a-flutter. The thick dust did not blow away, but did not settle either: it hung on the other side of the wattle fence among the transparent foliage of the trees in the garden. A little further away, on the threshing floor, the same voices and the same creaking of wheels could be heard, as the same yellow sheaves that had slowly moved past the fence flew through the air, and before my eyes oval-shaped houses rose, with their angular roofs sticking out and the figures of muzhiks swarming over them. In the foreground, on the dusty field, carts also moved, and the same yellow sheaves could be seen, the same sounds of carts, voices and singing heard. At one side the stubble was becoming more and more apparent, together with strips of boundary path overgrown with wormwood. A little further to the right, at the foot of the slope, on the inelegantly tangled, scythed field, the brightly coloured dresses of the women who were binding could be seen, as they stooped and waved their arms about, as the tangled field was cleared, and the elegant sheaves were placed at close intervals across it. Suddenly it was as if summer had been turned to autumn before my eyes. Dust and heat were everywhere, except for our favourite spot in the garden. Everywhere in this dust and heat, in the burning sun, there was the talk and noise and movement of the working folk.

But Katya snored so sweetly under her white cambric handkerchief on our cool bench, the cherries gleamed so black and juicy on the plate, our dresses were so fresh and clean, the water in the jug danced so brightly with rainbow colours in the sun, and I felt so happy! 'What can I do?' I thought. 'What fault is it of mine that I am happy? But how can I share my happiness? How and to whom can I give myself up, the whole of me, and all my happiness, too? . . .'

By now the sun had gone behind the treetops of the birch avenue, the dust was settling in the field, the distance was becoming clearer and brighter in the slanting light, the clouds had almost all disappeared, the roofs of two or three new stacks of corn were visible at the threshing floor behind the trees, and muzhiks came down from them; with loud shouts, the carts went hurrying past, evidently for the last time; women with rakes over their shoulders and straw bands for binding the sheaves on their sashes walked homeward, loudly singing, but there was still no sign of Sergey Mikhailych, even though I had seen him ride down the hill long ago. Suddenly, along the avenue, from a direction in which I had not at all expected him, his figure appeared (he had walked round through the dell). With a cheerful, beaming face and his hat off, he came swiftly towards me. When he saw that Katya was asleep, he bit his lip, closed his eyes, and walked on tiptoe; I noticed at once that he was in that special mood of groundless cheerfulness which was something I had always been dreadfully fond of in him, and which we called 'wild delight'. He was like a schoolboy who has broken away from his studies; his whole being, from his face to his feet, breathed contentment, happiness and childlike playfulness.

'Well, hullo, young violet, how are you? All right?' he said in a whisper, coming over to me and pressing my hand . . . 'Oh, I'm fine,' he replied to my question. 'I'm thirteen today, I want to play horses and climb trees.'

'In wild delight?' I said, gazing at his laughing eyes and feeling that this 'wild delight' was transmitting itself to me.

'Yes,' he replied with a wink, and restraining a smile. 'Only why do you have to punch Katerina Karlovna on the nose?'

As I gazed at him and continued to wave the branch, I had not even noticed that I had knocked Katya's handkerchief off and was stroking her face with the leaves. I began to laugh.

'And she will say she wasn't asleep,' I said in a whisper, as if in order not to wake Katya; but that was not the real reason at all: I simply liked talking with him in a whisper.

He began to move his lips, mimicking me, as though my voice was now so soft that it could not be heard. Catching sight of the plate of cherries, he made a show of seizing it as if by stealth, went off to Sonya under the lime tree and sat down on her dolls. Sonya was angry at first, but he soon made it up with her, arranging a game that consisted of a race to see which of them could eat cherries faster.

'If you like, I'll tell them to bring some more,' I said. 'Or let us go ourselves.'

He took the plate, placed the dolls on it, and the three of us walked towards the orchard. Sonya, laughing, ran after us, tugging at his coat, to make him give her back the dolls. He did so, and then turned to me in a serious manner.

'Well, there's no question that you are a violet,' he said to me, still softly, though there was no longer any need to fear waking someone. 'As soon as I came up to you after all that dust, heat and labour, I could unmistakably smell violets. And not those scented violets, but, you know, that early, rather dark little violet that smells of melted snow and spring grass.'

'So is everything all right on your estate?' I asked him, in order to cover up the joyful confusion his words had produced in me.

'It's going splendidly! These people are splendid wherever you find them. The more one knows them, the more one loves them.'

'Yes,' I said. 'Today, before you arrived, I watched them at work from the garden, and I suddenly felt ashamed that they were toiling while I was enjoying myself so much, that –'

'Do not play the coquette with this, my dear,' he interrupted me, with sudden seriousness, but also with an affectionate glance into my eyes. 'It is a sacred matter. May God save you from showing off about it.'

'But I'm telling this only to *you*.'

'Oh yes, I know. Well, what about the cherries?'

The orchard was locked, and there were no gardeners about

(he had sent them all off to work in the field). Sonya ran to fetch the key, but without waiting for her he climbed up on a corner of the wall, raised the netting, and jumped down to the other side.

'Do you want some?' his voice came to me from over there. 'Give me the plate.'

'No, I want to pick some for myself, I'll go and fetch the key,' I said. 'Sonya won't be able to find it . . .'

But at the same time I wanted to see what he was doing there, what he looked like, how he was moving, in the supposition that no one was watching him. And also, I simply did not want to lose sight of him for a single moment. I ran round the orchard through the nettles on tiptoe on the other side, where the wall was lower, and, standing on an empty tub, so that the wall was lower than my chest, leaned over into the orchard. I surveyed the interior of the orchard, with its bent old trees and broad, jagged leaves, beneath which the black, succulent fruits hung straight and heavy, and, pushing my head under the netting, from under the gnarled bough of an old cherry tree I caught sight of Sergey Mikhailych. He probably thought I had gone away, and that no one was watching him. With his hat off and his eyes closed, he was sitting in the fork of the old tree, busily rolling a piece of cherry-tree resin into a ball. Suddenly he shrugged his shoulders, opened his eyes and, saying something quietly, smiled. So unlike him were this word and this smile that I felt ashamed of myself for spying on him. It seemed to me that the word was 'Masha!'. 'This cannot be,' I thought. 'Dear Masha!' he repeated even more softly and even more tenderly. But now I heard those two words distinctly. My heart began to beat so violently and such a disturbing, almost forbidden joy suddenly assailed me that I clutched at the wall in order not to fall and give myself away. He heard my movement, looked round in alarm and, suddenly lowering his eyes, blushed crimson like a child. He wanted to say something to me, but could not, and again, again his face positively burned. But as he gazed at me, he smiled. I smiled back. His whole face shone with joy. This was no longer the old uncle, affectionately tutoring me, this was a man who was my equal, who loved and feared me and whom I feared and loved. We said nothing, and just looked at each other. But suddenly he frowned, the smile and the brilliance in his eyes disappeared, and he turned to me coldly, again in paternal fashion, as though we were doing something that was not right and as though he had come to his senses and was advising me to do likewise.

'I say, you'd better get down or you'll hurt yourself,' he said. 'And do put your hair right, just look at yourself.'

'Why is he pretending? Why does he want to cause me pain?' I thought with annoyance. And at that same moment I was visited by an irresistible desire to embarrass him and try out my strength on him again.

'No, I want to pick them for myself,' I said and, grasping the nearest branch, jumped up on the wall. He had not yet managed to support me, when I leapt down from the wall to the ground in the orchard.

'What silly things you do!' he said quietly, blushing again and trying to conceal his embarrassment under a show of annoyance. 'Look, you might have hurt yourself. And how are you going to get out of here?'

He was even more embarrassed than before, but now this embarrassment did not please me, but frightened me. It transmitted itself to me, I blushed and, avoiding his gaze and not knowing what to say, I began to pick cherries though I had nowhere to put them. I reproached myself, I repented. I felt afraid, and it seemed to me that by this action I had forever tarnished myself in his eyes. Neither of us said anything, and we both found the situation difficult. Sonya, who came running with the key, rescued us from it. For a long time after that we said nothing to each other, and addressed all our remarks to Sonya. When we returned to Katya, who assured us that she had not been asleep, but had heard everything, I felt calmer, and he once again tried to adopt his protective, fatherly tone, but he no longer had much success with it, and it did not take me in. I now vividly recalled a conversation that had taken place between us several days earlier.

Katya had been talking about how it is easier for a man to love and express love than for a woman.

'A man can say that he's in love, but a woman cannot,' she had said.

'Well, the way I see it, a man must not and cannot say that he is in love, either,' he said.

'Why?' I asked.

'Because it will always be a lie. What sort of revelation is it that a man is in love? It's as though as soon as he says it, something goes click – and he's in love. As though he has only to pronounce that word and something extraordinary is bound to happen, some kind of omens and auguries, all the cannons firing at the same time. It seems to me,' he continued, 'that people who solemnly pronounce those words "I love you" are either deceiving themselves or, even worse, deceiving others.'

'So how will a woman find out if she is loved, unless she is told it?' asked Katya.

'That I don't know,' he replied. 'Each person has their own words. But if the feeling is there, it will be expressed. When I read novels, I always imagine the puzzled face of Lieutenant Strelsky or of Alfred, when he says "I love you, Eleonora!",[4] thinking that something extraordinary will happen; and nothing happens, neither to her nor to him – their eyes and noses remain the same, and so does everything else.'

At the time, even in this joke I felt something serious that related to myself, but Katya would not permit the frivolous treatment of characters in novels.

'You and your paradoxes,' she said. 'Well, tell me the honest truth; have you really never told a woman that you loved her?'

'Never have I done so, nor even gone down on one knee,' he replied, laughing. 'Nor shall I.'

'Yes, he doesn't need to tell me that he loves me,' I thought now, vividly remembering that conversation. 'He loves me, I know that. And all his efforts to appear indifferent will not persuade me to the contrary.'

All that evening he said little to me, but in his every word to Katya and Sonya, in his every movement and glance I saw love, and did not doubt it. I merely felt annoyed and sorry for him, that he still felt he had to conceal his emotions and pretend coldness, when by now it was all clear, and when it would have been so easy and simple to be so impossibly happy. But the fact that I had jumped down to him in the orchard tormented me like a crime. I could not get rid of the idea that he would cease to respect me because of it, and was angry with me.

After tea I went to the piano, and he followed me.

'Play something, I haven't heard you for a long time,' he said, catching me up in the living-room.

'I was going to ... Sergey Mikhailych!' I said, suddenly looking him straight in the eye. 'You're not angry with me, are you?'

'What for?' he asked.

'For not obeying you after dinner,' I said, blushing.

He understood me, shook his head and smiled ironically. His look said that I ought to be scolded, but that he did not feel up to it.

'It was nothing; we're friends again,' I said, sitting down at the piano.

'Of course we are!' he said.

In the large, high-ceilinged drawing-room there were only two candles on the piano; the remaining expanse was in semi-darkness. In at the open windows gazed the bright summer night. Everything was quiet, and only Katya's footsteps creaked now and then in the dark living-room and Sergey Mikhailych's horse, tethered under the window, snorted and stamped in the burdock. He sat behind me, so I could not see him; but everywhere in the semi-darkness of that room, in the sounds, in myself, I could feel his presence. His every look, his every movement, which I could not see, found a response in my heart. I played Mozart's Sonata Fantasia,[5] which he had brought me and which I had learned in his presence, and for him. I did not think at all about what I was playing, but I think I played well, and it seemed to me that he liked it. I could feel the pleasure he was experiencing, and, without looking at him, feel the look that was fixed on me from behind. Quite without meaning to, continuing to move my fingers unconsciously, I glanced round at him. His head stood out against the light background of the night. He sat leaning his head on his hands, looking at me fixedly with brilliant eyes. I smiled at the sight of this gaze, and

stopped playing. He also smiled and shook his head reproachfully at the music, for me to continue. When I finished, the
moon had grown brighter, risen high, and now in addition to
the feeble light of the candles there came into the room from
the windows another, silvery light, which fell on the floor.
Katya said what was I doing, I had stopped in the best part of
the piece, and that I was playing badly; but he said that, on the
contrary, I had never played so well as I had this evening, and
he began to walk about the rooms, through the drawing-room
into the dark living-room and back to the drawing-room again,
each time looking round at me, and smiling. I smiled too, and
I even felt like laughing for no reason, so pleased was I about
something, only this evening, that had just taken place. As soon
as he vanished through the doorway, I would embrace Katya,
with whom I was standing at the piano, and begin to kiss her
in my favourite little place, her chubby neck under her chin; as
soon as he returned, I made my face look serious and tried my
best to stop myself from laughing.

'What has got into her today?' Katya would say to him.

But he made no reply, and merely laughed softly at me. He
knew what had got into me.

'Look what a night it is!' he said from the living-room,
stopping by the open French window that looked on to the
garden.

We went over to him, and, indeed, it was a night such as I
have never seen since. The full moon stood above the house
and us, so that it could not be seen, and half of the shadow of
the roof, the pillars and the awning on the terrace lay obliquely
and *en raccourci* on the gravel path in the circular lawn. Everything else was bright and suffused with the silver of dew and
moonlight. The broad path through the flowerbeds, on one
side of which lay the slanting shadows of the dahlias and
their supports, all radiant and cold, and shining with irregular
crushed stone, receded into the mist and distance. From behind
the trees the bright roof of the greenhouse was visible, and from
the dell rose a growing mist. By now a few bare lilac bushes
were bright all the way to their branches. All their flowers,
moistened with dew, could be distinguished one from the other.

In the avenues light and shadow mingled in such a way that the avenues seemed to consist not of trees and paths but of transparent houses that swayed and trembled. To the right, in the shadow of the house, all was black, indistinguishable and forbidding. On the other hand, all the more brightly from this murk emerged the capriciously spreading crown of a poplar, which for some strange reason had stopped here, close to the house, up aloft in the bright light, instead of flying away somewhere far over there, into the receding bluish sky.

'Let us go for a walk,' I said.

Katya agreed, but told me to put on galoshes.

'I don't need them, Katya,' I said. 'Sergey Mikhailych will give me his arm.'

As though this would prevent me from getting my feet wet. But at the time this was something all three of us understood, and did not seem in any way strange. He never normally offered me his arm, but now I took it of my own accord, and he did not find this strange. The three of us left the terrace. The whole of that world, that garden, that air, were not those that I knew.

When I looked ahead along the avenue down which we were walking, I kept imagining that it was impossible to walk any further that way, that there the world of the possible ended, that all this must be shackled forever in its beauty. But we continued to move, and the magic wall of beauty moved apart, let us in, and there too, it seemed, was our familiar garden, the trees, the paths, the dry leaves. And we really were walking along the paths, stepping on circles of light and shadow, and a dry leaf really did rustle under our feet, and a fresh twig brush against my face. And that really was him, walking steadily and quietly at my side, carefully supporting my arm, and that really was Katya who, with her creaking shoes, walked alongside us. And that must be the moon in the sky, shining on us through the motionless branches . . .

But with every step, from behind us and ahead of us the magic wall closed up again, and I ceased to believe that it was possible to go any further, ceased to believe in everything that existed.

'Oh! A frog!' Katya said quietly.

'Who is saying that, and why?' I thought. But then I remembered that it was Katya, that she was afraid of frogs, and I looked down at my feet. A tiny little frog hopped and froze in front of me, and I saw that it cast a little shadow on the bright clay of the path.

'Aren't you afraid?' he said.

I glanced round at him. At the spot we had reached in the avenue we were walking along, one of the lime trees was missing, and I could see his face clearly. It was so handsome and happy . . .

He had said: 'Aren't you afraid?' – but to my ears what he said was: 'Dear charming girl, I love you!' 'I love you! I love you!' his gaze and his arm said; and the light, and the shadow, and the air, and everything else repeated the same thing.

We had gone round the whole of the garden. Katya had walked beside us with her short little steps, and she was breathing heavily with tiredness. She said that it was time to go back, and I felt so, so sorry for her, the poor thing. 'Why does she not feel the same as we do?' I thought. 'Why isn't everyone young and happy, like this night and like he and I?'

We did return to the house, but it was still a long time before he rode away, in spite of the fact that the cocks were crowing, everyone in the house was asleep, and his horse kept beating its hoof more and more frequently on the burdock, snorting under the window. Katya did not remind us that it was late, and we, talking about the most trivial things, sat on, unaware of it ourselves, until after two. The cocks were crowing for the third time and the dawn had started to break when he left. He took his leave as he usually did, saying nothing in particular, but I knew that as of today he was mine and I would not lose him now. As soon as I had admitted to myself that I loved him, I told Katya everything. She was pleased and touched by what I told her, but the poor thing was able to fall asleep that night, while for a long, long time yet I strolled about the terrace, went down into the garden and, recalling every word, every movement, walked along those same avenues he and I had walked. I got no sleep at all that night and for the first time in my life saw the sunrise and the early morning. And never again, even later on, did I see such a night, such a morning. 'Only why won't he tell me simply that he loves me?' I thought. 'Why does he think up all these difficulties, call himself an old man, when everything is so simple and wonderful? Why does he waste this golden time which may perhaps never return? Let him say: "I love you", say it in so many words: "I love you"; let him take my hand, bend his head over it and say: "I love you." Let him blush and lower his eyes before me, and then I will tell him everything. And I won't say it in words, but embrace him, press myself close to him, and cry. But what if I'm mistaken, and he doesn't love me?' suddenly crossed my mind.

I was frightened by my own feeling – God knows where it might have taken me; his embarrassment, and mine, in the orchard, when I had jumped down to him, came back to me, and my heart felt heavy, so heavy. The tears poured from my eyes, and I began to pray. And a strange, reassuring thought and hope came to me. From today I decided to fast, to take communion on my birthday and on that same day become his fiancée.

For what reason? Why? How was it to happen? I had no idea, but from that moment I knew it would be so. It was broad daylight now, and the working folk had begun to get up as I returned to my room.

IV

It was the Fast of the Assumption,[6] and so no one in the house was surprised by my intention of going without food then.

Throughout the whole of that week he never once came to visit us, and not only was I not surprised, alarmed or angry with him, but was, on the contrary, pleased that he did not call, and did not expect him until it was my birthday. During that week I rose early each day and, while my horse was being got ready, alone, strolling about the garden, went over in my mind my sins of the previous day and thought about what I must do today in order to be satisfied with my day and not sin even once. At the time it seemed to me so easy to be entirely without sin. It seemed that all that was needed was a little effort. The horses were brought, I would get into the brake with Katya or one of the maids, and we would drive to the church some two miles away. On entering the church I always remembered to pray for all who 'come unto the Temple in the fear of God', and tried to mount the two grass-grown steps of the church porch with precisely this feeling. In the church at this time there were no more than a dozen fasting peasant women and servants; and with painstaking humility I tried to respond to their bows and all on my own – something that seemed to me a great feat – went over to the candle box to take candles from the old church elder, who was a soldier, and placed them. Through the royal gates one could see the altar cloth that my mother had embroidered; above the iconostasis stood two wooden angels with stars that had seemed so big when I was small, and the dove with a yellow radiance that had fascinated me then. Behind the choir one could see the crumpled font in which so many times I had baptized the children of our household servants and in which I too had been baptized. The old priest came out in a chasuble made from the pall on my father's coffin, and read the service in the same voice he had used for as long as I could remember at services in our house: at Sonya's christening, at my father's funeral, at my mother's burial. And the same tinkling voice of the deacon sounded in the choir, and the same old woman whom I always remember in the church, at every service, stood bent by the wall, looking at an icon in the choir with weeping eyes, and pressing her folded fingers to her faded handkerchief as she whispered something with her toothless mouth. And all this was no longer merely a curiosity, was close to me not because of memories alone – it was all now great and holy in my eyes, and seemed to me full of profound significance. I listened attentively to each word of the prayer that was being recited, tried to respond to it with feeling, and even though I did not understand, silently asked God to enlighten me, or thought up a prayer of my own in place of the one I had not been able to make out. When the prayers of penitence were read, I remembered my past, and so black did that innocent

childish past seem by comparison with the radiant condition of
my soul that I wept and felt horror at myself; but at the same
time I felt that all this would be forgiven and that even if I had
committed greater sins, repentance would be all the sweeter for
me. When at the end of the service the priest said: 'The blessing
of the Lord be upon you', it seemed to me that I experienced,
momentarily transmitted to me, a physical sensation of well-
being. As though some kind of light and warmth had suddenly
entered my heart. The service ended, and the priest came over
to me and asked whether he should come to our house to say
vespers, and when this should be; but I thanked him kindly for
what he wanted, so I thought, to do for me, and said I would
come myself either on foot, or driving,

'Do you really want to put yourself to that trouble?' he said.

And I did not know what to reply, as I was afraid to commit
the sin of pride.

After Mass, if Katya was not with me, I always sent the
carriage home, and returned alone on foot, bowing low, with
humility, to everyone I met, trying to find an opportunity of
giving aid or advice, of sacrificing myself for someone, helping
to lift a cart, rock a child, let others pass along the road and
get myself muddy. One evening I heard the steward, while
delivering his report to Katya, say that Semyon, a muzhik, had
come to beg for some planks to make his daughter's coffin and
a rouble for the costs of the funeral, and that he had given
them. 'Are they really so poor?' I asked. 'Very poor, miss. They
haven't a bean,' replied the steward. On hearing this, I felt a
pang in my heart, and yet at the same time I seemed to rejoice.
Deceiving Katya with the excuse that I was going out for a
walk, I ran upstairs, got out all my money (it was very little,
but it was everything I had) and, crossing myself, set off alone,
through the terrace and the garden, to Semyon's hut in the
village. It was at the edge of the village and, observed by no
one, I went up to the window, put the money outside it and
knocked on it. Someone came out of the hut, made the door
creak, and called to me; trembling and chilled with fear, like a
criminal, I came running home. Katya asked me where I had
been, and what was the matter with me, but I could not even

understand what she was saying, and did not reply to her. Everything suddenly seemed to me so trivial and petty. I locked myself up in my room and for a long time walked to and fro, unable to do or think anything, unable to account for my feeling. I thought of the joy of the whole family, of the words they would use about the person who had left the money, and I began to feel sorry I had not given it to them myself. I also thought about what Sergey Mikhailych would say if he learned of this action, and was glad that no one would ever learn of it. And such was the joy in me, and so bad did everyone seem to me, including myself, and with such gentle meekness did I look upon myself and on everyone, that the thought of death, like a dream of happiness, came to me. I smiled, and prayed, and wept, and with such passion and warmth did I love everyone in the world, including myself, at that moment. Between services I read the Gospels, and that book became more and more comprehensible to me, more moving and more simple the story of that divine life, and more terrible and impenetrable the depths of feeling and thought which I found in its teaching. On the other hand, however, how clear and simple everything seemed to me when, rising from that book, I once again studied and thought about the life that surrounded me. It seemed so difficult to live badly and so simple to love everyone and be loved. Everyone was so kind and gentle to me; even Sonya, to whom I continued to give lessons, was quite different, tried to understand, to oblige, and not upset me. As I treated others, so did others treat me. Going over my enemies then, whose forgiveness I had to ask before confession, outside of our household I could remember only one girl, a neighbour, whom I had made fun of in front of guests a year ago and who because of this had stopped coming to see us. I wrote her a letter, admitting I was to blame and asking her forgiveness. She replied to me with a letter in which she herself asked forgiveness and forgave me. I wept with joy as I read those simple lines, in which at the time I saw such deep and touching emotion. Nurse burst into tears when I asked her forgiveness. 'Why are they all so kind to me? What have I done to deserve such love?' I used to wonder. And I would find myself remembering Sergey Mikhailych, and think about him for a long time. I could not help it, and did not even consider it a sin. But I thought about him now in quite a different way than I had on that night when I had discovered for the first time that I loved him; I thought about him now as I thought about myself, involuntarily associating him with every thought about my future. The overwhelming influence I felt when he was near had completely vanished in my mind. I now felt myself his equal and, from the height of the spiritual mood in which I found myself, completely understood him. What had earlier seemed strange in him was now plain to me. Only now did I understand why he had said that happiness is only to be had in living for another, and I was now in complete agreement with him. It seemed to me that together the two of us would be so infinitely and serenely happy. And what I saw before me was not foreign travel, nor high society, nor glamour, but something quite different, a quiet family life in the country, with eternal self-sacrifice, eternal love for each other and an eternal awareness in all things of a gentle and enabling Providence.

I took communion, as I had planned to, on my birthday. So complete was the happiness within my breast when I returned from the church that day, that I was afraid of life, afraid of each impression, of anything that might disturb that happiness. But no sooner had we got out of the brake on to the front steps than the familiar cabriolet began to thunder from the bridge, and I caught sight of Sergey Mikhailych. He congratulated me, and together we went into the living-room. Never since I had known him had I been so calm and independent with him as I was that morning. I knew that within me there was a whole new world which he did not understand and which was above him. I did not feel the slightest embarrassment with him. He must have understood the origin of this, and was especially tender, gentle and piously deferential towards me. I was about to go over to the piano, but he locked it and put the key in his pocket.

'Don't spoil your mood,' he said. 'The music you have in your soul just now is better than any music in the world.'

I was grateful to him for this, yet at the same time I found it slightly unpleasant that he understood too clearly and easily everything within my soul that ought to be secret from everyone. At dinner he said that he had come to congratulate me and also to say goodbye, because tomorrow he was going to Moscow. As he said this, he looked at Katya; but then stole a fleeting glance at me, and I saw that he was afraid he might notice agitation in my face. But I was not surprised, was not alarmed, did not even ask him how long he would be away. I had known he was going to say this, and knew that he would not go. How did I know it? I cannot explain it to myself now; but on that memorable day it seemed to me that I knew everything that had been or would be. I was in a kind of happy dream, where all that happens seems to have happened already, and has long been known to one, and it will all happen again, and one knows that it will.

He wanted to go immediately after dinner, but Katya, who was tired after the service, went to lie down for a while, and he had to wait until she woke up in order to say goodbye to her. There was sun in the drawing-room, and we went out to the terrace. As soon as we sat down, I quite calmly began to say the things that were bound to decide the fate of my love. And I began to speak no sooner and no later, but at the very moment we sat down, and nothing had yet been said, the conversation had not taken any tone or turn that might have interfered with what I wanted to say. I myself do not know where this calm of mine came from, this determination and precision of speech. It was as though the speaker were not I, but someone independent of me, speaking in me. He sat opposite me, his elbows on the railing, and, pulling a twig of lilac towards him, tore the leaves from it. When I began to speak, he let the twig go and leaned his head on his hand. This could have been the posture of someone who was either perfectly calm or very agitated.

'Why are you going?' I asked meaningfully, in measured tones, and looking straight at him.

He took some time to reply.

'Business!' he said quietly, lowering his eyes.

I understood how hard it was for him to lie to me, and in response to a question that had been asked so sincerely.

'Listen,' I said. 'You know what kind of day this is for me. This day is very important for many reasons. If I ask you this question, it is not in order to show interest (you know that I have grown accustomed to you, and care about you), I ask because I need to know. Why are you going?'

'It's very hard for me to tell you the true reason why I am going,' he said. 'This week I have thought a great deal about you and about myself, and have decided that I must go. You understand the reason why, and if you do care about me you won't ask any more.' He rubbed his forehead with his hand, and covered his eyes with it. 'It's difficult for me . . . But you understand.'

My heart began to beat violently.

'I can't understand,' I said. 'I can't! You must tell me, for God's sake, and for the sake of this day, tell me, I can take anything calmly.'

He changed his posture, glanced at me and again pulled the twig towards him.

'However,' he said, after a short silence and in a voice which he vainly tried to make sound firm, 'though it's stupid, and impossible to put into words, and though it's painful for me, I will try to explain to you,' he added, frowning as if in physical pain.

'Very well, go on!' I said.

'Imagine that there was a gentleman – let us call him A.,' he said, 'an elderly man who had outlived his days, and a lady, B., who was young and happy, and had not yet seen anything of life or the world. Because of various family connections, he loved her as he would a daughter, and was not afraid that his love would ever be different.'

He fell silent, but I did not interrupt him.

'But he forgot that B. was so young that life for her was still a plaything,' he suddenly continued in a swift and decisive tone, and without looking at me, 'and that it was easy for her to love in a different way, and that this would appear to her as fun. And he made a mistake, and suddenly felt another emotion, as heavy as remorse, stealing its way into his soul, and was afraid. He was afraid that their previous friendly relations would be upset, and decided to go away before those relations could be upset.' Saying this, as if casually he again began to rub his eyes with his hand and covered them.

'But why was he afraid to love in a different way?' I said, barely audibly, restraining my excitement, and my voice was steady; but to him it probably seemed that I was being facetious. He replied in a tone that suggested he was hurt.

'You are young,' he said. 'I am not young. You want to play, but I need something else. Play, if you wish, only not with me, for otherwise I shall confess to you, and I will feel bad about it, and you will feel guilty. That is what A. said,' he added. 'Well, that's all nonsense, but you understand why I'm going. And let's not talk of it any more. Please!'

'No! No! Let's talk!' I said, and the tears began to tremble in my voice. 'Did he love her or didn't he?'

He made no reply.

'And if he didn't love her, then why did he play with her, as if she were a child?' I said quietly.

'Yes, yes, A. was to blame,' he replied, hurriedly interrupting me. 'But it was all over, and they parted . . . friends.'

'But that is dreadful! Is there no other ending?' I barely managed to get out, and was frightened of what I had said.

'Yes, there is,' he said, revealing a worried face, and looking straight at me. 'There are two different endings. Only for God's sake do not interrupt, and listen to me quietly. Some say,' he began, getting up and smiling a sickly, painful smile, 'some say that A. took leave of his senses, fell madly in love with B., and told her so . . . And she simply laughed. For her it was a joke, while for him it was a matter that involved his whole life.'

I gave a start, and tried to interrupt him, to say that he should not dare to speak for me, but restraining me he put his hand on mine.

'Wait,' he said in a trembling voice. 'Others say that she took pity on him, imagined, poor thing, who had seen nothing of the world, that she really could love him, and consented to be his wife. And he, the madman, believed it, believed that his whole life would start over again, but she saw that she had deceived him . . . and that he had deceived her . . . Let us not talk about it any more,' he concluded, plainly unable to go on, and began to pace the floor silently in front of me.

He had said: 'Let us not talk' – but I could see that, with every fibre of his being, he was waiting for me to speak. I wanted to, but could not: something was constricting my breast. I glanced at him: he was pale, and his lower lip was trembling. I felt sorry for him. I made an effort and suddenly, breaking through the force of the silence that had fettered me, began to speak in a voice that was quiet and inward, and one which I feared would break at any second.

'And the third ending,' I said, and paused, but he said nothing. 'The third ending is that he did not love her, but hurt her, and thought he was right, went away and even thought he had something to be proud of. It was you for whom it was all a joke, not me – I loved you, loved you from the very first day,' I repeated, and at the word 'loved' my voice involuntarily changed from being quiet and inward to one that was a wild shriek, which I myself found frightening.

He stood palely facing me, his lips trembled more and more violently, and two tears emerged on to his cheeks.

'It's not right!' I almost shouted, feeling that I was choking with angry, unwept tears. 'Why do this?' I said quietly, and rose in order to leave him.

But he would not let me go. His head was resting on my knees, his lips still kissed my trembling hands, and his tears wetted them.

'My God, if only I had known,' he said.

'Why? Why do you do it?' I kept on saying, but in my soul there was happiness, a happiness that had left forever, never to return.

Five minutes later Sonya was rushing upstairs to Katya and shouting, for the whole house to hear, that Masha wanted to marry Sergey Mikhailovich.

V

There were no reasons why our wedding should be postponed, and neither he nor I had any wish for that. Katya, it is true, began to express a desire to go to Moscow in order to buy and order the trousseau, and his mother was on the point of demanding that before he got married he should get himself a new carriage and furniture and have the house freshly wall-papered, but the two of us insisted that all this, if it really were so indispensable, should be done later, and that we should be married some two weeks after my birthday, quietly, without a trousseau, guests, best men, suppers, champagne and all those conventional trappings of a wedding. He told me how dis-pleased his mother was that the wedding should take place without music, without a mountain of trunks, and without the whole house being redecorated from scratch, so unlike her own wedding, which had cost thirty thousand; and how in secret from him, with serious intent, she rummaged through the trunks in the store room, conferring with Maryushka, the housekeeper, about carpets, drapes and salvers that were appar-ently most essential for our happiness. Katya did the same on my behalf with our nurse, Kuzminishna. And with Katya, too, it was impossible to talk about the matter in a less than serious manner. She was firmly convinced that when he and I talked about our future, we were merely billing and cooing, indulging in nonsense, as was characteristic of people in our situation; but that our real future happiness would depend merely on the correct cutting and sewing of camisoles and the stitching of tablecloths and napkins. Several times each day secret messages passed between Pokrovskoye and Nikolskoye about the prep-arations that were being made in both houses, and although outwardly it appeared that the relations between Katya and her mother were most affectionate, a rather hostile but most subtle diplomacy could already be sensed between them. Tatyana Semyonovna, his mother, with whom I now made closer ac-quaintance, was a prim, severe mistress of the household, a lady of the olden times. He loved her not merely as a son, out of duty, but as a person, from feeling, considering her to be the best, most intelligent, kind and loving woman in the world. Tatyana Semyonovna was always kind to us and especially to me, and was glad that her son was getting married, but when I visited her in my role of fiancée I had the impression that she wanted me to feel that as a match for her son I could have been better, and that it would do me no harm to remember that. I understood her perfectly, and agreed with her.

During those two last weeks we saw each other every day. He would come to dinner, and stay until midnight. But even though he said – and I knew he was speaking the truth – that he could not live without me, he never spent a whole day with me, and tried to go on attending to his business affairs. Right up to the wedding, our outward relations remained the same as before: we continued to use the polite form of address, he did not even kiss my hand, and not only did he not seek opportunities to be alone with me – he even avoided them. It was as if he were afraid to give in to the enormous, harmful tenderness that was in him. I do not know whether it was he or I who had changed, but now I felt quite equal to him, no longer found in him the pretence of straightforwardness that had previously annoyed me and often with pleasure saw before me not a man who inspired respect and fear, but a gentle child, bewildered with happiness. 'So that's all there was to him!' I often thought. 'He's just another person like myself, that's all.' It now seemed to me that he stood before me in his entirety, and that I had now learned to know him completely. And everything I had learned about him was so simple, and so congenial to me. Even his plans for how our life would be together were the same as my plans, only more clearly and better expressed in his words.

During those days the weather was bad, and we spent most of the time indoors. The best of our intimate talks took place in the corner between the piano and the window. The light of the candles was closely reflected on the black window; now and then drops struck the shiny pane and trickled down. The rain pattered on the roof, water splashed in the puddle under the roof-gutter, and there were gusts of damp air from the window.

And somehow this made our corner seem all the brighter, warmer and more cheerful.

'You know, there's something I've long wanted to tell you,' he said once, when we were sitting up late in that corner. 'I kept thinking about it while you were playing the piano.'

'Don't say anything, I know it all,' I said.

He smiled.

'Yes, you are right, let us not talk.'

'No, tell me, what is it?' I asked.

'Well, it's this. You remember the story I told you about A. and B.?'

'Of course I remember that silly story, how could I fail to? It's just as well it ended as it did . . .'

'Yes, a little more of that, and all my happiness would have perished by my own hand. You rescued me. But the main thing is that I lied all the time back then, and I'm ashamed, and I want to say it all now.'

'Oh, please, you don't need to.'

'Don't be afraid,' he said, smiling. 'I merely need to justify myself. When I began to speak, my intention was to present an argument.'

'Why do you need to do that?' I said. 'That's the last thing you need.'

'Yes, I presented my argument poorly. After all my disappointments and mistakes in life, when I came to the estate that day I told myself firmly that love was finished for me, that there remained for me only the obligations of old age, that for a long time I had not realized what my feeling for you was and what it might lead me to. I hoped, and I did not hope; at some moments it seemed to me that you were flirting, at others I had faith, and I really did not know what I was going to do. But after that evening – you remember, when we walked in the garden at night – I became afraid, my present happiness seemed to me too great, and outrageous. Well, what would have happened if I had allowed myself to hope, and in vain? But of course, I was thinking only of myself, because I'm a loathsome egoist.'

He was silent for a moment, as he looked at me.

'However, not everything I said then was nonsense. I mean, it was understandable and indeed right for me to feel afraid. I take so much from you and can give so little. You are still a child, you are a bud that is still to open, you are in love for the first time in your life, while I . . .'

'Yes, tell me the truth,' I said, but then suddenly felt afraid of what his reply might be. 'No, don't,' I added.

'Have I been in love before? Is that what you mean?' he said, guessing my thought immediately. 'I can tell you that. No, I haven't. Never anything like this feeling . . .' But some kind of painful memory seemed to flicker in his mind. 'No, here too I need your heart in order to have the right to love you,' he said sadly. 'So should I not have reflected before saying that I love you? What do I give you? Love – yes, there is that.'

'Is that not enough?' I asked, looking him in the eyes.

'No, my dear, for you it is not enough,' he continued. 'You have youth and beauty! Often I cannot sleep at nights now because of happiness, and I keep thinking of our future life together. I have lived through many things, and it seems to me that I have found what is necessary for happiness. A quiet, secluded life in our rural backwoods, with an opportunity of doing good to people to whom it is easy to do the good they are unaccustomed to having done to them; then labour, which one may suppose, will bring benefit; then rest, nature, books, music, the love of those who are close to one – there is my happiness, no loftier than which I have ever dreamed. And then, on top of all that, a friend such as you, a family, perhaps, and all that a man could possibly desire.'

'Yes,' I said.

'For me, who have lived out my youth – yes, but not for you,' he went on. 'You have not yet lived, you will perhaps want to seek happiness in something different, and find it, perhaps, in something different. You think now that this is happiness because you love me.'

'No, I have always desired and loved this quiet family life,' I said. 'And you are merely saying the same thing that I have thought.'

He smiled.

'That is just how it seems to you, my dear. But for you it is not enough. You have youth and beauty,' he said again, reflectively.

But I grew angry, because he did not believe me and seemed to be reproaching me for having youth and beauty.

'Then why do you love me?' I said angrily. 'For my youth, or for myself?'

'I don't know, but I love you,' he replied, looking at me with an attentive, magnetic gaze.

I made no reply and involuntarily looked into his eyes. Suddenly something strange happened to me: first I stopped seeing what was around me, then his face disappeared before me, and only his eyes shone, it seemed, facing my own, then it seemed to me that these eyes were inside me; everything grew dark, I could see nothing and had to screw up my eyes in order to tear myself away from the sense of pleasure and fear which that gaze was producing in me . . .

On the day before the day that had been appointed for our wedding, the weather cleared up towards evening. And after the rains that had begun in summer, the first cold and brilliant autumn evening gleamed in clarity. Everything was wet, cold and bright, and in the garden for the first time one could observe the spaciousness, the varied colour and the bareness of autumn. The sky was clear, cold and pale. I went to bed happy with the thought that tomorrow, the day of our wedding, the weather would be fine.

That day I awoke with the sun, and the thought that it was today . . . almost frightened and surprised me. I went out into the garden. The sun had just risen and was shining in fragments through the falling, yellowing leaves of the lime trees in the avenue. The path was strewn with rustling leaves. Bright, wrinkled clusters of red berries hung on the branches of the rowans, whose sparse leaves were shrivelled, killed by the frost, and the dahlias, too, were wrinkled and blackened. For the first time frost lay like silver on the pale green of the grass and on the broken burdock plants around the house. In the clear, cold sky there was not, nor could there be, a single cloud.

'Is it really today?' I wondered, unable to believe my own

happiness. 'Will I really wake up tomorrow not here, but in that strange house at Nikolskoye, the one with the pillars? Will I really not await his arrival and greet him and spend the evenings and nights talking about him with Katya any more? Will I not sit with him at the piano in the drawing-room at Pokrovskoye? Will I not see him off and fear for his safety on dark nights?' But I remembered that yesterday he had said that he was going to call for the last time, and Katya had made me try on my wedding dress and said: 'In memory of tomorrow'; and I believed for a moment, and then doubted again. Can it really be that after today I shall live over there with a mother-in-law, without Nadezha, without old Grigory, without Katya? Shall I no longer kiss Nurse goodnight or hear her say, from old custom, as she makes the sign of the cross over me: 'Goodnight, my lady'? Shall I no longer give Sonya her lessons and play with her and knock through the wall to her in the morning and hear her resonant laughter? Today shall I really become a stranger to myself, and will a new life, one in which my hopes and desires are realized, open out before me? Is this new life really to be for ever?' I waited for him with impatience, for I found it hard to be alone with these thoughts. He arrived early, and it was only when he was there that I quite believed that today I would be his wife, and that thought ceased to frighten me.

Before dinner we walked to our church to attend a memorial service for my father.

'If only he were alive now!' I thought as we returned home, and I silently supported myself on the arm of the man who had been the best friend of the one I was thinking about. During the prayer, as my head touched the cold stone of the chapel floor, I had such a vivid mental picture of my father, believed so profoundly that his spirit understood me and blessed my choice, that even now it seemed to me that his spirit was here, floating above us, and that I could feel his blessing on me. My memories, and my hopes, and my happiness and sadness all merged within me into one single solemn and pleasant feeling, which was in keeping with this motionless fresh air, this silence, the bareness of the fields, and the pale sky from which on

everything fell these brilliant but powerless rays that kept trying
to burn my cheek. It seemed to me that the one with whom I
was walking understood and shared my feeling. He walked
quietly and in silence, and in his face, at which I glanced up
from time to time, there was expressed that same not-quite-
sadness and not-quite-happiness that were both in nature and
within my heart.

Suddenly he turned to me, and I saw that he wanted to say
something. 'What if he starts talking about something else from
what I'm thinking about?' passed through my mind. But he
began to talk about my father, without even naming him.

'And once he said to me, jokingly: "Marry my Masha!"' he
said.

'How happy he would be now!' I said, pressing harder the
arm that carried my own.

'Yes, you were still a child then,' he continued, looking into
my eyes. 'I kissed those eyes then, and loved them only because
they were like his, and never thought they would be so dear to
me for their own sake. I used to call you Masha in those days.'

'Please say *thou* to me,' I said.

'I was just about to do that,' he replied quietly. 'Only now
do I feel that you, that *thou*, art wholly mine.' And his calm,
happy, magnetic gaze rested on me.

And we kept on walking quietly along the unbeaten path
across the trampled, flattened stubble field; and our footsteps
and voices were the only things we heard. On one side, across
a hollow to a distant leafless wood, stretched the browning
stubble field, across which, to the side of us, a muzhik with a
plough was making a black stripe that grew wider and wider.
A herd of horses that was scattered at the foot of the hill seemed
close. On the other side and ahead of us, as far as the garden
and our house, which was visible behind it, a thawed field of
winter crops showed black and sometimes green in places. On
everything shone a tepid sun, on everything lay long, fibrous
spiders' webs. They floated in the air around us and settled on
the frost-dried stubble, got into our eyes, our hair, our clothes.
When we spoke, our voices resounded and hung in the motionless air above us, as though we were alone in the whole world

and alone beneath this blue vault, on which, flashing and trembling, a tepid sun played.

I also felt I wanted to call him *thou*, but felt ashamed to.

'Why are you walking so fast?' I said, doing so, in a quick patter, almost in a whisper, and found myself blushing.

He began to walk more slowly, and looked at me even more affectionately, cheerfully and happily.

When we reached home, his mother and the guests, whom we could not avoid, were already there, and until we came out of the church and got into the carriage to go to Nikolskoye, I was not alone with him.

The church was almost empty, and I could just glimpse his mother, standing erect on a mat near the choir, Katya in a cap with purple ribbons and tears on her cheeks, and two or three of the servants, who were staring at me curiously. At him I did not look, but I could feel his presence there, beside me. I listened closely to the words of the prayers, repeated them, but nothing responded in my soul. I was unable to pray, and looked dully at the icons, the candles, the embroidered cross on the chasuble on the priest's back, at the iconostasis, at the window of the church – and took nothing in. My only feeling was that something extraordinary was happening to me. When the priest turned to us with the cross in his hand, congratulated us and said that he had christened me and 'Now God has brought me to marry you too', Katya and his mother kissed us, and old Grigory's voice was heard summoning the carriage, I felt surprise and alarm that it was all over so soon, but nothing unusual, nothing that corresponded to the mystery that had been performed over me, took place within my soul. He and I kissed each other, and that kiss was such a strange one, alien to our feeling. 'And is that all?' I wondered. We came out to the porch, the sound of wheels boomed thickly under the vault of the church, there was a smell of fresh air in one's face, he put on his hat and helped me into the carriage. From the carriage window I caught sight of a frosty moon with a halo round it. He got in beside me and closed the door after him. Something pricked my heart. The assurance with which he had done it seemed almost offensive to me. Katya's voice was shouting that I should cover my head, the wheels began to rumble on the stone, and then on the soft road, and we were off. Huddled up in the corner, I looked through the window at the distant, bright fields and the road that was receding in the cold radiance of the moon. And, without looking at him, I felt him there, beside me. 'What, is that all it had given me, this moment from which I expected so much?' I thought, and it still seemed somehow humiliating and offensive for me to be sitting alone with him, so close to him. I turned to him, intending to say something. But the words refused to be said, as though I no longer had my previous feeling of tenderness, and as though feelings of insult and fear had replaced it.

'Until this moment I did not believe that it could happen,' he replied quietly to my gaze.

'Yes, but I feel frightened for some reason,' I said.

'Frightened of me, my dear?' he said, taking my hand and lowering his head to it.

My hand lay lifelessly in his, and my heart was beginning to hurt with the cold.

'Yes,' I whispered.

But at that moment my heart suddenly began to beat more powerfully, my hand began to tremble and pressed his, I felt hot, my eyes sought his gaze in the semi-darkness, and I suddenly felt that I was not afraid of him, that this fear was love, a new and even more tender and more powerful love than the one I had experienced before. I felt that I was entirely his, and that I was happy in his power over me.

PART TWO

VI

Days, weeks, two months of secluded rural life passed unnotice-
ably, as it seemed at the time; and yet the feelings, excitements
and joys of those two months would have sufficed for a whole
lifetime. My dreams and his of how our life in the country
would be arranged were realized in quite a different way from
the one we had expected. But the life we led was not inferior to
our dreams. There was none of that austere toil, that fulfilment
of the duty of self-sacrifice and living for others which I had
pictured to myself during my engagement; there was, on the
contrary, merely a selfish feeling of love for each other, a desire
to be loved, a constant gaiety that had no apparent cause, and
a forgetting of everything in the world. To be sure, he sometimes
went off to do some work in his study, sometimes travelled into
town on business, and went about the management of the
estate; but I could see what an effort it cost him to tear himself
away from me. And he himself later confessed that everything
in the world, when I was not there, seemed to him such nonsense that he could not understand how anyone could ever
occupy himself with it. For me it was the same. I read, occupied
myself with my music, with Mother, with the school; but did it
all only because each of those occupations was connected with
him and earned his approval; but as soon as the thought of him
was not admixed with some matter or other, my hands would
grow idle, and it would seem to me quite amusing to think
that there could be anything in the world except him. That was
possibly a bad and selfish feeling; but that feeling gave me

happiness and raised me high above the whole world. He was all that existed for me, and I considered him the most wonderful and flawless human being in the world; and so I was unable to live for anything else but him, to be in his eyes what he considered me to be. And he considered me to be the first and most wonderful woman in the world, endowed with all possible virtues; and I tried to be that woman in the eyes of the first and finest man in the whole world.

On one occasion he came to my room while I was saying my prayers. I glanced round at him and went on praying. He sat down at the table in order not to distract me, and opened a book. But I had a feeling that he was looking at me, and I glanced round again. He smiled, and I burst out laughing, and could not go on with my prayers.

'What about you, have you already said your prayers?' I asked.

'Yes. And you carry on, for I am going now.'

'You do say your prayers, I hope?'

Without replying, he made to leave, but I stopped him.

'My dear, please, for my sake, say your prayers with me.'

He stood beside me and, awkwardly lowering his arms, with an earnest expression, stumblingly, began to recite. From time to time he turned to me, seeking help and approval in my face. When he had finished, I laughed and embraced him.

'Now, now! You're making me feel as if I were ten years old again,' he said, blushing and kissing my hands.

Our house was one of those old country houses in which, respecting and loving one another, several generations of kindred have lived their lives. It was all redolent of good, decent family memories, which suddenly, as soon as I entered that house, seemed to become my own memories, too. Tatyana Semyonovna supervised the order and decoration of the house in the old, time-honoured way. It could not be said that everything in it was elegant and beautiful; but from the servants to the furniture and the cooking, there was an abundance of everything, everything was neat, solid, tidy and inspired respect. In the drawing-room the furniture stood symmetrically, there were portraits on the walls, and the floor was covered with home-made carpets and mats. In the sofa room there was an old grand piano, with chests of drawers in two different styles, sofas and small tables with brass and inlaid work. My study, whose fittings had been arranged by Tatyana Semyonovna, contained the very best furniture of different periods and styles and, among other things, an old pier-glass, into which I was at first quite unable to look without bashfulness, but which later became dear to me, like an old friend. Tatyana Semyonovna kept a quiet profile, but everything in the house ran like clockwork, though there were far too many servants. But all those servants, who wore soft boots with no heels (Tatyana Semyonovna considered the creaking of soles and the stamping of heels the most unpleasant things in the world), all those servants seemed proud of their calling, trembled before the old *barynya*, looked on my husband and me with a protective kindness, and appeared to do their tasks with distinct satisfaction. Regularly every Saturday the floors in the house were washed and the carpets beaten, on the first of each month there was a religious service with sprinkling of holy water, on Tatyana Semyonovna's name-day and on her son's (and on mine, too – for the first time that autumn) there were feastings to which the whole neighbourhood was invited. And all this had been done invariably, for as long as Tatyana Semyonovna could remember. My husband did not involve himself in the running of the household, attending only to the farm work and the peasants, and spent much time on this. Even in winter he rose very early, so that when I woke up I would find he was gone. He usually returned for tea, which we drank alone, and was almost always at that time, after the chores and troubles of the farm work, in that special mood of cheerfulness that we called 'wild delight'. Often I would demand that he tell me what he had been doing that morning, and he would tell me such nonsensical things that we died of laughter; sometimes I demanded a serious account and, holding back a smile, he gave it to me. I gazed at his eyes, at his moving lips, and took in nothing, merely glad to see him and hear his voice.

'Well then, repeat it, what did I say?' he would ask. But I was unable to repeat any of it. It was so absurd that he should be talking not about himself and me, but about something else. As though it were not a matter of indifference, what took place out there. Only much later did I start to understand something of his concerns, and take an interest in them. Tatyana Semyonovna never appeared before dinner, took tea alone and greeted us only through emissaries. In our special, extravagantly happy little world a voice from her staid and orderly corner sounded so strange that I often could not restrain myself and merely burst out laughing in reply to the maid who with folded hands reported that Tatyana Semyonovna wished to know how I had slept after my walk yesterday, and of herself wished to inform us that she had had a pain in her side all night and that a stupid dog in the village had barked and kept her awake. 'And her ladyship also wished to inquire how you liked the baking this morning, and to inform you that it was not Taras who baked today but Nikolasha who was trying his hand for the first time, and actually it was not bad, she said, the pretzels especially, though he overbaked the rusks.' Before dinner we never spent much time together. I would play the piano, or read alone, while he wrote, or went out again; but towards dinner time, at four o'clock, we met in the drawing-room, my mother-in-law came sailing out of her room, and the impoverished gentlewomen, wandering pilgrims, of whom there were always two or three living in the house, made their appearance. Regularly every day my husband, in accordance with long-established custom, offered his arm to Mother, to take her in to dinner; but she would insist that he give me the other arm, and so regularly every day we jostled in the doorway and got into a muddle. His mother also presided at dinner, and the conversation was decorous, sensible and rather formal. The simple words my husband and I exchanged made a pleasant break from the formality of those dinner sessions. Sometimes disputes arose between mother and son, and they would poke gentle fun at each other; I was particularly fond of those disputes and banterings, because they were the most solid expression of the tender and unshakable love that united the two of them. After dinner *maman* would settle into a large armchair in the drawing-room and grind snuff or cut the pages of books that had been newly acquired, while we read aloud or went off to the piano in the sofa room. We read together a great deal at this time, but music was our favourite and best enjoyment, always touching new strings in our hearts and seeming to reveal us to each other once again. When I played his favourite pieces he sat on a distant sofa where I could hardly see him, and because of his embarrassment about showing emotion tried to conceal the effect that the music had on him; but often, when he was not expecting it, I would get up from the piano and go over to him in an attempt to catch on his face the traces of feeling and the unnatural brilliance and moistness of his eyes, which he tried in vain to hide from me. Mother often felt an inclination to watch us in the sofa room, but she was probably afraid of inconveniencing us, and sometimes, as if ignoring us, she would pass through the sofa room with a pretended expression of gravity and indifference; but I knew that she had no genuine reason to go to her room and return so soon. I poured out evening tea in the large drawing-room, and again everyone in the house gathered around the table. For a long time this formal session before the shining samovar, with the distribution of cups and glasses, made me uneasy. I kept feeling that I was not worthy of this honour, that I was too young and frivolous to turn the tap of such a large samovar, to put the glass on Nikita's salver and say: 'For Pyotr Ivanovich', 'For Marya Minichna' – to ask 'Is it sweet enough?' – and leave lumps of sugar for Nurse and deserving servants. 'Wonderful, wonderful,' my husband would often say. 'Just like a grown-up!' – and that upset me even more.

After tea *maman* played patience or listened to Marya Minichna's fortune-telling; then she kissed us both and made the sign of the cross over us, and we went off to our own part of the house. For the most part, however, we sat up together until after midnight, and that was the best and most pleasant time. He would tell me about his past life, we made plans, talked philosophy sometimes, and tried to keep our voices down so that no one upstairs would hear us and report us to Tatyana Semyonovna, who insisted that we go to bed early. Sometimes, when we got hungry, we would steal along to the buffet, obtain

a cold supper through the patronage of Nikita, and consume it
in my study by the light of a single candle. He and I lived
like strangers in that big old house, in which everything was
dominated by the stern spirit of the olden days and of Tatyana
Semyonovna. Not only she, but the servants, the old spinsters,
the furniture and the pictures inspired me with respect, a certain
fear and an awareness that he and I were a little out of place
here, and that we must conduct our lives here with great caution
and attention. Recollecting it now, I can see that many things
– the binding nature of that unvarying order, and those myriad
idle and inquisitive servants in our house – were uncomfortable
and oppressive; but at the time it was that very sense of con-
straint that vivified our love even more. Neither of us – not
only I, but he too – ever let it show that anything displeased
us. On the contrary, he even seemed to hide from what was
unpleasant. *Maman*'s lackey, Dmitry Sidorovich, was very fond
of smoking his pipe, and regularly went into my husband's
study to take his tobacco from the drawer; and it was a sight
to see the merry pretence of fear with which Sergey Mikhailych
tiptoed through to me and, wagging his finger and winking,
pointed to Dmitry Sidorovich, who had no idea that he was
being watched. And when Dmitry Sidorovich had gone away
without observing us, my husband, overjoyed that everything
had gone according to plan, as on all the other occasions, would
say that I was a darling, and kiss me. Sometimes I found his
calmness, his all-forgiving tolerance and apparent indifference
to everything less than appealing – never noticing that the same
things dwelt within me, too – and considered it weakness. 'It's
like a child who doesn't dare to show his will!' I thought.

'Ah, my dear,' he replied to me once, when I told him that I
found his weakness surprising, 'can one really be dissatisfied
with anything when one is as happy as I? It is easier to give way
oneself, than to bend the will of others, of that I have long
been convinced; and there is no situation in which it would be
impossible to be happy. And things are so good for us! I cannot
be angry; for me there is now nothing that is bad, there is only
the pitiful and the comical. And above all: *le mieux est l'ennemi
du bien*. Would you believe it, when I hear the doorbell ring,

or receive a letter, or simply when I wake up – I feel afraid. Afraid because one must go on living, and because something may change; but there can't be anything better than what there is now.'

I believed him, but did not understand what he meant. Things were good for me, but it seemed that all this was a matter of course, and was bound to be so, and not otherwise; that it was always like this for everyone, and that somewhere out there there was also another kind of happiness, which although no greater, was different.

Thus two months went by, winter arrived with its cold and snowstorms, and in spite of the fact that he was with me, I began to feel lonely, began to feel that life was repeating itself, that there was nothing new either in him or in me, and that, on the contrary, we seemed to be returning to what had been before. More than before, he began to occupy himself with business in which I had no part, and again I began to have the impression that there was within his soul a special world into which he did not want to admit me. His perpetual calmness irritated me. I loved him no less than before, and no less than before was happy in his love; but instead of growing, my love stood still, and beside it a new and disquieting emotion began to steal into my soul. Loving was not enough for me, after having experienced the happiness of loving him. I wanted move-ment, and not a calm flow of life. I wanted excitement, danger, and self-sacrifice for the sake of feeling. There was in me an excess of energy that could find no room in our quiet life. I had fits of depression, which was something unpleasant I tried to conceal from him, and also fits of violent tenderness and cheer-fulness, which frightened him. He noticed my condition before I did, and proposed a trip to town; but I begged him to forget this plan, and not to alter our way of life, not spoil our happi-ness. And indeed, I was happy; but I was tormented by the fact that this happiness cost me no effort, no sacrifice, when the forces of effort and sacrifice were wearing me out. I loved him and could see that I was everything to him; but I wanted every-one to see our love, for them to try to prevent me from loving him, while I went on loving him nonetheless. My mind and

even my feelings were engaged, but there was another emotion
– one of youth, the need for movement, that found no satisfaction in our quiet life. Why did he tell me that we could go to
town whenever I wanted to? Had he not told me this, I might
have realized that the feeling that was wearing me out was
harmful nonsense, my own fault, and that the sacrifice I sought
was right here, in front of me, in the overcoming of that feeling.
The thought that I could escape from the depression by merely
going to town for a while occurred to me involuntarily; and yet
at the same time the notion of tearing him away from all that
he loved, just for my own sake, made me feel ashamed of myself
and sorry for him. And the time went by, the snowdrifts grew
higher and higher around the walls of the house, and there we
were, alone as alone could be, and we were just the same to
each other as we had been before; but somewhere out there, in
the glitter, the noise, crowds of people were feeling, suffering
and rejoicing, oblivious of us and our withdrawn existence.
Worst of all for me was my sense that with each day that passed
the habits of our life were fettering it, so that it had only one
fixed shape, that our feeling for one another was losing its
freedom and becoming subjected to the even, dispassionate flow
of time. In the morning we were usually cheerful, at dinner
respectful, in the evening tender. 'Doing good! . . .' I would say
to myself. 'It's all very well to do good to others and live an
honest life, as he says; but there will be time for that later, and
there are certain things I only have strength for now.' That was
not what I wanted, I needed struggle; I needed feeling to govern
our lives, not life to govern feeling. I wanted to go to the edge
of a precipice with him and say: 'One step, and I'll throw myself
over, one movement and I perish!' And then, ashen-faced on
the edge of the precipice, for him to take me in his strong arms
and hold me above it, so that my blood froze, and carry me off
wherever it pleased him.

This state of mind even affected my health, and my nerves
began to go to pieces. One morning I felt worse than usual; he
had come back from the office in a bad mood, something that
rarely happened with him. I noticed it at once, and asked what
the matter was. But he did not want to tell me, saying it was of

no consequence. As I later found out, because of a dislike he felt for my husband the district police officer was conscripting our muzhiks, making illegal demands on them, and threatening them. My husband could not yet simply swallow this, pretend that it was all merely pitiful and comical: he was angry, and that was why he did not want to talk to me. But I had the impression that he did not want to talk to me because he considered me a child, who could not possibly understand what was on his mind. I turned away from him, said no more and gave instructions that Marya Minichna, who was staying with us, be invited to tea. After tea, which I brought to an end rather quickly, I led Marya Minichna to the sofa room and began to talk loudly to her about some nonsense that held not the slightest interest for me. He paced the room, looking at us from time to time. For some reason, those looks made me feel more and more that I wanted to talk or even laugh; everything I said seemed comical to me, and so did everything that Marya Minichna said. Without a word to me, he went off to his study and shut the door behind him. As soon as he was gone, all my cheerfulness suddenly vanished, prompting Marya Minichna to be surprised and begin to ask me what the matter was. I made no reply, sat down on a sofa, and felt like crying. 'And what is it he's thinking about, anyway?' I thought. 'Some nonsense or other that seems important to him, but if he were to try to tell me what it was, I'd show him that it's all rubbish. No, he needs to think that I wouldn't understand, he needs to humiliate me with his majestic calm, and always be right where I'm concerned. But I'm right too, when I feel bored and empty, when I want to live, to move,' I thought, 'and not stay in one place all the time and feel the time flowing through me. I want to go forward every day, with every hour I want something new, but he wants to stand still and make me stand still with him. And how easy it would be for him! He wouldn't need to take me to town, all he would need to do is be like me, not break himself, not hold himself back, but simply live, in a straightforward way. That is what he counsels me to do, but he isn't a straightforward man. That is the truth of it!'

I could feel the tears welling up within my heart, and with

them my anger at him. That anger frightened me, and I went in to see him. He sat in his study, writing. At the sound of my steps, he glanced round for a moment – indifferently, calmly – and continued his writing. That glance did not appeal to me; instead of going over to him, I stood beside the table at which he was writing, and, opening a book, began to look at it. Once again he broke off, and cast a gaze at me.

'Masha! Are you in a bad mood?' he said.

I replied with a cold look that said: 'You need not ask! Such courtesies!' He shook his head and smiled timidly and tenderly; but for the first time my smile did not respond to his.

'What was wrong today?' I asked. 'Why didn't you tell me?'

'It was trivial! A small unpleasantness,' he replied. 'But now I can tell you. Two of the muzhiks went off to the town . . .'

But I did not let him finish.

'Why didn't you tell me when I asked you over tea?'

'I would have said something stupid, I was angry then.'

'But that was when I needed to know.'

'Why?'

'Why do you always think I can never help you in anything?'

'Is that what I think?' he said, throwing down his pen. 'What I think is that without you, I cannot live. Not only do you help me in everything, everything, but you do everything. You've never noticed, have you?' he laughed. 'You are my whole life. Everything seems good to me only because you are here, because you are needed . . .'

'Yes, I know, I'm a sweet child who must be kept quiet,' I said in a tone that made him look at me in surprise, as though it was the first time he had seen something. 'I don't want quiet, there's enough of it in you, more than enough,' I added.

'Well anyway, now you see what the matter is,' he began hurriedly, interrupting me and evidently afraid to let me say all that was on my mind. 'How would you deal with it?'

'I don't want to now,' I replied. Though I wanted to hear what he had to say, I found it so pleasant to destroy his calm. 'I don't want to play at life – I want to live,' I said, 'like you do.'

His face, which reflected everything with such swiftness and liveliness, showed pain and close attention.

'I want to live with you on equal terms, with you . . .'

But I could not finish: such sadness, deep sadness showed in his face. He was silent for a while.

'In what way do you not live on equal terms with me?' he said. 'Because it is I and not you who has to deal with the district police officer and the drunken muzhiks . . .'

'Not that alone,' I said.

'For God's sake understand this, my dear,' he continued. 'I know that disturbance always brings us pain. I have lived through that and learned to know it. I love you and therefore I cannot but wish to save you from disturbance. In that is my life, in my love for you: so you must not prevent me from living.'

'You're always right!' I said, not looking at him.

I found it annoying that everything in his soul was once again clear and calm, when in me there was annoyance and a feeling similar to remorse.

'Masha! What's wrong?' he asked. 'It's not a question of whether I'm right or you are, it's something quite different: what do you hold against me? Don't answer at once, think about it and then tell me everything you're thinking. You're not pleased with me, and you are probably right not to be, but you must let me know where I am to blame.'

But how could I tell him all that was in my soul? The fact that he had understood me with such instant speed, that once more I was a child before him, that there was nothing I could do which he did not understand and had not foreseen, agitated me even more.

'There is nothing that I hold against you,' I said. 'I am simply bored, and I want not to be bored. But you say that that is how it must be, and again you are right!'

As I said this, I glanced at him. I had attained my goal: his calm was gone, and there was fear and pain in his face.

'Masha,' he began in a quiet, agitated voice. 'It's no trifling matter, what we are doing now. Now our destiny is being shaped. I beg you to hear what I have to say, and not to reply. Why do you want to torment me?'

But I interrupted him.

'I know, you'll be right. You'd do better not to say anything, you're right,' I said coldly, as though it were not me, but some evil spirit speaking within me.

'If you know what you are doing!' he said in a trembling voice.

I began to cry, and felt better. He sat beside me, and was silent. I felt sorry for him, and ashamed of myself, and annoyed about what I had done. I did not look at him. It seemed to me that if he were looking at me at that moment, it must be either with sternness or bewilderment. I glanced round: a meek, tender gaze, as if begging forgiveness, was fixed on me. I took his hand, and said:

'Forgive me! I myself don't know what I said.'

'Yes; but I know what you said, and you said the truth.'

'What?' I asked.

'That we must go to St Petersburg,' he said. 'There is nothing for us to do here just now.'

'As you wish,' I said.

He embraced me, and kissed me.

'You must forgive me,' he said. 'I am guilty before you.'

That evening I played the piano for him for a long time, while he walked about the room, whispering something. He had a habit of whispering, and I often used to ask him what it was he was whispering, and always, after thinking, he would tell me exactly what it was: mostly poetry, and sometimes dreadful nonsense, but the sort of nonsense that enabled me to know what sort of mood he was in.

'What are you whispering today?' I asked.

He stopped, thought and, smiling, quoted two lines of Lermontov:

> . . . And he, mad fellow, begs a storm,
> As though in storms there's calmness![7]

'No, he is more than human, he knows everything!' I thought. 'How can I not love him?'

I got up, took him by the arm and began to walk with him, trying to match my steps with his.

'Yes?' he asked, smiling, and looking at me.

'Yes,' I said in a whisper; and a merry disposition seized us both, our eyes laughed, and we took more and more steps, standing more and more on tiptoe as we did so. And in this same fashion, much to the indignation of Grigory and the astonishment of Mama, who was playing patience in the drawing-room, we set off through all the rooms to the dining-room, and there we stopped, looked at each other, and burst into laughter.

Two weeks later, before the holidays, we were in St Petersburg.

VII

Our trip to St Petersburg, a week in Moscow, his relations and mine, settling into the new apartment, the journey, the new cities and faces – all this went by like a dream. It was all so varied, new, cheerful, it was all illuminated so warmly and brightly with his presence, his love, that the quiet life in the country seemed to me something far in the past, and insignificant. To my great surprise, instead of pride and coldness of society which I had expected to find in people, everyone (not only my family, but strangers, too) greeted me with such unfeigned affection and delight that it seemed they had only to think of me, only to expect me, for them to feel happy, too. There was also something else which I found unexpected in society circles that seemed to me the very best there were: it turned out that my husband had many acquaintances of whom he had never told me; and it was often strange and disagreeable for me to hear him deliver such stern judgements on some of these people, who seemed to me so kind. I could not understand why he treated them so coldly and tried to avoid many acquaintances that to me seemed flattering. It appeared to me that the more kind people one knew, the better, and everyone was kind.

'Look, this is how we shall do it,' he said, before we left the estate. 'Here we are little Croesuses, but there we shall be not at all rich, and so we must only stay in town until Holy Week, and we shan't go into society, or we shall find ourselves in difficulties; and for your sake I would not want that, either . . .'

'What do we need society for?' I replied. 'We shall just take a look at the theatres, and our relations, go to the opera and hear some good music, and return to the country even before Holy Week.'

But as soon as we got to St Petersburg, these plans were forgotten. I suddenly found myself in such a new, happy world, so many joys enveloped me, so many new interests appeared before me, that at once, though unconsciously, I renounced the whole of my past and all its plans. 'All that was not really serious; my life had not really begun then; but now here it is, real life! And what will happen next?' I thought. All of a sudden the restlessness and the beginnings of depression that had troubled me in the country disappeared completely. My love for my husband grew calmer, and here I was never visited by the thought of whether he loved me less. And indeed I could not have any doubts about his love, for my every thought was instantly understood, my feeling shared, my wish fulfilled by him. Here his composure disappeared, or did not irritate me any more. Moreover, I felt that not only did he continue to love me as before – here, in these new surroundings, he also admired me.

Often after we had made a social visit, or made a new acquaintance, or held a soirée at our apartment, when I, inwardly trembling with fear of making a mistake, performed the role of hostess, he would say: 'That's a good girl! Well done! Don't be shy! Really, it's all right!' And I was always very pleased. Soon after our arrival he wrote a letter to his mother, and when he asked me to write a postscript, he would not let me read what he had written, whereupon I naturally demanded to read it, and did so. 'You would not recognize Masha,' he wrote, 'and I myself don't recognize her. Where does this charming, graceful self-confidence come from, this *affabilité*, and even social wit, and kindliness? And all with such simplicity, charm and good nature! Everyone is delighted with her, and indeed I myself can't admire her enough. Were it possible, I would love her even more.'

'Oh, so that's what I'm like!' I thought. And so cheerful and happy did I feel that it even seemed to me that I loved him even more. My success with all our acquaintances was quite unexpected for me. From every side I heard voices saying that there an uncle had taken especial liking to me, that here an aunt was in ecstasies over me; this person would tell me that there were no women like me in St Petersburg, while another assured me that if I felt so inclined I could be the most *exquisite* woman in society. In particular, a cousin of my husband's, the Princess D., a middle-aged society woman who suddenly fell in love with me, said flattering things to me that positively turned my head. On the first occasion that the cousin invited me to a ball and made a formal request to my husband, he turned to me and, with a sly and barely noticeable smile, asked me if I wanted to go. I nodded as a sign of agreement and felt I was blushing.

'She confesses like a criminal to what she wants,' he said, laughing good-naturedly.

'But I mean, you said that we couldn't go into society, and that anyway you didn't want to,' I replied, smiling and looking at him with an imploring gaze.

'If you very much want to go, we shall,' he said.

'Really, we had better not.'

'Do you want to? Very much?' he asked again.

I made no reply.

'There is no great harm in society as such,' he continued, 'but unsatisfied social aspirations are a bad and ugly thing. We must certainly go, and go we shall,' he concluded with determination.

'To tell you the truth,' I said, 'there is nothing in the world I would like so much as to go to this ball.'

We went, and the delight I experienced surpassed all my expectations. At the ball it seemed to me, even more than before, that I was the centre around which everything moved, that for me alone was this great room illuminated, this music played and this crowd of people assembled to admire me. Everyone, from the hairdresser and the lady's maid to the dancing partners and the old men who passed through the room, it seemed, told me or gave me to understand that they loved me. The general verdict formed about me at this ball and conveyed to me by the cousin was that I was quite unlike the other women, that there was something special, rustic, simple and charming about me. This success so flattered me that I openly informed my husband that I would like to go to two or three more balls this year, 'so that I'll get thoroughly fed up with them,' I added, dissembling in my soul.

My husband willingly agreed, and initially accompanied me with obvious pleasure, rejoicing in my success and, it seemed, having completely forgotten or renounced what he had said earlier.

As time went on, however, he plainly began to find the life we led tedious and burdensome. But I was too busy to think about that; if I sometimes noticed his attentive and serious gaze, questioningly fixed on me, I did not understand its significance. So befogged was I by this, as it seemed to me, unexpectedly awoken love for me on everyone's part, by this atmosphere of elegance, pleasure and novelty that I breathed here for the first time, so suddenly here had his moral influence, which had oppressed me, disappeared, so pleasant was it for me in this world not only to find myself his equal but to rise above him, and yet love him even more, and more independently, than before, that I could not understand what possible unpleasantness he could see for me in society life. I experienced a feeling, one that was new to me, of pride and self-satisfaction when, as I entered a ball, everyone's eyes turned towards me, and he, as if ashamed to confess his ownership of me before the crowd, made haste to leave me and disappeared from view in the throng of black tailcoats. 'Wait!' I often thought, seeking with my gaze his unnoticed, sometimes bored-looking figure at the end of the room. 'Wait!' I thought. 'When we get home, you will understand and see for whom it was I tried to be pretty and brilliant, and what it is I love out of all that surrounds me this evening.' I sincerely believed that my success pleased me only for his sake, only because it made it possible for me to sacrifice it for him. One thing that could be harmful for me in society life, I thought, was the possibility of my becoming infatuated with someone I might meet in society, and my husband being jealous; but he had such faith in me, seemed so calm and indifferent, and all these young men seemed so worthless by comparison with him that this one danger that might threaten me, so I believed, did not seem very great to me. But, in spite of this, the attention of many people in society gave me pleasure, flattered my vanity, and made me think that there was some merit in my love for my husband. It also made me more confident and almost casual in the way I behaved towards him.

'I saw you having a very lively conversation with N.N.,' I said one evening as we were returning from the ball, shaking my finger at him and naming one of the well-known St Petersburg ladies, with whom he really had been talking that evening. I said it in order to shake him up; he was particularly silent and bored looking.

'Oh, why do you put it like that? And you of all people, Masha!' he said through his teeth, and frowning, as though in physical pain. 'How little that suits you and me! Leave that to others; these false ways of relating may spoil the true ways we have, and I still have hopes that the true ones will return.'

I felt ashamed, and I fell silent.

'Will they return, Masha? What do you think?'

'They were never spoilt, nor will they be,' I said, and at the time this really was how it seemed to me.

'May God grant that it is so,' he said quietly. 'Otherwise it's time we went back to the country.'

But this he said to me only once. The rest of the time it seemed to me that he was just as content as I was, and I was so happy and cheerful! After all, if he was bored sometimes – I comforted myself – I too had been a bit bored in the country for his sake; if the relations between us had changed somewhat, it would all return as soon as we were alone with Tatyana Semyonovna in our house at Nikolskoye.

Thus, imperceptibly for me, the winter passed, and contrary to our plans we even spent Holy Week in St Petersburg. By the Feast of St Thomas, a week later, when we were already getting ready to leave, everything was packed up, and my husband, who had made some purchases of gifts, clothes, flowers for our rural life, was in a particularly cheerful mood, the cousin unexpectedly arrived to see us and begged us to stay until

Saturday in order to go to the reception at Countess R.'s. She said that the countess was very anxious to invite me, that a foreign prince, Prince M., was visiting St Petersburg, and that ever since the last ball he had wished to make my acquaintance, that he was only going to attend the reception for this purpose, and said that I was the prettiest woman in Russia. The whole of St Petersburg would be there, and, in a word, it would be a dreadful pity if I did not go.

My husband was at the other end of the drawing-room, talking to someone.

'So, what do you say? Will you go, Marie?' said the cousin.

'We were intending to go back to the country the day after tomorrow,' I replied uncertainly, with a glance at my husband. Our eyes met, and he hastily turned away.

'I'll persuade him to stay,' said the cousin, 'and on Saturday we shall go and turn heads. Yes?'

'It would upset our plans, and we've already packed,' I replied, beginning to give way.

'She'd do better to go and pay her compliments to the Prince this evening,' my husband said from the other end of the room in a tone of suppressed irritation which I had not heard from him before.

'Oh! He's jealous, that's the first time I've seen it,' the cousin laughed. 'But I mean to say, Sergey Mikhailovich, it's not for the Prince but for all of us that I'm trying to persuade her. You should have heard how Countess R. implored me!'

'It's up to her,' my husband said quietly, and left the room.

I saw that he was more agitated than usual; this worried me, and I did not promise the cousin anything. As soon as she had gone, I went to my husband. He was pacing reflectively to and fro, and did not see or hear me as I tiptoed into the room.

'He's already imagining his dear home at Nikolskoye,' I thought as I looked at him. 'He sees our morning coffee in the bright drawing-room, and his fields and muzhiks, and our evenings in the sofa room, and our secret nocturnal suppers. No!' I decided to myself. 'I would give up all the balls in the world, and the flattery of all the princes in the world, for his happy confusion and his quiet caress.' I was going to tell him that I would not attend the reception and did not want to go, when he suddenly glanced round and, catching sight of me, frowned and altered the gently reflective expression of his face. Once again there was shrewdness, wisdom and protective calm in his gaze. He did not want me to see him as an ordinary human being; he always needed to stand before me like a demigod on a pedestal.

'What is it, my dear?' he asked, turning towards me in a calm and casual manner.

I made no reply. I was annoyed that he was hiding from me, did not want to remain the person whom I loved.

'Do you want to go to the reception on Saturday?' he asked.

'I did,' I replied, 'but you don't like it. And anyway, everything is packed,' I added.

Never had he looked at me so coldly, never had he spoken to me so coldly.

'I shan't leave until Tuesday, and I'll tell them to unpack the things,' he said quietly. 'So you may go, if you want to. Do me the favour of going. I shan't leave.'

As always when he was agitated, he began to pace unevenly about the room, and did not look at me.

'I really don't understand you,' I said, staying where I was and following him with my eyes. 'You say that you are always so calm (he had never said this). Why do you talk to me so strangely? I am prepared to sacrifice this pleasure for your sake, yet now, in a tone that is almost ironic, and in a way you have never talked to me before, you demand that I go!'

'Well, I like that! You *sacrifice* (he put a special emphasis on this word), and I do too, what could be better? A battle of generosity. What more could one wish in the way of family happiness?'

It was the first time I had heard such bitterly mocking words from him. And his mockery did not put me to shame, but offended me, and his bitterness did not frighten me, but communicated itself to me. Was it he, who had always feared empty phrases in our relations with each other, who had always been sincere and straightforward, who was saying this? And why? Because I really did want to sacrifice for his sake a pleasure in which I could see nothing wrong, and because a moment ago I had understood him and loved him so much. Our roles had been altered: now he avoided words that were plain and straightforward, while I sought them.

'You've changed a great deal,' I said, with a sigh. 'What have I done wrong in your regard? It's not the reception, but something else, some old grievance you have in your heart against me. Why the insincerity? Wasn't it you who was so afraid of it before? Tell me straight, what do you have against me?' 'What is he going to say,' I thought, recalling with self-satisfaction that all that winter there had been nothing with which he could possibly reproach me.

I moved to the centre of the room, so that he had to pass close by me, and looked at him. 'He's going to approach me, embrace me, and then it will all be over,' was the thought that occurred to me, and I even felt sorry that I would not have a chance to prove him wrong. But he stopped at the end of the room and stared at me.

'Do you still not understand?' he said.

'No.'

'Well, then, I will tell you. I find loathsome, for the first time loathsome, what I feel, and cannot help feeling.' He stopped, evidently alarmed by the coarse sound of his voice.

'But what is it?' with tears of indignation in my eyes I asked.

'Loathsome, that the Prince thought you were pretty and that because of that you ran to meet him, forgetting your husband, yourself, and the dignity of woman, and that you refuse to understand that if there is no sense of dignity within you, your husband must feel it for you; on the contrary, you come to tell your husband that you are *sacrificing*, or in other words: "To show myself to his highness is a great happiness for me, but I am *sacrificing* it."'

The longer he spoke, the more he grew inflamed by the sound of his own voice, and that voice sounded malicious, hard and coarse. I had never seen him like this, nor had I ever expected to; the blood rushed to my heart, I was afraid, but at the same time a feeling of undeserved shame and injured pride excited me, and I wanted to take my revenge on him.

'I've been expecting this for a long time,' I said. 'Go on. Go on.'

'I don't know what you've been expecting,' he continued, 'but I could expect the worst, seeing you every day in the filth, idleness and luxury of this foolish society; and it arrived ... Arrived to a point where today I feel more shame and pain than I have ever felt; pain for myself, when your friend put her filthy hands in my heart and began to talk of jealousy, my jealousy, of whom? Of a man whom neither I nor you know. And you, as if deliberately, refuse to understand me and want to make sacrifices for me, and of what? ... Sacrifices!' he repeated.

'Ah! So this is a husband's power,' I thought. 'To insult and humiliate a woman who is not in any way to blame. This is what a husband's rights amount to, but I shall not submit to them.'

'No, I'm not making any sacrifices for you at all,' I said quietly, feeling my nostrils widen unnaturally as the blood left my face. 'I shall go to the reception on Saturday, and shall go without fail.'

'And may God grant you much enjoyment, but between us all is over!' he shouted, now in a fit of unrestrained fury. 'However, you shall not torment me any longer. I was a fool, to ...' he began again, but his lips started to tremble, and with a visible effort he contained himself, in order not to finish saying what he had begun.

I feared and hated him at that moment. There were many things I wanted to say to him, to take revenge for all his insults; but if I had opened my mouth I would have begun to cry, and would have discredited myself in his eyes. In silence I left the room. But as soon as I ceased to hear his footsteps, I felt sudden horror at what we had done. I was afraid that the bond that had made all my happiness would really be broken forever, and I wanted to go back. 'But will he have calmed down enough to understand me, if I stretch out my hand to him in silence and look at him?' I thought. 'Will he understand my magnanimity? What if he calls my grief a pretence? Or accepts my remorse with proud composure and a consciousness of his own rightness? And why did he, whom I love so, insult me so cruelly?'

I went not to him but to my own room, where I sat for a long time and cried, remembering with horror every word of the conversation that had taken place between us, substituting those words with others, adding other, kind words and again with horror and a sense of outrage remembering what had taken place. When in the evening I went down for tea and in the presence of S., who was staying with us, met my husband, I felt that from this day forward an entire abyss had opened between us. S. asked me when we were leaving. I did not manage to reply.

'On Tuesday,' my husband replied. 'We're staying for Countess R.'s reception. You're going, aren't you?' he said, turning to me.

I was frightened by the sound of this matter-of-fact voice and timidly glanced round at my husband. His eyes were looking straight at me, their gaze was cruel and mocking, and the voice was level and cold.

'Yes,' I replied.

In the evening, when we were alone, he came up to me and held out his hand.

'Please forget all that nonsense I told you,' he said.

I took his hand; there was a trembling smile on my face, and the tears were ready to flow from my eyes, but he took his hand away and, as though fearing a sentimental scene, sat down in an armchair quite some distance from me. 'Does he really still think he is in the right?' I thought, and my prepared explanation and request that we not go to the reception died on my lips.

'We must write and tell Mother that we've postponed our departure,' he said, 'or else she will worry.'

'And when are you thinking of leaving?' I asked.

'On Tuesday, after the reception,' he replied.

'I hope you're not doing it for me,' I said, looking him in the eyes; but those eyes merely looked, and told me nothing, as though they were somehow veiled from me. His face suddenly seemed to me old and unpleasant.

We went to the reception, and it seemed that good, friendly relations were once more established between us; but those relations were quite different from what they had been before.

At the reception I was sitting with the other ladies when the Prince came over to me, so that I had to stand up in order to talk to him. As I got up, I found my eyes involuntarily searching for my husband, and saw him look at me from the other end of the room, and then turn away. I suddenly felt such shame and pain that I suffered a fit of embarrassment and blushed all over my face and neck under the Prince's gaze. But I had to stand and listen as he spoke to me, surveying me from above. Our conversation did not last long: there was no room for him to sit down beside me, and he probably sensed that I felt very awkward with him. The conversation was of the last ball, of where I stayed in the summer, and so on. Leaving me, he expressed a wish to make the acquaintance of my husband, and I saw them meet and talk at the other end of the room. The Prince probably said something about me, because in the midst of their conversation he looked round smilingly in our direction.

My husband suddenly flushed, made a low bow and left the Prince, rather than the other way round, as would have been expected. I blushed too. I felt ashamed of the notion the Prince must have formed of me, and especially of my husband. It seemed to me that everyone had noticed my awkward shyness as I spoke to the Prince, and that they had noticed my husband's strange behaviour. God only knew how they would explain it: what if they already knew about the conversation my husband and I had had? The female cousin took me home, and on the way we fell to talking about my husband. I could contain myself no longer, and told her all that had taken place between us over this unfortunate reception. She tried to calm me, saying that it did not mean anything, that it was just a very ordinary tiff that would leave no traces; she explained my husband's character to me from her point of view, said she found he had become very uncommunicative and proud; I agreed with her, and now it seemed to me that I began to understand him better and more calmly.

But later, when I was alone with my husband, this judgement of him lay on my conscience like a crime, and I felt that the chasm that divided us from each other had become even greater.

VIII

From that day on, our life and our relationship changed completely. We were no longer as happy when we were alone together as we had been before. There were questions we avoided, and we found it easier to talk when someone else was present than face to face. The talk had only to turn to life in the country, or a ball, and we 'saw boys running',[8] and felt uncomfortable looking at each other. It was as if we both sensed where the abyss that divided us was, and were afraid of going near it. I was convinced that he was proud and irascible, and that one must be careful not to touch his weaknesses. He was sure that I could not live without society, that the country did not suit me, and that he must submit to this unfortunate taste. And we both avoided direct talk about these subjects, and both judged one another falsely. We had long ceased to be the most perfect people in the world for each other, and now we made comparisons with others, and judged each other in secret. Before our departure I became unwell, and instead of returning to the estate we moved to a dacha in the suburbs, from where my husband went back to his mother's. By the time he was leaving I had already recovered enough to be able to go with him, but he persuaded me to stay, seemingly concerned for my health. I felt that he was afraid, not for my health, but because we might find it unpleasant to be in the country; I did not insist very much, and stayed. In his absence I felt empty and alone, but when he returned I realized that he did not add to my life what he had added before. Our previous relationship, when every thought and impression I did not convey to him weighed on me like a crime, when his every word and action seemed to me a model of perfection, when for some reason we felt like laughing whenever we looked at each other – that relationship had changed into another so imperceptibly that we had not grasped that the old one no longer existed. Each of us now had our own separate interests and concerns which we no longer tried to share. We even ceased to be troubled by the fact that we each had our own world, foreign to the other. We grew accustomed to this idea, and with the passage of a year we no longer even 'saw boys running' when we looked at each other. His fits of gaiety with me, his boyishness, had disappeared, and so had the all-forgivingness and indifference that had earlier made me angry; that deep gaze which had earlier confused and delighted me was gone, along with the prayers and raptures we had shared together. We even met infrequently: he was forever off on his travels, and did not fear, did not regret leaving me alone; I was constantly in society, where I had no need of him.

There were no longer any scenes or tiffs between us; I tried to please him, he carried out all my wishes, and it was as though we loved each other.

When we were left by ourselves, which happened rarely, I experienced neither joy nor excitement nor confusion with him, as though I were alone. I was well aware that he was my husband, not some new man whom I did not know, but a good man – my husband, whom I knew like my own self. I was certain that I knew exactly what he would do, what he would say, how he would look; and if he acted or looked in a way that was not what I expected, it now seemed to me that he had made a mistake. I did not expect anything from him. In a word, he was my husband, and that was all. It seemed to me that it had to be this way, that this was how our relationship was, and even that it had never been any different. When he went away, especially during the initial period, I was lonely and afraid, and in his absence felt keenly how much his support meant to me; when he returned, I threw myself into his arms with joy, even though two hours later I had entirely forgotten that joy, and had nothing to say to him. Only at the moments of quiet, measured tenderness that occurred between us did it seem to me that there was something wrong, that something was paining my heart, and in his eyes I seemed to read the same thing. I felt that boundary of tenderness beyond which now he seemingly would not, and I could not, go. Sometimes this made me sad, but I had no time to reflect on anything at all, and I tried to forget this sadness about a vaguely sensed change in the diversions that were constantly ready for me. The life of society,

which had at first befogged me with its brilliance and its flattery
of my vanity, soon took complete possession of my inclinations,
became a habit, laid its fetters on me and occupied entirely that
place within my soul that was ready for feeling. I could never
be alone with myself and was afraid to meditate on my position.
The whole of my time from late in the morning until late at
night was taken up and did not belong to me, even if I did not
go out. By now I found this neither enlivening nor tedious;
instead, it seemed that this was how things had to be, and could
not be otherwise.

So three years went by, during which our relationship
remained the same, as if it had stopped, frozen and could
become neither worse nor better. In the course of those three
years two important events took place in our family life, but
neither of them changed my life. They were the birth of my first
child and the death of Tatyana Semyonovna. Initially maternal
feeling took hold of me with such force and produced such
unexpected rapture in me that I believed a new life would begin
for me; but after two months, when I began to go out again,
that feeling, growing weaker and weaker, became a habit and
the cold execution of a duty. My husband, on the contrary,
from the time of the birth of our first son became the meek,
calm stay-at-home he had been before, and he transferred his
former tenderness and cheerfulness to the child. Often, when I
went into the nursery wearing a ballroom dress in order to
make the sign of the cross over the child for the night, and
found my husband there, I would notice his gaze, which seemed
reproachful and sternly attentive, fixed on me, and I would feel
ashamed. I was horrified at my own indifference to the child,
and asked myself: 'Am I really worse than other women? But
what can I do?' I would think. 'I love my son, but I can't sit
beside him for whole days on end, I'd be bored; and on no
account am I going to pretend.'

His mother's death was a great sorrow to my husband; it
was, as he said, hard for him to go on living at Nikolskoye after
it, and although I was sorry about it and sympathized with my
husband's grief, I now found life in the country more pleasant

and tranquil. We spent most of those three years in the city; I only visited the estate once, for two months, and for the third year we went abroad.

We spent the summer at a spa.

I was then twenty-one years old, our material affairs were, I thought, in a flourishing condition, while of family life I demanded nothing beyond what it gave me; everyone I knew, it seemed to me, loved me; my health was good, my outfits were the best in the spa, I knew I was pretty, the weather was fine, a kind of atmosphere of beauty and elegance surrounded me, and I felt very cheerful. I was not as cheerful as I had been at Nikolskoye, when I felt that I was happy in myself, that I was happy because I deserved that happiness, that my happiness was great, but was bound to be even greater, that all I wanted was more and more happiness. Back then, things had been different; but this summer, too, I felt good. There was nothing I wanted, nothing I hoped for, nothing I was afraid of, and my life, it seemed to me, was full, my conscience untroubled. Of all the young men that season there was no single one whom I distinguished from the rest, or even from old Prince K., our emissary, who had paid court to me. One was young, another old, one was a fair-haired Englishman, another a Frenchman with a beard – to me they were all the same, but I needed them all. They were all equally indifferent personalities who together made up the cheerful atmosphere of the life that surrounded me. Only one of them, the Italian Marquis D., drew my attention more than the others because of the boldness with which he expressed his admiration to me. He missed no opportunity of being with me, danced with me, rode horseback with me, visited the casino with me, and so on, and told me that I was pretty. On several occasions I saw him near our house, and often the unpleasant, fixed gaze of his gleaming eyes made me blush and look round. He was young, handsome, elegant and, above all, his smile and facial expression resembled those of my husband, though far more attractive than his. He struck me by this similarity, though in general in his lips, eyes and long chin there was, not my husband's charming expression of kindness and ideal calm, but something coarse and animal. I supposed at the time that he was passionately in love with me, and sometimes thought about him with proud compassion. I sometimes tried to calm him, bring him round to a tone of quiet, half-friendly trust, but he violently rejected these attempts and continued to embarrass me with his unexpressed passion which was, however, ready to express itself at any moment. Although I did not admit it to myself, I was afraid of this man and often thought about him against my will. My husband knew him and behaved coldly and haughtily towards him, even more so than with our other acquaintances for whom he was only the husband of his wife.

Towards the end of the season I fell ill and did not leave the house for two weeks. When for the first time after my illness I went down to the concert at the bandstand, I learned of the arrival in my absence of Lady S., long awaited and renowned for her beauty. A circle had formed around me, and I was greeted with delight, but an even finer circle had formed around the visiting lioness. Everyone around me talked only of her and her beauty. She was pointed out to me and she really was lovely, but I was unpleasantly struck by the self-satisfied look on her face, and I said so. That day everything that had previously been such fun seemed tedious. On the next day, Lady S. organized a trip to the castle, but I decided not to go. Almost no one joined me in this, and everything changed completely in my eyes. Everything and everyone seemed stupid and boring, I felt like crying, wanted to finish the course of treatment as soon as possible and travel back to Russia. There was some ugly feeling in my soul, but I did not yet admit it to myself. Pleading infirmity, I stopped presenting myself at large social events, and went out only occasionally, in the morning, to take the waters or drive around the environs with L.M., a Russian lady friend. My husband was absent at this time: he had gone off to Heidelberg for a few days, waiting for my course of treatment to end so we could travel back to Russia, and only came to see me occasionally.

One day, Lady S. took the whole company away on a hunting trip, and after dinner L.M. and I made an excursion to the castle. As we drove slowly in our carriage along the winding

highway between the ancient chestnut trees, through which
those pretty and elegant environs of Baden opened further and
further, lit by the rays of the setting sun, we talked in earnest,
more seriously than we had ever done before. For the first time,
L.M., whom I had known for a long time, appeared to me now
as a good and intelligent woman, to whom it was possible to
say everything and with whom it was pleasant to be friends.
We spoke of our families, of our children, of the emptiness of
the life here, we wanted to go back to Russia, to the countryside,
and we somehow felt sad and happy. Under the influence of
this same serious emotion, we entered the castle. Within the
walls it was shady and cool, the sunlight played on the ruins
above, one could hear the footsteps and voices of others. From
a doorway, as in a picture frame, that Baden tableau was visible:
charming, but for us Russians – cold. We sat down to rest and
silently watched the setting sun. The voices were more distinct
now, and it seemed to me that someone mentioned my name. I
began to listen, and found myself overhearing every word. The
voices were familiar: they belonged to the Marquis D. and a
Frenchman, a friend of his, whom I also knew. They were
talking about me and about Lady S. The Frenchman was com-
paring me and her, and discussing the beauty of each of us. He
said nothing offensive, but the blood rushed to my heart as I
overheard his words. He explained in detail the things that
were good about me, and the things that were good about the
Lady. I already had a child, while Lady S. was only nineteen;
my hair was better, but the Lady had a more graceful figure;
the Lady was a *grande dame*, while 'yours,' he said, 'is just
so-so, one of those little Russian princesses who are starting to
turn up here so often now'. He concluded by saying that I did
well in not trying to compete with Lady S., and that I had been
decisively buried in Baden.

'I feel sorry for her. Unless, that is, she takes it into her head
to console herself with you,' he added with a cheerful and cruel
laugh.

'If she leaves, I'll follow her,' a voice said coarsely in an
Italian accent.

'Happy mortal! He can still love!' laughed the Frenchman.

'Love!' said the voice, and fell silent. 'I can't help loving! Without it there's no life. Making a romance out of life is the only good thing there is. And my romances never stop half way – this one too I shall carry through to the end.'

'*Bonne chance, mon ami!*' the Frenchman said quietly.

We did not hear any more of what was said, as they turned a corner, and we could hear footsteps from the other side. They came down the flight of steps, and a few minutes later they emerged from a side door and were thoroughly surprised to see us. I blushed when Marquis D. approached me, and I felt afraid when, as we left the castle, he gave me his arm. I could not refuse, and we went to the carriage behind L.M., who walked with his friend. I was offended by what the Frenchman had said about me, though I secretly admitted that he had only given expression to what I myself felt; but the Marquis's words had surprised and angered me with their coarseness. I was tormented by the thought that I had heard his words and yet, in spite of that, he was not afraid of me. I found it loathsome to feel him so close to me; and, without looking at him, without replying to him and trying to hold his arm in such a way as not to hear him, I hurriedly followed L.M. and the Frenchman. The Marquis spoke of the beautiful view, of the unexpected good fortune of meeting me, and of other things as well, but I was not listening to him. I was thinking all the while of my husband, of my son, of Russia; there was something I felt ashamed of, something I regretted, something I wanted, and I was in a hurry to get back as soon as possible to my solitary room at the Hôtel de Bade, in order to have the freedom to consider all the things that had just risen up within my soul. But L.M. walked slowly, it was still a long way to the carriage, and it seemed to me that my admirer was deliberately slowing his pace, as though trying to detain me. 'It cannot be!' I thought, and determinedly walked faster. But it was undeniable: he was trying to hold me back, and was even pressing my arm. L.M. turned a corner in the road, and we were quite alone. I felt afraid.

'Excuse me,' I said coldly and tried to free my arm, but the lace of my sleeve caught on a button of his. Bending towards me, his chest facing me, he began to undo the button, and his

ungloved fingers touched my arm. Some new feeling, somewhere between horror and pleasure, ran like a shiver of cold
down my back. I gave him a look, in order to express with my
cold gaze all the contempt I felt for him; but my gaze did not
express that, it expressed alarm and excitement. His moist,
burning eyes, right up against my face, looked passionately at
me, at my neck, at my breast, both his hands were fingering my
arm above the wrist, his parted lips were saying that he loved
me, that I was everything to him, and those lips were coming
closer to me, and those hands were pressing mine harder and
harder and burning me. A fire was coursing through my veins,
my eyes grew dim, I was trembling, and the words with which
I wanted to stop him were drying up in my throat. Suddenly I
felt a kiss on my cheek and, trembling all over and turning cold,
I stopped and stared at him. Unable to speak or move, and, in
horror, I waited and desired something. All this lasted a single
moment. But that moment was horrible! In it, I saw the whole
of him as he was. His face was so comprehensible to me: that
low, steep forehead under the straw hat, a forehead like my
husband's, that handsome straight nose with dilated nostrils,
that long, sharply pomaded moustache and beard, those close-
shaven cheeks and sunburned neck. I hated, I feared him, so
alien he was to me; but at that moment the excitement and
passion of this hateful, alien man echoed within me with such
power! So irresistibly did I want to give myself up to the kisses
of that coarse and handsome mouth, the embraces of those
white hands with their delicate veins and the rings on their
fingers. I felt such an urge to throw myself headlong into
the abyss of forbidden pleasures that had suddenly opened,
drawing me into it . . .

'I'm so unhappy,' I thought. 'So let more and more misfor-
tunes gather about my head.'

He embraced me with one arm and leaned towards my face.
'Let him, let more and more shame and sin accumulate about
my head.'

'*Je vous aime*,' he whispered in a voice that was so like the
voice of my husband. My husband and child were recalled to
me, as beings who had formerly long ago been dear to me, with

whom now all was over in my life. But suddenly just then from around the bend I heard the voice of L.M., who was calling me. I pulled myself together, tore my hand away and, not looking at him, almost ran after L.M. We got into the carriage, and only then did I look at him. He took off his hat and asked some question, smiling. He did not grasp the inexpressible revulsion I felt for him at that moment.

My life seemed so unhappy to me, the future so hopeless, the past so black! L.M. spoke to me, but I did not take in her words. It seemed to me that she spoke to me only out of pity, in order to hide the contempt I aroused in her. In every word, in every glance I fancied that I saw this contempt and offensive pity. The kiss burned my cheek with shame, and the thought of my husband and child was intolerable to me. Left alone in my room, I hoped to think about my position, but I was afraid to be alone. I did not finish the tea that was brought to me, and, without really knowing why, began at once with feverish haste to get ready to catch the evening train to Heidelberg, and my husband.

When I and my maid had found seats in an empty carriage, the train moved off and the fresh air wafted in on me through the window, I began to pull myself together and picture my past and future to myself more clearly. The whole of my married life from the day of our move to St Petersburg suddenly appeared to me in a new light, and lay on my conscience like a reproach. For the first time I vividly recollected our initial period in the country, our plans, and for the first time the question occurred to me: what joy had he had during all that time? And I felt guilty in his regard. 'But why did he not stop me, why did he play the hypocrite to me, why did he avoid explanations, why did he insult me?' I wondered. 'Why did he not use the power of his love over me? Or did he not love me?' But no matter how guilty he was, the kiss of that stranger sat right there on my cheek, and I could feel it. The closer I drew to Heidelberg, the more clearly did I imagine my husband, and the more I began to fear our imminent meeting. 'I'll tell him everything, everything, I'll weep it all out to him in tears of repentance,' I thought, 'and he will forgive me.' But I did not

really know myself what the 'everything' was that I was going
to tell him, nor did I really believe that he would forgive me.

However, as soon as I entered my husband's room and saw his
calm though surprised face, I felt that I had nothing to say to
him, nothing to confess or for which to ask his forgiveness. The
unexpressed sorrow and repentance had to remain inside me.

'What gave you this idea?' he said. 'I was going to come and
see you tomorrow anyway.' But then, studying my face more
closely, he seemed to grow alarmed. 'What is it? What's the
matter?' he said quietly.

'Nothing,' I replied, scarcely able to restrain my tears. 'I
shan't return. Let us go home to Russia, tomorrow, if you like.'

He looked at me silently and attentively for rather a long
time.

'But tell me, what has happened to you?' he said.

I found myself blushing, and lowered my gaze. In his eyes
there flashed a sense of outrage and anger. I was afraid of the
thoughts that might occur to him, and with a power of pretence
that I did not expect to find in myself, I said:

'Nothing has happened, I just got bored and sad being all on
my own, and I've been thinking a lot about our life, and about
you. Oh, I've been guilty for so long in your regard! Why do
you go with me to places you don't want to go to? I have long
been guilty in your regard!' I repeated, and again the tears
returned to my eyes. 'Let us go back to the country, and for
good.'

'Ah, my dear, please spare us the sentimental scenes,' he said
coldly. 'That you want to go back to the estate is well and good,
for we don't have much money; but as for its being for ever,
that is a dream. I know that you wouldn't settle down. Now
have some tea, that will make you feel better,' he concluded,
getting up in order to ring for the servant.

I imagined all the things he might be thinking about me, and
I was hurt by the terrible thoughts I ascribed to him as I met
his uncertain and almost shamefaced gaze, fixed upon me. No!
He will not and cannot understand me! I said I was going to
take a look at the child, and left his room. I wanted to be alone,
and cry, cry, and cry . . .

IX

The empty house at Nikolskoye, long unheated, revived, but what had lived in it before did not revive. Mother was gone, and we faced each other alone. But not only was solitude something we did not require now – we actually found it constraining. For me, the winter had been all the more trying because I was ill and did not recover until after the birth of my second son. The relationship between my husband and myself continued to be just as coldly amicable as it had been during our life in the city, but in the country each floorboard, each wall and sofa reminded me of what he had been to me, and what I had lost. It was as though there were some unforgiven injury between us, as though he were punishing me for something and at the same time pretending not to notice it. There was nothing to ask forgiveness for, no reason to appeal for pardon: he was simply punishing me by not giving me the whole of himself with all his heart and soul, as he had done previously; but he did not give it to anyone or anything, as though he no longer had it. Sometimes it struck me that he was merely pretending to be like this in order to torment me, that the old feeling was still alive within him, and I tried to call it forth. But every time it was as though he avoided being frank about it, as though he suspected me of pretending and was afraid of any tenderness as of something ridiculous. His gaze and tone of voice said: 'I know everything, I know it all, there is nothing to be said; I even know everything that you want to say. And I know that you will say one thing, but do another.' At first I was hurt by this fear of frankness, but then I got used to the idea that it was not a lack of frankness, but the absence of a need for it. I would not be able to bring myself to suddenly tell him now that I loved him, or to ask him to say prayers with me, or call him to listen to me playing the piano. Between us one could now sense certain conditions of propriety. We each lived separate lives. He with his pursuits, in which I was not needed, and in which I no longer felt like taking part, and I with my idleness, which did not offend or sadden him as it had done earlier. The children were still too young to be able to unite us yet.

But spring arrived, Katya and Sonya came to the country for the summer, our house at Nikolskoye began to undergo rebuilding, and we moved to the house at Pokrovskoye. The old house was just the same, with its terrace, its folding table, the piano in the well-lit drawing-room, and my old room with its white curtains and my girlish dreams, which seemed to have been forgotten there. In that room there were two beds – one formerly mine, where in the evenings I made the sign of the cross over sprawling, chubby Kokosha, and the other a small one, where Vanya's little face looked out from the swaddling clothes. When I had crossed them, I often stood still in the middle of the quiet room, and suddenly from every corner, from the walls, the curtains rose old, forgotten visions of my youth. Old voices would start to sing girlish songs. And where were those visions? Where were those dear, sweet songs? All that I had scarcely dared to hope for had been realized. My vague, intermingling dreams had become reality, and reality become a life that was painful, hard and joyless. Yet everything was still the same: the same garden visible through the window, the same stretch of grass, the same path, the same bench down there above the dell, the same nightingale songs drifting over from the pond, the same lilacs in full bloom, and the same moon shining above the house; but in everything such a terrible, unbearable change! So cold, everything that could have been so close and dear! Just as in the old days, Katya and I sit quietly in the living-room together talking, and talking about him. But Katya has grown wrinkled and sallow; her eyes do not shine with joy and hope but express a compassionate sadness and regret. We do not admire him as we used to, we judge him, we do not express surprise about why and for what we are so happy, and do not want to tell the whole world what we think, as we used to; like conspirators, we whisper to each other, and for the hundredth time ask each other why everything has changed so sadly. And he is still the same, except that the furrow between his eyebrows is deeper, and there is more white hair at his temples; but his deep, attentive gaze is constantly obscured from me as by a cloud. I, too, am the same, but there is in me no love, nor desire for love. I feel no need for work, have no contentment with myself. And so remote and impossible do they seem, my earlier religious ecstasies and my former love for him, the fullness of my former life. Now I would not understand what seemed to be so clear and right: the happiness of living for another. Why for another? When one does not even feel like living for oneself?

Since moving to St Petersburg, I had completely given up music; but now the old piano and the old sheet music gave me a taste for it again.

One day I felt unwell and stayed at home alone; Katya and Sonya had gone with him to Nikolskoye to look at the new building work. The tea-table was laid, I went downstairs and, while waiting for them, sat down at the piano. I opened the Sonata quasi una Fantasia and began to play it. No one could be seen or heard, the windows to the garden were open, and the familiar, sadly festive sounds rang out through the room. I finished the first movement and quite unconsciously, out of old habit, looked round at the corner where he once used to sit and listen to me. But he was not there; the chair, long unmoved, stood in its corner; but through the window one could see a lilac bush in the bright sunset, and the evening's freshness was pouring in through the open windows. I leaned both my elbows on the piano, covered my face with my hands, and thought. I sat like this for a long time, remembering with pain the old days that could never return and timidly trying to imagine the future. But it was as if nothing lay ahead, as if there were nothing I desired or hoped for. 'Is my life really over?' I thought, raising my head in horror and, in order to forget and not to think, I again began to play, the same *andante* once more. 'Oh God!' I thought. 'Forgive me, if I am guilty, or return to me everything that was so beautiful in my soul, or teach me what to do, and how to live now?' The sound of wheels was heard on the grass, and before the front steps and on the terrace I heard familiar, cautious footsteps, which then died away. But it was not the old feeling that responded to the sound of those familiar steps. When I had finished, I heard them behind me, and a hand was laid on my shoulder.

'What a clever one you are, to have played that sonata,' he said.

I said nothing.

'You haven't had tea?'

I shook my head without looking round at him, in order not to give away the traces of excitement that remained on my face.

'They'll be here in a moment; the horse began to play up, and they came down from the high road on foot,' he said.

'Let's wait for them,' I said, and went out on to the terrace, hoping that he would follow me; but he asked about the children, and went upstairs to see them. Again his presence, his simple, kindly voice persuaded me that I had not lost anything. What more could I wish? 'He is kind, gentle, he is a good husband, a good father, and I don't know myself what more I lack.' I went out to the balcony and sat down under the awning of the terrace on the same bench on which I had sat on the day of our engagement. By now the sun had gone down, it was beginning to grow dark, and a dark spring cloud hung over the house and garden; only from behind the trees could one see the clear rim of the sky with the dying embers of the sunset and an evening star that had just begun to burn. Over everything stood the shadow of the insubstantial cloud, and everything was waiting for the quiet spring shower. The wind died away, not a single leaf, not a single grass blade stirred; the smell of the lilacs and bird-cherry was so strong in the garden and on the terrace, as though the whole of the air were in blossom, its flow now weakening, now strengthening, that one wanted to close one's eyes and see and sense nothing but this sweet smell. The dahlias and the rosebushes, not yet in flower, motionlessly stretching on the black, dug-over bed, seemed to be slowly growing upward on their white shaven supports; the frogs, with all their might, as if making the most of their time before the rain, which would drive them into the water, croaked in piercing harmony from below the dell. The only thing that rose above this clamour was a thin, unbroken sound of water falling. Now and then nightingales called to one another, and one could hear them anxiously flying from place to place. Again this spring a nightingale had tried to make a nest in a bush under the window, and when I went out I could hear it move away to the other side of the avenue and give a single trill from there, also waiting. In vain I tried to calm myself; I was both waiting and regretting something. He came back from upstairs, and sat down beside me.

'I think Katya and Sonya are going to get wet,' he said.

'Yes,' I said quietly, and we were both silent for a long time.

And the cloud, with no wind, descended lower and lower; everything became quieter, more strong smelling, motionless, and suddenly a drop fell and seemed to bounce on the canvas awning of the terrace, while another shattered on the gravel of the path; there was a splashing in the burdock, and a heavy, fresh and steadily increasing shower began to fall. The nightingales and frogs fell completely silent; only the high-pitched sound of the waterfall, though it seemed further away through the rain, continued to hang in the air, and some bird which must have taken refuge in the dry leaves close to the terrace kept steadily repeating its two monotonous notes. He got up and began to go inside.

'Where are you going?' I asked, trying to hold him back. 'It's so nice here.'

'I'd better send them an umbrella and galoshes,' he replied.

'Don't bother, it will be over soon.'

He agreed with me, and we remained together by the railings of the terrace. I leaned my hand on the slippery, wet crossbar and put my head out. The fresh shower sprinkled drops unevenly on my hair and neck. The cloud, growing brighter and thinner, was passing over us; the steady sound of the rain was replaced by occasional drops that fell from above, and from the leaves. Again from below the frogs began to croak, again the nightingales startled up and began to call to one another from the bushes, now from this direction, now from that. Everything brightened up before us.

'How good!' he said quietly, sitting down on the railings, and passing his hand over my wet hair.

This simple caress acted on me like a reproach, and I felt like crying.

'And what more could a person need?' he said. 'I am now so content that I lack nothing; I'm completely happy!'

'That's not how you used to talk about your happiness,' I thought. 'You used to say that no matter how great your happiness was, you always wanted more and more. But now you are calm and contented, while my soul seems to be full of unexpressed remorse and unwept tears.'

'I too find it good,' I said, 'but I'm sad just because everything before me is so good. Inside me everything is incoherent, incomplete, wanting something all the time; but here it's so beautiful and calm. Is there really no element of anguish in your enjoyment of nature – as though one wanted something impossible and missed something that was in the past?'

He took his hand off my head, and said nothing for a while.

'Yes, I used to feel that way, too, especially in spring,' he said, as though remembering. 'And I also used to sit up at nights, full of desires and hopes, and they were good nights! . . . But then everything was still ahead of me, whereas now it's all behind me; now I'm content with what I have, and I feel marvellous,' he concluded with such casual confidence that, no matter how painful it was for me to hear it, I believed he was telling the truth.

'And there's nothing you want?' I asked.

'Nothing that's impossible,' he replied, guessing what I was feeling. 'Look, your head's getting wet,' he added, stroking me as though I were a child, and passing his hand over my hair again. 'You envy the leaves and the grass because they're wetted by the rain, and you would like to be the grass and the leaves and the rain. But I just rejoice in them, as in everything else in the world that is good, young and happy.'

'And you don't miss anything of the past?' I continued to ask, feeling my heart grow heavier and heavier.

He reflected and again fell silent. I could see that he was trying to give me a completely sincere reply.

'No!' he answered, shortly.

'Not true! Not true!' I said, turning towards him and looking into his eyes. 'You don't miss the past?'

'No!' he said again. 'I'm grateful for it, but I don't miss it.'

'But don't you wish you could bring it back?' I said.

He turned away and began to look at the garden.

'No, I don't, any more than I wish I could grow wings,' he said. 'It's impossible!'

'And you wouldn't alter the past? You don't reproach yourself or me?'

'Never! It was all for the best.'

'Listen!' I said, touching his arm to make him look round at me. 'Listen, why did you never tell me that you wanted me to live in the way that you wanted me to, why did you give me a freedom I was unable to avail myself of, why did you stop teaching me? If you'd wanted to, if you'd guided me differently, none of it, none of it would have happened,' I said in a voice that contained a stronger and stronger expression of cold vexation and rebuke, and not the former love.

'What would not have happened?' he said in surprise, turning to face me. 'It's all right as it is. Everything is fine. Just fine,' he added, smiling.

'Does he really not understand, or, even worse, doesn't he want to understand?' I thought, and tears came to my eyes.

'What would not have happened was that, while in no way guilty in your regard, I am punished with your indifference, contempt, even,' I suddenly blurted out. 'What would not have happened was that, without my being at all to blame, you suddenly took away from me everything that was dear to me!'

'What do you mean, my darling?' he said, as if unable to comprehend what I was saying.

'No, let me finish ... You have taken from me your trust, your love, even your respect; because I can't believe that you love me now, after what happened before. No, I need to speak out once and for all, and tell you what has long tormented me,' I interrupted him again. 'Am I to blame that I knew nothing of life, and you left me alone to find out ... Am I to blame that now, when I myself have understood what I must do, when I, for what will soon be a year now, have struggled in order to return to you, you push me away as though you don't understand what I want, and always in such a way that there is nothing to reproach you with, and that I am both guilty and unhappy? Yes, you want to cast me out into that life which could have been a disaster for both of us.'

'But how did I indicate that to you?' he asked with sincere alarm and surprise.

'Did you not tell me yesterday, and tell me constantly, that I will never settle down here, and that we must go back again and spend the winter in St Petersburg, which is hateful to me?' I continued. 'Instead of giving me support, you avoid all frankness, you never say a kind or sincere word to me. And then, when I fall utterly, you will reproach me and rejoice in my fall.'

'That will do, that will do,' he said, sternly and coldly. 'It's wrong, what you are saying. It merely proves that you are ill-disposed towards me, that you don't . . .'

'That I don't love you? Say it, say it!' I finished his sentence for him, and the tears streamed from my eyes. I sat down on the bench and covered my face with my handkerchief.

'So that's how he understood me!' I thought, trying to hold back the sobs that were choking me. 'It is finished, finished, our former love,' a voice in my heart was saying. He did not come over to me, did not comfort me. He was hurt by what I had said. His voice was calm and dry.

'I don't know what you're reproaching me for,' he began. 'If it's because I didn't love you as I used to . . .'

'Didn't love!' I said quietly into my handkerchief, and the bitter tears trickled on to it all the more abundantly.

'If that is so, then it's time that is to blame, and we ourselves. Each phase of life has its own love . . .' He was silent for a while. 'And shall I tell you the whole truth? If you really want frankness? Just as in that year when I had first made your acquaintance, I used to spend nights without sleep, thinking about you, and made my love for myself, and that love grew and grew within my heart, so in St Petersburg and abroad I had dreadful nights without sleep, when I tried to break that love in pieces and destroy it, for it had tormented me. I did not destroy it, but destroyed only what had tormented me; I grew calm again, and I still love, but with another kind of love.'

'Yes, you call it love, but it is torment,' I said quietly. 'Why did you let me live in society, if it seemed to you so harmful that you stopped loving me because of it?'

'It wasn't society, my dear,' he said.

'Why didn't you use your authority?' I continued. 'Why didn't you tie me up, or kill me? I'd be better off like that now, rather than being deprived of everything that formed my happiness, I'd be happy, I wouldn't be ashamed.'

I began to sob again, and hid my face.

At that moment Katya and Sonya, cheerful and wet, entered the terrace, loudly talking and laughing; but when they caught sight of us, they at once fell silent and left the terrace again.

We said nothing for a long time; I had cried all I wanted to, and felt better. I glanced at him. He was sitting with his head on his hand, and tried to say something in response to my look, but merely uttered a heavy sigh and leaned his head on his hand again.

I went over to him and took his hand away. His gaze turned thoughtfully to me.

'Yes,' he began, as though continuing his private thoughts. 'All of us, and especially you, women, must live through all life's nonsense in order to return to life itself; it's no good taking someone else's word for it. Back then you hadn't even begun to live through that dear and charming nonsense which I admired in you; and I left you to live it out and felt that I had no right to constrain you, though for me the time for all that had long passed.'

'But why did you live through that nonsense with me and let me live through it, if you love me?'

'Because you would have wanted to take my word for it, but were unable to; you had to find out for yourself, and you did.'

'You had it worked out, you really had it all worked out,' I said. 'You didn't love me much.'

Again we were both silent for a while.

'It's cruel, what you just said, but it's true,' he said quietly, suddenly getting up and starting to pace up and down the terrace. 'Yes, it's true. It was my fault!' he added, coming to a halt opposite me. 'I should either not have allowed myself to love you or I should have loved you in a simpler way, yes.'

'Let's forget it all,' I said timidly.

'No, what's past can't be returned, one can never get it back again.' And his voice softened as he said this.

'It has returned already,' I said, putting my hand on his shoulder.

He took my hand away and pressed it.

'No, I was wrong when I said that I don't miss the past; I do miss it, and I weep for that past love which no longer exists and can be no more. Who is to blame for that? I don't know. Love has remained, but not that love, its place has remained, but it has all wasted away, it no longer has any strength or succulence, the memories and the gratitude have remained, but . . .'

'Don't talk like that . . .' I interrupted. 'Let everything be as it was before . . . After all, it can be? Can't it?' I asked, gazing into his eyes. But his eyes were clear and calm and did not look deeply into mine.

Even as I spoke, I already felt that what I wanted and what I was asking him for were impossible. He smiled a calm, gentle smile which seemed to me like that of an old man.

'How young you are still, and how old I am,' he said. 'What you seek is no longer in me; why deceive ourselves?' he added, continuing to smile in the same way.

I stood silently beside him, and began to feel calmer inside.

'Let's not try to repeat life,' he continued. 'Let's not lie to ourselves. The old alarms and excitements are over, and thank God for that! We have no reason to go searching and stirring ourselves up. We've already found what we were looking for, and sufficient happiness has fallen to our lot. Now we must try to efface ourselves, make way for this fellow,' he said, pointing to the nurse who was carrying Vanya in, and had stopped by the terrace door. 'That's how it is, my dear friend,' he concluded, bending my head towards him, and kissing it. I was kissed, not by a lover, but by an old friend.

Meanwhile from the garden the fragrant freshness of the night rose ever stronger and sweeter, the sounds and the silence became more and more solemn, and the stars began to shine more thickly in the sky. I looked at him, and suddenly my heart grew light; it was as though that aching moral nerve that had made me suffer was now removed. I suddenly clearly and calmly understood that the feeling of that time had passed irrevocably, like the time itself, and that to bring it back now would be not only impossible, but painful and embarrassing. And come to think of it, was it really so good, that time that seemed to me so happy? And it was all so long, long ago!

'But anyway, it's tea time!' he said, and we went into the living-room together. In the doorway I again encountered the nurse with Vanya. I took the child in my arms, covered his red little legs which were now exposed, pressed him to me and, barely touching him with my lips, gave him a kiss. As if in his sleep, he moved his little hand with its parted, wizened fingers and opened his dim little eyes, as though he were looking for something or remembering something; suddenly those little eyes rested on me, a spark of thought gleamed in them, his chubby parted lips began to gather and opened in a smile. 'Mine, mine, mine!' I thought, pressing him to my bosom with a happy tension in all my limbs, and only with difficulty restraining myself from hurting him. And I began to kiss his cold little legs, his stomach and hands and head with its merest covering of hair. My husband came over to me, and I quickly covered the child's face and then uncovered it again.

'Ivan Sergeich!' my husband said softly, touching him with a finger under his little chin. But I quickly covered Ivan Sergeich up again. No one but me was to look at him long. I glanced at my husband: his eyes were laughing as they gazed at mine, and for the first time after all that long age I felt light and joyful as I looked into them.

From that day my romance with my husband was over; the old feeling became a dear, irrevocable memory, but my new feeling of love for my children and for the father of my children laid the beginning of another but now quite different happy life, which at the present moment I have not yet lived through . . .

THE KREUTZER SONATA

The original Russian text is to be found in L. N. Tolstoy, *Sobranie sochinenii v 22 tomakh*, vol. 12 (Moscow, 1978–85).

But I say unto you, That whosoever looketh on a woman to lust after her hath committed adultery with her already in his heart.   (Matthew v:28)

His disciples say unto him, If the case of the man be so with his wife, it is not good to marry.

But he said unto them, All men cannot receive this saying, save they to whom it is given.

For there are some eunuchs, which were so born from their mother's womb: and there are some eunuchs, which were made eunuchs of men: and there be eunuchs, which have made themselves eunuchs for the kingdom of heaven's sake. He that is able to receive it, let him receive it.
                                   (Matthew xix:10–12)

This took place in early spring. It was the second uninterrupted day of our journey. Every so often passengers who were only going short distances would enter the railway carriage and leave it again, but there were three people who, like myself, had boarded the train at its point of origin and were still travelling: a plain, elderly lady with an exhausted-looking face, who was smoking cigarettes and was dressed in a hat and coat that might almost have been those of a man; her companion, a talkative man of about forty, with trim, new luggage; and another man who was rather small of stature and whose movements were nervous and jerky – he was not yet old, but his curly hair had obviously turned grey prematurely, and his eyes had a peculiar light in them as they flickered from one object to another. He was dressed in an old coat that looked as though it might have been made by an expensive tailor; it had a lambskin collar, and he wore a tall cap of the same material. Whenever he unfastened his coat, a long-waisted jacket and a Russian embroidered shirt came into view. Another peculiar thing about this man was that every now and again he uttered strange sounds, as if he were clearing his throat or beginning to laugh, but breaking off in silence.

Throughout the entire duration of the journey this man studiously avoided talking to any of the other passengers or becoming acquainted with them. If anyone spoke to him he would reply curtly and abruptly; he spent the time reading, looking out of the window, smoking or taking from his old travelling-bag the provisions he had brought with him and then sipping tea or munching a snack.

I had the feeling that his solitude was weighing him down, and I tried several times to engage him in conversation. Each time our eyes met, however, which was frequently, as we were sitting obliquely opposite one another, he would turn away and start reading his book or gazing out of the window.

Shortly before evening on that second day, the train stopped at a large station, and the nervous man stepped outside, fetched some boiling water and made tea for himself. The man with the smart luggage, a lawyer, as I later discovered, went to have a glass of tea in the station buffet with his travelling companion, the cigarette-smoking lady in the man's coat.

During their absence several new passengers entered the carriage. They included a tall, clean-shaven old man whose face was creased all over in wrinkles; he was evidently a merchant, and he wore a polecat fur coat and a cloth cap that had an enormous peak. He sat down opposite the places temporarily vacated by the lawyer and the lady, and immediately launched into a conversation with a young man who looked like a sales clerk and who had also entered the carriage at this station.

My seat was diagonally opposite theirs, and since the train was not in motion I could, when no one was passing down the carriage, overhear snatches of what they were saying. The merchant started off by telling the other man that he was on his way to visit his estate, which lay just one stop down the line; then, as such men always do, they began to discuss trade and prices, the current state of the Moscow market, and eventually, as always, they arrived at the subject of the Nizhny Novgorod summer fair.[1] The sales clerk embarked on a description of the drinking and antics of a certain rich merchant they both knew, but the old man would not hear him out; instead, he began to talk about the jamborees he himself had taken part in at Kunavino[2] in days gone by. Of his role in these he was evidently proud, and it was with open delight that he related how once, when he and this same mutual acquaintance had been drunk together in Kunavino, they had got up to some mischief of a kind that he could only describe in whispers. The sales clerk's guffaw filled the entire carriage, and the old man laughed along with him, exposing a couple of yellow teeth to view.

Not expecting to hear anything of interest, I rose and left my seat with the aim of taking a stroll along the platform until it was time for the train to depart. In the doorway I bumped into the lawyer and the lady, who were chattering animatedly to one another as they found their way back to their seats.

'You won't have time,' the talkative lawyer said to me. 'The second bell's going to go any minute now.'

And so it was: before I had even reached the end of the line of carriages the bell rang. When I got back to my seat I found the lawyer and the lady deep in energetic conversation. The old merchant sat opposite them in silence, looking severely in front of him and chewing his teeth from time to time in disapproval.

'So then she just told her husband straight out,' the lawyer was saying with a smile as I made my way past him. 'She said she couldn't and wouldn't live with him any more, because . . .'

And he began to say something else, something I could not make out. More passengers came trooping in behind me; then the guard walked down the carriage, followed by a porter in a tremendous hurry, and for quite a long time there ensued such an uproar that no conversation could possibly be heard. When things had quietened down again and I could once more hear the lawyer's voice, the conversation had evidently passed from the particular to the general.

The lawyer was saying that the question of divorce was very much the object of public discussion in Europe just now, and that cases of this type were cropping up in our own country with an ever-increasing degree of frequency. Noticing that his voice had become the only one in the carriage, the lawyer cut short his homily and turned to the old man.

'There was none of that sort of thing in the old days, was there?' he said, smiling affably.

The old man was about to reply, but at that moment the train began to move and, taking off his cap, he began crossing himself and reciting a prayer in a whisper. The lawyer waited politely, averting his gaze. When he had finished his prayer and his thrice-repeated crossing of himself, the old man put his cap fairly and squarely back on his head, rearranged himself in his seat, and began to speak.

'Oh there was, sir. It's just that there wasn't so much of it, that's all,' he said. 'You can't expect anything else nowadays. They've all gotten that well educated.'

As the train began to gather speed it kept rattling over points, and it was not easy to hear what he was saying. I was interested, however, and I shifted my seat so as to be closer to him. The interest of my neighbour, the nervous man with the light in his eyes, had also plainly been aroused, and he continued to listen while staying where he was.

'But what's wrong with education?' said the lady, with a scarcely perceptible smile. 'Was it really better to get married in the old way, with the bride and bridegroom never even setting eyes on one another beforehand?' she continued, replying, as many women do, not to what the person she was addressing had actually said, but to what she thought he was going to say. 'You didn't know whether you were even going to like the man, let alone whether you'd be able to love him; you got married to the first man who came along and spent all the rest of your life in misery. Do you think that was better?' she said, making it clear that her words were addressed primarily to the lawyer and myself, and only in the last instance to the old man with whom she was talking.

'They've all gotten that well educated,' repeated the old merchant, surveying the lady contemptuously and letting her question go unanswered.

'I'd like to hear you explain the connection you see between education and marital discord,' the lawyer said, with a faint smile.

The merchant was about to say something, but the lady cut in before him.

'No, those days have gone,' she said. But the lawyer would not allow her to continue.

'Just a moment, let him say what's on his mind.'

'Education leads to nothing but a lot of silliness,' said the old man, firmly.

'People who don't love one another are forced to get married, and then everyone wonders why they can't live in harmony together,' said the lady hurriedly, turning an appraising eye on the lawyer, myself and even on the sales clerk, who had risen out of his seat and was leaning his elbows on its back, listening to the conversation with a smile. 'After all, it's only animals that can be mated at their masters' will; human beings have inclinations and attachments of their own,' she went on, apparently from a desire to say something wounding to the merchant.

'You're wrong there, missus,' said the old man. 'The true difference is that an animal's just an animal, but human beings have been given a law to live by.'

'Very well, but how are you supposed to live with someone you don't love?' asked the lady, still in a hurry to express her opinions, which doubtless seemed brand new to her.

'People didn't make such a fuss about all that in the old days,' said the merchant in a serious voice. 'That's all just come in lately. First thing you hear her say nowadays is "I'm leaving you." It's a fashion that's caught on even among the muzhiks. "Here you are," she says; "here's your shirts and trousers, I'm off with Vanka, his hair's curlier than yours." And it's no good arguing with her. Whereas what ought to come first for a woman is fear.'

The sales clerk looked first at the lawyer, then at the lady, and finally at me; he was only just keeping back a smile, and was preparing to treat what the merchant had said with either ridicule or approval, according to how it went down.

'What sort of fear?' asked the lady.

'Fear of her *hu-u-us*band, of course. That kind of fear.'

'Well, my dear man, those days have gone, I'm afraid,' said the lady, with an edge of malice in her voice.

'No, missus, those days can never be gone. Eve, the woman, was created from the rib of man, and so she will remain until the end of time,' said the old man, with such a stern and triumphant shake of his head that the sales clerk at once decided that victory was on the side of the merchant, and he burst into loud laughter.

'That's only the way you menfolk see it,' said the lady, not ceding defeat, and giving us all an appraising look. 'You've granted yourselves freedom, but you want to keep women locked up in a tower. Meanwhile you've decided you're going to allow yourselves anything you want.'

'No one's decided anything of the kind. It's just that a home profits nothing from a man's endeavours, and a woman is a fragile vessel,' the merchant continued earnestly.

The merchant's solemn, earnest tone of voice was evidently having a persuasive effect on his audience. Even the lady appeared to have had some of the wind taken out of her sails, though she showed no sign of giving up the struggle.

'Yes, well, but I think you would agree that a woman is a human being, and that she has feelings just as a man has, wouldn't you? So what's she supposed to do if she doesn't love her husband?'

'If she doesn't love him?' echoed the merchant darkly, making a grimace with his lips and eyebrows. 'She'd better love him.'

The sales clerk seemed to find this line of argument particularly attractive, and he made a noise of approval.

'Oh, no she hadn't,' said the lady. 'If there's no love there in the first place, you can't force it.'

'And what if the wife's unfaithful to the husband?' asked the lawyer.

'That mustn't happen,' said the old man. 'You have to be on the lookout for that kind of thing.'

'But what if it does happen? It does, after all.'

'There's some as it happens to, but not the likes of us,' said the old man.

No one ventured anything for a while. The sales clerk shifted a little closer. Apparently not wishing to be left out of things, he gave a smile and said: 'Oh, but it does, you know. There was a scandal with one of our lads. It wasn't easy to tell whose fault it was, either. Married a loose woman, he did. She started her flirting around, but he was the homely type, and he had a bit of education. First jump she had was with one of the clerks in the office. The lad tried to make her see reason, but there was no stopping her. All kinds of filthy tricks she got up to. Started stealing his money. So he beat her. Didn't do any good,

she just went from bad to worse. She started playing around –
if you'll pardon the expression – with a heathen, a Jew he was.
What was the lad supposed to do? He threw her out. Now he
lives as a bachelor, and she walks the streets.'

'So he was an idiot,' said the old man. 'If he'd never given
her any leeway in the first place but had kept her properly
reined in, she'd no doubt still be living with him to this day.
You mustn't allow them any freedom from the word go. Never
trust a horse in the paddock or a wife in the home.'

At this moment the guard arrived to take the tickets for the
next station. The old man gave up his ticket.

'Yes, you have to rein them in early on, those womenfolk,
otherwise it all goes to pot.'

'But what about that story you were telling us just then about
those married men going on the spree in Kunavino?' I could
not resist asking.

'That's something altogether different,' said the merchant,
and lapsed into silence.

When the whistle blew he got up, fetched his travelling-bag
from under his seat, drew his overcoat tightly around him and,
raising his cap to us, went out on to the brake platform.

II

As soon as the old man had gone, several voices took up the
conversation again.

'That fellow was straight out of the Old Testament,' said the
sales clerk.

'A veritable walking *Domostroy*,'[3] said the lady. 'What a
barbarous conception of woman and marriage!'

'Yes, we're a long way behind the European idea of marriage,'
said the lawyer.

'What these people don't seem to understand,' said the lady,
'is that marriage without love isn't marriage at all; love is the
only thing that can sanctify a marriage, and the only true
marriages are those that are sanctified by love.'

The sales clerk listened, smiling. He was trying to memorize as much of this clever talk as he could, for use on future occasions.

The lady's homily was interrupted halfway through by a sound that seemed to come from behind me and might have been a broken laugh or a sob. When we turned round, we saw my neighbour, the solitary, grey-haired man with the light in his eyes; he had evidently become interested in our conversation and had come closer to us without our noticing. He was standing up, his hands leaning on the back of his seat, and he was plainly in a state of great agitation. His face was red, and a muscle in one of his cheeks was twitching.

'What's this love . . . love . . . love . . . that sanctifies marriage?' he stammered.

Observing the state of agitation he was in, the lady tried to make her reply as gentle and thorough as possible.

'True love . . . if true love exists between a man and a woman, then marriage, too, is possible,' said the lady.

'Yes, but what's true love?' said the man with the light in his eyes, smiling timidly and awkwardly.

'Everybody knows what love is,' said the lady, visibly anxious to bring this conversation to an end.

'I don't,' said the man. 'You'd have to define what you mean . . .'

'What? It's very simple,' said the lady, though she had to think for a moment. 'Love? Love is the exclusive preference for one man or one woman above all others,' she said.

'A preference lasting how long? A month? Two days, half an hour?' said the grey-haired man, and he gave a laugh.

'No, not that kind of preference, you're talking about something else.'

'What she means,' said the lawyer, intervening and designating the lady, 'is firstly that marriage ought to be based primarily on affection – love, if you like – and that only if this is present does marriage offer something that is, as it were, sacred. Secondly, that no marriage which is not based on natural affection – love, if you like – carries with it any moral obligation. Have I understood you correctly?' he asked, turning to the lady.

By a movement of her head, the lady indicated her approval of this exposition of her views.

'It follows, therefore . . .' the lawyer began, pursuing his discourse. But by this time the nervous man, whose eyes were now on fire, was clearly restraining himself only with difficulty.

Without waiting for the lawyer to conclude, he said: 'Yes, that's exactly what I'm talking about, the preference for one man or one woman above all others, but what I'm asking is: a preference for how long?'

'How long? A long time, sometimes for as long as one lives,' said the lady, shrugging her shoulders.

'But that only happens in novels, not in real life. In real life a preference like that lasts maybe a year, but that's very rare; more often it's a few months, or weeks, or days, or hours,' he said, evidently aware that this opinion would shock everyone, and pleased at the result.

'What are you saying? No, no! Sorry, but no!' we all three of us burst out together. Even the sales clerk made a noise of disapproval.

'I know, I know,' said the grey-haired man in a raised voice, louder than any of us. 'You're talking about the way things are supposed to be, but I'm talking about the way things actually are. Every man experiences what you call love each time he meets a pretty woman.'

'Oh, but what you're saying is dreadful! Surely there's an emotion that exists between people called love, a feeling that lasts not just months or years, but for the whole of their lives?'

'Definitely not. Even if one admits that a man may prefer a certain woman all his life, it's more than probable that the woman will prefer someone else. That's the way it's always been and that's the way it still is,' he said, taking a cigarette from his cigarette case and lighting it.

'But there can be mutual affection, surely,' said the lawyer.

'No, there can't,' the grey-haired man retorted, 'any more than two marked peas can turn up next to one another in a pea-cart. And besides, it's not just a question of probability, but of having too much of a good thing. Loving the same man or woman all your life – why, that's like supposing the same candle could last you all your life,' he said, inhaling greedily.

'But you're just talking about physical love. Wouldn't you admit that there can be a love that's founded on shared ideals, on spiritual affinity?'

'Spiritual affinity? Shared ideals?' he repeated, making his sound again. 'There's not much point in going to bed together if that's what you're after (excuse the plain language). Do people go to bed with one another because of shared ideals?' he said, laughing nervously.

'I'm sorry,' said the lawyer. 'The facts contradict what you're saying. Our own eyes tell us that marriages exist, that the whole of humanity or at least the greater part of it lives in a married state and that a lot of people manage to stay decently married for rather a long time.'

The grey-haired man began to laugh again. 'First you tell me that marriage is founded on love, and then when I express my doubts as to the existence of any love apart from the physical kind you try to prove its existence by the fact that marriages exist. But marriage nowadays is just a deception!'

'No, sir, with respect,' said the lawyer. 'All I said was that marriages have existed and that they continue to exist.'

'All right, so they exist. But why? They've existed and they continue to exist for the sort of people who see in marriage something that's sacred, a sacrament that binds them in the eyes of God. Marriages exist for those people, but not for the likes of you and me. Our sort enter into a marriage without seeing in it anything except copulation, and it usually ends either in infidelity or violence. Infidelity is easier to put up with. The husband and wife simply pretend to everyone that they're living in monogamy, when in actual fact they're living in polygamy and polyandry. It's not very pretty, but it's feasible. But when, as is most often the case, the husband and wife accept the external obligation to live together all their lives and have, by the second month, come to loathe the sight of each other, want to get divorced and yet go on living together, it usually ends in that terrible hell that drives them to drink, makes them shoot themselves, kill and poison each other,' he said, speaking faster and faster, not letting anyone else get a word in, and growing hotter and hotter under the collar. No one said anything. We all felt too embarrassed.

'Yes, there's no doubt that married life has its critical episodes,' said the lawyer, endeavouring to bring to an end a conversation that had grown more heated than was seemly.

'I can see you've recognized me,' said the grey-haired man quietly, trying to appear unruffled.

'No, I don't think I have the pleasure . . .'

'It's not much of a pleasure. Pozdnyshev's the name. I'm the fellow who had one of those critical episodes you were talking about. So critical was it, in fact, that I ended up murdering my wife,' he said, making his noise again. 'Oh, I say, I'm sorry. Er . . . I didn't mean to embarrass you.'

'Not at all, for heaven's sake . . .' said the lawyer, not quite sure himself what he meant by this 'for heaven's sake'.

But Pozdnyshev, who was not paying any attention to him, turned round sharply and went back to his seat. The lawyer and the lady whispered to one another. I was sitting beside Pozdnyshev and I kept quiet, not knowing what to say. It was too dark to read, so I closed my eyes and pretended I wanted to go to sleep. We continued in this silent fashion until the train reached the next station.

While the train was at a standstill, the lawyer and the lady moved along to another carriage as they had arranged to do earlier on with the guard. The sales clerk made himself comfortable on the empty seat and went to sleep. As for Pozdnyshev, he continued to smoke cigarettes and sip the tea he had made for himself at the previous station.

When I opened my eyes and looked at him, he suddenly turned to me with an air of resolve and exasperation: 'I think perhaps you're finding it unpleasant to sit next to me, since you know who I am? If that's so, I'll move.'

'Oh, no, please don't.'

'Well, would you like some tea, then? It's strong, mind.' He poured me a glass of tea. 'What they were saying . . . It's all wrong, you know . . .'

'What are you talking about?' I asked.

'Oh, the same thing – that love they keep going on about, and what it really is. You're sure you'd not rather be getting some sleep?'

'Quite sure.'

'Well then, if you like, I'll tell you how that love of theirs drove me to the point where I did what I did.'

'By all means, if it's not too painful for you.'

'No, it's keeping quiet about it that's the painful part. Have some more. Or is it too strong for you?'

The tea was the colour of tar, but I swilled down a glass of it all the same. Just then the guard passed down the carriage. Pozdnyshev followed him angrily with his gaze and did not start speaking again until he was gone.

III

'Very well, then, I'll tell you ... You're absolutely sure you want me to?'

I repeated that I did, very much. He said nothing for a moment. Then, rubbing his face in his hands, he began: 'If I'm going to tell you, I'll have to start at the beginning, and tell you how and why I got married, and what I was like before my marriage.

'Before my marriage I lived the sort of life all men do, in our social circle, that is. I'm a landowner, I've got a university degree, and I used to be a marshal of nobility. As I say, I lived the sort of life all men do – a life of debauchery. And, like all the men of our class, I thought that this debauched existence was perfectly proper. I considered myself a charming young man, a thoroughly moral sort of fellow. I wasn't a seducer, had no unnatural tastes, and didn't make debauchery into my main aim in life, as many young men of my age did, but indulged in it with decency and moderation, for the sake of my health. I avoided women who might have succeeded in tying me down by having babies or forming attachments to me. Actually, there probably were both babies and attachments, but I behaved as if there weren't. Not only did I regard this as moral behaviour – I was proud of it.'

He paused and made his sound, as he apparently did whenever some new idea occurred to him.

'And that's the really loathsome thing about it,' he exclaimed. 'Debauchery isn't something physical. Not even the most outrageous physicality can be equated with debauchery. Debauchery – real debauchery – takes place when you free yourself from any moral regard for the woman you enter into physical relations with. But you see, I made the acquisition of that freedom into a matter of personal honour. I remember the agony of mind I once went through when I was in too much of a hurry to remember to pay a woman who had probably fallen in love with me and had let me go to bed with her. I just couldn't rest easy until I'd sent her the money, thereby demonstrating that I didn't consider myself morally obliged towards her in any way. Don't sit there nodding your head as if you agreed with me!' he suddenly shouted at me. 'I know what you're thinking! You're all the same, you too, unless you're a rare exception, you see things the way I did then. Oh I say, forget that, I'm sorry,' he continued. 'But the fact is that it's horrible, horrible, horrible!'

'What is?' I inquired.

'The abyss of error we live in regarding women and our relations with them. It's no good, I just can't talk calmly about it. It's not merely because of that episode, as the other gentleman called it, but because ever since I went through it my eyes have been opened and I've seen everything in a completely new light. Everything's been turned inside out, it's all inside out! . . .'

He lit a cigarette and, leaning forward with his elbows on his knees, began to tell me his story.

It was so dark that I could not see his face, only hear his forceful, pleasant voice raised above the rattling and swaying of the carriage.

IV

'Yes, it was only after the suffering I endured, only thanks to it that I came to understand what the root of the trouble was, saw the way things ought to be, and thus obtained an insight into the horror of things the way they were.

'If you want to know, this is how and when it all began, the sequence of events that led up to that episode of mine. It started shortly before my sixteenth birthday. I was still at grammar school then. My older brother was a first-year student at university. As yet I had no experience of women, but like all the wretched boys of our social class I was no longer innocent. For more than a year I'd been exposed to the corrupting influence of the other boys. Woman – not any woman in particular but woman as a sweet, ineffable presence – woman, any woman, the nakedness of woman already tormented me. The hours I spent alone were not pure ones. I suffered in the way ninety-nine per cent of our youngsters suffer. I was horrified – I suffered, prayed, and succumbed. I was already corrupted, both in my imagination and in reality, but I had still not taken the final step. In my lonely way I was going from bad to worse, but so far I had not laid my hands on any other human being. But then one of my brother's friends, a student, a *bon vivant*, one of those so-called "jolly good chaps" (an out-and-out villain, in other words), who had taught us to play cards and drink vodka, persuaded us to go with him to a certain place after a drinking bout one evening. My brother was still a virgin, like myself, and he fell that very same night. And I, a fifteen-year-old boy, defiled myself and contributed to the defilement of a woman without the slightest understanding of what I was doing. After all, never once had I heard any of my elders say that what I was doing was wrong. And it's not something you hear said nowadays, either. It's true that it's in the Ten Commandments, but you know as well as I do that they're only useful for giving the school chaplain the right answers on examination day, and even then they're not a great deal of help

– much less so, for example, than knowing when to use *ut* in conditional clauses.

'That's the way it was: none of the older people whose opinions I respected ever told me that what I was doing was wrong. On the contrary, the people I looked up to told me it was the right thing to do. I was told that, after I had done it, my struggles and sufferings would ease. I was told this, and I read it. My elders assured me that it would be good for my health. As for my companions, they said it entailed a kind of merit, a certain bravado. Accordingly, I could see nothing but good in it. The danger of infection? But that, too, is taken care of. Our solicitous government takes pains to see to it. It supervises the orderly running of the licensed brothels and ensures the depravation of grammar-school boys. Even our doctors keep an eye on this problem, for a fee of course. That is only proper. They assert that debauchery is good for the health, for it's they who have instituted this form of tidy, legalized debauchery. I even know mothers who take an active concern for this aspect of their son's health. And science directs them to the brothels.'

'Why science?' I asked.

'What are doctors, if not the high priests of science? Who are the people responsible for depraving young lads, claiming it's essential for their health? They are. And having made such a claim, they proceed to apply their cures for syphilis with an air of the utmost gravity.'

'But why shouldn't they cure syphilis?'

'Because if even one per cent of the effort that is put into curing syphilis were to be employed in the eradication of debauchery, syphilis would long ago have disappeared from memory. But our efforts are employed not in eradicating debauchery, but in encouraging it, making it safe. Anyway that isn't the point. The point is that I, like nine out of ten, if not more, young men, not only in our own class but in all the others as well, even the peasantry, have had the horrible experience of falling without succumbing to the natural temptation of the charms of any one woman in particular. No, it wasn't a case of my being seduced by a woman. I fell because the society I lived in regarded what was a fall either as a bodily function that was both legitimate and necessary for the sake of health, or as a diversion that was thoroughly natural for a young man and was not only pardonable, but even innocent. I myself didn't know it was a fall; I simply began to indulge in something that was half pleasure and half physical necessity – both, I was assured, perfectly proper for young men of a certain age. I began to indulge in this debauchery in the same way as I began to drink and smoke. Yet there was something strangely moving about that first fall. I remember that immediately after it was over, right there in the room, I felt terribly, terribly sad; I wanted to weep, weep for my lost innocence, for my relation to women which had been forever spoiled, corrupted. Yes, the simple, natural relation I had had to women had been ruined for ever. From that day on I ceased to have a pure relation to women, nor was I any longer capable of one. I had become what is known as a fornicator. Being a fornicator is a physical condition similar to that of a morphine addict, an alcoholic or a smoker of opium. Just as a morphine addict, an alcoholic or a smoker of opium is no longer a normal individual, so a man who has had several women for the sake of his pleasure is no longer a normal person but one who has been spoiled for all time – a fornicator. And just as an alcoholic or a morphine addict can immediately be recognized by his features and physical mannerisms, so can a fornicator. A fornicator may restrain himself, struggle for self-control, but never again will his relation to women be simple, clear, pure, that of a brother to a sister. A fornicator can be instantly recognized by the intent look with which he examines a woman. I, too, became a fornicator and remained one, and that was my undoing.'

V

'Yes, that's how it happened. After that it got worse and worse; I became involved in all kinds of moral deviations. My God! I recoil in horror from the memory of all my filthy acts! I, whom all my friends used to laugh at because of what they called my innocence! And when one looks at our golden youth, at our officers, at those Parisians! And when all those gentlemen and myself, debauchees in our thirties with hundreds of the most varied and abominable crimes against women on our consciences, go into a drawing-room or a ballroom, well scrubbed, clean-shaven, perfumed, wearing immaculate linen, in evening dress or uniform, the very emblems of purity – aren't we a charming sight?

'Just give some thought for a moment to the way things ought to be and the way things actually are. This is the way things ought to be: when one of these gentlemen enters into relations with my sister or my daughter, I go up to him, take him aside and say to him quietly: "My dear fellow, I know the sort of life you lead, how you spend your nights and who you spend them with. This is no place for you. The girls in this house are pure and innocent. Be off with you!" That's how it ought to be. Now how things actually are is that when one of these gentlemen appears and starts dancing with my sister or my daughter, putting his arms round her, we rejoice, as long as he's rich and has connections. Always supposing, of course, that after Rigolboche[4] he considers my daughter good enough for him. Even if there are consequences, an illness . . . it doesn't matter. They can cure anything nowadays. Good heavens, yes, I can think of several girls from the highest social circles whose parents enthusiastically married them off to syphilitics. Ugh, how vile! But the time will come when all that filth and deception will be shown for what it is!'

He made his strange sound several times and began to sip his tea. The tea was horribly strong, and there was no water with which to dilute it. I felt it was the two glasses of the stuff I had already drunk that were making me so agitated. The tea must also have been having an effect on him, for he was growing more and more excited. His voice was increasingly acquiring a singing, expressive quality. He shifted position constantly, now removing his hat, now putting it on again, and his face kept altering strangely in the semi-darkness where we sat.

'Well, and so that's the way I lived until I was thirty, without ever for one moment abandoning my intention of getting married and building for myself the most elevated and purest of family lives, and with that end in view I was keeping an eye out for a girl who might fill the bill,' he continued. 'I was wallowing in the slime of debauchery, and at the same time looking for girls who might be pure enough to be worthy of me! I rejected a lot of them because of that – because they weren't pure enough; but at last I found one whom I considered worthy of me. She was one of the two daughters of a Penza landowner who had once been very rich but had lost all his money.

'One evening after we'd been out boating and were going home together in the moonlight, I sat beside her and admired her curls and her shapely figure, hugged by the tight silk of the stockinet dress she was wearing. I suddenly decided that she was the one. That evening it seemed to me that she understood everything, all I was thinking and feeling, and that all my thoughts and feelings were of the most exalted kind. All it really was was that silk stockinet happened to suit her particularly well, as did curls, and that after a day spent close to her I wanted to get even closer.

'It's really quite remarkable how complete the illusion is that beauty is the same as goodness. A pretty woman may say the most stupid things, yet you listen, and you don't notice the stupidities, it all sounds so intelligent. She says and does things that are infamous, yet to you they seem delightful. And when at last she says something that is neither stupid nor infamous, as long as she's pretty, you're immediately convinced that she's quite wonderfully intelligent and of the very highest morality.

'I returned home positively beside myself with enthusiasm and decided that she was the acme of moral perfection and consequently worthy of being my wife. I proposed to her the very next day.

'What a tangled mess it all is! Out of a thousand men who get married, not only in our own class but also, regrettably, among the common people as well, there's scarcely one who hasn't already been married ten times, if not a hundred or even a thousand times, like Don Juan, before his marriage. (Nowadays there are, it's true, as I've heard and observed, pure young men who know and sense that this is no laughing-matter, but a great and serious undertaking. May God give them strength! In my day there wasn't one chap in ten thousand like that.) And everyone knows this, yet pretends not to. In novels the hero's emotions are described in detail, just like the ponds and bushes he walks beside; but while they describe his *grand amour* for some young girl or other, they say nothing about what has taken place in the life of this interesting hero previously: there's not a word about his visits to brothels, about the chamber-maids, the kitchen-maids, the wives of other men. Even if indecent novels of this type do exist, they're certainly not put into the hands of those who most need to know all this – young girls. At first we pretend to them that this debauchery, which fills up the lives of half the inhabitants of our towns and villages, doesn't exist at all. Subsequently we grow so accustomed to this pretence that we end up like the English, secure in the honest conviction that we are all of the very highest morality and that we live in a world that is morally perfect. The poor girls take it all very seriously. I know my own wretched wife did. I remember that after we'd got engaged I let her read my diary,[5] so she could get some idea of the sort of life I'd been leading previously and in particular some knowledge of my last affair, which she might have found out about from other people and which I therefore considered it necessary to tell her about. I remember her horror, despair and perplexity when she learned about it and the whole thing dawned on her. I could see she was thinking of leaving me. If only she had!'

He made his sound, fell silent, and took another mouthful of tea.

VI

'No, all the same, it's better the way it turned out, better the way it turned out!' he cried suddenly. 'It served me right! But that's all in the past now. What I was trying to say was that it's only the poor girls who are deceived. Their mothers know, especially the ones who've been "educated" by their husbands, they know perfectly well what goes on. And although they pretend to believe that men are pure, their actual behaviour is altogether different. They know the right bait to use in order to catch men, both for themselves and for their daughters.

'It's only we men who don't know, and we don't know because we don't want to know. Women know perfectly well that the most elevated love – the most "poetic", as we call it – depends not on moral qualities but on physical proximity and also on things like hairstyle, or the colour and the cut of a dress. Ask any experienced coquette who has set herself the task of ensnaring the attentions of a man which she would rather risk: to be accused of lying, cruelty and even of whorish behaviour in the presence of the man she is trying to attract, or to appear before his gaze in an ugly, badly made dress – and she will always choose the former. She knows that our man's lying when he goes on about lofty emotions – all he wants is her body, and so he will willingly forgive her the most outrageous behaviour. What he won't forgive, however, is an outfit that is ugly, tasteless or lacking in style. A coquette's knowledge of this is a conscious one; but every innocent young girl knows it unconsciously, as animals do.

'That's the reason for those insufferable stockinets, those fake posteriors, those bare shoulders, arms – breasts, almost. Women, especially women who've undergone the "education" provided by men, know very well that all talk about higher things is just talk, that all a man really wants is her body, and all the things that show it off in the most enticing fashion possible. And that's what they give him. You know, if only one is able to kick the habit of all this squalor that's become second nature to us and takes a look at the life of our upper classes as it really is in all its shamelessness, one can see that what we live in is a sort of licensed brothel. Don't you agree? I can prove it to you if you like,' he said, not letting me get a word in. 'You may say that women of our class act out of interests that are different from those of the women in the whorehouses, but I say that the contrary is true, and I can prove it. If people differ as regards the purpose, the inner content of their lives, that difference will inevitably be reflected in outward things, and those will differ, too. But look at those poor despised wretches, and then cast a glance at our society ladies: the same exposure of arms, shoulders, breasts, the same flaunted, tightly clad posteriors, the same passion for precious stones and shiny, expensive objects, the same diversions – music, dancing, singing. Just as the former seek to entice men by all the means at their disposal, so do the latter. There's no difference. At a rule, we may say that while short-term prostitutes are generally looked down upon, long-term prostitutes are treated with respect.'

VII

'Yes, and so I fell into the trap of all those stockinets, those curls and fake bottoms. I was an easy catch, because I'd been brought up under those special conditions created for amorous young people, who are cultivated in them like cucumbers in a greenhouse. Yes, the stimulating, superabundant food we eat, together with our complete physical idleness, amounts to nothing but a systematic arousal of lust. I don't know whether you find that astonishing or not, but it's a fact. I myself had no idea of all this until quite recently. But now I can see it. And that is what I find so infuriating, that no one has any idea of what's really going on, and everyone says such stupid things, like that woman just now.

'Yes, this spring there were some peasants working on the railway embankment close to where I live. The normal food of a young peasant is bread, kvas and onions; it keeps him lively, cheerful and healthy; he works at light tasks out in the fields.

He goes to work for the railway, and is fed on kasha and a pound of meat a day. But that day involves sixteen hours of labour, during which he has to trundle a wheelbarrow weighing some thirty poods, and he soon uses up the meat. It's just right for him. But look at us: every day each of us eats perhaps two pounds of meat, game and all kinds of stimulating food and drink. Where does it all go? On sensual excesses. If we really do use it up in that way, the safety valve is opened and everything is all right. If, on the other hand, we close the safety valve, as I did mine from time to time, there immediately results a state of physical arousal which, channelled through the prism of our artificial way of life, expresses itself as the purest form of love, sometimes even as a platonic infatuation. I, too, fell in love that way, like everyone else. And it was all there: all the ecstasy, the tender emotion, the poetry. In actual fact, this love of mine was the product of, on the one hand, the efforts of the girl's mother and dressmakers, and on the other, of the excessive quantities of food I had consumed during a life of idleness. If, on the one hand, there had been none of those boat trips, those dress-makers with their waistlines, and so on, and say my wife had gone around in an ill-fitting housecoat and spent her time at home, and if, on the other hand, I had been living the normal life of a man who consumes just as much food as is necessary for him to be able to do his work, and the safety valve had been open – it happened to be closed at the time – I would never have fallen in love and none of all this would ever have happened.'

VIII

'Well, this time it all clicked together: my state of mind, her dress and the boat trip. And it worked. Twenty times before it hadn't worked, but now it did – the way a trap does. I'm quite serious. Marriages nowadays are set like traps. Only stands to reason, doesn't it? The girl's grown up now, she'll have to be married to someone. It all seems so simple, as long as the girl's not a freak and there are men around who want to get married.

That's the way it was done in the old days. When a girl came of age, her parents arranged a marriage for her. That's how it was done, and that's how it's done all over the world to this very day: among the Chinese, the Hindus, the Muslims, among our own common people. That's how it's done among at least ninety-nine per cent of the human race. It's only we one per cent or less of debauchees who've decided that's not good enough and have thought up something new. And what is that something new? It's girls sitting in line while men come and go in front of them as if they were at a market, making their choice. As they sit there waiting, the girls think, not daring to say it out loud: "Choose me, dearest! No, me. Not her, me: look what nice shoulders and all the rest of it I have." We men walk up and down, take a look, and are very pleased with what we see. "I know what they're up to," we say to ourselves, "but I won't fall into their trap." We walk up and down, we take a look, we're thoroughly gratified that all this has been arranged for our benefit. We look, are taken off our guard for a moment – and slam! There's another one caught!'

'But how do you think it ought to be?' I asked. 'Should the woman be the one to propose?'

'I honestly don't know: but if we're going to have equality, then let's have real equality. It may well be that matchmaking is a degrading business, but this is a thousand times more so. At least under the old system the rights possessed by both parties and their chances of making a decent match were equal, but nowadays a woman is like a slave in a market or a piece of bait for a trap. Just you try to tell a mother or even the girl herself that all her activities are directed towards catching a husband. Dear Lord, what an insult! And yet that's all they do, and they've nothing else with which to fill their time. What's so awful is seeing even poor innocent young girls engaged in this activity. If only it were done out in the open, but no, it's all trickery, deceit. "Ah, the origin of species, how interesting! Oh, Liza's so interested in painting! And you'll be going to the exhibition? How educational! And the troika rides, and the theatre, and the symphony concert? How wonderful! My Liza's simply mad about music. Oh, do tell me why you don't share these convictions! And boating, too . . ." And all the while there's just one thought in her head: "Take me, take me, take my Liza! No, me! Go on, just for a trial!" Oh, horror! Lies!' he concluded, and, drinking up what was left of the tea, set about clearing away the glasses and the rest of the tea things.

IX

'You know,' he resumed, as he put the tea and sugar away in his travelling-bag, 'it's this domination by women we're suffering from, it all stems from that.'

'What domination?' I asked. 'All the rights and privileges are on the side of men.'

'Yes, yes, that's just the point,' he said, interrupting me. 'That's exactly what I'm trying to tell you, that's what explains this curious phenomenon: from one point of view, it's perfectly correct to say that woman has been brought to the lowest degree of subjection, but from another point of view it's equally true to say that she's the dominant one. Women are exactly like the Jews, who by their financial power compensate for the oppression to which they're subjected. "Aha, you just want us to be merchants, do you? All right, then, it's as merchants that we'll lord it over you," say the Jews. "Aha, you just want us to be the objects of your sensuality, do you? All right, then, it's as the objects of your sensuality that we'll enslave you," say women. Women's lack of rights has nothing to do with them not being allowed to vote or be judges – those matters don't constitute any sort of right. No, it has to do with the fact that in sexual relations she's not the man's equal. She doesn't have the right to avail herself of the man or abstain from him, according to her desire, to select the man she wants rather than be the one who's selected. You may say that would be monstrous. Very well. Then the man shouldn't have these rights, either. The way things are at present, the woman is deprived of the rights possessed by the man. And, in order to compensate for this, she acts on the man's sensuality, forces him into subjection by means of sensuality, so that he's only formally the one who chooses – in actual fact it's she who does the choosing. And once she has mastered this technique, she abuses it and acquires a terrible power over men.'

'But where's the evidence of this special power?' I asked.

'Where? All around us, in everything. Just go into the shops of any large town. There's millions of rubles worth of stuff there; you could never put a value on the amount of labour that's gone into producing it. Yet look: in nine out of ten of those shops is there even one article that's intended to be used by men? All life's luxury articles are made in order to meet the demands of women, and be consumed by them. Just look at all those factories. By far the majority of them produce useless ornaments, carriages, furniture, playthings for women. Millions of human beings, generations of slaves perish in factories doing this convict labour merely in order to satisfy the caprice of women. Women are like empresses, keeping nine-tenths of the human race in servitude, doing hard labour. And all because they feel they've been humiliated, because they've been denied the same rights men have. And so they take their revenge by acting on our sensuality and ensnaring us in their nets. Yes, that's where the trouble lies. Women have turned themselves into such effective instruments for acting on our senses that we can't even speak to them with equanimity. No sooner does a man go near a woman than he falls under her spell and loses his head. Even in my previous life I always used to get an uneasy sensation whenever I set eyes on a woman dressed in a ballgown, but now that sight inspires me with genuine terror: I really do see in her something that's dangerous to men, something that's against all law, and I feel like calling for the police and appealing to them for protection against this danger, demanding that the hazardous object be confiscated and taken away.

'Yes, you may laugh!' he shouted at me. 'But it's no laughing matter. I'm convinced that the day will come, and perhaps before very long, when people will realize this and be amazed that there could have existed a society which tolerated actions so disturbing to public order as the ornamentation of the body, something that's so openly provocative of sensuality, yet is permitted to women in our society. It's just as if we were to set traps along all the thoroughfares men use in their daily business ... it's even worse that that! Why is it that gambling's against the law, while women displaying themselves in prostitutes' garb that excites sensuality aren't? They're a thousand times more dangerous!'

X

'Well, anyway, that's how I too was caught. I was what's called "in love". It wasn't just that I thought she was the acme of perfection – during the time I was engaged to her I thought I was the acme of perfection, too. After all, there's no good-for-nothing who, after looking round for a bit, can't find other good-for-nothings worse than himself in certain respects, and thus find a reason for pride and self-congratulation. That's the way it was with me: I wasn't marrying for money – material interests weren't involved as they were for the majority of my friends, who were getting married for the sake of either money or connections – I was rich, she was poor. The other thing I was proud of was that while my friends were all getting married with the intention of continuing to live in polygamy as they had done before, I had the firm intention of remaining monogamous after my wedding – and my pride in this knew no bounds. Yes, I was a dirty pig, and I thought I was an angel.

'My engagement was a brief one. I can't recall that time now without a sense of shame. What an abomination! We usually assume, don't we, that love is something spiritual, not sensual? Well, if love is spiritual, a spiritual relation, its spirituality ought to be expressed in words, in our conversations, our chats with each other. Of that there was none. Whenever we were left alone together we had a dickens of a job finding anything to say to one another. It involved a kind of Sisyphean labour. As soon as you thought of anything to say, you said it – then you had to be silent again, and try to think of something else to say.

There was nothing to talk about. Everything we could think of to say about the life that lay ahead of us, about our plans and our living arrangements, we had already said, and what was there left? If we'd been animals, we'd have known that talking was not what we were supposed to be doing. In this situation, however, we were supposed to talk – yet there was nothing to talk about, since what occupied our thoughts was not something that could be dealt with by means of conversation. Add to this the outrageous custom of offering each other sweetmeats, our brutish gorging on candies and desserts, and all those revolting wedding preparations: the talk about the apartment, the bedroom, the beds, the dressing-gowns, the night clothes, the linen, the toilettes. You'd agree, I think, that if people get married according to the *Domostroy*, in the manner that old man was describing, all those things like feather quilts, trousseaus and beds are just details that accompany the sacrament. But in our day, when out of ten men who get married there's hardly one who believes in the sacrament or even that what he's doing carries any particular obligation with it, when out of a hundred men there's hardly one who hasn't been married before, and out of fifty hardly one who hasn't married with the intention of being unfaithful to his wife at the first opportunity, when most men view the trip to church merely as a peculiar condition set down for their being able to possess a certain woman – think what a dreadful significance all those details acquire. In the end they turn out to be what the whole thing boils down to. It's a kind of sale: an innocent girl is sold to some debauched individual, and the sale is accompanied by certain formalities.'

XI

'I got married the way everyone gets married, and the much-vaunted honeymoon began. What vulgarity there is in the very name!' he spat contemptuously. 'When I was in Paris once, I went on a tour of all the city sights; lured by a billboard, I went in to have a look at a bearded lady and a so-called "aquatic dog". The first turned out to be nothing but a man in a woman's low-cut dress, and the second a dog that had been forced into a seal-skin, swimming around in a bath-tub. It was all of very little interest; but as I was on my way out, the man in charge of the show politely followed me to the door and, when we got outside, pointed to me, saying to the people who were standing there: "Ask this gentleman if it's worth seeing! Roll up, roll up, one franc a time!" It would have pricked my conscience to say that the show wasn't worth a visit, and the man was no doubt banking on that. That's probably how it is for people who've experienced the entire beastliness of a honeymoon and who refrain from disillusioning others. I didn't disillusion anyone, either, but now I can see no reason why I shouldn't tell the truth. I even think it's necessary for the truth about this matter to be told. A honeymoon is an embarrassing, shameful, loathsome, pathetic business, and most of all it is tedious, unbearably tedious! It's something similar to what I experienced when I was learning how to smoke: I felt like vomiting, my saliva flowed, but I swallowed it and pretended I was enjoying myself. It's like the pleasure one gets from smoking: if there's to be any, it comes later on. A husband and wife have to educate themselves in this vice if they're to get any pleasure out of it.'

'Why vice?' I asked. 'I mean to say, you're talking about one of the most natural human activities there is!'

'Natural?' he said. 'Natural? No, I tell you, quite the contrary's true, I've come to the conclusion that it isn't . . . natural. No, not . . . natural, at all. Ask children about it, ask any uncorrupted young girl. When my sister was still very young she married a man twice her age, a thoroughly debauched character. I remember how startled we were when, on the night of her wedding, pale and in tears, she came running out of the bedroom and, trembling all over, declared that not for anything, not for anything in the world would she do what he wanted her to do – she couldn't even bring herself to say what it was.

'You claim it's natural. Eating is natural. Eating is something joyful, easy and pleasant which by its very essence involves no shame. But this is something loathsome, ignominious, painful.

No, it's unnatural! And an uncorrupted young girl – of this I'm convinced – never fails to hate it.'

'But,' I said, 'how else can the human race continue?'

'Oh yes! As long as the human race doesn't perish!' he said with malevolent irony, as if he had been expecting this response as a familiar one, made in bad faith. 'To preach that one must abstain from procreation so that the English lords may continue to gorge themselves at their ease ... that's all right. To preach that one must abstain from procreation in order to make the world a more agreeable place to live in ... that's all right, too. But just try to insinuate that one ought to abstain from procreation in the name of morality ... God in heaven, what an uproar will ensue! Is the human race going to disappear from the face of the earth just because a couple of dozen men don't want to go on living like pigs? But I'm sorry, excuse me. The light's getting in my eyes – do you mind if we pull the shade over it?' he said, pointing to the lamp.

I said I had no objection, and then with the haste that marked all his actions he got up on his seat and pulled the woollen shade over the lamp.

'All the same,' I said, 'if everyone thought like that, the human race would disappear.'

He did not reply at once.

'You ask how the human race would continue?' he said, settling himself down again opposite me; he had spread his legs wide apart and was leaning his elbows on his knees. 'Why should it continue, the human race?' he said.

'Why? We wouldn't exist, otherwise.'

'And why should we exist?'

'Why? So we can live.'

'But why should we live? If life has no purpose, if it's been given us for its own sake, we have no reason for living. If that really is the case, then the Schopenhauers and the Hartmanns,[6] as well as all the Buddhists, are perfectly right. And even if there is a purpose in life, it seems obvious that when that purpose is fulfilled life must come to an end. That's the conclusion one reaches,' he said, visibly moved, and obviously treasuring this idea. 'That's the conclusion one reaches. Observe that if the purpose of life is happiness, goodness, love or what-ever, and if the goal of mankind is what it is stated to be by the prophets, that all men are to be united by love, that swords are to be beaten into ploughshares and all the rest of it, what prevents it from being attained? The passions do. Of all the passions, it is sexual, carnal love that is the strongest, the most malignant and the most unyielding. It follows that if the passions are eliminated, and together with them this ultimate, strongest passion, carnal love, the goal of mankind will be attained and there will be no reason for it to live any longer. On the other hand, for as long as mankind endures, it will follow some ideal – not, needless to say, the ideal of pigs and rabbits, which is to reproduce themselves as abundantly as possible, nor that of monkeys and Parisians, which is to enjoy sexual pleasure with the greatest degree of refinement possible, but the ideal of goodness, goodness that is attained by means of abstinence and purity. Men have always striven for this ideal, and they continue to do so. But just look at the result.

'The result is that carnal love has become a safety valve. If the present generation of men hasn't yet attained its goal, that's merely because it has passions, the strongest of which is the sexual one. And since that passion exists, a new generation also exists, and thus a possibility of the goal being attained in the next generation. If this generation doesn't manage to do it, there will always be another one to follow it, and so it will continue until the goal has been attained and men have been united with one another. What would things be like if this were not the case? Imagine if God had created human beings in order to achieve a certain goal and had created them either mortal, but without the sex instinct, or immortal. If they'd been made mortal, but without the sex instinct, what would the result have been? They would have lived for a while, and failed to attain their goal; in order to achieve his aim, God would have had to create a new human race. If, on the other hand, they'd been created immortal, let us suppose (though it would be more difficult for beings of this sort to correct the error of their ways and approach perfection than it would for new generations to do so) that after many thousands of years they attained their goal ... what good would they be then? What could be done with them? Things are still best the way they are at present ... But perhaps you don't care for that sort of an argument, perhaps you're an evolutionist? The outcome's still the same. In order to defend its interests in its struggle with the other animals, the highest form of animal life – the human race – has to gather itself into a unity, like a swarm of bees, and not reproduce infinitely: like the bees, it must raise sexless individuals, that's to say it must strive for continence, not the excitement of lust, towards which the entire social organization of our lives is directed.' He fell silent for a moment. 'The human race disappear? Is there anyone, no matter how he views the world, who can doubt this? I mean, it's just as little in dispute as death is. All the churches teach the end of the world, and all the sciences do the same. So what's so strange about morality pointing to the same conclusion?'

He said nothing for a long time after this. He drank some more tea, put his cigarette out, and transferred some fresh ones from his bag to his old, stained cigarette case.

'I follow your meaning,' I said. 'It's a bit like what the Shakers[7] preach.'

'Yes, and they're right,' he said. 'The sex instinct, no matter how it's dressed up, is an evil, a horrible evil that must be fought, not encouraged as it is among us. The words of the New Testament, that whosoever looks on a woman to lust after her has already committed adultery with her in his heart, don't just apply to the wives of other men, but expressly and above all to our own.'

XII

'In our world it's exactly the other way round: even if a man's thoughts run on sexual abstinence while he's still single, as soon as he gets married he ceases to think it of any importance. Those trips away after the wedding, that seclusion into which the young couple retires with the sanction of their parents – all that's nothing more nor less than a licence for debauchery. But the moral law has a way of paying us back if we ignore it. No matter how hard I tried to make our honeymoon a success, nothing came of it. The whole episode was repellent, embarrassing and tedious. And it was not long before it became unbearably irksome. It started to get that way very early on. On the third day, or maybe it was the fourth, I noticed that my wife seemed to be in a listless frame of mind; I asked her what the matter was and tried to put my arms around her, thinking that was what she wanted. But she pushed me away and burst into tears. Why? She was unable to tell me. She felt depressed and ill at ease. Probably her worn-out nerves had given her an insight into the truth about the vileness of our relationship: but she couldn't express it. I continued to question her and she told me she was missing her mother. Somehow I suspected this wasn't really true. I began to reason with her, but without pursuing the subject of her mother. I didn't realize she was just depressed, and that this talk about her mother was simply an excuse. But she immediately flew into a temper because I'd passed her mother over in silence, as if I hadn't believed what she'd been telling me. She said she could see I didn't love her. I scolded her for being capricious, and suddenly her face completely altered: now, instead of depression, it expressed irritation, and she began to accuse me in the most biting terms of cruelty and egotism. I looked at her. Her entire countenance expressed the most consummate hostility and coldness – hatred, almost. I remember how horrified I was when I saw this. "How can this be?" I thought. "Love is supposed to be the union of souls, and now this! It isn't possible, this isn't the woman I married!" I tried to calm her down, but I ran up against an intransigent wall of such cold and embittered hostility that before I'd had time to gather my wits I was seized with irritation, and we began to say a whole lot of nasty things to each other. That first quarrel had a terrible effect on me. I call it a quarrel, but it wasn't really a quarrel; it was just the revelation of the abyss that actually separated us. Our amorous feelings for each other had been drained by the gratification of our senses, and we were now left facing each other in our true relation, as two egotists who had nothing whatever in common except our desire to use each other in order to obtain the maximum amount of pleasure. I said it was a quarrel, what took place between us. It wasn't a quarrel, it was just the bringing out into the open of our true relationship, which followed upon the appeasement of our sensual desire. I didn't realize that this cold and hostile attitude was actually the one that was normal to us, and that was because at the beginning of our life together it was very soon obscured from us by a new sublimation of our sensuality, a new infatuation with each other.

'I thought what had happened was that we had quarrelled and then made it up, and that nothing of this kind would happen again. During this same first month of our honeymoon, however, we soon reached a second stage of satiety: once again we stopped being necessary to each other, and we had another quarrel. This second quarrel had an even worse effect on me than the first one had had. "So the first one wasn't an accident," I thought. "It was bound to happen, and it'll happen again." Our second quarrel struck me all the more forcibly because it arose from the most improbable of pretexts. It had something to do with money. I've never been stingy with money, and I certainly would never have been grudging with it where my wife was concerned. All I remember is that she managed to interpret something I had said to imply that I was attempting to use my money in order to dominate her, that I'd made my money into the basis of an exclusive right over her – some absurd, stupid, evil nonsense that was unworthy of either of us. I lost my temper, and began to shout at her for her lack of tact, she accused me of the same thing, and thus it started all over again. Both in what she was saying and in the expression of her face and eyes I once again saw that cold, cruel hostility that had so shaken me previously. I remembered quarrels I had had with my brother, my friends, my father. But never had there been between us the personal, envenomed hatred that made its appearance here. After some time had passed, however, this mutual hatred was once again obscured by our "love" – our sensuality, in other words – and once again I consoled myself with the thought that these two quarrels had been mistakes that could be made up for. But then there came a third, and a fourth, and I realized that they were no accidents, that this was how it was bound to be, that this was how it was going to be in future, and I was appalled at the prospect. I was tortured, moreover, by the dreadful thought that I was alone in having such a wretched relationship with my wife, and that everything was quite different in other people's marriages. At that stage I was still unaware that this is the common experience, that everyone believes, as I did, that theirs is an exceptional misfortune, and that everyone hides their shameful and exceptional misfortune not only from the eyes of others but also from themselves, and that they refuse to admit its existence.

'It set in right at the start of our married life together, and it continued without a break, increasing in intensity and bitterness. Even in the very first weeks I knew in the bottom of my heart that I'd been *trapped*, that this wasn't what I'd been expecting, that not only was marriage not happiness, it was something exceedingly painful and distressing. But, like everyone else, I refused to admit this to myself (I'd still not have admitted it to myself even now if the whole thing hadn't come to an end) and I hid it not only from others, but also from myself. It amazes me now that I didn't realize the situation I was in. I ought to have understood it then, for our quarrels used to start from the kind of pretexts that made it impossible, later on, when it was all over, to remember what they'd been about. Our intelligences had no time in which to lay a foundation of satisfactory pretexts beneath the increasing hostility we felt for one another. But even more remarkable were the flimsy reasons we would find for patching up our differences. Sometimes there were talks, explanations, even tears, but sometimes . . . ugh, how vile it is to remember it even now – sometimes, after we had both said the cruellest things to one another, suddenly, without a word, there would be looks, smiles, embraces . . . Ugh! What loathsomeness! How could I have failed to see the vile mediocrity of it all even then . . . ?'

XIII

Two passengers got on and found seats for themselves further up the carriage. He remained silent until they had seated themselves, but as soon as they were settled he continued, evidently never losing the thread of his thought for a second.

'The vilest thing of all about it,' he began, 'is that in theory love's supposed to be something ideal and noble, whereas in practice it's just a sordid matter that degrades us to the level of pigs, something it's vile and embarrassing to remember and talk about. After all, nature didn't make it vile and embarrassing for no reason. If it's vile and embarrassing, it ought to be seen as such. And yet it's quite the contrary: people behave as though what was vile and embarrassing were something beautiful and noble. What were the first signs of my love? They were that I abandoned myself to animal excesses, not only quite unashamedly, but even taking pride in the fact that it was possible for me to indulge in them, without ever once taking thought for her spiritual or even her physical well-being. I wondered in astonishment where this relentless animosity we felt towards each other could possibly be coming from, yet the reason for it was staring me in the face: this animosity was nothing other than the protest of our human nature against the animality that was suffocating it.

'I was astounded at the hatred we felt for one another. Yet it couldn't have been otherwise. This hatred was nothing but the mutual aversion experienced by accomplices to a crime – both for inciting to it and for perpetrating it. What other word can there be for it but crime, when she, poor creature, became pregnant in the very first month, and yet our piglike relationship continued? Perhaps you think I'm losing the thread of my thought? Not a bit of it! I'm still telling you the story of how I murdered my wife. They asked me in court how I killed her, what I used to do it with. Imbeciles! They thought I killed her that day, the fifth of October, with a knife. It wasn't that day I killed her, it was much earlier. Exactly in the same way as they're killing their wives now, all of them . . .'

'But how did you kill her?' I asked.

'Look, this is what's really astounding: no one is willing to admit what's so clear and self-evident, the thing doctors know and ought to tell people about, instead of keeping quiet on the subject. It's so simple. Men and women are made like animals, so that carnal love is followed by pregnancy, and then by the nursing of young, both states in which carnal love is harmful for the woman and her child. There's an equal number of men and women. What follows from that? The answer would seem to be quite clear. It surely doesn't require a great deal of intelligence to come to the conclusion the animals arrive at – abstinence, in other words. But oh, no. Science has managed to discover things called leucocytes that float about in our bloodstream, and has come up with all sorts of other stupid bits of useless information, yet it's unable to grasp this. At any rate, one's never heard it say anything on the subject.

'And so for the woman there are really only two ways out: one is to turn herself into a freak of nature, to destroy or attempt to destroy in herself her faculty of being a woman – a mother, in other words – so that the man can continue to take his pleasure without interruption; the other isn't really a way out at all, just a simple, gross and direct violation of the laws of nature, one that's practised in all so-called "decent" families. In other words, the woman has to go against her nature and be expectant mother, wet-nurse and mistress all at the same time; she has to be what no animal would ever lower itself to be. And she doesn't have the strength for it, either. That's where all the hysteria and "nerves" come from, and it's also the origin of the klikushi, the "possessed women" that are found among the common people. You don't need great powers of observation to see that these klikushi are never pure young girls, but always grown women, women who have husbands. It's the same in our class of society. It's equally the case in Europe. All those nerve clinics are full of women who've broken the laws of nature. But after all, the klikushi, like the patients of Charcot, are out-and-out cripples; the world's full of women who are only semi-crippled. To think of the great work that's accomplished in a woman when she bears forth the fruit of her womb, or when she gives suck to the child she's brought into the world. What's in the process of growing there is what will give us perpetuity, what will replace us. And this sacred work is violated – by what? It's too dreadful even to contemplate! And we carry on with our talk of freedom and women's rights. It's just as if a tribe of cannibals were to fatten up its captives before eating them, all the while assuring them of its concern for their rights and freedom.'

This was all rather original, and it made an impression on me.

'Yes, but what then?' I said. 'If that's really how it is, a man would only be able to make love to his wife once every two years, but men . . .'

'Men can't survive without it,' he chipped in. 'Once again our dear priests of science have managed to convince everyone that this is true. I'd like to see those witch-doctors compelled to perform the duties they say women must carry out as being so necessary to men, what would they have to say for themselves then, I wonder? Tell a man he needs vodka, tobacco and opium, and all those things will become necessities for him. The way they see it is that God had no idea of what human beings needed, and that he made a mess of things because he didn't consult them, the witch-doctors. You only have to take a look round to see there's something wrong. The witch-doctors have decided that men must satisfy their lust – it's a need, a necessity, and yet here are things like child-bearing and breast-feeding getting in the way. What's to be done about it? Send for the witch-doctors, they'll sort it out. And so they have. Oh, when will those witch-doctors and all their tricks be shown up for what they really are? It's high time. Now it's even got to the point where people go insane and shoot themselves, and all because of this. How can it be otherwise? The animals seem to know that their offspring assure the continuation of their species, and they stick to certain laws in this regard. It's only man who doesn't know these laws, and doesn't want to know them. He's only concerned with obtaining the greatest possible amount of pleasure. And who is this? The king of nature – man. You'll notice that the animals copulate with one another only when it's possible for them to produce offspring; but the filthy king of nature will do it any time, just so long as it gives him pleasure. More than that: he elevates this monkey pastime into the pearl of creation, into love. And what is it that he devastates in the name of this love, this filthy abomination, rather? Half of the human race, that's all. For the sake of his pleasure he makes women, who ought to be his helpmates in the progress of humanity towards truth and goodness, into his enemies. Just look around you: who is it that's constantly putting a brake on humanity's forward development? Women. And why is this so? Solely because of what I've been talking about. Yes, yes,' he repeated several times, and began to rummage about in search of his cigarettes. At last he found them and lit one, in an obvious attempt to calm himself down.

XIV

'So that's the sort of pig's existence I led,' he resumed, in the same tone of voice. 'And the worst of it was that, living in this filthy way, I imagined that because I didn't allow myself to be tempted by other women, I was leading a decent, married life, that I was a man of upright morality with not a stain of guilt on my conscience, and that if we had quarrels, it was her fault, the fault of her character.

'Needless to say, it wasn't her fault. She was just like all women, or the majority of them, anyway. She'd been brought up in the way the situation of women in our society demands, the way in which all upper-class women without exception are and have to be brought up. You hear a lot of talk these days about a new type of education for women. That's all hot air: women's education is exactly the way it ought to be, given the prevailing attitude towards women in our society – the real attitude, that is, not the pretended one.

'The type of education women receive will always correspond to the way men see them. After all, we know what men think of women, don't we? *Wein, Weiber und Gesang* – even the poets write things like that in their verses. Examine the whole of poetry, painting and sculpture, starting with love-poetry and all those naked Venuses and Phrynes, and you'll see that in them woman's an instrument of pleasure, just as she is on Trubnaya Street, on the Grachevka,[8] or at the court balls. And observe the devil's cunning: if pleasure and enjoyment are what's being offered, we might as well know that there's enjoyment to be had, that woman's a sweet morsel. But that's not the way of it: from the very earliest times the knights of chivalry professed to deify woman (they deified her, but they still viewed her as an instrument of pleasure). Nowadays men claim to have respect for woman. Some will give up their seats to her, pick up her handkerchief, recognize her right to occupy any post whatsoever, participate in government and so forth. They say this, but their view of her remains the same. She's an instrument of pleasure. Her body's a means of giving pleasure. And she knows it. It's like slavery. Slavery's just the exploitation by the few of the forced labour of the many. And so, if there's to be no more slavery, men must stop exploiting the forced labour of others, they must come to view it as a sin or at least as something to be ashamed of. But instead of this, all they do is abolish the outer forms of slavery – they arrange things so that it's no longer possible to buy and sell slaves, and then imagine, and are indeed convinced, that slavery doesn't exist any more; they don't see, they don't want to see, that it continues to exist because men go on taking satisfaction in exploiting the labour of others and persist in believing that it's perfectly legitimate for them to do so. And for as long as they believe this, there will always be those who are able to do it with more strength and cunning than others. It's the same where the emancipation of woman is concerned. The reason for the condition of slavery in which woman is kept hasn't really got much to do with anything except men's desire to exploit her as an instrument of pleasure, and their belief that this is a very good thing. Well, and so they go emancipating woman, giving her all sorts of rights, just the same as men have, but they still continue to regard her as an instrument of pleasure; that's how she's brought up as a child and how later on she's moulded by public consensus. And there she is, still the same humiliated and debauched slave, while men continue to be the same debauched slave-masters.

'They've emancipated woman in the universities and the legislative assemblies, but they still regard her as an object of pleasure. Teach her, as is done in our society, to consider herself in the same light, and she will for ever remain an inferior being. Either, with the help of those sharks of doctors, she'll prevent herself conceiving offspring, and so will be a complete whore, will descend to the level, not of an animal, but of a material object; or else she'll be what she is in the majority of cases: mentally ill, hysterical and unhappy, as are all those who are denied the opportunity of spiritual development.

'Schools and universities can do nothing to change this. It can only be changed by a radical shift in the opinion that man has of woman, and that woman has of herself. That shift will only occur when woman comes to consider virginity the most exalted condition a human being can aspire to, and doesn't, as she does at present, regard it as a shame and a disgrace. As long as this is lacking, the ideal of every girl, no matter how well educated, will be to attract as many men, as many males, as she can, so she can make her choice from among them.

'The fact that this one is rather good at mathematics, and that one can play the harp – that alters nothing. A woman's happy and gets everything she wants when she succeeds in bewitching a man. That's her main task in life. That's the way it's always been, and that's the way it'll go on being. A young girl in our society lives that way, and she continues to live that way after she gets married. She needs to live like this when she's a young girl so she can make her choice, and she needs to do it when she's a married woman so she can dominate her husband.

'The only thing that can put a stop to it or at least suppress it for a time is children, and then only if the woman isn't a monster, that's to say, if she breast-feeds them herself. But here again the doctors interfere.

'My wife, who wanted to breast-feed and did breast-feed our five subsequent children, had a few problems with her health after the birth of our first child. Those doctors who cynically made her undress and probed every part of her body, actions for which I had to thank them and pay them money, those pleasant doctors decided that she shouldn't do any breast-feeding, and thus throughout that early phase of our life together she was deprived of the only thing that might have prevented her from indulging in coquetry. Our child was fed by a wet-nurse – in other words, we exploited the wretchedness, poverty and ignorance of a peasant woman, and enticed her away from her own child in order to look after ours, to which purpose we dolled her up in a fancy bonnet trimmed with silver lace. But that wasn't the problem. The problem was that no sooner had she escaped from pregnancy and breast-feeding than the female coquetry that had lain dormant within her made a quite flagrant reappearance. And, every bit as flagrantly, the torments of jealousy reawoke in me: they continued to plague me throughout the whole of my married life, as they can't fail to plague men who live with their wives the way I lived with mine – immorally, in other words.'

XV

'Never once, throughout all my married life, did I cease to experience the tortures of jealousy. And there were periods when I suffered particularly badly in this way. One of those periods occurred when, after the trouble with her first child, the doctors told her not to do any breast-feeding. At this time I was particularly jealous, in the first instance, because my wife was undergoing that restlessness that is characteristic of a mother and is inevitably brought on by such an arbitrary interruption of her life's natural rhythm; and, in the second instance, because when I saw with what ease she threw aside the moral obligations of a mother, I correctly, though uncon-sciously, drew the conclusion that she would find it just as easy to throw aside her obligations as a wife, especially since she was in perfect health and, in spite of what the dear doctors told

her, subsequently breast-fed all our other children herself, and
did it excellently.'

'I can see you don't like doctors,' I said. I had observed that
at the very mention of them his voice acquired a peculiarly
malevolent intonation.

'It isn't a question of liking them or not liking them. They've
ruined my life, just as they've ruined and continue to ruin the
lives of thousands, hundreds of thousands of people, and I can't
help putting two and two together. I can see they're just trying
to earn money, like lawyers and the rest, and I'd gladly give
them half my income – anyone who understands what it is they
do would gladly give them half of what they own – provided
only that they shouldn't interfere with our marriages or ever
come anywhere near us. I mean, I haven't got any statistics,
but I know of dozens of cases – there's a vast number of them
– where they've murdered the child while it was still in its
mother's womb, claiming she was unable to give birth to it,
and where the mother has subsequently given birth to other
children without difficulty; or else it's the mothers they've murdered, on the pretext of carrying out some operation or other
on them. No one even bothers to count these murders, just as
no one ever counted the murders of the Inquisition, because they
were supposed to be for the good of mankind. It's impossible to
put figures on the number of crimes they've committed. But all
those crimes are as nothing compared to the moral rot of
materialism they've brought into the world, especially through
woman. And all that's quite apart from the fact that if they
were to follow the doctors' instructions regarding the infection
they say is rife everywhere and in everything, people would
have to seek not union but disunion; according to the doctors'
version of things, everyone ought to keep apart from one
another and never take the spray-syringe of phenol acid (which
they've found doesn't have any effect, anyway) out of their
mouths. But even that's not important. No, the real poison is the
general corruption of human beings, of women in particular.

'Nowadays it's simply not done to say: "You're living badly,
you ought to try to live better." It's not done to say that either

to yourself or to someone else. If you're living badly, it's because your nerves aren't functioning properly, or something of that sort. So you have to go to the doctors. They'll prescribe you thirty-five copecks' worth of medicine, and you'll take it. You'll just make yourself worse, and then you'll have to take more medicines and consult more doctors. As a trick, it fairly takes your breath away!

'But again, that's not important. What I was trying to say was that she breast-fed her children herself, perfectly well, and that it was only her pregnancies and breast-feeding that saved me from the tortures of jealousy. If it hadn't been for that, everything would have happened sooner than it did. Our children protected both of us. In the space of eight years she had five of them. And she breast-fed them all herself.'

'Where are they now, your children?' I asked.

'My children?' he echoed, in a frightened tone of voice.

'I'm sorry, perhaps you don't want to be reminded of them.'

'No, it's all right. The children were taken into custody by my sister-in-law and her brother. They wouldn't let me have them back. I'm supposed to be a kind of madman, you know. I'm on my way home from visiting them now. I saw them, but they won't let me have them back. They think I might bring them up so they're not like their parents. And they have to be the same. Well, what can I do? Naturally they won't let me have them back, and they don't trust me. I don't even know myself whether I'd have the strength to bring them up. I think probably I wouldn't. I'm a wreck, a cripple. I've only got one thing. It's what I know. Yes, I know something it'll take other people quite a while to find out about.

'At any rate, my children are alive, and they're growing up to be the same savages as everyone else around them. I've seen them, three times I've seen them now. There's nothing I can do for them. Nothing. I'm going down south now, home. I've got a little house and garden down south.

'No, people aren't going to find out what I know for quite a while to come. If it's a question of whether there's a lot of iron or other metals in the sun or the stars, they soon get to the bottom of it; but if it's something that exposes our pigsty behaviour – they find that hard, terribly hard!

'At least you're listening to me, and I'm grateful for that.'

XVI

'You mentioned children just now. Again, what awful lies we spread about children. Children are God's blessing on us, children are a delight. It's all lies, you know. All that may have been true once upon a time, but it isn't nowadays. Children are a torment, nothing more. Most mothers know this, and will sometimes be quite frank about it. Most mothers in our well-off section of society will tell you they're so scared their children are going to fall ill and die, they don't want to have any, and even if they do have children, they don't want to breast-feed them in case they grow too attached to them and suffer as a result. The pleasure their baby gives them with the grace and charm of its being, of its little arms and legs, of the whole of its young body, the enjoyment they receive from their baby is not as great as the suffering they endure – not even because it falls ill or dies, but because of their fear that it may do so. Once they've weighed the advantages against the disadvantages, it seems to them that having children is disadvantageous, and therefore undesirable. They say this boldly and frankly, imagining that these feelings stem from their love of children, from a good and praiseworthy sentiment they're proud of. They don't notice that by talking like this they do nothing but negate love and affirm their own selfishness. They find less enjoyment than suffering in the grace and charm of their baby because of the fear they have for its safety, and so they don't really want this child which they are going to love. They don't sacrifice themselves for a being they love, what they do is sacrifice to themselves a being that's intended to be loved.

'It's obvious that this isn't love but selfishness. But not one hand will be raised to condemn them, these mothers from well-off families, for their selfishness, when it's remembered what agonies of suffering they go through on account of the health of their children, thanks once again to those doctors and the role they play in the lives of our better-off citizens. Even now I have only to recall the manner of my wife's existence, the condition she was in, during that early phase of our life together when she had three, then four children and was entirely absorbed in them, in order to be seized with horror. That was no life we led. It was a kind of perpetual state of danger, escape from it, then fresh danger, again followed by desperate efforts at escape, and then – another escape; constantly the sort of situation there is on board a ship that's in the process of sinking. It sometimes used to seem to me that it was all an act she was putting on, that she was just pretending to be worried about the children in order to score points over me. This way of behaving settled every problem so simply and flatteringly in her favour. It sometimes seemed to me that everything she said and did on these occasions had some kind of ulterior motive. Yet she herself suffered terribly, and constantly punished herself with guilt about the state of her children's health, about their illnesses. It was an ordeal for her, and for me as well. And she couldn't have done anything else but suffer. After all, her attachment to her children, her animal instinct to feed, caress and protect them, were just as strong in her as they are in the majority of women; she did not, however, have what the animals have – an absence of reason and imagination. The hen isn't afraid of what may happen to her chick, knows nothing of all the diseases that may attack it, or of all those remedies human beings imagine will save them from sickness and death. And the hen's chicks are not a source of torment to her. She does for them what it's natural and agreeable for her to do: her children are a delight to her. And when one of her chicks starts to show signs of being ill, the range of her concerns is very limited: she feeds the chick and keeps it warm, secure in the knowledge that what she's doing is all that is necessary. If the chick dies, she doesn't ask herself why it has died, or where it's gone, she merely clucks for a while, then stops, and goes on living as before. But that's not how it is for our unfortunate women, and that's not how it was for my wife. Quite apart

from all the talk about illnesses and their treatment, about
the best methods of rearing children and educating them, she
was surrounded on all sides by a great mass of divergent and
constantly changing rules and regulations, both printed and
spoken. Children should be fed like this, with this; no, not like
that, not with that, but like this; how they should be dressed,
what they should be given to drink, how they should be bathed,
put to bed, taken out for walks, how to see they get enough
fresh air – every week we (or rather she) discovered new rules
affecting all this. As if it were only yesterday that children had
started being brought into the world. And if the feeding method
was wrong, if the bathing was done in the wrong way or at the
wrong time, and the child fell ill, then it was all her fault, as
she hadn't done what she was supposed to do.

'That was if the child was healthy. And even that was torture.
But just wait till it fell ill – then the fat was really in the fire. All
hell would be let loose. There's a common notion that illness
can be treated, and that there's a science devoted to this purpose, with people – doctors – who know all about it. Not all of
them do, but the very best ones do. Right, so your child's been
taken ill, and your task is to find one of those very best doctors,
one who's able to save lives, and then your child will be all
right; but if you can't find one of those doctors, or you don't
live in an area where there is one – your child's had it. And this
wasn't a faith in any way exclusive to her, it was the faith
adhered to by all the women in her set, and all she ever heard
from every side was: "Yekaterina Semyonovna's lost two of
hers, because they didn't call in Ivan Zakharych; Ivan Zakharych saved Marya Ivanovna's eldest girl, you know. And then
look at the Petrovs: they took the doctor's advice in time, he
told them to get the children out of the home and they were
split up and moved into various hotels and they survived – if
they hadn't been separated they'd have died. And then there
was that woman who had the delicate child; the doctor advised
her to move down south, they did, and the child was all right."
How could she have not been plagued by misery and anxiety
all her life when the lives of her children, to whom she was
devoted as an animal is devoted, were dependent on her being

able to find out in time what Ivan Zakharych had to say? And what Ivan Zakharych would say, nobody knew, least of all Ivan Zakharych himself, since he was very well aware that he didn't really know anything at all and was quite unable to offer any kind of help, but just kept improvising blindly so that people wouldn't stop believing he did know something. After all, if she'd really been an animal, she wouldn't have suffered like that; if she'd really been a human being, she'd have believed in God, and she'd have said and thought what the peasant women say: "The Lord gave, and the Lord hath taken away; we're all in the hands of God." She'd have considered that the lives and deaths of all God's creatures, her own children included, fell outside the jurisdiction of human beings and were dependent upon God alone, and then she wouldn't have been tormented by the thought that it was in her power to prevent the deaths and illnesses of her children – but this she didn't do. The way she saw the situation was like this: she'd been given some extremely weak and fragile creatures to look after, creatures that were susceptible to an infinite number of disasters. For these creatures she felt a passionate, animal devotion. What was more, although these creatures had been delivered into her care, the means by which they could be preserved from danger had been concealed from us, but revealed instead to complete strangers, whose services and advice could only be obtained for large sums of money, and even then not always.

'The whole of the existence my wife led with her children was for her, and consequently for me as well, not a joy but a torment. How could she not have suffered? She suffered continually. We might just have calmed down after some scene of jealousy or outright quarrel and be thinking that now we'd be able to get on with our lives for a while, do a bit of reading or thinking; yet no sooner had one settled down to some task or other than the news would arrive that Vasya was being sick, or there was blood in Masha's stool, or Andryusha had a rash, and then it would all be over, life would once more cease to be possible. Where would one have to go galloping off to now, which doctors would have to be sought out, where would the child have to be taken? And then the enemas would start, the temperatures, the mixtures and the doctors' visits. No sooner would this be at an end than something else would crop up. We had no stable, regular family life. All we had was, as I've told you, a constant running battle against dangers both real and imaginary. That's the way it is for the majority of families nowadays, you know. In my own family it took a particularly nasty form. My wife was the maternal type, and she was easily gulled.

'So it wasn't just that our having children made our lives no better – it actually poisoned them. More than that: the children constantly gave us new pretexts for quarrelling. The older they grew, the more frequently they themselves were the reason for our falling out with one another; not only that – they were the weapons in a battle. It was as if we were fighting one another through our children. We each had a favourite child – a favourite weapon. My weapon was usually our son Vasya, the eldest child, while hers was usually our daughter Liza. And that wasn't all: when the children started getting a bit older and their personalities started to mature, they turned into allies whom we each tried to win over to our own side. They suffered terribly because of that, the poor children, but we were far too preoccupied with our never-ending war to pay any attention to them. The girl was on my side, while the eldest, our son, who looked like his mother and was her favourite, was often really nasty to me.'

XVII

'Well, that's the way we lived. We grew more and more hostile to each other. And it finally got to the point where it was no longer our disagreements that were responsible for our hostility to one another – it was our hostility that created our disagreements. Whatever she might say to me, I would disagree with it before she had even opened her mouth, and exactly the same was true of her.

'By the fourth year of our marriage we both seemed to have

accepted, almost as if it had been decided for us, that we were never going to be able to understand each other or agree about anything. We'd already given up trying to settle our arguments. We each obstinately stuck to our own point of view about even the most simple things, but particularly about the children. Thinking back on it now, I can see that the opinions I used to defend were by no means so dear to me that I couldn't have got along without them; no, the point was that the opinions she held were the opposite of mine, and yielding to them meant yielding to . . . her. This I was not prepared to do. Neither was she. I think it's probable she always considered herself entirely in the right where I was concerned, and as for me, I saw myself as a saint in comparison with her. When we were left alone together we either had to remain silent or else carry on the sort of conversations I'm convinced animals have with one another. "What's the time? Bedtime. What's for dinner today? Where are we going to go? Is there anything in the newspaper? Send for the doctor. Masha's got a sore throat." We had only to stray out of this impossibly narrow focus of conversation by as much as a hair's breadth, and our mutual irritation would flare up again. Quarrels would erupt over things like the coffee, a table-cloth, a cab, or a lead at whist – none of them things that were of the slightest importance to either of us. I used to boil inwardly with the most dreadful hatred for her! Sometimes I'd watch the way she poured her tea, the way she swung her leg or brought her spoon to her mouth; I'd listen to the little slurping noises she made as she sucked the liquid in, and I used to hate her for that as for the most heinous act. I didn't notice it then, but I was regularly affected by bouts of animosity that used to correspond to the bouts of what we called "love". A bout of "love" would be followed by one of animosity; a vigorous bout of "love" would be followed by a long bout of animosity, while a less intense bout of "love" would be followed by a correspondingly shorter bout of animosity. We didn't realize it then, but this "love" and animosity were just two sides of the same coin, the same animal feeling. To live like that would have been insufferable if we'd understood the situation we were in, but we didn't understand it – we weren't even aware of it. It's the salvation as well as the punishment of human beings that when they're living irregular lives, they're able to wrap themselves in a blanket of fog so that they can't see the wretchedness of their situation. That's what we did. She tried to forget herself in a frantic round of concerns, always hastily attended to: the furniture, her clothes and those of her children, the children's health and their education. As for myself, I had my own anaesthetic, the anaesthetic of work, hunting and cards. We were both constantly busy. We both sensed that the busier we were, the more opportunity we would have for being nasty to one another. "It's all very well for you to make faces," I used to think, "but you've plagued me all night with your scenes and I've got a meeting today." "It's all very well for you," she used not only to think, but say out loud, "but I haven't been able to get a wink of sleep all night because of the baby."

'And so we continued to live, in a perpetual fog, without ever becoming aware of the situation we were in. If what finally happened hadn't happened, and I'd gone on living like that until my old age, I think that even when I was dying I'd have thought I'd had a good life, not an unusually good one, perhaps, but not a bad one either, the sort of life everyone has; I would never have come to perceive the abyss of unhappiness, the loathsome falsehood in which I was wallowing.

'We were like two prisoners in the stocks, hating each other, yet fettered to each other by the same chain, poisoning each other's lives and trying not to be aware of it. I didn't know then that ninety-nine per cent of all married couples live in the same hell I lived in, and that this can't be otherwise. I didn't know that then, either with regard to other people or with regard to myself.

'It's amazing what coincidences can take place in a life that's regularly led, or even in one that's not! Just at the point where the parents have made life intolerable for each other, an urban environment becomes necessary for the sake of the children's education. And thus the need for a move to town becomes apparent.'

For a while he said nothing, but made his peculiar noises a

couple of times. Now they really did sound like stifled sobs.
The train was approaching a station.

'What time is it?' he asked me.

I looked at my watch. It was two a.m.

'You're not tired?' he asked.

'No, but you are.'

'Oh, I'm just short of breath. Look, excuse me, I'm just going
out for a moment to get myself a drink of water.'

And he went stumbling off up the carriage. As I sat there on
my own I ran over in my mind all the things he had been telling
me, and so absorbed in my thoughts did I become that I failed
to notice him returning through the door at the opposite end.

XVIII

'Yes, I keep getting led off the point,' he said when he had sat
down again. 'I've changed a lot of the ideas I used to have,
there are a lot of things I see differently now, and I have this
need to talk about it all. Well, anyway, we went to live in town.
Life's more bearable for unhappy people there. In town a man
can live for a hundred years and never notice that he's long
been dead and buried. There's never any time to study your
conscience; you're busy all the time. There's business, social life,
looking after your health, keeping up with the arts, attending to
the health of your children, arranging their education. One
moment you may have to receive this person, go and visit that
person; the next, you may have to go and see this or that
exhibition, attend this or that concert. You know how it is: at
any given moment there are one, two or even three celebrities
in town whom you simply mustn't miss. One moment you're
taking some treatment or other, or arranging treatment for
somebody else; the next, it's teachers, tutors, governesses, and
yet life is as empty as it can possibly be. Well, that's how we
lived, and that way we didn't feel so acutely the pain caused by
the fact of our living together. More than that: in those early
days we were kept busy in the most marvellous fashion, setting

ourselves up in a new town, in a new apartment, with the added diversion of trips from the town to the country and back again.

'We spent one whole winter like that. During the second winter there took place an event no one noticed at the time, one which seemed quite trivial but which lay at the root of all that was to happen subsequently. She was ill, and those reptiles had forbidden her to have any more children and had taught her a method of contraception. I found this revolting. I struggled against it, but she held firm with a frivolous obstinacy, and I yielded to her. The last excuse for our pigsty existence – children – had been removed, and our life together became even more repulsive. Even though it may be hard for him to feed them, a muzhik or a working man's children are necessary to him, and for this reason his marriage relationship has a justification. But for our sort of people children aren't necessary – they're a superfluous worry, an extra expense, co-inheritors, a burden. And the pigsty existence we lead has no justification whatsoever. We either get rid of our children by artificial methods, or we view them as a misfortune, a consequence of imprudent behaviour, which is even more loathsome. There's no justification for it. But morally we've sunk so low that we don't even see the need for a justification. Nowadays the greater part of the educated classes indulges in this debauchery without the slightest shadow of remorse.

'There's no remorse left because in our section of society there's no moral conscience except the conscience – if you can call it that – represented by public consensus and criminal law. Yet neither of these are violated. There's no reason for anyone to feel guilty in the face of public opinion, since *everyone*, from Marya Pavlovna to Ivan Zakharych, does it. Why should one add to the number of paupers there already are, or deprive oneself of the possibility of leading a social life? No more is there any reason to feel guilty in the face of the criminal law or to be afraid of it. It's only whores and soldiers' wives who drown their children in ponds or throw them down wells; they, of course, should be locked up in prison, but we do it all in our own good time and without any mess.

'We lived like that for another two years. The method the reptiles had prescribed was obviously beginning to be effective; she had rounded out physically and had grown as pretty as the last ray of summer. She was aware of it, and she started to take an interest in her appearance. A kind of provocative beauty radiated from her, and people found it disturbing. She was thirty years old, in the full flower of her womanhood; she was no longer bearing children; she was well fed and emotionally unstable. Her appearance made people uneasy. Whenever she walked past men she attracted their gaze. She was like an impatient, well-fed horse that has had its bridle taken off, the same as ninety-nine per cent of our women. I could sense this, and it scared me.'

XIX

Suddenly he got up, moved over to the window and sat down there.

'Excuse me,' he said and, fixing his gaze on the window, sat there in silence for something like three minutes. Then he gave a deep sigh and came back to sit opposite me once more. His face had now altered completely; his eyes wore a beseeching expression, and something that might almost have been a smile creased his lips strangely. 'I'm getting a bit tired, but I'll tell you the rest of it. There's a lot of time yet; it's still dark out there. Yes,' he began once more, as he lit a cigarette. 'She'd rounded out a bit since she'd stopped having children, and that illness of hers – her constant suffering on account of the children – had begun to clear up; well, it didn't really clear up, but it was as though she'd come to after a bout of drunkenness, as though she'd recovered her senses and realized that God's world was still there with all its delights, the world she'd forgotten about and had no idea of how to live in, God's world, of which she knew absolutely nothing. "I mustn't let it slip! Time flies, and one doesn't get it back again!" I reckon that's the way she thought, or rather felt, and it was impossible she could have thought or felt any differently. She'd been brought up to believe that there was only one thing in the world worth bothering about – love. She'd got married, she'd managed to get a bit of that love she'd been told about, but it was far from being what she'd been promised, what she'd expected, and it had brought her a lot of disillusionment and suffering; what was more, it had involved this quite unforeseen torment – children! This torment had worn her out. And then, thanks to those obliging doctors, she'd discovered it was possible to avoid having children. She'd been overjoyed, had tried the method for herself and had started to live again for the one thing she knew anything about – love. But love with a husband who was bemired in jealousy and rancour wouldn't do. She began to imagine another love that was fresh and pure – that's the way I figure it, at any rate. And then she started looking around her as though she were expecting something to come her way. I could see this, and I couldn't help feeling uneasy. Quite often it would happen that as she carried on a conversation with me through the intermediary of others – that's to say, she'd be talking to other people while really addressing herself to me – she'd come out boldly and half seriously, completely oblivious to the fact that an hour ago she'd said the exact opposite, with the statement that a mother's cares are simply an illusion, a worthless one at that, and that it's not worth sacrificing oneself for the sake of one's children when one's young and able to enjoy life. She had started to devote less attention to the children, and no longer had such a desperate attitude towards them; she was spending more and more time on herself and on her appearance (though she tried to conceal the fact), on her amusements and also her accomplishments. She took up the piano again with enthusiasm – previously she had let it go completely. That was how it all started.'

Again he gave the window a weary look. Almost immediately, however, he made a visible effort to pull himself together, and continued: 'Yes, and then this man appeared.' He faltered and made his peculiar nasal sounds a couple of times.

I could see it was torture for him to mention this man, to remember him and talk about him. But he made the effort and, as if he had tugged clear some obstacle that was in his way, he continued in a resolute tone of voice: 'He was a rubbishy fellow, as far as I could see or judge, and not because he'd acquired this importance in my life, but because he really was what I say he was. Anyway, the fact that he was so mediocre only went to prove how irresponsible she was being. If it hadn't been him, it would have been someone else, it had to happen.' Once again he fell silent. 'Yes, he was a musician, a violinist; not a professional musician, but part professional, part man of the world.

'His father was a landowner, one of my own father's neighbours. He – the father – had suffered financial ruin, and his children – he had three boys – had all found settled positions; only this one, the youngest, had been delivered into the care of his godmother in Paris. There he'd been sent to the Conservatoire, as he was musically gifted, and he'd emerged from it as a violinist who played at concerts. As a man, he was . . .' Obviously experiencing an impulse to say something bad about him, he restrained himself and said quickly: 'Well, I don't really know what sort of a life he led, all I know is that during that year he turned up in Russia, and turned up, what's more, in my own home.

'He had moist eyes, like almonds, smiling red lips, and a little moustache that was smeared with fixative; his hair was styled in the latest fashion; his face was handsome in a vulgar sort of way, and he was what women call "not bad-looking". He was slight of physique, but not in any way malformed, and he had a particularly well-developed posterior, as women have, or as Hottentots are said to have. I believe they're also said to be musical. He tried to force a kind of brash familiarity on to everyone as far as he could manage, but he was sensitive and always ready to drop this mode of address at the slightest resistance, and he never lost his outward dignity. He dressed with that special Parisian nuance: buttoned boots, brightly coloured cravats and the like – all the sort of garb foreigners adopt when they're in Paris, the sort of thing that makes an impression on women because of its distinctiveness and novelty. His manner had a superficial, affected gaiety. You know that way of talking all the time in allusions and desultory snatches, as if to say, "You know all that, you remember, you can fill in the rest for yourselves."

'He and his music were the real cause of it all. At my trial the whole thing was made to look as though it had been caused by jealousy. Nothing could have been further from the truth. I'm not saying jealousy didn't play any part at all, mind – it did, but it wasn't the most important thing. At my trial they decided I was a wronged husband who'd killed his wife in order to defend his outraged honour (that's the way they put it in their language). So I was acquitted. During the court hearings I tried to explain what was really at the bottom of it all, but they just thought I was trying to rehabilitate my wife's honour.

'Whatever her relationship with that musician was, it wasn't important to me, any more than it was to her. What was important was what I've been telling you about – my pigsty existence. It all happened because of that terrible abyss there was between us, the one I've been talking about, the terrible stress of our mutual hatred for each other that made the first pretext that came along sufficient to cause a crisis. In the last days our quarrels became terrifying; they were particularly shattering because they alternated with bouts of animal sensuality.

'If it hadn't been him, it would have been some other man. If jealousy hadn't been the pretext, some other one would have been found. I insist on the fact that all husbands who live as I lived must either live in debauchery, get divorced, or kill themselves or their wives, as I did. If there's any man alive to whom this doesn't apply, he's an extremely rare exception. You know, before I brought it all to an end in the way I did, I was several times on the verge of suicide, and she'd also tried to poison herself on several occasions.'

XX

'Yes, that's the way it was, even quite a short time before it happened.

'It was as though we were living in a kind of truce and

couldn't find any reason for breaking it. One day as we were talking, the subject of a dog came up. I said it had won a medal at a dog show. She said it hadn't been a medal, just a special mention. An argument began. We started to jump from one subject to another, and the accusations began to fly: "Yes, yes, I've known that for ages, it's always the same: you said . . ." "No, I didn't." "I suppose you think I'm lying!" I suddenly got a feeling that at any moment now that terrible quarrel was going to start, the one that would make me either want to kill myself or kill her. I knew it was about to begin, and I was afraid of it in the way one's afraid of a fire starting. I tried to keep myself under control, but the hatred had gained complete mastery over me. She was in the same sort of state, only worse, and she was purposely misinterpreting my every word, twisting its meaning. Everything she said was steeped in venom; she was trying to hurt me where she knew I was most sensitive. The longer it went on, the worse it got. I shouted: "Shut up!" or something like that. She went skittering out of the room and into the nursery. I tried to detain her in order to finish what I was saying and prove my point, and I seized her by the arm. She pretended I was hurting her, and she screamed: "Children, your father's beating me!" "Don't tell lies!" I shouted. "This isn't the first time he's done it!" she screamed, or something of the kind. The children went running to her, and she calmed them down. "Stop play-acting!" I said. "Everything's play-acting to you," she replied. "You'd kill someone and then say they were play-acting. Now I can see what you're really like. You actually want things to be like this!" "Oh, I wish you were dead!" I shouted. I remember the horror those terrible words filled me with. I had never thought I'd be capable of uttering such terrible, primitive words and I was amazed at the way they leapt out of me. I shouted those terrible words and then fled to my study, where I lay down and smoked one cigarette after another. Eventually I heard her going out into the hall and getting ready to go off somewhere. I asked her where she was going. She didn't answer. "Well, she can go to hell for all I care," I said to myself. I went back to my study, lay down again and continued to smoke. A thousand different plans of how

I might take my revenge on her and get rid of her, making it look as though nothing had happened, came into my head. I thought about all this, and as I did so I smoked, smoked, smoked. I thought of running away from her, of hiding, of going to America. I got to the point where I dreamed that I had in fact got rid of her and of how marvellous it was going to be now: I'd meet another, beautiful woman, entirely different from my wife. I'd get rid of my wife because she'd die, or I'd get a divorce, and I thought of how I'd do it. I was aware I was getting muddled, that I wasn't thinking about the right things – but I went on smoking to stop myself being aware of it.

'But the life of the household went on as before. The governess arrived, and asked "Where's madame? When's she coming back?" The butler appeared, to ask if he should serve the tea. I went into the dining-room; the children, especially Liza, the eldest girl, who already knew what was going on, looked at me questioningly and disapprovingly. We sipped our tea in silence. She still hadn't returned. The whole evening passed, she still didn't come back, and two emotions kept alternating inside me: animosity towards her making my life and the lives of all the children a misery by her absence when I knew she intended to come back again; and fear that she might not come back, that she might do away with herself. I wanted to go and look for her. But where would I look? At her sister's? It would have been stupid to go there asking for her. Oh, let her go: if she wanted to make our lives a misery, let her make her own life miserable too. That was probably what she wanted, anyway. And next time it would be even worse. But what if she wasn't at her sister's, what if she was trying to do away with herself, or had even done so already? Eleven o'clock, twelve, one a.m. I didn't go into our bedroom, it would have been stupid to lie there alone, waiting, and I didn't want to sleep in my study. I wanted to be busy with something, write letters, read; I couldn't do anything. I sat alone in my study, suffering, angry, listening. Three a.m., four a.m. – still no sign of her. Towards morning I fell asleep. When I woke up, she still wasn't back.

'Everything in the house continued as before, but everyone was perplexed and looked at me questioningly and reproachfully, assuming it was all my fault. And still the same struggle was going on inside me: animosity because she was making my life a misery, and worry lest anything should have happened to her.

'At about eleven o'clock that morning her sister arrived, acting as her emissary. And the usual things were said: "She's in a terrible state. What on earth have you been doing?" "Oh, it was nothing." I said something about how impossible she was, and that I hadn't done anything.

'"Well, it can't go on like this, you know," said her sister.

'"It's all up to her, not to me," I said. "I'm not going to take the first step. If she wants a divorce, we'll get a divorce."

'My sister-in-law went away empty-handed. I'd spoken boldly, on the spur of the moment, when I'd told her I wouldn't take the first step, but as soon as she'd left and I'd gone out of the room and seen the children looking so scared and wretched, I suddenly felt ready to take that first step. I would even have been glad to take it, but I didn't know how to. Once again I started to wander about the house; I smoked cigarettes, drank vodka and wine with my lunch and attained the goal I unconsciously desired: not to see the stupidity, the vulgarity of the situation I was in.

'She arrived at about three o'clock that afternoon. She didn't say anything when we met. I thought perhaps she'd calmed down a bit, and I started to tell her that I'd been provoked by her accusations. With the same severe look of terrible suffering on her face she told me she hadn't come for explanations but in order to fetch the children; it was impossible for us to go on living together. I started to say it wasn't I who was the guilty one, that she'd driven me beyond the limits of my endurance. She gave me a solemn, severe look, and then said: "Don't say any more, you'll regret it."

'I said I couldn't bear melodramatics. Then she shrieked something I couldn't make out, and rushed to her room. I heard the sound of the key turning in her door: she'd locked herself in. I knocked, but there was no answer, and I went away in a fuming rage. Half an hour later, Liza came running to me in tears.

'"What is it? Has something happened?"

'"It's gone all quiet in Mummy's room!"

'We went to investigate. I pulled at the double door with all my might. She hadn't fastened the bolt properly, and both halves of the door opened. I went over to her bed. She was lying awkwardly atop her bed with her petticoat and her high boots still on, and she was unconscious. On the bedside table there was an empty phial of opium. We brought her round. There were more tears and, at last, a reconciliation. Yet it was not really a reconciliation: within each of us the same animosity continued to burn, mingled now with irritation at the pain this fresh quarrel had caused, pain for which each of us blamed the other. In the end, however, we had to bring it to some sort of conclusion, and life took its accustomed course. Quarrels of this kind, and occasionally even worse ones, were constantly breaking out, sometimes once a week, sometimes once a month, sometimes every day. On one occasion I even went to the lengths of getting myself a passport for foreign travel – the quarrel had been going on for two days – but then once more we had a semi-explanation, a semi-reconciliation – and I stayed put.'

XXI

'So that's the way things were between us when this man appeared. This man – Trukhachevsky's his name – arrived in Moscow and came to see me. It was in the morning. I asked him in. There'd once been a time when we'd been on familiar "thou" terms with one another. Now he tried, by means of phrases inserted between his use of "thou" and "you", to commit us to the "thou" form, but I put the emphasis fairly and squarely on "you", and he immediately complied. I didn't like the look of him from the very outset. But it was a strange thing: some peculiar, fatal energy led me not to repulse him, get rid of him, but, on the contrary, to bring him closer. After all, what could have been simpler than to speak to him coldly for a couple of minutes and then bid him farewell without introducing him to my wife? But no, of all things, and as if on purpose, I started to talk about his playing, saying that I'd heard he'd given up the violin. He said that, on the contrary, he was playing more than ever before nowadays. He recalled that I had been musical too, in the old days. I said that I'd let my playing go, but that my wife played the piano rather well.

'It was quite remarkable! From the very first day, the very first hour of our meeting, my attitude towards him was such as it ought really to have been only after what eventually took place. There was something fraught in my relations with him: I found a special significance in each word, each expression either of us uttered.

'I introduced him to my wife. The conversation immediately turned to music, and he offered to play duos with her. My wife was, as she always was during those last days, very elegant and alluring, disturbingly beautiful. It was obvious that she *did* like the look of him from the very outset. What was more, she was delighted at the prospect of having someone to play the violin with her – so fond of playing duos was she that she used to hire the services of a violinist from the local theatre orchestra – and her joy was written all over her face. Having cast a glance at me, however, she immediately understood the way I felt and altered her expression accordingly, and a game of mutual deception got under way between us. I smiled pleasantly, trying to make it look as though nothing could be more agreeable to me than the thought of them playing duos together. He, surveying my wife in the way all debauched men look at pretty women, tried to make it appear as though all he was interested in was the subject of the conversation, which was of course what interested him least of all. She tried to appear indifferent, but the combination of my jealous-husband look, with which she was familiar, and his lustful ogling evidently excited her. I saw that right from that first meeting her eyes began to shine in a peculiar way and that, probably as a result of my jealousy, there was immediately established between them a kind of electric current which seemed to give their faces the same expression, the same gaze, the same smile. Whenever she blushed or smiled, so did he. They talked for a while about music, about Paris, about various trivial matters. He got up to go and, with a smile on his lips, his hat resting on his thigh which from time to time gave a sudden quiver, he stood looking now at her and now at me, as if he was waiting for what we would do next. I remember that moment so well, as it was then that I could have decided not to invite him back, and then nothing would have happened. But I looked at him, and at her. "Don't think I'm jealous," I said to her mentally. "Or that I'm afraid of you," to him. And I invited him to bring his violin with him one evening and play duos with my wife. She looked at me in surprise, blushed and began to make excuses, saying that her playing wasn't good enough. This excuse-making irritated me even further, and I became all the more insistent. I remember the strange feeling I had as I looked at the nape of his neck, at its white flesh with the black hairs standing out against it, parted in the middle, as he moved away from us with his peculiar, bobbing, almost birdlike gait. I'm not exaggerating when I tell you that man's presence used to drive me out of my mind. "It's up to me to arrange things so I need never set eyes on him again," I thought. Yet to act like that was tantamount to admitting I was afraid of him. No, I wasn't afraid of him! That would be too degrading, I told myself. And right there and then in the hallway, knowing that my wife could hear me, I insisted that he should bring his violin along that very same evening. He promised to do so, and left.

'That evening he arrived with his violin and they played duos. It took them quite a while to get their playing organized: they didn't have the music they wanted, and my wife couldn't sight-read. I was very fond of music, and I took an interest in their playing, fixed his music stand for him, and turned the pages. And they managed to play a few pieces: some songs without words, and a Mozart sonata. He played excellently, with what they call a good tone. More than that: he played with a refinement and nobility of taste that were quite out of keeping with the rest of his character.

'He was, of course, a far better player than my wife, and he helped her along, at the same time managing to say nice things about her playing. He was a model of good behaviour. My wife seemed only to be interested in the music, and she behaved in a simple, natural sort of way. I, on the other hand, although I pretended to be interested in the music, spent the entire evening being tortured by jealousy.

'From the first moment that his eyes met those of my wife, I saw that the beast which lurked in them both, regardless of all social conventions and niceties, asked "May I?", and replied "Oh yes, certainly." I saw that he hadn't at all expected to find in the person of my wife, a Moscow lady, such an attractive woman, and was clearly delighting in his discovery. For there was no doubt at all in his mind that she was willing. The only problem was how to stop her insufferable husband from getting in the way. If I'd been pure, I wouldn't have understood this, but, like the majority of men, I too had thought this way about women before I'd got married, and so I could read his mind as if it were a printed book. I was particularly tormented by the fact that I could see beyond any doubt that the only feeling she had in my regard was a constant irritation, broken only by our habitual bouts of sensuality, and that this man, because of his outward elegance, his novelty and undoubted musical talent, would, as a result of the intimacy arising out of their playing together, and of the effect produced on impressionable natures by music, especially violin music, inevitably not only appeal to her, but would unquestionably and without the slightest hesitation conquer her, crush her, twist her round his little finger, do with her anything he wanted. I couldn't fail to see this, and I suffered horribly as a result. Yet in spite of this or perhaps in consequence of it, some force compelled me against my will to be, not simply extra-polite, but even kindly disposed towards him. Whether it was for my wife's sake that I did this, or for his, in order to show him I wasn't afraid of him, or whether it was in order to pull the wool over my own eyes – I don't know. All I do know is that right from the start of our dealings with each other I found it impossible to be straight-forward with him. I had to be nice to him, if I wasn't to end up killing him on the spot. I regaled him with expensive wine at dinner, expressed my admiration of his playing, smiled particularly amicably whenever I spoke to him and invited him to come to our house again and play duos with my wife the following Sunday. I told him I would invite some of my musical friends to come and listen to him. And that's how it ended.'

Pozdnyshev, greatly agitated now, changed his position and made his peculiar noise.

'It's strange, the effect that man's presence had on me,' he began again, making a visible effort to remain calm. 'Coming home from an exhibition the following day or the day after, I entered the hallway and suddenly felt something heavy, like a stone, fall on my heart. At first I couldn't work out what it was. It had to do with the fact that as I'd walked through the hallway I'd noticed something that had reminded me of him. It was only when I got to my study that I was able to work out what it had been, and I went back into the hallway to make sure. No, I hadn't been seeing things: it was his overcoat. You know, one of those fashionable men's overcoats. (Though I wasn't aware of doing so at the time, I paid the most minute attention to everything that was connected with him.) I made inquiries: yes, I was right, he was here. I made for the ballroom, entering it from the schoolroom, not the drawing-room end. My daughter Liza was in the schoolroom, reading a book, and the nurse was sitting at the table with the youngest girl, helping her to spin a saucepan lid or something of the kind. The door into the ball-room was closed: I could hear regular arpeggios coming from inside, and the sound of their voices, talking. I listened, but I couldn't make out what they were saying. It was obvious that the piano-playing was meant to drown out their voices, and perhaps their kisses, too. My God! The feelings that rose up in me! I'm seized with horror whenever I think of the wild beast that lived in me during that time. My heart suddenly contracted, stopped beating, and then started again like a hammer. The principal feeling I had was the one there is in all angry rage, that of self-pity. "In front of the children, in front of the nurse!" I thought. I must have been a dreadful sight, for Liza gave me a strange look. "What should I do?" I wondered. "Go in? I can't. God knows what I might do." But I couldn't go away, either. The nurse was looking at me as though she understood my situation. "No, there's nothing for it, I'll have to go in," I said to myself, and swiftly opened the door. He was sitting at the grand piano, playing those arpeggios with large, white, arched fingers. She was standing in the crook of the piano, looking at some musical scores she had opened out. She was the first to see me or hear me, and she glanced up at me quickly. Whether she was frightened but pretending not to be frightened, or whether she really wasn't frightened at all, I don't know, but she didn't bat an eyelid, didn't even move, but just blushed, and then only after a moment or two.

' "How nice that you're back; we can't decide what to play on Sunday," she said, in a tone of voice she wouldn't have used if we'd been alone. This, together with the fact that she'd said "we", meaning the two of them, made me furious. I greeted him in silence.

'He shook my hand and, with a smile that to me seemed downright mocking, began to explain to me that he'd brought some music over so my wife could practise it before Sunday, and that they couldn't come to an agreement as to what they should play – whether it should be something more on the difficult, classical side, like a Beethoven sonata, or just short pieces. It was all so normal and straightforward that there was nothing I could find any fault with, yet at the same time I was convinced it was all a pack of lies, that they had agreed on a plan to deceive me.

'One of the most tormenting things for jealous husbands (and in our section of society all husbands are jealous) is that peculiar set of social conventions which permits the greatest and most dangerous degree of intimacy between the sexes. You'd make a laughing-stock of yourself if you were to try to prevent the kind of intimacy there is at balls, the intimacy there is between a doctor and his female patients, the intimacy that's associated with artistic pursuits – with painting, and especially music. People practise the noblest art of all, music, in pairs; the art necessitates a certain intimacy, yet there's nothing at all suspect about it – it's only a stupid, jealous husband who will see anything undesirable in it. Yet at the same time everyone knows that it's precisely these pursuits, music in particular, that cause

most of the adulteries in our class of society. I'd evidently
embarrassed them by the embarrassment I myself had shown.
For a long time I could find nothing to say. I was like an
upturned bottle from which the water won't flow because it's
too full. What I wanted to do was shout at him and turn him
out of the house, but once again I felt I had to be nice to him,
affable to him. So I was. I made it appear as though I approved
of it all, and again under the influence of that strange feeling
that made me treat him all the more kindly the more unbearable
I found his presence, I told him that I had the greatest confidence
in his taste, and advised my wife to do the same. He stayed just
long enough in order to dispel the unpleasant atmosphere that
had been created by my walking into the room in silence,
looking afraid – and left in the pretence that now they had
decided what they would play the following evening. I, on the
other hand, was fully convinced that in comparison with what
was really on their minds, the question of what they were going
to play was a matter of complete indifference to them.

'I accompanied him out through the hallway with especial
politeness (how could one fail to accompany out a man who
had arrived with the express purpose of shattering one's peace
of mind and destroying the happiness of a whole family?).
I shook his soft, white hand with a peculiar effusiveness.'

XXII

'All that day I didn't say a word to my wife – I couldn't. The
mere sight of her aroused such hatred in me that I even frightened myself. At dinner she asked me in front of the children
when it was I was leaving. The following week I was due to
travel to the provinces to attend a meeting of the local zemstvo.[9]
I told her the date of my departure. She asked me if I needed
anything for the journey. I made no reply, but sat at the table
for a while in silence, and then, just as silently, went off to my
study. During those last days she never came into my room,
particularly at that hour. I lay there in my study, fuming with

anger. Suddenly I heard familiar footsteps. And into my head
came the terrible outrageous thought that, like the wife of
Uriah, she wanted to conceal the sin she had already committed,
and that with this purpose in view she was coming to see me in
my room at this unprecedented hour. "Can she really be coming
to my room?" I wondered, as I listened to her approaching
footsteps. "If she is, it means I was right." And an unutterable
hatred of her arose within me. The footsteps came nearer,
nearer. Perhaps she would go past, into the ballroom? No, the
door creaked, and there in the doorway was her tall, beautiful
silhouette. Her face and eyes had a timid, ingratiating look
which she was trying to conceal but which was evident to me
and the meaning of which I knew only too well. I had nearly
choked, so long had I held my breath, and, continuing to look
at her, I grabbed my cigarette case and lit a cigarette.

'"Well, what's this? A woman comes to sit with you for a
while and all you do is light a cigarette," she said, and sat down
on the sofa close to me, leaning against me.

'I moved away so as to avoid touching her.

'"I see you're unhappy about me wanting to play duos on
Sunday," she said.

'"I'm not in the slightest unhappy about it," I replied.

'"Do you think I haven't noticed?"

'"Well, I congratulate you for noticing. I haven't noticed
anything, except that you're behaving like a flirt."

'"Oh, if you're going to start swearing like a cabby, I'd
better go."

'"Go then, but just remember that even if you don't think
our family's good name's of any importance, I do, and it's not
you I care about (you can go to hell for all I care) but our
family's good name."

'"What? *What* did you say?"

'"Just go. For God's sake go!"

'I don't know whether she was just pretending, or whether
she really didn't have any idea of what I was talking about, but
she took offence and flew into a temper. She got up, but didn't
go away; instead she remained standing in the middle of the
room.

' "You've really become impossible," she began. "You'd wear out the patience of a saint." And trying, as always, to be as wounding as she possibly could, she reminded me of how I had behaved towards her sister (on one occasion I'd lost my temper with her sister and been rudely offensive to her; she knew that this had caused me a lot of pain, and it was here that she chose to insert her dart). "Nothing you say or do will surprise me after this," she said.

' "Yes, go on, insult me, humiliate me, drag my good name in the mire and then claim I'm the guilty one," I said to her inwardly, and suddenly I was seized by a feeling of animosity towards her more terrible than any I'd ever experienced before.

'For the first time I felt a desire to give my animosity physical expression. I leapt to my feet and went up to her; I remember that at the very moment I got up I became aware of my animosity and asked myself whether it was a good thing for me to abandon myself to this feeling, and then told myself that it was a good thing, that it would give her a fright; then immediately, instead of fighting off my animosity, I began to fan it up in myself even further, rejoicing in its steadily increasing blaze within me.

' "Go, or I'll kill you!" I shouted suddenly, going up to her and seizing her by the arm, consciously exaggerating the level of animosity in my voice. I must really have appeared terrifying, as she suddenly lost her nerve to the point where she didn't even have the strength to leave the room, but merely said: "Vasya, what is it, what's wrong with you?"

' "Go!" I roared, even more loudly. "Otherwise you'll drive me mad, and I won't be responsible for my actions any more!"

'Having given vent to the full frenzy of my rage like this, I revelled in it, and was filled with a desire to do something extraordinary, something that would illustrate the pitch of rabid fury I had reached. I had a horrible wish to beat her, to kill her, but knew I couldn't do it, and so in order to continue giving expression to my frenzied rage, I grabbed a paperweight from my writing-desk, and with another shout of "Go!", I hurled it to the floor, narrowly missing her. I judged the shot excellently. She ran for the door, but stopped on her way out.

And then without further ado, while she could still see it (I did it for her to see), I began to take other things – the candle-holders, the inkwell – off my desk and threw them to the floor as well, shouting: "Go! Away with you! I won't be responsible for my actions!"

'She left – and I immediately stopped what I'd been doing.

'An hour later, the nurse came to me and told me my wife was having a fit of hysterics. I went to have a look; she was sobbing, laughing, unable to get a word out. Her whole body was trembling. She wasn't shamming – she really was ill.

'Towards dawn she calmed down, and we had a reconciliation under the influence of the feeling to which we gave the name "love".

'In the morning, when after our reconciliation I confessed to her that I'd been jealous of her and Trukhachevsky, she wasn't at all upset and burst into the most artless laughter, so strange, as she said, did it seem to her, this idea that she might be interested in a man like that.

' "Do you really think any woman with self-respect could feel anything for a man like that beyond the enjoyment of hearing him play? I tell you what, if you like, I'll never see him again. I won't even have him here on Sunday, even though all the guests have been invited now. You can write and tell him I'm not well, and that'll be that. The worst thing would be for anyone, especially him, to think that he's dangerous. And I'm far too proud to let anyone think that."

'And, you know, she wasn't lying, she really believed what she was saying. By saying this she was hoping to make herself feel contempt for him, and so protect herself from him, but she couldn't manage it. Everything was against her, particularly that damned music. So that's how it all ended up: on Sunday evening the guests arrived as invited, and the two of them played together again.'

XXIII

'I think I need hardly tell you that I was very vain. In the sort of life our set leads, if a man's not vain he doesn't have much to live for. Well, that Sunday I went out of my way to see to it that the dinner and the musical evening were organized with the maximum possible good taste. I personally supervised the buying of the food for the dinner, and I issued all the invitations myself.

'By six that evening the guests had all assembled, and he appeared wearing tails and a dicky with vulgar diamond studs on it. He was behaving in a free and easy manner, replying hastily to any question that was put to him, with an understanding, acquiescent smile – you know, the kind of expression that conveyed that everything others said or did was exactly what he'd been expecting. I noted all the things that were *mauvais ton* about him now with especial satisfaction, because they helped to put my mind at rest and demonstrate to me that he was so much my wife's inferior that she would never be able, as she put it, to stoop that low. By now I'd stopped allowing myself to feel jealous. For one thing, I'd had a basinful of that particular torture, and I needed a rest; for another, I wanted to believe my wife's assurances, and so I did believe them. But in spite of not being jealous, I couldn't behave naturally towards either of them, and this was true both during dinner and throughout all the earlier part of the evening, before the music started. I kept watching their movements, their looks.

'The dinner was as such dinners usually are – tedious and artificial. The music began fairly early. Oh, how well I remember all the details of that evening. I remember how he produced his violin, the way he opened the case, removed the cloth that had been specially sewn for him by some lady or other, took the instrument out and began tuning it. I remember the way my wife sat down at the piano, trying to appear indifferent, while in actual fact she was extremely nervous – her nervousness being mostly due to fears about her own ability – and then the customary As on the piano, the plucking and tuning of the violin, the setting up of the music. Then I remember how they looked at one another, glanced round at the audience and began to play. She took the first chord. His face assumed a stern, severe, sympathetic expression and, as he gave attention to the sounds he was making, he searched the strings with careful fingers and provided a response to the piano. And so it began . . .'

He paused and made his sounds again several times in succession. He seemed to be on the point of continuing, but sniffed and paused once again.

'They played Beethoven's "Kreutzer Sonata". Do you know its first movement, the presto? You know it?' he burst out. 'Ah! It's a fearful thing, that sonata. Especially that movement. And music in general's a fearful thing. What is it? I don't know. What is music? What does it do to us? And why does it do to us what it does? People say that music has an uplifting effect on the soul: what rot! It isn't true. It's true that it has an effect, it has a terrible effect on me, at any rate, but it has nothing to do with any uplifting of the soul. Its effect on the soul is neither uplifting nor degrading – it merely irritates me. How can I put it? Music makes me forget myself, my true condition, it carries me off into another state of being, one that isn't my own: under the influence of music I have the illusion of feeling things I don't really feel, of understanding things I don't understand, being able to do things I'm not able to do. I explain this by the circumstance that the effect produced by music is similar to that produced by yawning or laughter. I may not be sleepy, but I yawn if I see someone else yawning; I may have no reason for laughing, but I laugh if I see someone else laughing.

'Music carries me instantly and directly into the state of consciousness that was experienced by its composer. My soul merges with his, and together with him I'm transported from one state of consciousness into another; yet why this should be, I've no idea. I mean, take the man who wrote the "Kreutzer Sonata", Beethoven: he knew why he was in that state of mind. It was that state of mind which led him to perform certain actions, and so it acquired a special significance for him, but none whatever for me. And that's why that kind of music's just an irritant – because it doesn't lead anywhere. A military band plays a march, say: the soldiers march in step, and the music's done its work. An orchestra plays a dance tune, I dance, and the music's done its work. A Mass is sung, I take communion, and once again the music's done its work. But that other kind of music's just an irritation, an excitement, and the action the excitement's supposed to lead to simply isn't there! That's why it's such a fearful thing, why it sometimes has such a horrible effect. In China, music's an affair of state. And that's the way it ought to be. Can it really be allowable for anyone who feels like it to hypnotize another person, or many other persons, and then do what he likes with them? Particularly if the hypnotist is just the first unscrupulous individual who happens to come along?

'Yet this fearful medium is available to anyone who cares to make use of it. Take that "Kreutzer Sonata", for example, take its first movement, the presto: can one really allow it to be played in a drawing-room full of women in low-cut dresses? To be played, and then followed by a little light applause, and the eating of ice-cream, and talk about the latest society gossip? Such pieces should only be played on certain special, solemn, significant occasions when certain solemn actions have to be performed, actions that correspond to the nature of the music. It should be played, and as it's played those actions which it's inspired with its significance should be performed. Otherwise the generation of all that feeling and energy, which are quite inappropriate to either the place or the occasion, and which aren't allowed any outlet, can't have anything but a harmful effect. On me, at any rate, that piece had the most shattering effect; I had the illusion that I was discovering entirely new emotions, new possibilities I'd known nothing of before then. "Yes, that's it, it's got absolutely nothing to do with the way I've been used to living and seeing the world, that's how it ought to be," I seemed to hear a voice saying inside me. What this new reality I'd discovered was, I really didn't know, but my awareness of this new state of consciousness filled me with joy. Everyone in the room, including Trukhachevsky and my wife, appeared to me in an entirely new light.

'After the presto they played the attractive but unoriginal

andante with its rather trite variations, and then the finale, which is really weak. Then, at the request of members of the audience, they played things like Ernst's "Elégie", and various other brief encores. These were all quite pleasant, but none of them made one tenth of the impression on me that the presto had done. They all came filtering through the impression the presto had made on me. I felt cheerful and buoyant all evening. As for my wife, I'd never seen her looking as she did that evening. Her radiant eyes, her serenity, the gravity of her expression as she played, and that utterly melting quality, the weak, pathetic, yet blissful smile on her lips after they'd finished – I saw all this, but I didn't attach any particular significance to it, beyond supposing that she had experienced the same feelings as I had, and that she, like myself, had discovered, or perhaps rather remembered, emotions that were new and unfamiliar. The evening ended satisfactorily, and everyone went home.

'Knowing that I was due to travel away for the zemstvo meeting in two days' time, Trukhachevsky told me on his way out that he hoped to repeat the pleasure of that evening when he was next in town. I took this to mean that he didn't consider it permissible to visit my house when I wasn't there, and this pleased me. It turned out that, since he would have left town by the time I was back, we wouldn't see one another again.

'For the first time I shook his hand with real satisfaction, and thanked him for the pleasure he had given me. He also said a final goodbye to my wife. Their mutual farewells seemed to me the most natural and proper thing in the world. Everything was fine. My wife and I were both very pleased with the way the evening had gone.'

XXIV

'Two days later, having said goodbye to my wife in the best and most tranquil of moods, I went off to the provinces. In my particular district there was always an enormous amount of

business to attend to, and the place had a life of its own; it was
a little world apart. On each of my first two days in the district
town I spent ten hours in the zemstvo headquarters. On the
second day a letter from my wife was brought to me in the
council chamber. I read it there and then. She wrote about
the children, about our uncle, about the nurse, about things she
had bought and then in passing, as if in reference to the most
ordinary event, about a visit she'd had from Trukhachevsky:
he'd apparently brought her the music he'd promised her and
had suggested they play together again, but she had refused.
I couldn't remember him having promised to bring any music:
it had seemed to me at the time that he'd said a definitive goodbye, and what she described gave me a nasty jolt. However, I
had so much to do that there wasn't any time to reflect about
it, and it was only in the evening, when I got back to my
lodgings, that I read her letter through again properly. It wasn't
just the fact that Trukhachevsky had been to the house again
in my absence. The whole tone of the letter seemed forced to
me. The rabid beast of jealousy began to snarl in its kennel,
trying to get out, but I was afraid of that beast, and I hastily
locked it up inside me. "What a loathsome thing jealousy is!"
I told myself. "Nothing could be more natural than what's in
her letter."

'And I lay down on the bed and began to think about the
matters I had to attend to the following day. I always had a lot
of trouble getting to sleep when I was away at those zemstvo
meetings – it also had to do with the unfamiliar surroundings
– but on this occasion I managed to fall asleep almost at once.
But then – you know the way it sometimes happens, that you're
seized by a sort of electric shock, and you wake up? I woke up
like that, with my head full of thoughts about her, about my
carnal love for her, about Trukhachevsky and about the two of
them making love together. I shrank inwardly with rage and
horror. But I began to reason with myself. "What rubbish," I
told myself. "You've got absolutely no grounds for thinking
like that, nothing of the kind's happening, nor has it happened
already. And how can you humiliate yourself and her by supposing such horrors? Some hired fiddler, known to be a worth-

less individual, suddenly taking up with an honourable woman, the respectable mother of a family, *my* wife? What an absurdity!" was what one part of me was thinking. "How could it possibly be otherwise?" was what the other part thought. "There couldn't be anything more simple or straightforward: it was for the sake of that simple, straightforward thing that I married her, for the sake of it that I've lived with her, it's the only thing about her which I actually want and which other men, including that musician, therefore also want. He's an unmarried man, in good health (I can still remember the way he used to crunch the gristle in his chop and greedily seize the rim of his wineglass in his red lips), sleek and well fed, and not merely quite without principles but obviously an adherent of certain special ideas of his own about how best to take full advantage of the pleasures that come his way. And between them they have the bond of music, the most refined form of sensual lust. What can possibly hold him back? Nothing. On the contrary, everything is drawing him in that direction. Would she be able to hold him back? I don't even know who she is. She's a mystery, just as she's always been, just as she'll always be. I don't know her. I only know her as an animal. And nothing can or should hold an animal back."

'It was only then that I began to remember the way they had looked that evening when, after they'd finished the "Kreutzer Sonata", they played some passionate little encore – I don't recall the composer – some piece that was so voluptuous it was obscene. "How could I have gone away like that?" I wondered, as I began to remember the look on their faces. "Surely it must have been obvious that everything took place between them that evening? And surely I must have seen then that there was no longer any barrier between them? Not only that, but that both of them, especially her, were experiencing a kind of shame after what had occurred between them?" I remembered how weakly, pathetically and blissfully she had smiled as I came up to the piano, how she had wiped the perspiration from her blushing face. Even then they had been avoiding each other's eyes, and it was only at supper, when he was passing her a glass of water, that they looked at each other and gave each other a little smile. With horror now I recalled those looks, those barely perceptible smiles. "Yes, it's all taken place between them," said a voice inside me, yet almost immediately another voice said something quite different. "What's come over you? That's impossible," said that other voice. I started to get a sinister feeling, lying there in the dark, and I struck a match: the little room with its yellow wallpaper suddenly filled me with a kind of terror. I lit a cigarette; you know how it is when your mind starts to spin round in the same circle of insoluble problems – you smoke. I smoked one cigarette after another, in an endeavour to cloud my intelligence and make the problems go away.

'I didn't get any sleep at all that night, and at five a.m. I decided I couldn't stand any more of this nervous tension and would go home immediately. I got up, woke the caretaker who acted as my servant and sent him off to fetch some horses. I sent a note to the zemstvo, saying I'd been called away to Moscow on urgent business and asking them to replace me with one of the other members. At eight a.m. I got into a carriage and began my journey.'

XXV

The guard came in and, noticing that our candle had burned down, he extinguished it without putting a new one in its place. Outside it was beginning to get light. Pozdnyshev kept silent, sighing heavily all the time the guard was in the carriage. He continued his story only when the guard had left; and all that could be heard in the semi-darkness was the rattling of the windows of the moving carriage, and the sales clerk's regular snoring. In the half-light of the dawn I could no longer make out Pozdnyshev's features. All I could hear was his voice, which was growing more and more agitated, fuller and fuller of suffering.

'I had to go thirty-five versts[10] by horse and carriage, and then after that there was an eight-hour rail journey. The conditions were just right for a carriage ride. It was frosty autumn

weather, with brilliant sunshine. You know, the time of the
year when the calks in the horseshoes leave their imprints on a
road surface that's even, without a single rut in it. The roads
were smooth, the light was bright and the air was invigorating.
I really enjoyed that carriage ride. Once it had got light and I'd
started my journey, I'd felt a load lift from my shoulders. As I
looked at the horses, the fields, the passers-by, I forgot where
it was I was going. At times I had the illusion that I was just
out for a drive, and that none of what had given rise to this
journey had ever taken place. And I experienced a strange joy
in those moments of self-oblivion. Whenever I remembered
where I was going, I would say to myself: "It'll all be clear soon
enough; don't worry your head about it." Moreover, halfway
through the journey there occurred an event that delayed me
and proved even more diverting: the carriage broke down and
had to be repaired. This breakdown was very significant, as it
meant that I got to Moscow not at five p.m., as I'd planned,
but at midnight, and didn't reach home until one in the morning
– I missed the fast mail train, and had to take the ordinary
passenger service. All the business of being towed by a cart,
getting the repair done, paying the bill, having tea at the inn,
chatting with the innkeeper – all that took my mind off things
even further. By twilight everything was ready, and I set off
once more; it was even better driving by night than it had been
by day. There was a new moon, the frost was light, the road
still perfect, the horses galloped, the coachman was in a good
mood; I rode along, enjoying myself, because I was completely
unmindful of what awaited me; or perhaps it was because I
knew only too well what awaited me, and was saying farewell
to the joys of life. But this tranquillity of spirit I experienced,
this ability to suppress my emotions, all that came to an end
when the carriage journey was over. As soon as I got into the
railway coach I lost all control over my imagination: it began
to paint for me, in the most lurid fashion, a rapid sequence of
pictures which inflamed my jealousy, and each of which was
more cynical than the last. They were all of the same thing – of
what was happening there, in my absence, of her being unfaithful to me. I was consumed with rage, indignation and a kind of

strange, drunken enjoyment of my own hurt pride as I contemplated these pictures, and I couldn't tear myself away from them. I couldn't help looking at them, I couldn't erase them from my mind, and I couldn't stop myself dreaming them up. But that wasn't all: the more I contemplated these imaginary pictures, the more I believed they were real. The luridness with which they appeared before me seemed proof that what I was imagining was in fact reality. It was as though some devil was inventing the most abominable notions and suggesting them to me against my will. I suddenly remembered a conversation I'd once had long ago with Trukhachevsky's brother, and I used it in order to lacerate my feelings with a kind of triumphant ecstasy, making it relate to Trukhachevsky and my wife.

'It had been a very long time ago, but I still remembered it. Once, when I'd asked Trukhachevsky's brother if he ever went to brothels, he'd replied that a respectable man wouldn't go to some dirty, loathsome place where he might run the risk of catching an infection, when it was always possible to find a respectable woman. And now his brother had found my wife. "It's true that she's not all that young any more, she's lost one of her side teeth and she's a bit on the puffy side," I imagined him thinking, "but there you are, you have to make the best of what's available." "Yes, he thinks he's doing her a favour by taking her as his mistress," I reflected. "And what's more, she's safe. No, that's outrageous! What am I thinking of?" I said to myself in horror. "There's nothing of that kind, nothing. There aren't even any grounds for supposing anything of that kind. After all, didn't she tell me herself that she found the very idea of my being jealous of him degrading to her? Yes, but she was lying, she's always lying!" I cried out loud – and it started again ... There were only two other passengers in the carriage, an old woman and her husband, both of whom were very untalkative, and when they got out at one of the stations I was left alone. I was like a wild animal in a cage: at one moment I'd leap up and go to the window, at another I'd pace stumblingly up and down, willing the train to go faster; but the carriage just went on shaking and vibrating all its seats and windows, exactly like ours is doing now ...'

And Pozdnyshev leapt to his feet, took a few paces and then sat down again.

'Oh, I'm so afraid, so afraid of railway carriages; I get stricken with horror in them. Yes, it was horrible,' he continued. 'I told myself I was going to think about something else; I'd think about the keeper of the inn, say, where I'd had tea. And immediately I saw him in my mind's eye, the old, long-bearded inn-keeper with his grandson, a boy the same age as my Vasya, standing beside him. My Vasya! Now he was seeing a musician embracing his mother. What must be taking place in his poor soul? But what did she care? She was in love ... And it all began to seethe within me again. "No, no ... Very well," I thought, "I'll fix my mind on the hospital I inspected yesterday. And that doctor who had a moustache like Trukhachevsky's. And the way he impudently ... They were both deceiving me when they told me he was leaving town." And again it began. All my thoughts led back to him. I suffered horribly. I suffered mainly because of my ignorance, my doubts, my ambivalence, my not knowing whether I ought to love her or hate her. So intense was my suffering that I remember that the thought occurred to me – I found it greatly appealing – that I might get out on to the track and throw myself on the rails under the train, and thus make an end of it all. Then at least I wouldn't be able to doubt and hesitate any more. The only thing that prevented me from doing this was my own self-pity, which immediately gave way to a surge of hatred for my wife. For him I felt both a strange hatred and a consciousness of my humiliation and of his triumph, but for her I felt nothing but the most terrible hatred. "I'm not just going to commit suicide and let her off that way; she's at least got to suffer a bit, and realize how I've suffered," I said to myself. At every station I got out of the train in an attempt to take my mind off it all. I saw some men drinking in one of the station buffets, and I went in and ordered some vodka. There was a Jew standing beside me. He too was drinking. He started talking to me and, willing to do anything rather than sit alone in my carriage, I accompanied him along to his grimy, smoky, third-class compartment, the interior of which was spattered with the husks of sunflower seeds. There I sat down beside him, and he droned away, telling me various anecdotes. I listened to him, but I couldn't follow what he was telling me, as I was still thinking about my own problems. He noticed this, and began to demand that I pay more attention. At that point I got up and went back to my own carriage. "I must think about it carefully," I said to myself. "Is it really true, what I suspect, and is there really any reason for me to torture myself like this?" I sat down and tried to think it over calmly and quietly; but no sooner had I done so than it all started up again: instead of following a calm, reasoned argument, my head was filled with pictures and imaginings. "Think how often I've tortured myself like this," I said to myself, as I remembered the similar attacks of jealousy I'd had previously. "Yet every time it was a false alarm. That's probably the way it'll be this time, as well. I'll find her peacefully asleep; she'll wake up, be delighted to see me, and her words and eyes will tell me that nothing's happened and that all my suspicions are groundless. Oh how good that would be!" "Oh no, it's happened that way too often, this time it's going to be different," said a voice inside me, and it started again. Yes, that was the nature of my punishment! If I'd wanted to discourage a young man from running after women, I wouldn't have taken him to a syphilis clinic, I'd have taken him into my own soul and shown him the devils that were tearing it apart! What was really so horrible was that I felt I had a complete and inalienable right to her body, as if it were my own, yet at the same time I felt that I wasn't the master of this body, that it didn't belong to me, that she could do with it whatever she pleased, and that what she wanted to do with it wasn't what I wanted. And that there was nothing I could do to stop either him or her. He was like some Vanka-Klyuchnik[11] before the gallows, singing a song about how he'd kissed her sweet lips, and so forth. And he had the upper hand. With her there was even less I could do. Even if she hadn't been unfaithful to me yet, she wanted to, and I knew she wanted to, and that made it even worse. It would have been better if she'd actually done it and I'd known about it, so there wouldn't have been this uncertainty. I wouldn't have been capable of saying what it was I wanted. I wanted her not to want what she couldn't help wanting. It was complete and utter madness.'

XXVI

'At the station before the terminus, after the guard had been along to collect the tickets, I got my things together and went out on to the brake-platform. My awareness of what now lay close at hand – the resolution of the entire conflict – was making me even more nervous. I was cold and my jaws started to shake so that my teeth chattered. I shuffled mechanically out of the station with the rest of the crowd, hailed a cab, got into it and set off home. As we rode along I observed the few passers-by, the yard-keepers,[12] the shadows thrown by the street-lamps and by my cab, now in front, now behind, and thought very hard about nothing. After we'd gone about half a verst, my feet started to feel chilled, and it came back to me that I'd taken off my long woollen socks in the train and had put them in my travelling-bag. But where was my travelling-bag? Had I left it in the train? No, I hadn't, it was there. But where was my wicker trunk? It flashed into my mind that I'd forgotten all about my luggage. However, when I discovered that I still had the luggage ticket, I decided it wasn't worth going back just for the trunk, and we travelled on.

'Even though I try hard now, I can't remember the state of mind I was in at that moment. What were my thoughts? What did I want? I've absolutely no idea. All I can remember is that I knew some terrible and very important event was about to take place in my life. Whether that important event did in fact take place because I was thinking like this, or whether it took place because I had a foreboding that it would, I don't know. It may even be that after what happened, everything that went before has taken on a gloomy tinge in my memory. The cab drove up to the porch of our house. It was one o'clock in the morning. There were several cabs standing outside the house; their drivers were waiting for fares, as there were lights in the windows (the lights were on in the ballroom and drawing-room of our apartment). Not stopping to ask myself why there might be lights on so late in our apartment, I climbed the stairs in the same expectation of some terrible event, and rang the doorbell. The door was opened by Yegor, our good, hard-working, but not very intelligent manservant. The first thing that struck my eyes was Trukhachevsky's overcoat hanging with the other coats on the coat-stand in the hallway. I ought to have been surprised, but I wasn't – it was as if I'd been expecting this. "So it's true," I said to myself. When I'd asked Yegor who the visitor was, and he'd told me it was Trukhachevsky, I asked him if there were any other visitors. '"No others, sir," he said.

'I remember the tone of voice in which he replied to me, as if he were anxious to please me and to dispel any uneasiness I might have that there might be other visitors. "No others, sir." "I see, I see," I said, as if I were talking to myself. "And the children?"

'"All well, sir, praise be to God. They're all asleep long ago."

'I could hardly breathe, and I couldn't stop the shaking in my jaws. "That means it's not the way I thought it was," I said to myself. "I used to think, 'disaster' – and yet everything would turn out to be just the same as before. It isn't like that this time; this time it's all happened, everything I used to think about and imagine, only now it isn't imaginings but reality. It's here, all of it . . ."

'I almost burst out sobbing, but the Devil immediately whispered to me: "If you go and cry and be sentimental, they'll just part quietly, there won't be any evidence, and you'll spend the rest of your life in doubt and agony." And immediately my self-pity evaporated, and was replaced by a strange feeling – you won't believe this – a feeling of joy, that now my suffering was at an end, that now I'd be able to punish her, get rid of her, give my hatred free rein. And indeed, I did give free rein to my hatred – I became a wild beast, a ferocious and cunning wild beast.

'"No, don't, don't," I said to Yegor, who was about to go into the drawing-room. "I tell you what you can do: take a cab down to the station and fetch my luggage. Look, here's the ticket. Off you go, now."

'He went along the passage to get his coat. Afraid that he might disturb them, I followed him to his little room and waited while he put his coat on. From the drawing-room, which lay through another room, voices and the sound of plates and knives were audible. They were eating, and hadn't heard the bell. "If only they don't come out now," I thought. Yegor put on his coat, which had an astrakhan collar, and went out. I opened the door for him and closed it behind him, and I felt an eerie sensation at being alone and knowing what I had to do next. How I was going to do it, I didn't yet know. All I knew was that now it had all taken place between them, that the fact of her guilt was now established beyond all question and that now I was going to punish her and bring my relations with her to an end.

'Previously I had always hesitated, and told myself: "But what if it's all untrue, what if I'm mistaken?" This time there was none of that. It had all been irrevocably settled. Without my knowledge, alone with him, at night! That showed a disregard that was total. Or perhaps it was even worse: the audacity and the insolence of her crime were intentional, and aimed at serving as a mark of her innocence. It was all quite transparently obvious. There could be no doubt whatsoever. I was only afraid that they might try to make a run for it, think up some new way of pulling the wool over my eyes, thus depriving me of my evidence and my chance of punishing her. And in order the more quickly to catch them, I crept on tiptoe to the ballroom where they were sitting, not through the drawing-room, but through the passage and the two nurseries.

'The boys were asleep in the first nursery. In the second, the nurse was stirring, on the point of waking up, and I pictured to myself what she would think when she discovered what had happened; at this notion I was seized by such self-pity that I couldn't keep my tears back, and so as not to wake the children I ran back into the passage on tiptoe and along to my study, where I threw myself on the sofa and wept out loud.

'"I'm an honest man, I'm the son of my parents, all my

life I've dreamt of family happiness, never once have I been unfaithful to her ... yet look! Five children, and she's kissing a musician because he's got red lips! No, she isn't human, she's a bitch, a repulsive bitch! Right next door to a room full of children she's pretended to love all her life. And to have written me the things she did! To throw herself into his arms so brazenly! For all I know, it may have been this way all along. Perhaps all these children that are considered mine were really sired by the manservants! And tomorrow I'd have arrived home and she'd have come out to greet me with hair done in that special way, with that twist of hers and those graceful, indolent movements" – I saw before me the whole of her loathsome, attractive presence – "and the wild beast of jealousy would have taken possession of my heart for ever and torn it to shreds. What will the nurse think, and Yegor? And poor little Liza? She already knows something. This brazenness! This lying! This animal sensuality which I know so well," I said to myself.

'I wanted to get up, but I couldn't. My heart was beating so violently that I couldn't stay standing upright. That was it, I was going to die of a stroke. She was going to kill me. That was exactly what she wanted. What did killing matter to her? Oh no, that would be doing her far too great a favour, I wasn't going to give her that satisfaction. Yes, here I was to sit, while in there they ate and laughed and ... Even though she'd lost the first freshness of her girlhood, he wasn't going to turn his nose up at her; actually she wasn't at all bad-looking, and, most important of all, she didn't pose any danger to his precious health. "Why didn't I just strangle her there and then?" I asked myself, remembering the moment when, a week ago, I'd shoved her out of my study and then smashed things. I vividly remembered the state of mind I'd been in at the time: not only did I remember it, I now felt the same desire to smash and destroy that I'd felt then. I wanted to act. All considerations other than those related to action went abruptly out of my head. I entered that state a wild animal knows, or the state that's experienced by a man who is under the influence of physical excitement at a time of danger, and who acts precisely, unhurriedly, but without ever wasting a moment, and with only one end in view.'

XXVII

'The first thing I did was to take off my boots. Then, in my stockinged feet, I went over to the wall above the sofa where I kept my guns and daggers hanging, and took down a curved, damask-steel poniard that had never once been used and was horribly sharp. I removed it from its sheath. I remember that the sheath fell down behind the sofa, and that I said to myself: "I'd better see I find it afterwards, otherwise it'll get lost." Then I took off my overcoat, which I'd been wearing all this time and, treading softly in my stockinged feet, made for the drawing-room.

'I crept quietly up to the door, and then suddenly opened it. I remember the look on their faces. I remember it because it gave me an excruciating joy. It was a look of terror. That was exactly what I wanted. I'll never be able to forget the expression of desperate terror that came over both their faces in the first split-second they caught sight of me. As I remember it, he was sitting at the table, but when he saw me, or heard me, he leapt to his feet and froze with his back to the cupboard. His features wore a quite unmistakable look of terror. So did hers, but there was something else there, too. If all she had done was look terrified, it's quite possible that what took place might never have happened; but in that facial expression of hers – at least that's how it seemed to me in that first split-second – there was also a kind of annoyance, she looked as though she were put out at having her love-life interrupted, her happiness with him. It was as if all she cared about now was that no one should prevent her from being happy. These expressions stayed on their faces only for an instant. His terrified look quickly gave way to one that asked a question: was it going to be possible to lie or not? If it was, then they'd better start now. If it wasn't, then something else was going to begin happening. But what? He threw her a questioning look. When she looked back at him, it seemed to me that her expression of annoyance had turned into one of concern for him.

'For an instant I froze there in the doorway, clutching the poniard behind my back. At that same moment he smiled and started to say, in a tone of voice that was nonchalant to the point of being absurd: "Oh, we were just playing a little music together . . ."

'"Goodness, I wasn't expecting . . ." she began simultaneously, adopting the same tone of voice.

'But neither of them managed to get to the end of their sentences. That same rabid frenzy I had experienced a week previously once more took possession of me. Once again I felt that compulsion to destroy, to subjugate by force, to rejoice in the ecstasy of my furious rage, and I abandoned myself to it.

'Neither of them managed to finish what they were saying . . . That something else, the thing he was afraid of, the thing that blew all their words to kingdom come in one instant, began to happen. I rushed at her, still keeping the poniard hidden in case he tried to stop me plunging it into her side, under the breast. That was the spot I'd chosen right from the outset. In the very moment I attacked her, he saw what I was doing, and seized my arm – something I'd never expected he'd do – shouting: "Think what you're doing! Someone help!"

'I wrenched my arm free and went for him without a word. His eyes met mine, and suddenly he turned as white as a sheet, even his lips turned pale; his eyes started to glitter in a peculiar way, and then suddenly – this was something else I hadn't been expecting – he ducked under the piano and was out of the room in a flash. I was about to rush after him, but there was something weighing me down by my left arm. It was her. I tried to pull myself away, but she hung on to me even more heavily and wouldn't let go. This unexpected impediment, her weight and the physical contact with her, which I found revolting, inflamed me even further. I was in a rabid frenzy, and I knew I must be a fearful sight, and was glad of it. I swung my left arm round as hard as I could, and my elbow struck her full in the face. She screamed and let go of my arm. I wanted to run after him, but I reflected that it would be ridiculous to run after one's wife's lover in one's stockinged feet; I didn't want to look ridiculous, I wanted to look terrifying. In spite of the terrible fury that gripped me, I was constantly aware of the impression I was making on others, and this consideration even guided my actions to a certain extent. I turned and looked at her. She'd slumped on to a chaise longue; snatching with one hand at her eyes, which I'd hurt, she was observing me. In her face there was fear and hatred of me: I was the enemy. It was the kind of fear and hatred that could only be inspired by her love for another man. Yet I might still have held myself in check and not done what I did, if only she hadn't said anything. But she suddenly began to speak, as she attempted to seize the hand in which I was holding the poniard.

'"Think what you're doing! What is this? What's wrong with you? There's nothing, nothing, nothing . . . I swear it!"

'I might still have managed to put it off a little longer, but what she had just said – from which I drew quite the opposite conclusion, namely that everything *had* taken place between them – demanded a reply. And the reply had to be in keeping with the state of mind into which I'd worked myself, which was rising in a non-stop crescendo, and which could not but continue to rise. Even frenzied rage has its laws.

'"Don't lie, you repulsive bitch!" I began to yell, grabbing her arm with my left hand. But she tore herself free. Then, without letting go of the poniard, I gripped her throat in my left hand, threw her back and started to strangle her. How hard her neck was . . . She seized my hands in hers, trying to tear them free of her throat, and as if this were the signal for which I'd been waiting, I struck her with the poniard as hard as I could in her left side, beneath the ribs.

'When people tell you they don't remember what they did when they are in a mad fit of rage, don't believe a word of it – it's all lies, nonsense. I remembered everything afterwards, and I've never ceased to remember it for one second. The more steam my rage got up, the more brilliantly the light of consciousness flared within me, making it impossible for me not to be aware of everything I was doing. I can't claim that I knew in advance what I was going to do, but I was aware of each action I took at the moment I performed it, and sometimes, I think, a little before. It was as if it had been arranged like this so I could repent, so I could tell myself I was capable of stopping if I wanted to. I knew that I was striking her with the poniard under the ribs, and that it was going to go in. At the moment I did it, I knew I was doing something horrific, something the like of which I had never done before, and that it was going to have terrible consequences. But that awareness came and went like a flash of lightning, and was instantly followed by the act itself. I was blindingly aware of that act, too. I felt – I can remember it now – the momentary resistance of her corset, and of something else as well, and then the way the poniard sank into something soft. She grabbed at the poniard with both hands, lacerating them on the blade, but she couldn't stop it from going in. For a long time afterwards, in prison, when a change of heart had taken place in me, I used to think about that moment, remembering what I could of it, and weighing it up in my mind. I would remember that for a split-second – only a split-second, mind you – before I did what I did, I had a terrible awareness that I was killing, that I'd killed a woman, a defenceless woman, my wife. I remember the horror of that awareness even now, and putting two and two together I think that once I'd stuck the poniard into her, I must have pulled it out again (I even have a dim memory of doing this), in an attempt to set right what I'd done and put a stop to it all. For a second I stood without moving, waiting to see what would happen, and whether everything was going to be all right again. She leapt to her feet and screamed: "Nurse, he's killed me!"

'The nurse had heard the noise, and was standing in the doorway. I continued to stand there, waiting, unable to believe what had happened. But then suddenly the blood came gushing out from under her corset. It was only then that I realized it couldn't be put right again, and I immediately made up my mind that there was no need for it to be put right, that this was just what I'd wanted, and what I'd been obliged to do. I waited a little, until she'd fallen down, and the nurse, with a scream of

"Lord Almighty!", had run to her side, and only then did I throw down the poniard and stalk out of the room.

' "It's no good getting all worked up, I must be aware of what I'm doing," I told myself, looking neither at her nor at the nurse. The nurse was screaming, calling for the maid. I stalked along the passage, and, after I'd told the maid to go and help, went into my room. "What am I going to do now?" I wondered, and immediately knew the answer to my question. As I walked into my study, I made straight for the wall, took down a revolver, examined it – it was loaded – and placed it on the desk. Then, taking care to retrieve the sheath from behind it first, I sat down on the sofa.

'I sat there for a long time. I thought about nothing, remembering nothing. Along the passage I could hear people moving about. I heard someone come into the house, followed by someone else. Then there was a noise, and I saw Yegor come into my room carrying the wicker trunk he'd fetched from the station. As if anyone needed it now!

' "Haven't you heard what's happened?" I asked him. "Tell the yard-keeper to inform the police."

'He made no reply, and went away. I got up, locked the door, found my cigarettes and matches, and had a smoke. I'd hardly finished my cigarette when sleep overcame me and rendered me senseless. I remember I dreamed that she and I were on friendly terms again, that we'd had a quarrel but had made it up; we still had a few outstanding differences, but we were friends once more. I was woken by a knocking at the door. "That'll be the police!" I thought. "After all, I've just committed a murder, I think. Or maybe it's her, and nothing has happened." There was more knocking. I didn't go to see who it was, I was trying to make up my mind whether it had all really happened or not. Yes, it had. I had a memory of her corset's resistance, of the way the poniard had sunk into her, and a chill ran down my spine. "Yes, it happened, all right," I said to myself. "And now it's my turn." But even as I silently formed these words, I knew I wasn't going to kill myself. It was a strange thing: I remembered how many times before I'd been on the point of committing suicide; even that day in the train it had seemed easy to me, easy because I'd thought of how it would put the fear of God into her. Now, however, not only was I unable to kill myself – nothing could have been further from my thoughts. "Why should I?" I asked myself, and there was no reply. The knocking came again. "Right," I said to myself. "The first thing I must do is find out who that is. I'm not in any hurry." I put the revolver back on the desk and covered it with a newspaper. Then I went to the door and undid the latch. It was my wife's sister, that kind-hearted, brainless widow.

'"Vasya! What's happened?" she said, and the tears she always had ready started to flow.

'"What do you want?" I asked her, rudely. I knew there was absolutely no excuse for my being rude to her, nor would any purpose be served by it, but I couldn't think of any other tone of voice to adopt.

'"Vasya! She's dying! Ivan Fyodorovich said so." Ivan Fyodorovich was my wife's doctor and adviser.

'"Is he here?" I asked, and all my hatred for her seethed up again. "Well, what of it?"

'"Vasya, go in and see her. Oh, this is terrible," she said.

'"Go in and see her?" I said, phrasing the words in the form of a question to myself. And I immediately knew the answer, knew that I must go in and see her, that when a husband had murdered his wife, as I had done, the correct thing was for him to go in and see her. "If that's the correct thing to do, then I must go in," I told myself. "And if I have to, I'll still have time," I thought, apropos of my intention to commit suicide. I followed my sister-in-law out.

'"Wait," I said to her. "I'll look ridiculous without my boots, let me at least put a pair of slippers on."'

XXVIII

'And it really was quite remarkable! Once again, as I emerged from my study and passed through the familiar rooms, once again there rose within me the hope that nothing at all had happened. But then the smell of that vile stuff doctors use – iodoform, phenol acid – or whatever it is – hit my nostrils. No, it had happened all right, all of it. As I passed the nursery I caught sight of Liza. She was looking at me with frightened eyes. For a moment it even seemed to me that all five children were in there, and that they were all looking at me. I went up to her bedroom. The maid came to the door, let me in and left. The first thing that leapt to my gaze was her light-grey dress draped over a chair; the dress was stained black all over with blood. She was lying on our double bed, on my side of it (it was easier of access), her knees raised. She was lying almost supine, on a pair of pillows, and she was wearing an unbuttoned bed-jacket. Some stuff or other had been applied to the place where the wound was. There was a heavy smell of iodoform in the room. What struck me most forcibly was her face: it was swollen, and along part of her nose and under one eye it was blue with bruises. This was the result of the blow I'd given her with my elbow when she'd been trying to hold me back. She had no beauty at all now, and I felt there was something repulsive about her. I stood still on the threshold.

' "Go in, go in to her," said my sister-in-law.

' "Yes, I expect she wants to confess," I thought. "Shall I forgive her? Yes, she's dying, and so can be forgiven," I said to myself, trying to be magnanimous. I went in and walked right up to her. She looked up at me with difficulty – she had a black eye – and she said, haltingly: "You've got what you wanted, you've killed me . . ." And through all her physical suffering, her nearness to death, even, I saw displayed on her face the same inveterate look of cold, animal hatred I knew so well. "Even so . . . I won't . . . let you have . . . the children . . . She" – her sister – "will look after them . . ."

'The thing I thought most important – the question of her guilt, her unfaithfulness – she didn't even seem to think worth mentioning.

' "Yes, admire what you've done," she said, looking towards the door, and she gave a sob. Her sister was standing in the doorway with the children. "Yes, there it is, there's what you've done."

'I looked at the children, at her battered face with its bruises, and for the first time I forgot about myself, about my marital rights and my injured pride; for the first time I saw her as a human being. And so insignificant did all that had hurt me and made me jealous appear, and so significant what I'd done, that I wanted to press my face to her hand and say: "Forgive me!" – but I didn't dare to.

'She fell silent, closing her eyes, and obviously without the strength to speak any more. Then her disfigured face began to quiver and was creased with a frown. Feebly, she pushed me away.

'"Why did all this happen? Why?"

'"Forgive me," I said.

'"Forgive? That's all nonsense! . . . If only I wasn't going to die! . . ." she screamed, heaving herself up and transfixing me with her feverishly glittering eyes. "Yes, you've got what you wanted! . . . I hate you! . . . Ah! Ah!" she cried, evidently in delirium now, and afraid of something. "Go on, kill me, kill me, I'm not afraid . . . Only kill all of us, all of us, him too. He's gone, he's gone!"

'After that, her fever became continuous. She couldn't recognize anyone any more. She died towards noon that same day. Before then, at eight a.m. to be precise, I'd been taken to the local police station and from there to prison. And there I remained for eleven months awaiting trial. During that time I thought a great deal about myself and my past life, and I grasped what it had all been about. I began to grasp it on my third day. It was on that third day that they took me there . . .'

He was about to say something else, but could not hold back his sobbing, and had to stop. Pulling himself together with an effort, he continued:

'I only began to grasp it when I saw her in her coffin . . .' He gave a sob, but continued hastily, at once: 'It was only when I saw her dead face that I realized what I'd done. I realized that I'd killed her, that it was all my doing that from a warm, moving, living creature she'd been transformed into a cold, immobile waxen one, and that there was no way of setting this to rights, not ever, not anywhere, not by any means. If you've never experienced that, you can't possibly understand . . . Oh! Oh! Oh!' he cried several times, and fell silent.

For a long time we sat there saying nothing. He sobbed and shook silently, and I looked at him.

'Well, *prostite*[13], forgive me . . .'

He turned away from me and lay down on the seat, covering himself up with his plaid. When we reached the station where I had to get off – this was at eight a.m. – I went over to him in order to say goodbye. Whether he was asleep or merely pretending, he didn't stir. I touched him with my hand. He threw off the plaid, and it was clear he had not been asleep.

'*Proshchayte*, goodbye,' I said, offering my hand.

He took it, and gave me the barest smile, though it was so pathetic that I felt like crying.

'Yes, *prostite*, forgive me . . .' he said, repeating the word with which he had brought his story to an end.

THE DEVIL

The original Russian text is to be found in L. N. Tolstoy, *Sobranie sochinenii v 22 tomakh*, vol. 12 (Moscow, 1978–85).

But I say unto you, That whosoever looketh on a woman to lust after her hath committed adultery with her already in his heart.

And if thy right eye offend thee, pluck it out, and cast it from thee: for it is profitable for thee that one of thy members should perish, and not that thy whole body should be cast into hell.

And if thy right hand offend thee, cut it off, and cast it from thee: for it is profitable for thee that one of thy members should perish, and not that thy whole body be cast into hell.

(Matthew v:28–30)

I

A brilliant career lay ahead of Yevgeny Irtenev. He had all that it took: an excellent home education, a first-class degree from the Faculty of Law at St Petersburg University, connections, obtained through his recently deceased father, in the very highest social circles, and even the beginnings of a position in a government ministry under the patronage of the minister himself. He also had a private income; it was quite a large income, though not very secure. His father had lived abroad for part of the year and had spent the rest of his time in St Petersburg, making an annual allowance of six thousand rubles to each of his two sons – Yevgeny and Andrey, who was a bit older and served in the Horse Guards. He himself, together with his wife, had managed to get through a fortune. The only time he had ever visited his estate had been for two months each summer, and he had never concerned himself with the running of it, leaving all that to an overfed manager who never concerned himself with the running of it either, but whom he had trusted completely.

When, after the death of their father, the brothers came to divide up the property, there proved to be so many debts outstanding that the family attorney advised them to renounce their inheritance and make do with the estate of their grandmother, which was valued at a hundred thousand rubles. However, a neighbour of the estate, a landowner who had had dealings with old man Irtenev, had one of his promissory notes and had come to St Petersburg especially on that account, told the young men that in spite of all the debts there was a very good chance that they could clear up all the practical business and still manage to keep back a large capital sum. All they had to do was sell the wood and a few bits of vacant land, keeping the 'goldmine' – Semyonovskoye, with its four thousand desyatinas[1] of black earth, its sugar factory and its two thousand desyatinas of water meadows – for themselves. It just required a bit of application. They would have to settle in the village on a permanent basis and run the place sensibly, with a due regard for economy.

So it was that, when he paid a visit to the estate that spring (his father had died during Lent) and made a tour of inspection, Yevgeny decided to give up his government position, settle in the village with his mother, and devote himself to getting the most out of the property. With his brother, to whom he was not particularly closely attached, he came to the following arrangement: he undertook to pay him either an annual allowance of four thousand rubles, or a lump sum of eighty thousand, in return for which the elder brother would agree to give up his share of the inheritance.

This done, he went with his mother to live in the manor house at Semyonovskoye, and set about running the estate with zeal, but also with caution.

It is usually considered that old men are the natural conservatives, while young men are natural innovators. This is not really so. Young men are the natural conservatives – young men who want to live but who don't think, or don't have time to think, about how they ought to live and who therefore take as their model the lifestyle of those who have lived before them.

Yevgeny was no exception. Ensconced now in Semyonovskoye, he had as his dream, his ideal, the resurrection of the type of life that had been lived there not in his father's day – his father had been hopeless at practical things – but in the day of his grandfather. In all that affected the house, the garden and the way things were run, he now began – making certain adjustments in keeping with the times, of course – to resurrect the general spirit that had reigned during his grandfather's lifetime: everything on a grand scale, concern for the welfare of all, good order, the organization of services and amenities – all of which involved a great deal of hard work. The demands of the creditors and the banks had to be met, and to this end land had to be sold and terms of credit arranged. Money also had to be found with which to continue (in some places by renting out land, in others by the use of hired labour) the farming of Semyonovskoye's enormous, four-thousand-desyatina tillage and the running of the sugar factory; the house and garden had to be taken in hand so they did not give an impression of dereliction and decay.

There was a lot of work to do, but Yevgeny had a good deal of strength, both physical and intellectual. He was twenty-six years old, of average height, powerfully built, with muscles that had been developed by physical exercises. He was a sanguine type, and his cheeks had a high, vivid colour; his teeth were brilliantly white, his lips bright red, and his hair was thin, soft and curly. His only physical defect was his near-sightedness, which he had brought upon himself by using spectacles; now he could not manage without a pince-nez, which had already set its imprints upon his aquiline nose. Such was his physical appearance. As for his personality, it could be said that the better you knew him, the better you liked him. His mother had always been fonder of him than of any of her other children, and now that her husband had died she not only lavished all her attention on her favourite son, she made him into the focus of her entire life. But she was not the only one who felt this way about him. The friends he had made at school and university had not only had a special place in their hearts for him, they had held him in respect. He had always had this kind of effect on other people, as well. It was impossible for anyone not to believe what he said, impossible to suspect any deceit or untruth when confronted with such an open, honest face, and especially such open, honest eyes.

Indeed, his personality was of great assistance to him in the business matters he now had to attend to. A creditor who might have turned down another man had confidence in him. A manager, an elder or a muzhik who might have played dirty and hoodwinked another man, forgot all about such trickery under the benign effect of dealing with someone who was so

kind-hearted and straightforward, and who, most important of
all, was as good as his word.

It was the end of May. After some wheeling and dealing,
Yevgeny had finally managed to make arrangements in the
town for the vacant land to be released from its mortgage so
that it could be sold to a merchant. He had then borrowed
money from this same merchant with which to renovate his
stock of horses, bulls and carts, and, even more importantly,
with which to start the construction of a badly needed farmhouse. The work got under way. Timber was being carted in,
the carpenters had already got down to business, and eighty
cartloads of manure were in the process of arriving, even though
the entire project still hung by a thread.

II

Right in the middle of all these concerns, something happened
which, although it was not important, caused Yevgeny rather
a lot of trouble at the time. Up till now he had lived the way all
young, healthy single men live: he had had relations with various kinds of women. He was not a libertine, but neither, as he
liked to tell himself, was he a monk. And he had only indulged
in this in so far as it was necessary for his physical wellbeing
and his intellectual freedom, as he put it. It had started when
he was sixteen. And so far it had all gone smoothly – smoothly
in the sense that he hadn't given himself up to debauchery, had
never once lost his head over any of the women he had had,
and had never caught any diseases. Initially he had had relations
with a seamstress in St Petersburg, but then she had become
infected, and he had made other arrangements for himself. This
side of his life had been so well organized that it had never
given him any trouble.

But now here he was in his second month at Semyonovskoye,
and he had not the faintest idea of how to make the necessary
arrangements. The involuntary abstinence was beginning to
have a bad effect on him. Would he have to go into town to get

what he wanted? But whereabouts in town? And how was he
going to arrange it? Such were the questions that troubled
Yevgeny Ivanovich; and since he had made himself believe that
this was what he had to do, and this was what he needed, it
really did become a necessity for him. He felt he was no longer
a free agent. Every time he caught sight of a young woman, he
found himself following her with his eyes.

He did not think it would be right for him to have relations
with a girl or a woman in Semyonovskoye. From what he had
been told, he knew that both his father and his grandfather had
differed completely from other landowners of their day in this
respect, and had never had liaisons with their female serfs. He
determined that he would not, either. As time went by, however,
and he began to feel more and more constrained and pictured
to himself with horror what might befall him in the godforsaken
town, he told himself that since serfs were a thing of the
past nowadays, there was really nothing to stop him making
arrangements in the village. The main thing was to do it in such
a way that no one found out about it, and to do it not out of
lust but for the sake of his health, as he said to himself. Having
taken this decision, he became even more uneasy. Whenever he
talked to the elder, the muzhiks or the carpenter he found
himself bringing the conversation round to the subject of
women, and if women were what they already happened to be
talking about he would try to spin the conversation out as long
as possible. As for women themselves, he found himself paying
more and more attention to them.

III

To take a decision like this in private was one thing, however;
to carry it out in practice was another. He couldn't just
approach some woman all by himself. Which one would he
choose? Where would they do it? It would have to be arranged
through some third party, but who could he turn to?

One day when he was out in the woods he happened to call

in at a gamekeeper's hut in order to get himself a drink of water. The gamekeeper had been one of his father's huntsmen. Yevgeny Ivanovich started to talk to him, and the gamekeeper began telling stories about the high old times they'd had on hunting expeditions in days gone by. It occurred to Yevgeny Ivanovich that it might not be such a bad idea to arrange what he had in mind out here in the hut, or in the woods. The trouble was that he didn't know how to go about it, or whether old Danila would arrange it for him. 'Perhaps if I suggest it to him he'll be horrified, and then I'll look really silly; but maybe he'll agree to it without any bother,' he thought, as he listened to Danila's stories. Danila went on to relate how they had once strayed rather far afield and had ended up staying the night with the deacon's wife, and how he had once fixed up a woman for the landowner Pryanichnikov.

'Yes, I can ask him,' thought Yevgeny.

'Your father, God rest his soul, never went in for that kind of nonsense.'

'No, I can't,' thought Yevgeny. However, in order to test the ground, he said: 'How did you ever come to get mixed up in an unpleasant business like that?'

'What's unpleasant about it? She was glad to do it and my Fyodor Zakharych was well satisfied. He gave me a ruble. Anyway, how was he going to manage, otherwise? Needed his oats, he did, same as other men. Never said no to a drop of vodka, either.'

'Yes, I can ask him,' thought Yevgeny, and without further ado took the plunge.

'You know, Danila...' He could feel himself blushing scarlet. 'You know, I've been having an awful time.' Danila smiled. 'I'm not a monk, after all. I'm not used to it.'

He felt stupid saying this, but was relieved to see that Danila's attitude was one of approval.

'Why, sir, you should have told me ages ago, that's easily seen to,' he said. 'All you have to do is tell me which one you want.'

'Oh, it's really all the same to me. Well, of course, as long as she isn't ugly and hasn't any diseases.'

'I take your meaning!' said Danila, cutting him short. He

thought for a bit. 'Ha, there's one really nice bit of stuff,' he began. Once again Yevgeny blushed. 'A lovely bit of stuff. She was married last autumn,' said Danila, starting to whisper now, 'but her husband can't do anything. Think what that's worth to a hunter, eh?'

Yevgeny was well and truly frowning with embarrassment by this time.

'No, no,' he managed to get out. 'That's not what I want at all. On the contrary (what could possibly be on the contrary?), all I want is one who's free of disease and won't cause any trouble. A soldier's wife, or something like that . . .'

'I've got the very one for you, sir. It's Stepanida you'll be wanting. Her husband works in the town, she's just like a soldier's wife. And she's that good-looking, and clean with it. You'll be well satisfied, sir. I was just saying to her the other day, you ought to go looking elsewhere, and she . . .'

'All right, so when can it be?'

'Tomorrow, if you want. I'll look in and fetch her on my way to buy tobacco. When it's dinner-time come here, or to the bath-house behind the kitchen garden. There won't be a soul about. Everybody sleeps after dinner.'

'Very well, then.'

As he made his way home, Yevgeny was gripped by a terrible sense of unease. 'What will it be like? What's a peasant woman like? What if she's horrible and ugly? No, they're pretty,' he said to himself, remembering the ones he had seen. 'But what will I say to her? How will I behave with her?'

He was not himself for the whole of the rest of that day. At twelve noon the following day he went back to the game-keeper's hut. Danila was standing in the doorway. He said nothing, but turned his head meaningfully in the direction of the wood. Yevgeny felt all the blood rush to his head, and he made for the kitchen garden. There was no one there. He approached the bath-house. There was no one there, either. He took a quick look inside, came out again and suddenly heard the snap of a twig breaking. He looked round, and there she was, standing in a thicket on the other side of a small ravine. He rushed down into the ravine in order to get across to her.

There were nettles in the ravine, he hadn't noticed them. He got badly stung, his pince-nez fell from his nose, and he scrambled up the opposite bank. Dressed in a white embroidered apron and a red-brown peasant skirt, her head covered by a bright red kerchief, barefoot, fresh, firm and pretty, she stood there, smiling shyly.

'There's a path, you should have gone round,' she said. 'I've been here for ages. Ever so long.'

He went up to her and, looking quickly around him first, touched her.

A quarter of an hour later they parted company. He found his pince-nez, and went off to the hut to see Danila. When Danila asked him 'Satisfied, master?', he gave the old man a ruble. Then he went home.

He was satisfied. It was only at the beginning that he had felt embarrassed. But his sense of shame had quickly passed. And it had been good. What was especially good was that now he felt calm, relaxed and cheerful. As for her, he hadn't really been able to see her properly. He remembered her as being clean, fresh, quite good-looking, and natural, with no airs and graces. 'Who's her husband?' he wondered. 'Pechnikov, did he say? Which Pechnikov would that be, now? There are two families of them, aren't there? She must be old Mikhaila's daughter-in-law. Yes, that's probably who she is. He's got a son who lives in Moscow. I must ask Danila about it some time.'

From that day on, the major drawback to life in the country – involuntary abstinence – was removed. Yevgeny's thoughts were no longer subject to distraction, and he was able to concentrate on the business of running the estate without interference.

The task Yevgeny had taken on was, however, very far from being an easy one: it sometimes seemed to him that he would not be able to last the course and that it would end with him having to sell the estate, and all his labours going for nothing. Worse still, that it might end with it being perfectly obvious that he hadn't been able to last the course, that he had failed to complete the task he had set himself. That was what worried him most. No sooner would he manage to plug up one gap than another, unexpected one would appear.

During all this time, more and more of his father's old debts, previously unknown, came to light. It became clear that during the latter days of his life his father had borrowed right, left and centre. When in May the property had been divided up, Yevgeny had believed that at last he knew everything. But suddenly, in the middle of the summer, he received a letter from which it transpired that a widow named Yesipova was still owed a sum of twelve thousand rubles. There was no promissory note, just a plain receipt which the family attorney said could be disputed. All Yevgeny wanted to know was whether the debt was a valid one or not.

'Mother, who's Kaleriya Vladimirovna Yesipova?' he asked, when he met his mother at dinner as usual.

'Yesipova? Oh, she was one of your grandfather's pupils. Why do you ask?'

Yevgeny told his mother about the letter.

'She ought to be ashamed of herself. After your father giving her all that money!'

'But do we owe her *this* money?'

'Well, I don't quite know how to put it. It isn't really a debt; your father, in his infinite goodness . . .'

'Yes, but did Father consider it as a debt?'

'I really couldn't tell you. I don't know. All I know is that you've enough troubles already without that one.'

Yevgeny could see that Marya Pavlovna, his mother, didn't know what to say, and was testing him.

'From what you say it sounds as though it's a debt that will have to be paid,' he said. 'I'll go and have a word with her tomorrow. We'll see if the payment can't be deferred.'

'Oh, I'm so sorry for you. But you know, it's best this way. Yes, tell her she'll have to wait for a bit,' said Marya Pavlovna, evidently put at ease by this response, and proud of her son's determination.

Another thing that made Yevgeny's life particularly difficult was the fact that his mother, although she lived in the same house with him, had not the slightest understanding of the position he was in. All her life she had been accustomed to living on such a grand scale that she could not even imagine her son's predicament, which was that one of these days things might work out in such a way as to leave them destitute; Yevgeny might have to sell everything and support her by paid employment, which given his situation could earn him no more than two thousand rubles a year at the very most. She did not understand that they could only avoid such an outcome by cutting down their expenditure on all sides, and so was unable to comprehend why Yevgeny was so careful about little things like gardeners, coachmen, servants and even the meals they ate. What was more, like most widows she held the memory of her departed husband in a kind of reverential awe, quite unlike the attitude she had had towards him when he had been alive, and she would never have admitted that things he had done or arrangements he had made might have been bad ones, and needed to be put right.

By dint of great exertions, Yevgeny was managing to run the garden with only two gardeners, and to keep up the stables with only two coachmen. In her innocence, his mother thought that by not complaining about the meals which the old manservant-cook prepared, or about the fact that the paths in the park were not all swept clean, or that instead of proper footmen they only had a boy, she was doing all that a mother could by way of sacrificing herself for her son. Similarly, in this matter of the new debt, which for Yevgeny was more or less the death-blow to all his attempts at good management, she saw merely one more instance of her son's noble character. Another reason why she was not particularly worried about his material situation was that she was sure he would make a brilliant marriage which would set everything to rights again. And indeed, it was in his power to make the most brilliant of marriages. She could think of a dozen families who would be happy to see their daughters married to him. And she wanted to arrange it as soon as possible.

IV

Yevgeny, too, dreamed of marrying, but not in the way his mother envisaged it. He found her view of marriage as a means of setting his financial affairs in order a repellent one. He wanted to marry honourably, for the sake of love. As it was, he eyed the girls he knew, and those who came his way, and tried to imagine what it would be like to be married to one of them, but so far nothing had come of it. Meanwhile, to his considerable surprise, he found that his relations with Stepanida showed no signs of abating; indeed, they were even acquiring a certain degree of steadiness. So far was Yevgeny from being a libertine, so ashamed had he been of performing that secret and, he sensed, ignoble act, that on no account could he bring himself to make arrangements to repeat it. After that first rendezvous he had rather hoped he would never see Stepanida again. It turned out, however, that after a while he was once more overtaken by the restlessness he ascribed to that cause. But this time the restlessness was not an anonymous one: into his consciousness this time floated those same black, brilliant eyes, that same low voice, saying 'ever so long', that same smell of something fresh and strong, and those same high breasts lifting up the apron, and all of this in that thicket of hazels and maples, awash with vivid light. In spite of the shame he felt, he went to see Danila again. And a second midday rendezvous in the woods was arranged. This time Yevgeny managed to get a better look at her, and everything about her seemed appealing to him. He tried to engage her in conversation a little, asked her about her husband. As he had thought, her husband was Mikhaila's son, and lived in Moscow where he was employed as a coachman.

'But look here, I mean, how is it you can . . .' Yevgeny was about to ask how she could be unfaithful to him like this.

'How is it I can what?' she asked. She was obviously intelligent and quick off the mark.

'Well, how is it you can make love with me like this?'

'Oh, that,' she said, full of high spirits. 'I'm pretty sure he gets his fun over there. Why shouldn't I have mine, too?'

She was obviously putting on this display of pertness and bravado especially for his benefit, and he found it charming. Even so, he could not bring himself to make another rendezvous with her. Not even when she suggested they might meet without involving Danila, towards whom she seemed somewhat coolly disposed, did he give his assent. He was hoping that this meeting would be their last. He found her appealing. He thought that such intercourse was a necessity for him, and that there was nothing wrong in it; deep within him, however, sat a sterner judge who did not approve and who hoped this was going to be the last time – or, if he did not hope that, at least did not wish to be party to the arrangement and did not want to make preparations to repeat it.

In this way the entire summer went by; during its course they met on perhaps a dozen occasions, each time through the mediation of Danila. There was one time when she was unable to show up because her husband had arrived back from town, and Danila suggested another woman. Yevgeny refused with disgust. Then her husband went back to town again, and their rendezvous continued. Initially it was all done through Danila, but later on Danila would merely fix a time, and Stepanida would make her way to the rendezvous in the company of a woman called Prokhorova, as married peasant women were not allowed to go around on their own. Once, at the very time for which one such rendezvous had been arranged, a family came to visit Yevgeny's mother, bringing with them the one girl she really wanted for her son, and there was no way that he could escape. When at last he managed to get away, he made as though for the barn, and then took the path round through the woods to the place where they were to meet. She was not there. However, in the place where they usually made love, all the shrubs and saplings – the bird-cherry, the hazel, even the young maple as thick as a fence-post – had been snapped and broken. She had waited, become worked up and angry, and had playfully left this for him as a reminder. He stood around for a while, then for a while longer, and finally went off to see Danila in order to ask him to tell her to come the following day. She did, and was just the same as ever.

Thus the summer went by. It was always in the woods that they arranged to meet. Only once, when autumn was approaching, did they meet in the barn that stood in Stepanida's back yard. It never entered Yevgeny's head that this relationship might be important to him in any way. Stepanida – he never thought about her. He gave her money, and that was that. What he didn't know and didn't suspect was that the entire village knew about the affair, that she was the object of envy, that her people at home were taking money from her and egging her on, and that all her ideas of right and wrong had been completely undermined by the influence of money and family. The way she saw it was that if people were envious of her then what she was doing must be all right.

'It's only for the sake of my health,' Yevgeny told himself. 'I know it isn't right, and even if no one's saying anything, they all, or at least some of them, know about it. The woman who comes with her knows. And since she knows, she's bound to have told others. But what can I do about it? I know I'm behaving badly,' he would say to himself, 'but what am I supposed to do? Anyway, it's not going to be for very long.'

Yevgeny's main worry was Stepanida's husband. For some reason he felt at first that her husband must be a sorry-looking fellow, and that this to a certain extent justified his behaviour. But then one day he saw the husband and was quite taken aback. The husband was a handsome, well-dressed man who looked no worse than he did, and probably even better. When he next met Stepanida he told her he had seen her husband and had been most impressed by his fine appearance.

'There isn't another man like him in all the village,' she said with pride.

This surprised Yevgeny. From then on, the thought of the husband started to worry him even more. Once, when he happened to be at Danila's hut, Danila said to him in the course of conversation: 'Mikhaila was asking me the other day: is it true the young master's living with my son's wife? I said I didn't know. Well, I said, better the master than some muzhik.'

'And what did he say?'

'"Oh, it's all right," he said. "Just wait, though, I'll find out what's going on, and then I'll give her what for."'

'Well, if her husband came back I'd give her up,' thought Yevgeny. But the husband went on living in town, and for the time being their relationship continued. 'When I have to, I'll break it off, and that'll be that,' he thought.

This seemed to him beyond all doubt. His certainty had much to do with the fact that during the summer he was intensely preoccupied with various matters: the layout of the new farmhouse, the harvest, the building work and, above all, the payment of the debts and the sale of the vacant land. These were things that absorbed him to the exclusion of all else; they occupied his thoughts all day, from the time he got up in the morning till the time he went to bed at night. They represented the life that was real. His relations – he did not even use the word 'affair' – with Stepanida were, on the other hand, something of very little account. It was true that when he was taken by the desire to see her, it was so overwhelming that he couldn't think of anything else. But this was of short duration: a rendezvous was arranged, and afterwards he would forget about her for weeks on end, sometimes even as long as a month.

That autumn Yevgeny had to make frequent trips to the town, and it was there that he made the acquaintance of the Annensky family. The Annenskys had a daughter who had just finished a course at a young ladies' institute. To the great chagrin of Marya Pavlovna, it came about that her son, as she put it, 'cheapened himself' by falling in love with Liza Annenskaya and asking for her hand in marriage.

After that his relations with Stepanida came to an end.

V

In the way that it is always impossible to say why a man chooses one woman rather than another, so it is impossible to say why Yevgeny chose Liza Annenskaya. There were all sorts of reasons, both positive and negative. One reason was that she was not the very rich girl his mother wanted him to marry; another was that towards her own mother she displayed an attitude of naive helplessness; yet another was that while she was no self-advertising beauty, she was not bad-looking either. The principal reason was, however, that Yevgeny had come to know her just at a time when he was ready to marry. He fell in love because he knew he was going to get married.

At first he had merely taken a fancy towards Liza Annenskaya; but once he had made up his mind that she was to be his wife, he conceived a much stronger emotion towards her: he felt he was in love with her.

Liza was tall, slender and long. Everything about her was long: her face, her nose, which pointed not outwards but downwards, her fingers and her feet. The colour of her face was very delicate, yellowy-white with a soft glow; her hair was long, soft, light brown and curly, and she had beautiful eyes that were clear, gentle and artless. These eyes made a particular impression on Yevgeny, and whenever he thought of Liza he saw them looking at him – clear, gentle and artless.

Such was her physical appearance. He knew nothing of what she was like as a person – all he could see was those eyes. They told him everything he needed to know. And what they told him was this.

Ever since, at the age of fifteen, she had started at her institute, Liza had consistently fallen in love with all the attractive men who had come her way, and had only been happy when she was in love. When she had left the institute she had continued to fall in love with all the young men she had met and, needless to say, had fallen in love with Yevgeny on her very first acquaintance with him. It was this susceptibility that gave her eyes the curious expression which so fascinated Yevgeny.

That particular winter she had already fallen in love with two young men at the same time, thrilling with excitement not only whenever they came into the room, but whenever their names were mentioned. When, however, her mother let it drop that Irtenev might have serious intentions towards her, so infatuated with him did she immediately become that she almost stopped thinking about the other two; and when Irtenev

started to attend their balls and social gatherings, danced with
her more than he did with the other girls, and only seemed to
be interested in whether she loved him or not, her infatuation
with him became positively morbid – she had dreams about
him and fancied she saw him in her room at night, and all
other men ceased to have any significance for her. But when he
proposed to her, and their planned union received its blessing,
when they kissed and were formally betrothed, she had no
desire other than to be with him, to love him and be loved by
him. She was proud of him, was touched and moved by him
and by herself, and by her love for him. The better he got to
know her, the more he returned her love. He had never expected
to encounter such a love, and it made his own feelings all the
more powerful.

VI

At the onset of spring he went to Semyonovskoye in order to
take a look round and give instructions concerning the running
of the estate, with particular regard to the house, which was
being redecorated in preparation for the wedding.

Marya Pavlovna was unhappy about the choice her son had
made, but only because the match was not as brilliant as it
could have been, and because she disliked Varvara Alekseyevna,
Yevgeny's future mother-in-law. She had no idea of whether
Varvara Alekseyevna was a nice person or not, and she had not
given the matter any reflection. She had, however, perceived at
their very first meeting that Varvara Alekseyevna was not a
woman of social distinction, not *comme il faut*, not a lady, as
Marya Pavlovna expressed it to herself, and this vexed her
bitterly. It vexed her because she set great store by social distinction; she knew that Yevgeny, too, was very sensitive in this
regard, and foresaw no end of problems arising from it. On the
other hand, she did like the girl. She liked her mainly because
Yevgeny did. She had to like her. And Marya Pavlovna was
quite prepared to do so and be completely sincere about it.

Yevgeny found his mother in a state of joyful happiness. She was putting the house in order and had intended to leave as soon as her son arrived with his young wife-to-be. Yevgeny urged her to stay. And the issue remained unresolved. In the evening, after tea, Marya Pavlovna played her usual game of patience. Yevgeny sat with her and took an interest in the game. This was the time of day when they had their most intimate chats with one another. As she was finishing one game of patience, and before beginning another, Marya Pavlovna gave Yevgeny a quick look and began, somewhat hesitantly, 'Oh, there was something I've been meaning to say to you, Zhenya. Of course I don't know anything about it, but as a general rule I'd advise you that before you marry it's absolutely essential that you wind up all your bachelor affairs, so that nothing can upset you or, pray God, your wife. Do you understand what I mean?'

And indeed, Yevgeny was not slow to gather that Marya Pavlovna was alluding to his relations with Stepanida, which had come to an end as long ago as the previous autumn, and that, as lonely women are prone to do, she ascribed a far greater importance to those relations than what they had actually possessed. Yevgeny went rather red in the face, not so much from embarrassment as out of annoyance that his dear, kind mother should go meddling – even if it was only out of love for him – in things that were none of her business, things she did not and could not possibly understand. He said he had nothing to hide, and had always taken care to behave in such a way that there could never be anything to interfere with his marriage.

'Well, my dear, that's wonderful news. Please, Zhenya, don't be angry with me,' said Marya Pavlovna in embarrassment.

But Yevgeny could see that she hadn't finished, and had not said what she really wanted to say. Such indeed proved to be the case. After a little while she began to tell him how, when he had been away, she had been asked to be a godmother by . . . the Pchelnikovs.

This time it was not annoyance nor even embarrassment that made Yevgeny go red in the face, but a strange presentiment of the importance of what he was about to be told, an involuntary

recognition that ran quite counter to his normal way of thinking. It was as he expected. As if she were simply making pleasant
conversation, Marya Pavlovna happened to mention that this
year all the women in the village seemed to be having boys, and
that this must mean there was going to be a war soon. The
young Vasin woman and the young Pchelnikov woman had
both had their first children recently, and both had been boys.
Marya Pavlovna had meant to slip this in casually, but when
she saw how red in the face her son had gone and observed the
nervous way in which he removed his pince-nez, gave it a flick,
put it back on his nose again and hurriedly lit a cigarette, she
herself grew embarrassed. She fell silent. He too said nothing,
unable to think of anything with which to break the silence.
That was how they knew that each had understood the other.

'Yes, the main thing is that there should be fair dealing in the
village, and no favourites, as there were in your grandfather's
day.'

'Mother,' said Yevgeny all of a sudden, 'I know why you're
saying this. You're worrying your head over nothing. My marriage is so sacred to me that there's nothing for which I'd ever
put it in jeopardy. Anything that may have happened when I
was a bachelor is all over and done with now. I never got
involved in any serious affairs, and there's no woman who's
entitled to anything from me.'

'Well, I'm glad to hear it,' said his mother. 'I know how
fastidious you are in such matters.'

Yevgeny interpreted these words of his mother's as a tribute
that was his due, and made no reply.

Next morning he set off for town, his head full of his bride-
to-be, or anything at all, in fact, except Stepanida. But almost
as if it had been planned that way in order to remind him of
her, as he drove up to the church he started meeting people
who were going home from it on foot and in carriages. He met
the old man Matvey with his son Semyon, some young lads and
girls, and then two married women; one of these women was
rather older than the other, who was smartly dressed and wearing a bright red kerchief, and who looked vaguely familiar. She
was walking along lightly and cheerfully, carrying a baby in her

arms. As he drew level with them, the older woman stopped short and bowed to him in the old-fashioned way, while the younger one with the baby merely inclined her head; from under the kerchief he caught the brilliance of smiling, merry eyes that were familiar to him.

'Yes, it's her, but that's all over now, and there's no point in giving her a second glance. And the child's probably mine,' flashed through his mind. 'No, that's all rot. She had a husband, she used to make love with him, too.' He did not even bother to start doing the necessary calculations, so firmly was it implanted in his head that it had been necessary for his health, that he had paid his money, and that had been that; there was no bond of any kind between her and himself, there never had been, nor could there or must there ever be. It was not a matter of him suppressing the voice of his conscience; no, it was simply that his conscience had nothing to tell him. And after the talk he had had with his mother, and this encounter, he dropped her completely from his mind. Nor did he encounter her again.

The week after Easter, Yevgeny and Liza were married in town. They left for Semyonovskoye immediately after the wedding. The arrangements at the house were of the kind usually made for a young couple. Marya Pavlovna wanted to leave, but they both – Liza, especially – prevailed upon her to stay. So instead of leaving, she merely moved into one of the annexes.

And so for Yevgeny a new life began.

VII

The first year of Yevgeny's marriage was a difficult one. It was difficult because after the wedding all the business to do with the estate which he had somehow managed to put off dealing with during his courtship now suddenly descended on him.

It was going to be impossible for them to free themselves from all the debts. The dacha had been sold, and the major debts paid; yet there still remained debts outstanding, and there was no money with which to meet them. The estate brought in a fair amount, but he had had to send some of that money to his brother, and then on top of that there had been all the expense of the wedding, which had left them with hardly any ready cash at all; the sugar factory would be unable to operate and would have to be closed down. The only way out of this mess was for him to use his wife's money. When she discovered the plight her husband was in, Liza herself insisted he do this. Yevgeny gave his consent, but only on condition that they took out a deed of purchase on half of the estate in her name. He did this not for his wife's sake, needless to say – she found it rather offensive – but in order to placate his mother-in-law. These concerns, with their varying alternations of success and failure, were one of the things that poisoned Yevgeny's life during that first year. Another was his wife's ill health. In the autumn of that same first year, seven months after the wedding, Liza had an unpleasant accident. She had taken the charabanc out to meet her husband, who was returning from town. The horse, normally a very docile creature, had suddenly started to frisk and prance; she had taken fright and had jumped out. The jump had been a relatively lucky one – a wheel might have caught her – but she was pregnant, and that same night the pains started. She had a miscarriage, and it took her a long time to recover from it. The loss of the expected child, his wife's illness, the attendant upset to his routine and, more than anything else, the presence of his mother-in-law, who had arrived the moment Liza had been taken ill – all this made the year even more trying for Yevgeny.

Despite all these trying circumstances, however, towards the end of the first year Yevgeny began to feel better. For one thing, the aim he had set himself of reconstituting his family's fortune and reviving in a new form the sort of life that had been led on the estate in his grandfather's day was, albeit slowly and with difficulty, in the process of being achieved. Now there could be no more talk of their having to sell the whole estate in order to meet their debts. The most important part of the estate – even if it had been transferred to his wife's name – had been saved, and as long as the beet harvest was a good one and the prices favourable, in the new year they could expect their situation of tension and economic need to give way to one of complete prosperity. There was that for a start.

The other thing was that, however much he had expected of his wife, he had never expected to find in her what he had in fact discovered. Not only was this not what he had expected – it was far better. Tender scenes, ecstatic expressions of affection – these there had not been, or only very mutedly, even though he had tried to arrange them. What there had been was something quite different: life had not only become more cheerful, more pleasant – it had become easier. He had no idea why this should be, but it was so.

The reason was that immediately after the wedding Liza had made up her mind that Yevgeny Irtenev was the loftiest, cleverest, purest and most noble man in the whole world, and that it was therefore incumbent upon everyone to serve him and do whatever was pleasing to him. But since it was impossible to make everyone do this, she was going to have to do it herself, as far as she could. So she did, and all her emotional energy went into finding out and guessing what he wanted, and then doing it, no matter what it was or how difficult it might be.

She possessed, too, what constitutes the principal charm of association with a loving woman: the ability, derived from her love for her husband, to see into his innermost thoughts. She perceived – often, he used to think, better than he himself did – his slightest change of mood, his slightest inflection of feeling, and adapted her behaviour accordingly. So it was that she never gave him cause for offence, but invariably exerted a moderating influence on his depressions and a heightening one on his moods of elation. And it was not only his feelings she understood, but also his thoughts. She had an instant understanding of matters one might have thought would have been completely alien to her – agricultural problems, for instance, or questions to do with the factory and the assessment of personnel – and she was not only able to chat with him about all this, but often, as he himself said, to be a useful and irreplaceable adviser to him about it all. She viewed people, objects and everything else in the world exclusively through his eyes. She loved her mother, but when she saw that Yevgeny disliked her mother's interference in their lives, she immediately took her husband's part, and went about it with such determination that he had to chide her for it.

In addition to all this, she possessed an enormous amount of tact and good sense. Most important of all, she had about her an air of silent calm. Everything she did, she did so it was not noticed; all that could be observed were the results of her industry; cleanliness, order and elegance in all things. Liza had understood at once what the ideal of her husband's life consisted of, and she strove to attain, and by the orderly way in which she ran the house indeed did attain, the very things he wanted. As yet they had no children, but of that, too, there were hopes. That winter they took a trip to St Petersburg, where they consulted an obstetrician who assured them that Liza was in perfect health and that there was absolutely nothing to prevent her having children.

This dream, too, was realized. Towards the end of the year she became pregnant again.

The one thing that . . . poisoned would be too strong a word, let us say threatened their happy life together was her jealousy. She kept it in check and did not display it, but she suffered from it frequently. It was not simply that Yevgeny could not love anyone else, because there was no woman on earth who was worthy of him (the question of whether she herself was worthy of him did not arise) – it was that, for this same reason, no woman might dare to love him.

VIII

This was the pattern of their daily lives: he would get up early, as he always did, and make himself busy about the estate, paying a visit to the factory where work would already be in progress, and sometimes going out into the fields. When it got round to ten o'clock he would come back to the house for coffee, which he had on the terrace in the company of Liza, Marya Pavlovna and an uncle who lived with them. After conversation – which was often quite heated – over coffee, they

would go their separate ways until it was time for dinner. They
dined at two. Afterwards they might take a walk or go out for
a drive. In the evening, when he came back from the estate
office, they would have a late glass of tea together, and sometimes he would read aloud while she worked, or, if guests were
present, there would be chamber music or conversation. If he
went away on a business trip somewhere he would write her a
letter and receive one from her every day. Sometimes she would
travel along with him, and then they would have a particularly
happy time. On their name-days they would have guests to the
house, and he would derive pleasure from her talent for seeing
that everyone had an enjoyable time. He would see and hear
that everyone was full of admiration for her, this young, charming hostess, and he loved her for it all the more. Everything was
going swimmingly. She bore her pregnancy with ease and they
both began, if somewhat timidly, to make plans about the way
they would rear their child. The method of upbringing, the
principles to be applied in it – all this was in Yevgeny's hands.
Her only desire was to carry out his wishes obediently. Yevgeny
even started to dip into medical textbooks, and had every intention of rearing his child according to all the precepts of medical
science. It went without saying that she was in complete agreement with everything he told her; she began to sew up 'warm'
and 'cold' swaddling blankets, and got a cradle ready. Thus
began the second year of their marriage, and the second year
they had spent together.

IX

It was just before Whitsun. Liza was in the fifth month of her
pregnancy and, although she was being careful, she was cheerful
and active. Both their mothers were staying with them under
the pretext of being there to keep an eye on her and look after
her, and were, needless to say, only succeeding in making her
thoroughly nervous by their constant bickering. Yevgeny had
taken up farming with particular zeal, and was completely

immersed in the details of a new large-scale processing technique for sugar beet.

Just before Whitsun, Liza decided that the house would have to be given a thorough cleaning, which it had not had since Easter, and she called in two charwomen to help the servants wash the floors and the windows, beat the furniture and carpets, and spread loose covers over everything. The charwomen arrived early in the morning, put their iron cauldrons of water on to heat, and set to work. One of the women was Stepanida, who had recently weaned her little boy and had gone pestering the estate clerk, with whom she was now having an affair, to let her do cleaning work up at the house. She wanted to get a good look at the new mistress. Stepanida was living alone, as previously, without her husband, and she had had a series of affairs, first with Danila, who had caught her stealing firewood, then with Yevgeny, and now with this young lad, the clerk. Of Yevgeny she had no thoughts whatsoever. 'He's got a wife now,' she said to herself. 'But it'll be fun to see the mistress, and the way she's running the house; they say she's had it done up really nicely.'

Yevgeny had not seen her since that day he had met her with her child. Since she had had the baby to look after, she had not been doing any work, and he seldom passed through the village. That morning, the day before the Whit holiday, he got up early, at five a.m., and set off to visit a field which was lying fallow and was due to be spread with phosphorite. He left the house before the charwomen came in, while they were still busy out at the stove with their cauldrons.

Cheerful, satisfied and with a good appetite, Yevgeny came back to the house to have his breakfast. At the gate he dismounted from his horse and, having given it into the charge of a gardener who happened to be passing, he walked the remaining distance to the house, swiping at the tall grass with his whip and, in the way that people often do, repeating to himself something he had said not long ago. The words he kept repeating were 'Phosphorite will repay'; but what or whom they would repay, he neither knew nor greatly cared.

Someone was beating a carpet on the lawn. All the furniture

had been carried out of the house. 'Good Lord! What a cleaning Liza's organized! Phosphorite will repay. There's a wife for you. Yes, a wife among wives,' he said to himself, quickly summoning up a mental picture of her in her white housecoat, her face radiant with happiness, as it nearly always seemed to be whenever he saw her. 'Yes, I'd better change my boots, or else that phosphorite will repay, or smell like manure, rather, and my wife's in that way of hers again. What way might that be? Ah yes, another little Irtenev's growing inside her,' he thought. 'Yes, phosphorite will repay.' And, smiling at his own thoughts, he made to push open the door of his study.

But no sooner had he started to apply pressure to the door than it seemed to open of its own accord, and he collided face to face with a woman who was coming towards him carrying a bucket; she had tucked up her skirt, she was barefoot, and her sleeves were rolled up as high as they would go. He moved to one side to let her past, but she also moved to one side, adjusting her kerchief, which had been knocked askew, with the back of a wet hand.

'Come along, I won't go in, if you . . .' Yevgeny began; then suddenly, recognizing her, he stopped.

She glanced at him with eyes that were merrily smiling. Then, untucking her skirt so that it covered her legs, she went out through the doorway.

'What nonsense is this? What on earth? . . . It can't be true!' said Yevgeny to himself, giving his head a toss as though to drive away a fly, annoyed with himself for having noticed her. In spite of his annoyance, however, he could not take his eyes off her body as it swayed to the rhythm of her supple and powerful walk, off her bare feet, her arms, her shoulders, the attractive folds of her chemise and her red peasant skirt, which was tucked up high above her white calves.

'And what am I looking at her for, anyway?' he wondered, and he lowered his eyes so as not to see her. 'Yes, I'll have to go in as if nothing had happened, and fetch another pair of boots.' He turned and faced his room again, but had hardly gone five paces into it when, not knowing why or on whose command, he looked round once more in order to catch another

glimpse of her. At that moment she was turning the corner of
the passage, and as she did so she also looked round to get a
glimpse of him.

'Oh! What am I doing?' he exclaimed inwardly. 'She'll only
get ideas into her head. In fact, she's probably got them already.'

He went into his wet study. Another woman, old and
emaciated, was still in there, scrubbing. Yevgeny tiptoed his
way across the dirty puddles towards the wall, where his other
pair of boots was. He was just about to go out again when the
woman herself left.

'Now she's gone, the other one, Stepanida, will come back –
on her own,' someone inside him started to predict.

'Oh God! What am I thinking of, what am I doing?' He
grabbed his boots and ran with them out into the hallway; there
he put them on, brushed himself down and went on to the
terrace where both mothers were already sitting having their
coffee. Liza had obviously been waiting for him, and she came
out on to the terrace at the same time as he did, but through a
different door.

'Oh God, if only she knew, she who thinks I'm so honest, so
pure, so innocent, if only she knew!' he thought.

Liza greeted him as always, with a radiant countenance.
Today, however, he thought she looked somehow especially
pale and yellow, long and weak.

X

Over coffee, as often happened, there was one of those conversations, peculiar to ladies, in which there is no logical
connecting thread whatsoever, but which are evidently held
together by something, as they go on interminably.

The two ladies were exchanging barbed remarks with one
another, and Liza was artfully manoeuvring between them.

'I'm awfully sorry we didn't manage to finish cleaning your
room for you before you got back,' she said to her husband.
'It's just all the clearing out there is to do.'

'Well, how are you? Did you manage to get some sleep after I left?'

'Yes, I slept. I feel fine.'

'How can a woman in her condition possibly feel fine in this unbearable heat when all the windows in her house face straight into the sun?' said Varvara Alekseyevna, Liza's mother. 'And not a screen or an awning anywhere. I always had awnings.'

'But the terrace is in the shade from ten o'clock onwards,' said Marya Pavlovna.

'That's the way to catch a chill, sitting in the damp,' said Varvara Alekseyevna, quite oblivious to the fact that this completely contradicted what she had just finished saying. 'My doctor always says that you can never diagnose an illness if you don't know the character of the patient. And he knows, believe me; he's a leading physician and we pay him a hundred rubles a visit. My late husband didn't hold much with doctors, but he never spared any expense for my sake.'

'How can a man spare expense on the woman he's married when her life and that of their child may depend . . . ?'

'Well, of course, if she's got money she doesn't have to depend on her husband so much. But a good wife defers to her husband in all matters,' said Varvara Alekseyevna. 'Liza's simply still rather weak after her illness, that's all.'

'Oh no, Mother, I feel absolutely fine. Haven't they given you any boiled cream?'

'I don't want it. Fresh cream will do.'

'I did ask Varvara Alekseyevna if she wanted any. She said she didn't,' said Marya Pavlovna, as if in self-justification.

'That's right, I don't want any.' And, in order to bring this awkward conversation to a close, and as if she were making some magnanimous concession, Varvara Alekseyevna turned to Yevgeny and asked him: 'Well, and so have you finished spreading those phosphates?'

Liza went dashing off to fetch the boiled cream.

'But I don't want any, I don't want any.'

'Liza! Liza! Not so quickly, dear,' said Marya Pavlovna. 'Those quick movements are so bad for her.'

'There's nothing will do her any harm as long as her mind's at rest,' said Varvara Alekseyevna, as though hinting at something, even though she knew perfectly well that there was nothing to hint at.

Liza returned with the cream. Yevgeny sipped his coffee and listened gloomily. He was used to this kind of conversation, but today he found its absurdity particularly irritating. He wanted to reflect on what had just happened to him, and this empty prattle was getting in the way. Having finished her coffee, Varvara Alekseyevna left the terrace in a worse frame of mind than she had been in before. Liza, Yevgeny and Marya Pavlovna stayed on, and their conversation was simple and pleasant. Even so, Liza, whom love had rendered more sensitive, noticed at once that something was troubling Yevgeny, and she asked him if he had something on his mind. He had not been prepared for this question, and he answered somewhat hesitantly, saying it was nothing. This reply made Liza ponder even more. There was something troubling him, and troubling him very deeply; that was as plain to her as the fact that a fly had landed in the milk. But he would not tell her what it was.

XI

After breakfast they all attended to their separate tasks. Yevgeny, according to a time-honoured habit, went off to his study. There, instead of getting on with the business of reading and writing letters, he sat down and began to smoke one ciga-rette after another as he turned things over in his mind. He had been shocked and upset by the reawakening within him of the unclean feeling from which, since the time of his marriage, he had believed himself to be immune. Since his wedding, he had never once experienced that feeling either for Stepanida or for any other woman apart from his wife. On many occasions now he had felt a profound relief at this sense of immunity, yet now this one seemingly trivial incident had revealed to him that he was not immune after all. What troubled and tormented him now was not that he had given into this feeling, that he desired

her – he did not even want to think about that – but that the
feeling was alive in him and that he would have to be on his
guard against it. He had not the slightest doubt that he would
succeed in conquering it.

He had one letter to answer, and a document to draw up. He
sat down at his writing-desk and began to work. By the time
he had finished, he had forgotten all about what had been
worrying him, and he went outside with the intention of visiting
the stables. But again, as ill luck would have it – he did not
know whether it was by accident or design – no sooner had he
emerged on to the porch than a red peasant skirt and a red
kerchief came round the corner, and she walked past him,
swinging her arms and swaying her hips. Not only that – once
she had gone by, she started to run almost playfully, and caught
up her female companion.

Once again it all rose in his imagination: the brilliant noon,
the nettles and, in the shade of the maples behind Danila's hut,
her smiling face as she bit some leaves.

'No, I can't let it go on like this,' he told himself. He waited
until the women were out of sight, and then went over to the
office. It was right in the middle of the dinner-break, and
he hoped he might catch the estate manager there. He did.
The estate manager had just woken up from his nap. He was
standing in the office, stretching, yawning and surveying the
cattleman, who was saying something to him.

'Vasily Nikolayevich!'

'At your service, sir.'

'I want to have a word with you.'

'At your service, sir.'

'Finish your business with the cattleman first.'

'Can't you just carry it?' said Vasily Nikolayevich to the
cattleman.

'It's too heavy, Vasily Nikolayevich.'

'What's he talking about?' asked Yevgeny.

'Oh, a cow's gone and had her calf out in the fields,' said
Vasily Nikolayevich. 'Well, all right, then, I'll have a horse
harnessed up right away. Tell Nikolay Lysukh to get an open
cart ready.'

The cattleman went off.

'Well, you see, it's like this,' began Yevgeny, blushing and conscious of doing so. 'It's like this, Vasily Nikolayevich. When I was a bachelor here, I did a few things I shouldn't have ... Maybe you've heard? ...'

Vasily Nikolayevich smiled with his eyes and, obviously feeling sorry for his master, said: 'Is it about Stepashka, sir?'

'Well yes, it is. Look, this is what I wanted to say to you. Please, please don't hire her to do cleaning work up at the house. You must understand that it puts me in a very difficult situation ...'

'Yes, I think you've got Vanka the clerk to thank for that, sir.'

'So please ... Well, and are they going to spread the rest of the phosphorite today?' asked Yevgeny, in order to cover up his embarrassment.

'Yes, I'm just off to see to it now, sir.'

And there the matter rested. Yevgeny regained his calm, in the hope that since he had gone for a whole year without seeing her, things would continue like that. 'Besides, Vasily will tell Ivan the clerk, Ivan will tell her, and she'll realize I don't want her in the house,' he told himself, and was glad he had summoned up the courage to have a word with Vasily, however hard it had been for him to do so. 'Anything, anything's better than that uncertainty, that shame.' He shuddered at the mere recollection of the crime he had committed in his thoughts.

XII

It had cost Yevgeny a certain moral effort to overcome his sense of shame and tell Vasily Nikolayevich about what was troubling him. The effort had brought him calm. Now he felt that everything was all right again. Liza noticed at once that he seemed quite to have regained his composure and that he even appeared to be in a better mood than usual. 'It was probably our mothers getting at one another that upset him,' she thought. 'It really is a bit much, especially for a sensitive, high-minded man like him, constantly to be exposed to those hostile, vulgar hints at nothing in particular.'

The following day was Whit Sunday. The weather was glorious, and according to custom the women of the village went into the woods to wreathe garlands for themselves; on their way there they came up to the big house and began to sing and perform dances. Marya Pavlovna and Varvara Alekseyevna came out on to the porch dressed in fine clothes and carrying parasols, and went down to stand near the circle of dancers. This year the two women were accompanied by one of Yevgeny's uncles, a corpulent lecher with a weakness for alcohol, who was spending the summer at the house; he was wearing a little Chinese tunic.

As always, a gaily coloured circle of young married women and unmarried girls, vivid with flowers, formed the central axis, around which in succession and from every side, like planets and satellites that had torn themselves free of it and were now in orbit around it, went girls holding hands, rustling the new silk of their peasant gowns, young boys sniggering at something and chasing one another to and fro, older lads in red shirts, black long-waisted coats and black caps, keeping up an incessant spatter of sunflower-seed husks, and the manor serfs and bystanders looking on from a distance. The two ladies went right up to the circle. They were followed by Liza, who was wearing a light-blue dress and had ribbons of the same colour and material in her hair; the dress had wide sleeves that exposed her long, white arms and her angular elbows.

Yevgeny did not really want to go out, but it would have looked odd for him to hide himself away. He too came out on to the porch, smoking a cigarette; he exchanged greetings with the lads and muzhiks and had a brief conversation with one man. All the while the peasant women continued to yell out a dance tune at the tops of their voices, snapping their fingers, clapping their hands and dancing.

'The lady of the house is calling you, sir,' said a young boy, coming over to Yevgeny, who had not been able to hear his wife's voice above the din. Liza wanted him to come and watch the dancing of one of the peasant women she thought looked particularly charming. It was Stepanida. She was dressed in a yellow skirt, a sleeveless cotton-velvet jacket and a silk kerchief; she was wide-hipped, energetic, flushed and elated. No doubt she was dancing wonderfully. He saw nothing of it.

'Well, well,' he said, taking off his pince-nez and putting it back on his nose again. 'Well, well,' he thought. 'So I'm not going to get away from her, after all.'

He could not bring himself to look at her, as he was afraid of her attractiveness. For that very same reason, in the brief glimpse he had of her she seemed to him particularly attractive. What was more, he could tell from the way her eyes had flashed that she had seen him and seen that he was enthralled by her. He remained there just as long as good manners dictated and then, having seen Varvara Alekseyevna summon Stepanida to her side and address her rather awkwardly and artificially, calling her 'my dear', turned away and went back to the house. He had left so as to avoid seeing her, yet as he reached the house's top storey, not knowing why he did it, not even aware of doing it, he found himself going to a window. For as long as the peasant women remained below the porch, he stood at that window and looked and looked at her, feeding his eyes on her.

Before anyone could catch sight of him, he ran downstairs and quietly went out on to the balcony. There he lit a cigarette and, as if he merely had the intention of taking a walk, set off into the garden following the direction she had taken. He had hardly gone a couple of yards along the path when behind some trees he caught a glimpse of a cotton-velvet jacket against a pink skirt and a red kerchief. She was going off somewhere with another woman. Where could they be going?

Suddenly he was burned by a terrible lust that gripped hold of him like a hand. As if in obedience to some alien will, he looked round and went towards her.

'Yevgeny Ivanych, Yevgeny Ivanych! May I have a word with your honour?' came a voice from behind him. Yevgeny saw that it was the old man Samokhin, who was digging a well on his land. Turning quickly, he went back towards Samokhin. As he talked to him, he looked to one side and saw Stepanida and the other woman going down the hill, evidently to the well or at least with the well as a pretext. They stayed by the well for a short time, and then went back to the dancing.

XIII

When he had finished talking to Samokhin, Yevgeny returned to the house. He felt completely crushed, like someone who has committed a crime. It was perfectly obvious that she had read his mind, knew that he wanted to see her, and wanted it herself. What made it even worse was that the other woman – this Anna Prokhorova – clearly knew what was going on.

What he felt more than anything else was that he had been beaten, that he no longer had any will of his own, that he was being propelled along by some force that was extraneous to him. He felt that today he had only been saved by a lucky chance, and that if not today, then tomorrow, or the day after, he would be ruined.

'Yes, ruined.' There was no other way of putting it. 'To be unfaithful to one's young and loving wife with a peasant woman from the village, for everyone to see, is that not ruin, the most terrible ruin, after which life must cease to be possible? No, I must act, I must do something.

'Oh God! God! What can I do? Am I really to go to my ruin like this?' he said to himself. 'Is there really nothing I can do? There must be something. You mustn't think about her,' he ordered himself. 'You mustn't!' And immediately he began to think about her, saw her in front of him, in the shade of the maples.

He recalled once having read about a *starets*, a holy man, who when faced with the holy duty of laying his hand on a woman in order to cure her had, in order to ward off temptation, placed his other hand in a brazier and burned his fingers to ash. He reflected on this. 'Yes, I'd sooner burn my fingers to ash than be ruined.' And, taking a quick look round to make sure there was no one else in the room, he lit a match and put his finger in the flame. 'Right, now think about her,' he said to himself, ironically. He started to feel pain, withdrew his soot-blackened finger, threw the match away, and laughed at himself. 'What rot. This isn't what I ought to be doing. What I ought to be doing is making sure I never see her again – I ought either to go away myself or make arrangements for her to go away. Offer her husband money to move to town or to another village. People would find out, the word would get around. So what, anything would be better than this constant risk. Yes, that's what I must do,' he told himself, continuing to watch her from the window. 'Where's she going now?' he wondered, suddenly. He had a feeling she had seen him at the window. She was going off in the direction of the garden, arm in arm with some other woman, letting her free arm swing briskly as she went. Without knowing why or for what purpose, allowing his thoughts to take over, he went along to the estate office.

Vasily Nikolayevich, wearing his Sunday best, his hair sleeked with pomade, was sitting in the office having tea with his wife and a female visitor in a carpet shawl.

'I wonder if I might have a word with you for a moment, Vasily Nikolayevich?'

'Why, certainly, sir. Go right ahead. We've finished our tea.'

'No, I think it would be better if you came outside with me.'

'Just as you wish, sir. Wait till I get my cap. You can let the samovar go out now, Tanya,' said Vasily Nikolayevich gaily as he went outside.

Yevgeny thought Vasily Nikolayevich looked as though he had been drinking, but there wasn't anything to be done about that; anyway, it might even help matters – make Vasily Nikolayevich more sympathetic.

'It's the same thing I was telling you about last time,' said Yevgeny. 'It's that woman.'

'What? I told them on no account should they hire her.'

'No, it isn't that. You see, what I've been thinking, and what I wanted to ask your advice about, was whether it wouldn't be possible to have them move, have the whole family move?'

'Where would you have them move to?' asked Vasily, in a displeased, mocking tone of voice, Yevgeny thought.

'Well, I thought I might give them some money, or even a bit of land at Koltovskoye – anything, so long as she isn't here.'

'But how would you ever get them to move? It would mean him having to tear up his roots. And what's it to you? What harm has she ever done to you?'

'Oh, Vasily Nikolayevich, surely you must understand what a dreadful thing it would be for my wife if she were ever to find out about this.'

'But who's going to tell her?'

'And how can I go on living in this constant fear? Anyway, the whole business is just too awful for words.'

'I don't know what you're getting so worked up about, sir, truly I don't. You must allow bygones to be bygones. Let him that is without sin . . .'

'All the same, it would be better if they could be made to go away. Couldn't you have a word with her husband?'

'There'd be no point, sir. Dear me, Yevgeny Ivanovich, what's got into you? That's all over and done with now. It was just one of those things. Anyway, who is there that's going to say anything bad about you now? After all, you are in the public eye, you know.'

'Yes, but I want you to have a word with him, all the same.'

'Very well, sir, I'll talk to him.'

Even though he knew already that nothing was going to come of it, this conversation did have the effect of calming Yevgeny down a little. Above all, what it made him feel was that in his disturbed state of mind he had exaggerated the danger.

Had he really come out in order to meet her? No, of course he hadn't. He had simply taken a walk in the garden and she had happened to be there, too.

XIV

On the afternoon of that very same Whit Sunday, Liza went for a walk in the garden with Yevgeny. As she was crossing a little ditch on her way out of the garden into the meadow, where her husband wanted to take her in order to see the clover, she missed her step and fell down. Her fall was a gentle one, and she landed on her side; but she gave a moan, and in her features her husband could read an expression not only of fear, but of pain. He made as if to help her to her feet, but she pushed his hand away.

'No, wait a moment, Yevgeny,' she said, smiling weakly, and looking up at him rather guiltily, he thought. 'I went over on my foot, that's all.'

'It's what I'm forever telling her,' said Varvara Alekseyevna. 'How can she possibly expect to go jumping over ditches in her condition?'

'Oh Mother, it's nothing. I'll be on my feet in a second.'

With her husband's help she managed to get up, but the moment she did so she turned pale, and looked frightened.

'No, there's something wrong,' she said, and whispered in her mother's ear.

'Oh, merciful heavens, what have you done to yourself?' exclaimed Varvara Alekseyevna. 'I told you not to go out walking. Wait here, all of you – I'll call the servants. She mustn't try to walk. She'll have to be carried.'

'Liza, you won't be afraid if I carry you, will you?' said Yevgeny, putting his left arm around her. 'Put your arms round my neck. Like this.'

And, bending down, he took hold of her legs with his right arm and lifted her up. The expression of beatific martyrdom on her face remained in his memory for ever after.

'I'm quite heavy, you know, darling,' she said with a smile. 'Mother's running, do tell her!'

And she tilted her head towards him and gave him a kiss. She obviously wanted her mother to see him carrying her.

Yevgeny shouted to Varvara Alekseyevna not to hurry, he would carry Liza back to the house. Varvara Alekseyevna stopped running and began to shout in a voice even louder than his: 'You'll drop her, you're bound to drop her. Do you want to kill her? You've absolutely no conscience.'

'I'll manage perfectly.'

'I don't want to watch you murdering my daughter, I don't want to look and I can't look.' And off she ran, until she disappeared round the corner of the pathway.

'Don't worry, it'll pass,' said Liza with a smile.

'Just as long as there aren't any consequences like there were the other time.'

'No, I'm not talking about that. There's nothing wrong with me, it's Mother I'm talking about. You're tired, you ought to take a rest for a minute.'

But even though she was rather heavy, Yevgeny carried his burden all the way to the house with proud delight. He did not even give her up to the housemaid and the cook whom Varvara Alekseyevna had found and sent out to meet them, but carried her up to their bedroom and put her down on the bed.

'All right, you can go now,' she said and, pulling his hand towards her, kissed it. 'Annushka and I will manage.'

Marya Pavlovna also came running in from her annexe. Together the women undressed Liza and put her to bed. Yevgeny sat in the drawing-room with a book in his hand, waiting. Varvara Alekseyevna swept past him with an expression of such gloom and reproach on her face that he was gripped by a sudden fear.

'How is she?' he asked.

'How is she? I'm surprised you bother to ask. She's just the way I expect you wanted her to be when you made her leap over those dikes.'

'Varvara Alekseyevna!' he burst out. 'This is intolerable. If you want to torment people and make their lives a misery . . .' he was going to add, 'go somewhere else and do it,' but managed to restrain himself in time. Instead he said: 'Don't you feel sorry for us?'

'It's too late for feeling sorry now.'

And with a triumphant toss of her cap she went out through the doorway.

Liza's fall had really been quite a bad one. She had gone over on her foot in an awkward way, and there was a real danger that she might have a miscarriage. Everyone knew there was nothing to be done, that she would just have to lie quietly, yet all the same they decided to send for the doctor.

'Dear Nikolay Semyonovich,' Yevgeny wrote to the doctor. 'You have always been so kind to us in the past that I hope you will not refuse to come to the aid of my wife on this occasion.

A few days ago she . . .' and so it went on. When he had finished the letter, he went to the stables to see about the horses and the carriage. It was necessary to get ready one set of horses to bring the doctor, and another to take him home again. When a household is not run on a grand scale, such things cannot be arranged at once, but require careful thought. By the time he had sorted the matter out and dispatched the coachman on his way, it was nearly ten o'clock. When he got back to the house, he found his wife lying down as usual. She told him she felt fine and was not in any pain; but Varvara Alekseyevna was seated by a lamp that was shielded from Liza by a book of music, and was knitting a large red coverlet with a look on her face which plainly said that after what had happened there could be no reconciliation. 'Whatever anyone else may have done, I at least have performed my duty,' was what that look declared.

Yevgeny was aware of this, but in order to pretend he hadn't noticed anything, he tried to simulate a cheerful, light-hearted air, telling them how he had fitted out the horses, and how the mare Kavushka had made an excellent left-side trace-horse.

'Yes, of course, you couldn't have thought of a better time for breaking in wild horses, just at the very moment when you have to send for help. I dare say the doctor will end up in a ditch, too,' said Varvara Alekseyevna, casting a swift glance through her lorgnette at her knitting, bringing it right up under the lamp as she did so.

'But we had to send someone to get him. I did the best I could.'

'Yes, Yevgeny, I well remember how your horses went charging under that train with me.'

This was an old exaggeration of hers, and now Yevgeny was careless enough to protest that it had really not been like that at all.

'It just goes to prove what I'm always saying. I'm forever telling the Prince the same thing, that there's nothing more terrible than living with people who are untruthful and lacking in sincerity. Anything I can endure, but not that.'

'Well, if anyone's sorry about what's happened, it's me,' said Yevgeny.

'Yes, that's obvious.'

'What do you mean by that?'

'Oh, nothing, I'm counting my stitches.'

At that moment Yevgeny was standing beside the bed; Liza was looking at him. With one of her moist hands, which were resting on top of the coverlet, she caught his and pressed it. 'Put up with her for my sake. After all, she can't stop us loving each other,' her gaze said.

'I won't do it again. Really I won't,' he whispered, kissing first her long, moist hand, and then her lovely eyes, which closed as his lips brushed against them.

'It's not the same thing again, is it?' he asked.

'I'm frightened to say in case I'm wrong, but it feels as though it's alive and it's going to be all right,' she said, looking down at her abdomen.

'Oh, it's terrible, too terrible even to think of.'

Even though Liza insisted that he should go away, Yevgeny spent the night by her bedside, only occasionally allowing himself to nod off to sleep, and ready to attend to her at any moment. But she passed the night without incident, and might have got up next morning, had it not been for the fact that the doctor had been sent for.

The doctor arrived towards noon, and announced, predictably, that although a recurrence of the symptoms might give cause for concern, there were no positive indications that anything was wrong, but that as there were no counter-indications it was possible to suppose one thing, while from another point of view it was possible to suppose something else entirely. And so she must go on lying down, and although he did not like prescribing drugs, she must take this medicine none the less, and not get out of bed. The doctor also delivered a lecture to Varvara Alekseyevna on the subject of the female anatomy, in the course of which Varvara Alekseyevna nodded her head meaningfully. When he had taken his fee, slipping the money, as doctors do, into the rearmost part of his palm and securing it there with his thumb, the doctor left, and the patient was consigned to a week of lying on her back.

XV

Yevgeny spent the greater part of his time by his wife's bedside, attending to her needs, talking to her, reading to her and, most difficult of all, putting up with Varvara Alekseyevna's shows of hostility without a murmur, and even contriving to make light of them.

But he could not spend all his time at home. For one thing, his wife kept sending him away, declaring that he would fall ill if he stayed with her all the time, and, for another, the practical affairs of the estate were developing in such a way that his presence was required at every step. He could not stay at home; he had to be out in the fields, in the wood, in the garden, at the threshing barn – and wherever he went he was haunted not only by the thought of Stepanida, but also by her living image, to such an extent that only rarely was she absent from his mind. Not that that in itself was so significant; he might have been able to overcome that feeling. What made it so much worse was that while previously he had gone for months without seeing her, now he was constantly running into her, she was constantly before his eyes. She evidently understood that he wanted to renew his intimacy with her, and she contrived to cross his path whenever she was able to. Neither of them ever spoke to the other, and they made no arrangements to meet, but simply tried to be in the same place as often as possible.

This was most likely to happen in the woods where the women from the village went with sacks to cut grass for their cows. Yevgeny knew about this, and took a walk along the edge of the wood every day. Each day he would tell himself he was not going to go there, and each day he would end by going off to the wood; hearing the sound of voices, he would stand still behind a bush and peep out, his heart beating violently, to see if it was her.

Why he wanted to know if it was her, he was not sure. If it was her – so he imagined, at any rate – he would run away; but he did want to see her. On one occasion he did encounter her: as he was going into the wood, she emerged from it with two other women; she was carrying a heavy sack full of grass on her shoulders. A little earlier, and he might perhaps have come across her in the wood itself. Now, however, with the other two women looking on, it was out of the question for her to turn back and join him. But even though he knew it was out of the question, he stood behind a hazel bush for a long time, running the risk of attracting the other women's attention. Needless to say, she did not come back. But he continued to stand there for a long time. And, merciful heaven, how lovely did she appear to him in the picture his imagination painted for him! Not only once did she appear, but five, six times, and each time she seemed lovelier than the last. Never had she seemed so attractive to him. Not only that: never had she had such a complete hold over him.

He felt he was losing control of himself, was going insane, even. His severe attitude towards himself had not slackened by one iota. On the contrary, he was perfectly aware of the utter loathsomeness of his desires, and of his actions – for his going to the wood was an action. He knew that it would be enough for him to meet her unexpectedly in the dark, close to, and for him to touch her, and he would give himself up to his passions. He knew it was only shame – before others, before her and before himself – that was holding him back. And he knew that he was looking for circumstances in which that shame would not be noticeable – darkness, or the kind of physical contact in which shame is anaesthetized by animal passion. It was for that reason that he knew he was a loathsome criminal, and he despised and hated himself with all the strength of which his soul was capable. He hated himself because he still had not succumbed. Each day he prayed to God to give him strength, to save him from ruin, each day he resolved that from now on he would not take so much as one step in her direction, would never look at her again, would erase her from his memory. Each day he thought up new methods of delivering himself from his infatuation, and he put these methods into practice. But it was all to no avail.

One of the methods he used was to keep himself constantly occupied; another was fasting, combined with strenuous physical

labour; yet another was imagining to himself in vivid detail
the shame that would descend upon him when everyone – his
wife, his mother-in-law, the servants and farm-hands – got to
know about his affair. He would do all these things, and think
he was gaining the upper hand; but then a certain time of day
– noon, the time of their former rendezvous and the time he
had met her carrying the grass – would arrive, and he would
go into the wood.

Five agonizing days went by like this. He only glimpsed her
from a distance, and never once met her face to face.

XVI

Liza gradually recovered. Now she was up and about, but she
was perturbed by the change that seemed to have taken place
in her husband, which she did not understand.

Varvara Alekseyevna had gone away for a while, and now
the uncle was the only guest in the house. Marya Pavlovna was
there, as ever.

Yevgeny was still in the same state of semi-insanity when, as
often happens after thunderstorms in June, there were two
successive days of pouring rain. The rain made it impossible for
anyone to work. They even had to give up carting the manure
because of the mud and damp. Everyone stayed at home. The
herdsmen had a terrible time rounding up the cattle, but finally
managed to drive them back to the houses. Cows and sheep
strayed on to the common pasture and went scampering about
all over the grounds. The peasant women, barefoot and in
shawls, ran splashing through the mud in search of cows that had
got loose. The roads became rivers, the leaves and grass were
saturated in water, and steady rivulets flowed from the roof-
gutters into bubbling pools. Yevgeny stayed at home with his
wife, who was being particularly trying that day. Several times
now she had asked him why he was so unhappy, and on each
occasion he had irritably replied that nothing was the matter.
Now she had stopped asking, though she was obviously annoyed.

After lunch they sat in the drawing-room. For the hundredth time, Yevgeny's uncle was telling invented stories about his acquaintances in high society. Liza was knitting a bed-jacket and sighing, complaining about the weather and the pains in the small of her back. Yevgeny's uncle advised her to lie down, and told the servant to bring him some vodka. Yevgeny was horribly bored. Everything was so insipid, so tedious. He smoked cigarettes and tried to read a book, but took in nothing of what he read.

'Well, I'll have to be getting along now. I must take a look at the new beet grater; it was only delivered yesterday,' he said. He got up and went out.

'See you take an umbrella with you.'

'Oh no, I've got my leather coat. Anyway, I'm only going as far as the refinery.'

He put on his boots and leather coat and set off in the direction of the sugar factory; but he had hardly gone twenty paces when he suddenly caught sight of her coming towards him, her skirt tucked up high above her white calves. As she walked along she held down with both hands the shawl in which her head and shoulders were swathed.

'What are you doing?' he asked, not recognizing her at first sight. By the time he had recognized her, it was too late. She stopped and looked at him slowly, smiling.

'I'm looking for a calf. Where are you off to in this weather?' she said, as if she were used to seeing him every day.

'Come to the hut,' he said suddenly, hardly aware of doing so. It was as if someone else had uttered the words from inside him.

She bit her shawl, flashed him a look of assent, and ran off in the direction she had been following when he had met her – into the garden, towards the hut. Meanwhile he continued on his way, intending to turn back under cover of the lilacs and go to the hut as well.

'Master,' he heard a voice behind him say. 'The mistress is asking for you, sir, she wants you to go in and see her for a moment.' It was Misha, their servant.

'My God, that's the second time I've been saved like this,'

thought Yevgeny, and he went back to the house immediately. His wife wanted to remind him that he had promised to deliver later that day some medicine to a woman who was ill, and to ask him to take it with him now.

It was some five minutes before the medicine was ready. When he emerged from the house with it, he decided not to go to the hut, in case someone saw him from a window. As soon as he was out of sight, however, he turned back and went to the hut after all. He could already see her in his imagination, halfway inside the hut, smiling and laughing; but she wasn't there, and there was nothing in the hut to say that she had been there. He was already beginning to suspect she was not going to turn up, had not heard or had misunderstood the words he had spoken to her. He had muttered them under his breath, as if he had been afraid she might hear them. Perhaps she had not wanted to come? And anyway, where had he got the idea that she would just fling herself at him? She had a husband. It was only he, Yevgeny, who was such a low individual. He had a wife, and a good one, too, yet here he was running after the wife of someone else. Such were his thoughts as he sat down in the hut, the thatched roof of which leaked in one place, letting in a steady drip of water. 'How good it would be if she did come, though. Alone here in the rain, just the two of us. If only I could have her again, just once, and then let things turn out as they may. Yes, of course,' he reflected, 'if she's been here I'll be able to tell by her footprints.' He examined the area of trodden ground that led up to the hut and the path where it was overgrown with grass, and found the fresh imprints of a bare foot that had slithered on the mud. 'Yes, she's been here all right. But I'm fed up with this. Wherever I see her now, I'll go to her. It's as simple as that. I'll even go to her at night.' For a long time he remained sitting in the hut. When he emerged from it, he felt exhausted and depressed. He delivered the medicine, and then went home and lay down in his room to wait for dinner.

XVII

Before dinner was served, Liza came to see him in his room. Still trying to fathom why he seemed so unhappy, she began to tell him that she had been afraid he would disapprove of her being taken to Moscow to have her baby, and that she had decided to remain at Semyonovskoye. There was nothing that would induce her to go to Moscow. He knew that it was really the birth she was afraid of, and the risk that she might have a deformed or sickly child, and he could not help being touched when he saw how ready she was to make this sacrifice because of her love for him. Everything in the house was so pleasant, so cheerful, so clean; everything in his soul was so dirty, loathsome and foul. All evening Yevgeny was tormented by the knowledge that, in spite of the outright disgust he felt at his weakness, in spite of his firm intention of breaking off all relations with Stepanida, everything would be the same again tomorrow.

'No, this is impossible,' he told himself, as he paced up and down his room. 'Surely there must be something I can do? Oh God, what can I do?'

Someone knocked at the door, in the foreign manner. He knew this would be his uncle.

'Come in,' he said.

His uncle had come to see him of his own accord, as a kind of emissary from Liza. 'You know, I really have noticed a change in you recently, old chap,' he said, 'and I can understand how worrying Liza must find it. I'd advise the two of you to go and take a vacation somewhere. I can see it will be hard for you to leave all the fine work you've started here, but what can you do, *que veux-tu*? It'll be better for both of you. My advice to you both would be to go to the Crimea. The climate there's better than any obstetrician, and you'll arrive right in the middle of the grape season.'

'Uncle,' said Yevgeny, suddenly, 'can you keep a secret – a terrible, shameful secret?'

'My dear boy, surely you trust me?'

'Uncle, you've got to help me. Not only help me, but save

me,' said Yevgeny. And the thought that now he was going to
reveal his secret to his uncle, whom he did not respect, that he
was going to show himself to his uncle in a most disadvantageous light and degrade himself before him, this thought was
pleasing to him. He felt loathsome and guilty, and he wanted
to punish himself.

'Go right ahead and tell me all about it, dear boy. You know
how fond of you I am,' said his uncle, obviously tickled that
there was a secret, that it was a shameful secret, that he was
about to be told it and that his services were required.

'First of all I must tell you that I'm a loathsome individual, a
good-for-nothing, a real cad.'

'I say, what's got into you?' said his uncle, puffing himself
up angrily.

'How can I possibly be anything but a cad when what I want,
I, Liza's husband – you know how pure she is, how much she
loves me – when what I, her husband, want is to be unfaithful
to her with a peasant woman?'

'What do you mean, want? Are you saying you haven't been
unfaithful to her?'

'Yes, but it's the same as if I had, because the matter wasn't
under my control. I was ready to do it. Something happened
to stop me, but if it hadn't, by now I'd have . . . I'd have . . .
I don't know what I'd have done.'

'I'm afraid you'll have to explain it to me.'

'Look, it's like this: I was once stupid enough to get physically
involved with a woman here, one of the women in the village.
What I'm saying is that I used to meet her out in the woods, in
the fields . . .'

'And was she pretty?' asked his uncle.

This question made Yevgeny frown, but so desperate was he
for some outside support that he pretended not to have heard,
and continued: 'Well, I didn't think anything of it at the time,
I thought I'd break it off eventually, and then it would all be
over. And I did break it off before I got married, and I didn't
see her or think about her for nearly a year.' Yevgeny had a
strange feeling as he heard himself giving this description of his
situation. 'And then suddenly, I don't know how it happened

– you know, sometimes I really do believe in witchcraft – I saw her, and a worm crept into my heart – and it's gnawing me away. I curse myself, and I'm conscious of the utter hideousness of that act, that act I may commit at any moment, and yet I go looking for an opportunity to commit it, and if I haven't committed it yet it's only because God has saved me. I was on my way to see her yesterday when Liza called me to the house.'

'What, out in the rain?'

'Yes. Uncle, I've had all I can take, and I've decided to confide in you and ask you to help me.'

'Well, of course, you know, it's not a good idea on your own estate. People will get to hear of it. I realize Liza isn't strong, of course, and that you have to go easy on her. But why on your own estate?'

Once again Yevgeny tried to ignore what his uncle was saying, and proceeded instead to the heart of the matter.

'Please save me from myself. That's what I'm asking you to do. Today it was chance that prevented me; but tomorrow, or another time, it may not prevent me. And she knows about it now. Please don't leave me all on my own.'

'Yes, very well, then,' said his uncle. 'But are you sure you're really so in love with her?'

'Oh, it's nothing like that. It's a kind of force that's taken hold of me and won't let me go. I don't know what to do. Perhaps I'll recover my strength, and then . . .'

'Well, what about my suggestion?' asked his uncle. 'Why don't we go to the Crimea?'

'Yes, yes, let's go – and in the meantime I'll stay with you, talk with you.'

XVIII

Confiding his secret to his uncle, in particular the agonies of guilt and shame he had experienced after that rainy day, had a sobering effect on Yevgeny. A trip to Yalta was arranged, and the date of their departure fixed for a week hence. During that week Yevgeny visited town in order to draw the money for the trip, and made the necessary practical arrangements for the running of the house and the estate office while they were away; he became noticeably more cheerful, was on friendly terms with his wife again, and his mental state began to improve.

So it was that, without once having seen Stepanida since that rainy day, he set off with his wife for the Crimea. There they spent two wonderful months. There were so many new impressions that it seemed to Yevgeny as though all that had gone before had been completely wiped from his memory. In the Crimea they met some old friends with whom they got along extremely well; they made some new friends, too. For Yevgeny, this time in the Crimea was a perpetual holiday; what was more, it was instructive and useful for him. While they were there they became friendly with the ex-marshal of their province, an intelligent man of liberal views who conceived a liking for Yevgeny, took him in hand and won him over to his side. At the end of August, Liza gave birth to a fine, healthy baby girl; the birth passed off with surprising ease.

In September the Irtenevs went home with two additions to their ménage – the baby and a nurse, since Liza could not breast-feed the baby herself. Completely free now of his former black mood, Yevgeny returned home a new and happy man. Having gone through everything a man usually goes through when his wife is having a baby, he loved her even more. The feeling he had for his new daughter, when he took her into his arms, was an amusing, novel, pleasant one, the sort of sensation one has on being tickled. Another novel aspect of his life was that now his mind was occupied not only with the running of the estate, but also, thanks to his recent contact with Dumchin (the ex-marshal), with a new-found interest in the affairs of the local zemstvo, an interest that stemmed partly from personal vanity and partly from a sense of duty. In October there was to be an extraordinary session of the zemstvo at which he was to be a candidate for election as a member. When he got home he made one visit to town, and another to see Dumchin.

The tortures of his former allurement and his struggle with it had slipped from his mind; now he could only recall them with difficulty. They seemed to him like some fit of temporary insanity he had undergone.

So free of all that did he feel now that, on the first occasion he was alone with the estate manager, he was not afraid to ask about her.

'How's Sidor Pchelnikov getting along these days – still living away from home?' he asked.

'Yes, sir, still living in town.'

'And what about his wife?'

'Some wife, if you ask me, sir. Gallivanting around with Zinovy now, she is. Gone right off the rails.'

'Well that's fine,' thought Yevgeny. 'I really feel extraordinarily indifferent. How I've changed!'

XIX

Everything had worked out as Yevgeny had wanted it to. He had managed to retain the estate, the sugar factory was in operation, the beet crop had given an excellent yield and they could expect to make a large profit from it; his wife had had her baby without mishap, his mother-in-law had gone, and he had been elected to the zemstvo by a unanimous vote of all the members.

Yevgeny was returning home from the town after his election. People had congratulated him, and he had thanked them. Afterwards there had been a dinner at which he had drunk about five glasses of champagne. Entirely new plans as to the way his future life would develop had risen before him. During the drive home, he thought about these. They were having an Indian summer that year. The road surface was excellent, the sun was shining brightly. As his carriage approached the house, Yevgeny reflected that as a consequence of his election he would now be able to serve the people of the village in the way he had always dreamed of doing, not merely by providing work for them but by exercising a direct influence on them. He wondered what his peasants, and the others, would be saying about him three years from now. 'That man, for example,' he thought, as he drove through the village and in front of the carriage saw a muzhik carrying a full tub of water across the road, helped by a peasant woman. They halted to let the carriage go past. The muzhik was the old man Pchelnikov, and the woman was Stepanida. Yevgeny glanced at her, recognized her, and found to his satisfaction that he was able to remain quite calm. She was as pretty as ever, but that had no effect on him now. As he arrived at the house, his wife came out to meet him on the porch. It was a beautiful evening.

'Well, can I congratulate you?'

'Yes, I was elected.'

'Why, that's marvellous. We'll drink to it!'

Next morning Yevgeny went for a ride around the estate, which he had been neglecting. A new threshing-machine was being tried out at one of the farms. As he watched it at work, Yevgeny strolled among the peasant women. He tried not to pay any attention to them, yet no matter how hard he tried, he could not help once or twice catching sight of Stepanida's black eyes and red kerchief. She was carrying the chaff away. Once or twice he took a surreptitious glance at her, and felt that something was taking place inside him again, though he wasn't sure what it was. It was only the day after, when he took another ride over to the farm to watch the threshing, and spent two hours there, quite unnecessarily, unable to take his eyes off the young woman's familiar, appealing figure, that he suddenly knew he was lost, utterly and irrevocably lost. Once again he experienced those torments, that fear and horror. And there was no way out.

It happened to him, the very thing he had been dreading. The following evening he somehow found himself outside her back yard, opposite the hay barn where they had once made love the previous autumn. As if he were merely out taking a stroll, he stopped there and lit a cigarette. A woman who lived in one of the neighbouring cottages saw him, and as he started to turn back he heard her say to someone: 'Go on, he's waiting for you. Cross my heart, it's him. Go on, you silly idiot!'

He saw a woman – it was her – run towards the barn, but it was too late for him to retrace his steps now, as a muzhik was coming, and he went home.

XX

When he entered the drawing-room, everything somehow seemed wrong and not as it should be. That morning, when he had got out of bed, he had still been in a cheerful frame of mind; he had formed a resolve to cast the whole matter aside, to forget about it and forbid himself to think about it. But somehow, without even really being aware of it, all that morning he found that not only could he not arouse any interest in his work, he was even trying to avoid it. Everything that had previously been important to him and had brought him such satisfaction now seemed utterly insignificant. Unconsciously he found himself trying to get out of attending to the business of the estate. He felt he must get away from it in order to be able to review the situation and think things over. And get away from it he did, and kept himself to himself. As soon as he was alone, however, he began to make forays into the garden or the wood. Each place he visited bore the taint of memories, memories that obsessed him. He told himself he was just taking a walk in the garden and thinking things over, whereas in actual fact he wasn't thinking anything over at all, but simply waiting for her, waiting quite irrationally in the hope that by some miracle she would realize that he desired her and would come either here to the garden or over there to the wood where no one would see anything or better still to either place, but under cover of night, when there was no moon, and no one, not even she herself, would be able to see anything – that was the time she would come to him, the time when he would touch her body . . .

'Yes, I thought I could break it off when I wanted to,' he said to himself. 'I thought I could make love with a clean, healthy woman for the sake of my health! No, it's obvious I can't play around with her like that. I thought I'd taken her, but it's she who has taken me, she's taken me and she won't let me go. I thought I was free, but I wasn't free at all. I was deceiving myself when I got married. All that was mere nonsense and deception. From the first time I made love with her, I experienced a new feeling, the true feeling of a husband. Yes, it was her I should have lived with.

'There are two lives open to me: one is the life I've begun with Liza, involving my work at the zemstvo, the running of the estate, our child, the respect of other people. If that's the life I'm to lead, there's no room for Stepanida. She'll have to be induced to move, as I was talking of doing, or else done away with, so she doesn't exist any more. The other life is right here: I'd have to take her away from her husband, give him money, close my eyes to the shame and disgrace, and live with her. But then there would be no place for Liza and Mimi, our child. No, that's not right, Mimi wouldn't be any problem, but there'd be no room for Liza, she'd have to go away. She'd have to find out about it, curse me and go away. She'd have to find out that I'd exchanged her for a peasant woman, that I'm a trickster and a cheat. No, it's too dreadful to contemplate! It's out of the question. But what if,' he continued to reflect, 'what if Liza were to fall ill and die? If she were to die, everything would be perfect!

'Perfect? You miserable worm! No, if anyone's got to die, it had better be the other one. If only Stepanida were to die, how wonderful everything would be.

'Yes, that's how it's done, that's how a man poisons or shoots his wife or his mistress. He just takes a revolver, tells her to come to him and then, instead of embracing her, he fires a bullet into her breast. And that's that.

'After all, she's a devil. Just that – a devil. She's taken possession of me against my will. Shall I kill her? Yes. There are only two ways out: either I kill Liza or I kill her. Because I can't go on living like this.* I can't. I must think things over and look to the future. If I leave everything as it is, who knows what may happen?

* The alternative ending begins here (see Appendix 2).

'What will happen will be that I'll start telling myself I'm going to give her up, but it'll just be words, and by the time it's evening I'll be standing in her back yard again, and she'll see me and come out. And either the servants will find out and tell my wife, or I'll tell her myself, because I can't go on lying, I can't go on living like that. I can't. I'll be found out. They'll all get to know about it – Parasha, the blacksmith, all of them. Well, honestly, how can I live like that?

'I can't. There are only two ways out: either I kill Liza or I kill her. Or . . .

'Ah, yes, there's a third way: I can kill myself,' he said aloud, softly, and a sudden shiver ran over his flesh. 'Yes, if I kill myself, I won't have to kill either of them.' He grew afraid, because he knew that this was in fact the only possible way out. 'I've got a revolver. Am I really going to kill myself? I'd never have thought of that before. How strange it will be.'

He returned to his study and without further ado opened the cupboard where he kept his revolver. No sooner had he opened it, however, than his wife came in.

XXI

He threw a newspaper over the revolver.

'Again,' she said, giving him a frightened look.

'What do you mean, "again"?' he asked.

'You've got the same look on your face again, the one you had before, that time when you wouldn't tell me what was wrong. Zhenya darling, tell me what's wrong. I can see you're dreadfully worried about something. Tell me what it is, then you'll feel better. Whatever it is, tell me – anything's better than seeing you suffer like this. Anyway, I know it's nothing so very terrible.'

'You know? I'll tell you what it is presently.'

'Tell me, tell me. You're not going to get away without telling me.'

He smiled at her pathetically.

'Tell you? No, I can't do that. Anyway, there isn't really anything to tell.'

He might very well have gone ahead and told her, had not the nurse come in just then to ask if it was all right for her to take the baby out in the pram now. Liza went off to get the baby dressed.

'All right, so you'll tell me, then? I'll be back in a moment.'

'Yes, perhaps . . .'

She never forgot the look of suffering he gave her as he said this. She went out.

Quickly, furtively, like a burglar, he whipped the revolver out of its case. 'It's loaded, but that was ages ago, and one of the cartridges is missing. Well, so be it.'

He put the muzzle to his temple, and then hesitated. Almost immediately, however, he remembered Stepanida, his decision not to see her any more, his struggle, temptation, fall and resumed struggle. He shuddered with horror. 'No, it's better this way.' And he pulled the trigger.

When Liza came running into the room – she had only just left the balcony – she found him lying on the floor, face down. Warm, dark blood was spurting from the wound, and his body was still twitching.

There was an inquest. No one was able to understand or explain the causes of Yevgeny's suicide. It never even entered his uncle's mind that it might be in some way linked with the confession his nephew had made to him two months previously.

Varvara Alekseyevna claimed to have seen this coming all along. She said she had observed it in his eyes on all those occasions when he had argued with her. Neither Liza nor Marya Pavlovna had the slightest notion as to why it should have happened; on the other hand, neither of them believed what the doctors said, that he had been mentally ill. On no account could they agree with this diagnosis, as they knew he had been more sensible and level-headed than hundreds of people of their acquaintance.

And indeed, if Yevgeny was mentally ill, then everyone is mentally ill, and most of all those who see in others symptoms of the madness they fail to see in themselves.

FATHER SERGIUS

Tolstoy began writing 'Father Sergius' in 1890–91 and finished it some ten years later. It was first published after Tolstoy's death, in volume 2 of his *Posthumous Literary Works* (Moscow, 1911). The translation is from the text in L. N. Tolstoy, *Sobranie sochinenii v duadtsati tomakh*, vol. 12 (Moscow, 1964).

I

In the 1840s there took place in St Petersburg an event which caused general surprise: a handsome prince, commander of the sovereign's squadron of a regiment of cuirassiers, whom everyone expected to become an *aide-de-camp* and have a brilliant career at the court of Nicholas I, a month before his marriage to a beautiful lady-in-waiting who enjoyed the special favour of the empress, suddenly resigned his commission, broke with his fiancée, made over his modest estate to his sister, and retired to a monastery with the intention of becoming a monk. To those who knew nothing of the circumstances the whole thing was odd and unaccountable, but for Prince Stepan Kasatsky himself it was all so natural that he could not conceive of any other possible course of action.

Stepan Kasatsky's father, a retired guards colonel, had died when his son was twelve. Much as the boy's mother regretted sending him away, she felt obliged to carry out the wishes of her late husband, whose instructions were that in the event of his death his son should not be kept at home but sent to the cadet school.[1] So she entered him at the school and with her daughter Varvara moved to St Petersburg in order to be near her son and to take him out at holidays.

The boy was remarkable for his brilliant ability and colossal ambition, qualities which took him to the top of his class both in his school work (particularly in mathematics, on which he was especially keen) and in drill and horse-riding. Although more than usually tall, he was lithe and handsome. In conduct, too, he would have been a model cadet, had it not been for his quick temper. He did not drink or go in for debauchery; he was remarkably upright in character. All that prevented him from being a paragon was that he was given to outbursts of anger in which he lost all control of himself and became like a wild animal. On one occasion he practically threw another cadet out of a window for poking fun at his collection of minerals. Another time he almost came to grief: he threw a dishful of cutlets at the catering officer, attacked him and, it was said, struck him because he had gone back on his word and told a barefaced lie. He would certainly have been reduced to the ranks had it not been for the head of the cadet school who dismissed the catering officer and hushed the matter up.

When he was eighteen Kasatsky passed out as an officer and joined an aristocratic guards regiment. The Emperor Nicholas had known him when he was still a cadet and continued to take notice of him now that he had joined his regiment, so it was predicted that he would become an imperial *aide-de-camp*. And this was Kasatsky's own earnest desire, not just because he was ambitious, but also – and chiefly – because ever since his days as a cadet he had passionately – literally passionately – loved the emperor. Every time that Nicholas visited the cadet school (which he did often), as soon as his tall, military-coated figure with swelling chest, aquiline nose, moustache and trimmed side-whiskers strode in and boomed a greeting to the cadets, Kasatsky felt the rapture of a lover, the same feeling he experienced later on meeting the woman he loved. Only his rapturous affection for Nicholas was stronger. He wanted to demonstrate the utterness of his devotion, to sacrifice something, his whole self, for him. And Nicholas was aware that he aroused this ecstasy and purposely evoked it. He played with the cadets, gathered them round him, and varied his treatment of them, being one moment boyishly simple, then friendly, then solemnly majestic. After the recent episode involving Kasatsky and the officer Nicholas said nothing to him, but when Kasatsky came near he theatrically rebuffed him, frowned and wagged his finger. Then, as he was going, he said:

'Understand that I am aware of everything. Certain things, however, I do not wish to know. But they are here!'

He pointed to his heart.

When the cadets appeared before Nicholas on passing out, he made no further mention of this, but said, as always, that each of them could approach him directly, that they should loyally serve him and their fatherland, and that he would always be their best friend. They were all, as always, moved by this, and Kasatsky, recalling the past, shed tears and swore to serve his beloved tsar with all his strength.

When Kasatsky joined his regiment, his mother and sister moved first to Moscow and then to the country. Kasatsky gave half his property to his sister, keeping for himself only sufficient to pay his way in the smart regiment in which he served.

Outwardly Kasatsky appeared to be a perfectly ordinary brilliant young guards officer making his career, but within him there was an intense and complex process at work. Ever since childhood he had had this impulse; it had taken various apparent forms, but basically it was always the same – the urge to attain perfection and success in everything that it fell to him to do and thus attract the praise and wonder of other people. If it was a matter of study and learning he buckled down and worked until he was lauded and held up as an example to others. Once one object was attained, he took on something new. So it was that he made himself top in his class; so it was that, when still a cadet, having noticed on some occasion how awkwardly he expressed himself in French he taught himself to speak it as perfectly as he did Russian; so it was that later, when he took up chess, he became an excellent player, though still only a cadet.

Apart from his general vocation in life, which was to serve the tsar and his country, he always had some set purpose to which, however insignificant it was, he would devote himself wholeheartedly and live only for the moment of its achievement. But no sooner had one aim been achieved than another immediately took shape in his mind and supplanted the one before. This urge to excel, and to achieve the aims he set himself in order to excel, dominated his whole life. So when he was

commissioned he made it his object to achieve a complete
mastery of his duties and soon became an exemplary officer,
though he still suffered from the same uncontrollable temper
which in his service life too caused him to do things which were
bad in themselves and prejudicial to his career. Once, later,
when conversing on some social occasion, he had been conscious of his lack of general education, so he determined to
make good this deficiency, got down to his books and achieved
what he intended. He decided then to win for himself a brilliant
place in high society, became an excellent dancer, and was soon
invited to all the society balls and to certain receptions as well.
But this did not satisfy him. He was used to being first, and in
the social world he was far from that.

High society at that time consisted (as, indeed, I think it
consists at all times and in all places) of four kinds of people:
(1) the wealthy who attend court; (2) the not wealthy who
nonetheless have been born and brought up in court circles; (3)
the wealthy who fawn on those at court; and (4) the not
wealthy, unconnected with the court, who fawn on those in the
first and second categories. Kasatsky did not belong to the first
group, though he was readily received in the last two circles.
On his very first entry into the social world Kasatsky set his
sights on forming a liaison with some society lady and, contrary
to his expectations, it was not long before he succeeded. But he
very quickly saw that the circles in which he moved were the
lower circles of society and that there were circles above these
and that, though he was received in these higher court circles,
he did not belong there. People were polite, but everything in
their manner made it clear that he was not one of their set. And
this Kasatsky wished to be. But for this it was necessary to be
an *aide-de-camp* (which he had hopes of becoming) or to marry
into the circle. And that is what he decided to do. The girl he
selected was beautiful and one of the court circle; she was not
only part of that society which he wished to enter, but someone
whose acquaintance was actually sought after by all the highest
and most established members of this higher circle. She was
the Countess Korotkova. It was not merely on account of his
career that Kasatsky began courting her: she was extraordi-

narily attractive and he was soon in love with her. At first she
was distinctly chilly towards him, but then everything suddenly
changed. She began to show signs of affection and her mother
became particularly pressing with invitations.

Kasatsky proposed and was accepted. He was surprised how
easily he had won such happiness; he was surprised, too, by
something peculiar and odd in the behaviour of both mother
and daughter towards him. He was deeply in love and blinded
by his feelings and so was unaware of what practically everyone
else in the city knew: that the year before his fiancée had been
Nicholas's mistress.

II

Two weeks before the day fixed for their wedding Kasatsky
was sitting at his fiancée's summer villa at Tsarskoe Selo. It was
a hot day in May. The engaged couple had been walking in the
garden and now sat on a bench in the shade of a lime avenue.
Mary was looking more than usually pretty in a white muslin
dress and seemed a picture of innocence and love. She sat with
lowered head, looking up now and then at the great handsome
man who was talking to her with particular tenderness and
caution, fearing that his every word and gesture might injure
or defile the angelic purity of his betrothed. Kasatsky was
one of those men of the forties – not met with today – who,
while consciously allowing themselves to be unchaste in sexual
matters and inwardly seeing nothing wrong in it, nonetheless
expected their wives to possess an ideal celestial purity; they
assumed this quality to exist in all the girls of their society and
behaved towards them accordingly. There was much that was
false in this attitude and much that was harmful in the dissol-
ution indulged in by the men, but as far as the women were
concerned this attitude – so different from that of young people
today who see in every girl a female looking for a mate – was,
I think, beneficial. Seeing themselves worshipped, girls actually
tried to be more or less like goddesses. This attitude towards

women was shared by Kasatsky, and it was thus that he
regarded his bride-to-be. He was especially in love that day; he
felt no sensual attraction towards her, but regarded her rather
with tender awe as something unattainable.

He rose to his full height and stood before her with his hands
resting on his sabre.

'It is only now that I have discovered how happy a man can
be. And it is you, you – my dear,' he said with a bashful smile,
'that I have to thank for this.'

He was still at the stage of being unused to addressing her
affectionately,[2] and to him, conscious of his moral inferiority
to this angel, it seemed terrible that he should do so.

'I have come to know myself through you, ... dear, and
I have found that I am better than I thought.'

'I have known it long since. That is the reason why I love
you.'

A nightingale trilled nearby; a sudden breeze rustled the
young leaves.

He took her hand and kissed it. Tears came into his eyes. She
understood that he was thanking her for saying that she loved
him. He walked a little in silence, then came and sat down.

'You know, my dear, at first I had an ulterior motive in
getting to know you. I wanted to form connections in society.
But then, when I came to know you, how trivial that was in
comparison with you! This does not make you angry?'

She made no answer, but merely touched his hand with hers.
He understood its meaning: 'No, I am not angry.'

'You said just now . . .' he broke off, feeling it was too much
of a liberty. 'You said that you love me, but – forgive me – I
believe there is something else, too, which troubles you and
stands in your way. What is it?'

It's now or never, she thought. He is bound to find out
anyway. And he will not cry off now. Oh, but how terrible if
he did!

She looked lovingly at his large, noble, powerful figure. She
loved him more than Nicholas now and, but for Nicholas being
emperor, she would not have preferred him to Kasatsky.

'Listen. I cannot be untruthful and must tell you everything.

You ask me what is the matter. It is that I have loved someone before.'

She pleadingly put her hand on his. He did not speak.

'You want to know who it was? It was him, the emperor.'

'But we all love him. When you were at school, I suppose . . .'

'No, it was after. It was an infatuation, then I got over it. But I must tell you . . .'

'Well, what?'

'That there was more to it.'

She covered her face with her hands.

'What? You gave yourself to him?'

She said nothing.

'You were his mistress?'

She said nothing.

He leapt to his feet and stood before her pale as death, his face quivering. He remembered now the kindly greeting Nicholas had given him when he met him on the Nevsky.[3]

'My God! What have I done, Steve?'

'Don't touch me, don't touch me! Oh, how insufferable!'

He turned and went to the house. There he met her mother.

'What is it, Prince? I . . .' Seeing his face, she stopped. Suddenly he flushed with rage.

'You knew about this and were going to use me as a cover. If you were not both women . . .' he cried, raising his enormous fist over her – then he turned and fled.

If the man who had been his fiancée's lover had been a private citizen he would have killed him. But it was his adored tsar.

The next day he took leave from his duties and resigned his commission. To avoid seeing anyone he said that he was ill, and went to the country.

He spent the summer on his estate putting his affairs in order. At the end of the summer he did not return to St Petersburg, but went to the monastery which he entered as a monk.

His mother wrote trying to dissuade him from such a decisive step. He replied that the call of God was more important than any other consideration, and that he felt this call. Only his sister, who was as proud and ambitious as her brother, understood him.

She understood that he had become a monk in order to be superior to those who wanted to demonstrate their superiority over him. And she understood him correctly. By becoming a monk he was showing his scorn for all those things which seemed so important to others and which had seemed so important to him when he was an officer; he was placing himself on a new eminence from which he could look down on the people he had previously envied. But he was swayed not by this feeling alone, as his sister thought. Within him there was another, truly religious feeling of which she knew nothing, a feeling which, mingled with his pride and desire for supremacy, now governed him. His disillusionment with Mary (his fiancée), whom he had supposed so angelic, and his sense of injury were so strong that he was brought to despair, and despair brought him – to what? To God and to the faith of his childhood which had remained intact within him.

III

On the Feast of the Intercession[4] Kasatsky entered the monastery.

The abbot was of gentle birth, he wrote scholarly works and was *starets* – that is he belonged to that succession of monks which stemmed from Wallachia, monks who submit without murmur to a chosen preceptor. The abbot was a pupil of the famous *starets* Amvrosii, who had been the pupil of *starets* Makary, the pupil of Paisy Velichkovsky.[5] And to the abbot Kasatsky subjected himself as pupil.

In the monastery, enjoying the sense of his own superiority, Kasatsky took the same pleasure as elsewhere in attaining the highest perfection in both inward and outward things. Just as in his regiment he had been not merely an impeccable officer but one who did more than was necessary and set new standards of perfection, so too as a monk he strove to be perfect: constantly working, abstemious, meek, gentle, pure in thought as in deed, and obedient. This last quality (or attainment) in

particular made life easier for him. Many of the demands made
on him by living in a much visited monastery close to the capital
he disliked and found corrupting, but all such feelings were
dispelled by the obedient fulfilment of his duties. It was not his
business to think, but to carry out his appointed task, which
might be to keep vigil over the relics, to sing in the choir or
to keep the accounts of the hospice. All possibility of doubt
on any conceivable matter was removed by this obedience to
his *starets*. It was only obedience that stopped him feeling
oppressed by the length and monotony of the church services,
by the triviality of the visitors, and by the negative features of
the brethren; but all these things he not only joyfully endured,
but found in them a source of consolation and support. 'I do
not see the point of hearing the same prayers several times a
day, but I know that it has to be done, and knowing that it has
to be done I take pleasure in the prayers.' The *starets* told him
that just as one needs material food to sustain life, so, too, one
needs spiritual food – praying in church – to sustain the life of
the spirit. Kasatsky believed this, and indeed the church services
for which he sometimes found it hard to get up in the morning
undoubtedly brought him comfort and happiness. He was made
happy by the consciousness of his own humility and of the
absolute rightness of his actions, all of which were determined
by the *starets*. His concern in life was not only to work for the
fuller subjugation of his own will and for greater humility; he
wished also to attain all the Christian virtues which seemed to
him at first so easy to attain. He gave all his property to the
monastery and felt no regret. Sloth was unknown to him.
Demeaning himself before lesser men was not only easy for
him, but even a source of joy. He even found it easy to overcome
the sin of lust – both gluttony and concupiscence. The *starets*
warned him particularly against this sin, and Kasatsky rejoiced
in the knowledge that he was free from it.

Only the memory of his fiancée tormented him. It was not
just the memory, it was also the vivid picture he had of what
might have been. He kept thinking of one of the emperor's
favourites whom he knew. She had subsequently married
and become a fine wife and mother; her husband occupied an

important position, had power, honour, and a good wife who repented of her past.

In his better moments Kasatsky was not troubled by these thoughts. At such times his recollections simply made him glad that he was freed from these temptations. But there were other times when that by which he now lived suddenly faded, and though he never ceased to believe in that by which he lived, he lost sight of it, was unable to summon it up within him, and he was overwhelmed by his memories and – a terrible thing – by remorse for his conversion.

His only salvation in this situation was obedience – work and the whole day occupied in prayer. He said his prayers and performed his devotions as usual; he prayed even more than usual, but he prayed in body alone and his spirit was not in it. This state would last for a day, sometimes two, and then pass of itself. But these one or two days were terrible. Kasatsky felt he was in the power not of himself or of God but of some other being. And all that he could do – and did – at such times was to follow the counsel of his *starets*: hold on, attempt nothing for the present, and wait. In general, the whole of this time Kasatsky lived not by his own will, but by the will of his *starets*, and he felt a curious sense of tranquillity in this submission.

In this way Kasatsky spent seven years in the monastery which he first entered. At the end of the third year he took his vows and was ordained, adopting the monastic name of Sergius. Taking his vows was inwardly an important event for Sergius. He had always in the past felt much comfort and spiritual uplift when he took communion, and now, when he himself was the celebrant, the act of preparing the bread and wine filled him with ecstasy and spiritual joy. But this feeling in the course of time became gradually less intense, and once when he was celebrating in the depressed mood that came on him from time to time he sensed that this feeling, too, would one day pass. And indeed it did lose its force, though the habit remained.

By the seventh year of his life in the monastery Sergius was generally bored. He had learnt all there was to learn and achieved all there was to achieve, and there was nothing left to do.

His apathy on the other hand grew steadily worse. During this time he had learnt of his mother's death and Mary's marriage. Both pieces of news he received with indifference. All his attention and interest were focused on his own inner life.

In his fourth year as a monk the bishop showed him special favour and the *starets* told Sergius that if an appointment to some higher sphere were offered him he should not refuse it. At this the monastic ambition which Sergius in other monks had found so repellent was sparked in him. He was appointed to a monastery near the capital. He wished to refuse, but the *starets* ordered him to take the appointment. He accepted it, took leave of the *starets* and moved to the new monastery.

This move to a monastery near the capital was an important event in Sergius's life. There were many temptations of every kind and he devoted his entire strength to withstanding them.

In his previous monastery Sergius had been little troubled by the temptations of women, but here this temptation presented itself with terrifying force and even took specific form. A certain lady well known for her wayward conduct began making advances to Sergius. She spoke to him and asked if he would visit her. Sergius sternly refused, but was horrified at the distinctness of his desire. Such was his alarm that he wrote to the *starets*; and in addition, to keep himself in check he sent for his young novice and, overcoming his shame, confessed to him his weakness and begged him to follow him and make sure that he went nowhere except to the services and about his appointed tasks.

It was also a great trial to Sergius that the abbot of the monastery was a clever, worldly man making his career in the church, for whom he felt the deepest aversion. However he struggled against it, Sergius could not overcome this aversion. He made himself submit, but at the bottom of his heart he never ceased to condemn him. And in the end this evil feeling burst out.

It was in his second year at the monastery and it happened as follows. On the Feast of the Intercession the Vigil service[6] was conducted in the main church of the monastery. There were many visitors, and the abbot himself was the celebrant.

Father Sergius was in his usual place, praying – that is, he was in that state of conflict which regularly came on him during services, especially in the main church, when he himself was not celebrating. This conflict came from the annoyance caused him by the visitors, the gentlemen and especially the ladies. He tried not to see them, to pay no attention to all that went on: the soldier who showed them to their places, pushing aside the ordinary people, the ladies pointing out the monks to each other – often himself and another monk who was known for his good looks. He tried to blinker himself, to see nothing but the shining candles by the icon-screen, the icons and the clergy conducting the service, to hear nothing but the words of the prayers as they were sung and spoken, and to have no other feeling but that sense of self-abandon in the consciousness of fulfilling an obligation, which he always experienced as he listened and anticipated the words of the prayers he had heard so many times before.

As he stood, bowing and crossing himself when necessary, in conflict with himself, one moment coldly censorious, the next deliberately suspending all thought and feeling, he was approached by the sacristan, Father Nicodemus (he was another great trial for Father Sergius, who could not avoid reproaching him for the way he flattered and toadied to the abbot). Father Nicodemus bowed, bending to the ground, and said that the abbot wished to see him in the sanctuary. Father Sergius straightened his robe, put on his monk's cap and carefully made his way through the throng.

'*Lise, regardez à droite, c'est lui,*' he heard a woman's voice say.

'*Où, où? Il n'est pas tellement beau.*'[7]

He knew they were speaking of him. Hearing them, he repeated as he always did in moments of temptation: 'And lead us not into temptation,' then with head and eyes lowered he passed by the ambo, stepped round the precentors in their vestments who were crossing in front of the icon-screen, and went through the north door into the sanctuary. On entering he bowed to the ground and crossed himself as usual before the icon; he then raised his head and, without turning, glanced from the corner of his eye at the abbot. He saw him standing with another person wearing something that glittered.

The abbot in his vestments was standing by the wall; his short podgy hands were thrust from under the chasuble that covered his portly body and stomach and he rubbed the gold lace on it as he spoke, smiling, to an officer in the uniform of a general of the imperial suite with royal ciphers and aiguillettes, which Father Sergius noted at once with his practised military eye. The general had been the commander of his own regiment. He evidently now held an important post and Father Sergius saw at once that the abbot knew it and took pleasure in it and that was why he was beaming all over his fat red face with the receding hair. Father Sergius felt grieved and offended and this feeling was increased when he discovered from the abbot that he had been summoned for no other purpose than to satisfy the curiosity of this general who had wanted to see, as he put it, his 'former comrade in arms'.

'Very glad to see you have taken your vows,' said the general, extending his hand. 'I hope you have not forgotten an old comrade.'

The abbot's face, red amidst the whiteness of his hair, smiling as if in approval of the general's words, the well-groomed face of the general with its complacent smile, the reek of wine on his breath and of cigars from the whiskers on his cheeks were too much for Father Sergius. He bowed once more to the abbot and said:

'Did your reverence wish to see me?'

He stopped. The whole expression of his face and posture asked the question: Why?

The abbot said:

'Yes, I wanted you to meet the general.'

'Your reverence,' said Father Sergius, turning pale, his lips quivering, 'I abandoned the world in order to save myself from temptations. Why do you put temptations in my way here in God's house and at a time of prayer?'

'Go then, go!' said the abbot, angry and frowning.

The next day Father Sergius asked forgiveness of the abbot and the brethren for his pride, but after spending the night in prayer he also decided that he must leave this monastery. He wrote to his *starets* telling him this and begging to be allowed to return to the *starets'* monastery. He wrote that he was conscious of his weakness and of his inability to maintain the struggle against temptation on his own without the *starets'* help. And he repented of his sinful pride. By the next post a letter came from the *starets* in which he wrote that the cause of all the trouble was Sergius's pride. He explained to him that his outburst of anger came about because he had humbled himself by refusing religious honours not for the sake of God, but to satisfy his own pride, as if to say: 'See the sort of man I am: I want nothing.' That was why he had found the abbot's action intolerable – that *he* who had scorned everything for God should be displayed like a wild animal! 'If you scorned fame for God,' he wrote, 'you would have borne this. Worldly pride is still not extinguished in you. I have thought and prayed about you, Sergius, my son, and this is what God has spoken to me concerning you: that you should live as before and submit. It has recently become known that the saintly hermit Hilarion has died in the hermitage. He lived there eighteen years. The abbot of Tambino asked if there is any brother who would like to live there, and just then your letter arrived. Go to Father Paisy in the monastery at Tambino. I will write to him. Ask if you may occupy Hilarion's cell. You cannot replace him, but you need solitude in which to subdue your pride. God bless you.'

Sergius did as the *starets* said. He showed his letter to the abbot and with his permission gave up his cell, left all his belongings to the monastery, and went to the hermitage at Tambino.

The prior there, who was of merchant stock and ran things extremely well, received Sergius simply and calmly; at first he gave him a lay brother, but then, at Sergius's request, left him to himself. The cell was a cave hollowed in the hill. There Hilarion was buried. His burial-place was in the rear chamber of the cave; in the front chamber there was a recess where Sergius could sleep on a straw mattress, a small table and a shelf with icons and books on it. By the outside door which could be locked there was another shelf on which was placed

the food brought daily from the monastery by one of the monks.
And Father Sergius became a hermit.

IV

At Shrovetide in the sixth year of Sergius's life of seclusion a
merry party of well-to-do men and women, after their pancakes
and wine, set off on a troika ride. The party was made up of a
couple of lawyers, a wealthy landowner, an officer and four
women – the wives of the officer and the landowner, the landowner's unmarried sister, and an attractive divorcée, a wealthy
eccentric whose escapades were a continual source of surprise
and consternation in the town.

The weather was splendid and the road as smooth as a ballroom floor. When they had gone eight or nine miles from the
town they stopped to consider whether they should go back or
carry on.

'Well, where does this road lead?' asked Makovkina, the
attractive divorcée.

'It goes to Tambino – that's another eight miles,' said one of
the lawyers, who was making advances to Makovkina.

'Where does it go then?'

'It goes on to L— by way of the monastery.'

'You mean the place where that Father Sergius lives?'

'That's it.'

'You mean Kasatsky? The handsome hermit?'

'Yes.'

'Mesdames! Gentlemen! Let's go and see Kasatsky. We can
have a breather in Tambino and get a bite to eat there.'

'But we would never get back tonight.'

'That doesn't matter. We can spend the night at Kasatsky's.'

'We could do. The monastery has a guest-house which is very
good. I stayed there when I was defending Makhin.'

'That's not for me. I'm going to spend the night at
Kasatsky's.'

'That you'll never do, not even the great almighty you.'

'Won't I? Do you want to bet?'

'All right. You spend the night in Kasatsky's cell and I'll pay you what you like.'

'The winner decides.'

'Yes. And the same for you.'

'Very well. Let's go then.'

They gave the drivers some wine and themselves fetched a hamper containing pies, wine and bonbons. The ladies wrapped themselves up in their white dog-fur coats. The drivers had an argument about who should lead; one of them, a young fellow, turned half about in devil-may-care style, brandished his long whip and gave a shout, then with harness-bells jingling and sledge-runners screeching they were off.

The sledge slightly shook and swayed; the trace-horse galloped evenly and merrily along, its tightly lashed tail lifting over the brass-studded breeching; the level, slippery road sped away behind; the driver drove in dashing style, giving an occasional flick of the reins. One of the lawyers and the officer opposite him bantered with the lady sitting by Makovkina. Makovkina herself sat still, wrapped tight in her fur coat. She was thinking: It's the same revolting thing all the time: shiny red faces smelling of wine and tobacco, saying the same thing, thinking the same thing, and all the time for the same revolting purpose. And they are all quite happy and convinced that that is the way it must be, and they can go on living like that until they die. But I can't. I'm tired of it all. I want something that would shatter all this, turn it upside down. Perhaps like those people – in Saratov, wasn't it – who went for a drive and got frozen to death. What would our lot do? How would they react? Despicably, I suppose. Everyone for himself. Yes, and I would be as bad as the rest. At least I am good-looking, though. They know it too. But what about this monk? Does he really no longer have any idea of these things? Of course he does. It's the one thing they do understand. Like that cadet last autumn, and what a fool he was . . .

'Ivan Nikolaich,' she said.

'Yes, what can I do for you?'

'How old is he?'

'Who?'

'Kasatsky, of course.'

'He's in his forties, I think.'

'And does he receive everybody?'

'Yes, he does, though not all the time.'

'Cover my legs for me. Not like that, clumsy! A bit more, more – that's right. But you don't have to squeeze them.'

And so they came to the forest where Kasatsky's cell was.

Makovkina got out and told the others to drive on. They tried to talk her out of it, but she became cross and insisted on their going. The sledge moved on and she in her white dog-fur coat set off along the track. The lawyer got out and stayed to watch.

V

It was the sixth year of Father Sergius's life as a hermit. He was forty-nine. It was a hard life, though the hardship lay not in the fasting and prayer (these were no hardship), but in an inner conflict which he had never expected. There were two causes of this conflict: doubt and carnal desire. And these two adversaries always raised their heads together. He saw them as two different adversaries, but in fact they were one. When he banished doubt he also banished desire. But he thought of them as two separate devils and struggled separately against them.

'Oh, God, why dost thou not give me faith?' he thought. 'Lust is one thing. St Antony struggled against it, and others, too. But they had faith, and there are times – minutes, hours, days – when I have none. What is the point of the whole world and its delights, if it is sinful and has to be renounced? Why didst thou create temptations to sin? Sin? But is it not sinful fancy for me to leave the pleasures of the world and prepare for myself a reward in a place where there may after all be nothing?' At his words he was seized with horror and self-loathing, and castigated himself: 'Vile creature – you, who would be a saint!' And he knelt to pray. But no sooner had he begun than he pictured himself vividly as he had been in the monastery and how grand he had looked in his monk's cap and robe. And he shook his head. 'No, this is no good. It is a deception. But it is others I deceive, not myself or God. There is nothing grand about me. I am just pitiful and absurd.' He drew back the sides of his cassock, looked at his pathetic legs clad in underdrawers, and smiled.

He let the cassock fall back into place and began to say his prayers, crossing himself and bowing. 'And shall this bed be unto me a coffin?' he prayed. And a devil seemed to whisper: 'A solitary bed is a coffin, anyway. It's all a lie.' And in his mind he saw the shoulders of the widow with whom he had lived. He shook himself and went on with his prayers. When he had finished the set prayers, he took the Gospels, opened them and lighted on a passage which he often repeated and which he knew by heart: 'Lord, I believe: help thou mine unbelief.' He suppressed all his rising doubts. As one stands an unstable object, so he propped his faith on its tottering leg and backed carefully away in order not to knock it and cause it to collapse. Once more the blinkers were on, and he was calm again. He repeated his childhood prayer: 'Lord, take me, take me', and he felt not only easy in mind, but joyfully content. He crossed himself and lay down on the narrow bench on his thin mattress, his summer cassock under his head. He fell asleep. Sleeping lightly, he fancied he heard harness-bells. He did not know if it was real or a dream. But then he was woken from his sleep by a knocking at the door. He got up, thinking he must be mistaken. But the knocking came again. Yes, it was a knock near by, at his door, and there was a woman's voice.

'Lord! Is it then true what I read in the Saints that the devil takes on woman's form? ... Yes, it is a woman's voice. A tender, shy, sweet voice. Pshah!' He spat. 'No, it is just my imagination,' he said and walking over to the corner where there was a small lectern, he knelt down with that accustomed regular movement which was in itself a comfort and pleasure to him. He bent forward, his hair falling over his face, and pressed his now sparsely covered forehead on the cold, damp mat. (There was a draught through the floor.)

He read the psalm which old Father Pimen had told him gave help against manifestations of the devil. Effortlessly he raised his light, wasted body on his powerful, restless legs, and was going to go on reading, but instead of reading he involuntarily strained his ears to see if he could hear anything. He wanted to hear. It was perfectly still. Water went on dripping from the roof into the butt at the corner. There was a fine drizzling mist outside eating away the snow. It was very, very still. Then suddenly by the window there was a rustling and the distinct sound of a voice – a tender, shy voice which could only belong to an attractive woman. It was saying:

'Let me in. For the Lord's sake . . .'

Every drop of blood seemed to rush to his heart and stop. He could not breathe. 'Let God arise; and let his enemies be scattered . . .'

'I'm no devil . . .' he could hear the lips smiling as they spoke. 'I'm no devil. I'm just a sinful woman who has gone astray – not metaphorically, literally.' (She laughed.) 'I'm frozen through and want to shelter . . .'

He put his face to the pane. The glass shone from the reflection of the icon-lamp. He put his hands to the sides of his face and peered out. He saw mist and drizzle, a tree. Yes, there to the right, yes, she was there. A woman in a white long-haired fur coat and hat, with a very sweet, kind, frightened face: she was there two inches from his own face, leaning towards him. Their eyes met and there was a moment of recognition. Not that they had ever seen each other, for they had never met, but in the look that passed between them they (he in particular) felt that they knew one another, understood one another. After this look all doubt was dispelled: this was no devil, but a woman, simple, kind, sweet and shy.

'Who are you? What do you want?' he asked.

'Come on, open up,' she said, skittishly peremptory. 'I'm frozen stiff. I've lost my way, I tell you.'

'But I am a monk, a hermit.'

'Well, open up then. Or do you want me to freeze to death on your doorstep while you go on praying?'

'But what will you . . .'

'I shan't eat you. For God's sake, let me in. I'm chilled to the bone.'

She was beginning to feel scared herself, and there was a catch in her voice as she spoke.

He stepped back from the window and looked at the icon of Christ in his crown of thorns. 'Help me, oh Lord. Help me, oh Lord,' he said, crossing himself and bowing to the ground. Then he went to the door leading into the porch and opened it. In the porch he felt for the latch and began unfastening it. He heard footsteps outside as she walked from the window round to the door. There was a sudden cry of 'Ah!' and he realized that she had stepped into the puddle that had formed outside the door. His hands trembled and he was quite unable to lift the latch against the pressure of the door.

'What are you up to? Let me in. I'm soaked through and absolutely frozen. There are you worrying about saving your soul while I freeze to death.'

He pulled the door towards him, lifted the latch and without thinking jerked the door outwards so that it bumped against her.

'I beg your pardon,' he said, suddenly slipping back into his old accustomed way of addressing a lady.

Hearing his apology, she smiled. 'He's not so frightening after all,' she thought.

'Oh, it's all right,' she said, stepping past him. 'It's for you to pardon me. I would never have dreamt of it if there had not been a special reason.'

'Please come in,' he said, allowing her to pass. He was struck by the powerful scent of fine perfume, something not experienced by him for a long time. She went through the porch into the inner room. He closed the outer door without replacing the latch, crossed the porch and went inside.

'Lord Jesus Christ, Son of God, have mercy upon me, a sinner, have mercy upon me, a sinner,' he prayed incessantly, not just inwardly but outwardly, too, involuntarily shaping his lips to the words.

'What can I do for you?' he said.

With water dripping off her on to the floor she stood in the middle of the room. There was laughter in her eyes.

'Pardon me for disturbing your seclusion, but you see the fix I am in. It was all because we went for a drive out of town and I bet that I could walk back on my own from Vorobevka. But then I lost my way and if I hadn't come across your cell . . .' she lied. But she was so disconcerted by his face that she could not go on. She had expected him to be quite different. He was not as handsome as she had imagined him, but she thought him a fine-looking man. His curling grey-streaked hair and beard, his thin straight nose, and his eyes which burned like coals when he looked at you straight made a deep impression on her. He saw that she was lying.

'Yes, well . . .' he said, looking at her and again lowering his eyes. 'I shall go in here and you can make yourself at home.'

Taking down the lamp, he lit a candle, bowed low to her and went into the tiny room behind the partition. She heard him moving things about. 'Probably barricading himself in,' she thought, smiling. She then threw off her white dog-fur cloak and began taking off her hat, which was caught in her hair, and the knitted scarf she wore underneath it. When she stood at the window she had not been soaked at all and had only said she was as a pretext to make Kasatsky let her in. But she had stepped in the puddle by the door and the water had gone over her left ankle, filling her bootee and overshoe. She sat down on his bed – a mere board with a rug over it – and began taking off her shoes. She thought the tiny cell charming. The narrow inner room, some eight feet by ten, was absolutely spotless. There was nothing in it but the bed on which she sat, a shelf over it containing books, a small lectern in the corner, and nails by the door with a top-coat and cassock, above the lectern an icon of Christ in his crown of thorns and an icon-lamp. There was a curious smell of oil, sweat and earth. She liked it all, even the smell.

She was worried about her wet feet, particularly the left one, and she hurried to take off her shoes, smiling all the time, pleased not so much at having achieved her aim as at seeing how she had disturbed this charming, striking, strange and attractive man. 'He didn't respond, well that's no great matter,' she told herself.

'Father Sergius,' she called. 'Father Sergius, that's your name, isn't it?'

'What do you want?' came his quiet voice.

'You will forgive me, won't you, for disturbing your solitude? There really was nothing else I could do. I would have been ill and I can't be sure that I'm not as it is. I'm all wet and my feet are like ice.'

'I'm sorry,' said the quiet voice, 'but there is nothing I can do.'

'I wouldn't disturb you for the world. I shall just stay till it's light.'

He did not reply. She heard him whispering something – he was obviously praying.

'You won't be coming in here?' she asked, smiling. 'I ought to take my things off to dry out.'

He did not reply and went on praying in even tones on the other side of the partition.

'He is a man all right,' she thought, struggling to pull off her squelching overshoe. She tugged at it, but it would not come off and she thought how funny it was. She laughed quietly but, aware that he could hear her and that her laughter would affect him in the way she wished, she laughed more loudly, and this gay, natural, good-natured laughter did indeed affect him, and precisely in the way she wished.

'Yes, you could fall in love with a man like him. Those eyes. And that straightforward, noble and – pray as he will – that passionate face!' she thought. 'It's no good pretending to us women. As soon as he put his face to the window and saw me, he knew, he realized. There was a glint in his eyes, then down came the shutters again. He was in love with me, wanted me. Yes, wanted me,' she said, at last succeeding in removing her overshoe and bootee, and now trying to take off her long gartered stockings. In order to get them off she had to lift her skirts. She had a qualm of conscience and said: 'Don't come in.' But there was no answer from behind the partition. The steady murmuring continued and there were also sounds of movement. 'He will be bowing to the ground,' she thought, 'but bowing won't help him. He is thinking about me, just as I am about him. He has got the same feeling as he thinks about these legs,' she said, as she pulled off the wet stockings, treading her bare feet on the bed and drawing them up beneath her. She sat for a moment like that, hugging her knees and gazing pensively into space. 'This remote and quiet place, and no one would ever know . . .'

She got up, took her stockings to the stove and hung them over the damper. It was an unusual kind of damper: she turned it, then stepping lightly on her bare feet went back and again sat with her feet up on the bed. Behind the partition all was quiet. She looked at the tiny watch hanging from her neck. It was two o'clock. 'They should be here about three,' she thought. There was only an hour to go.

'Am I just to sit here on my own then? Nonsense!' she thought. 'I'm not going to do that. I'll call him.'

'Father Sergius, Father Sergius! Sergey Dmitrievich! Prince Kasatsky!'

There was no sound through the door.

'Really, it's too bad of you. I wouldn't call you if I didn't need something. I'm ill. I don't know what it is,' she said in a suffering voice. 'Ah! Ah!' she groaned, falling on to the bed. And oddly enough, she did feel genuinely weak and faint, full of aches and pains and seized with feverish shivering.

'Listen. You must help me. I don't know what it is. Oh, oh!' She unhooked her dress, baring her breast, and threw out her arms which were uncovered to the elbow. 'Oh, oh!'

All this time he stood praying in the store-room. He had finished the evening prayers and was now standing motionless, his eyes fixed on the end of his nose as he prayed mentally, repeating in spirit: 'Lord Jesus Christ, Son of God, have mercy on me.'

But he heard everything. He heard the rustle of silk as she took off her clothes, the tread of her bare feet across the floor; he heard her as she rubbed her feet with her hand. He felt his own weakness and how close he was to perdition; and for that reason went on praying without cease. He felt rather like the hero in the fairy-tale must have felt when he had to walk on and never look round. In the same way Sergius heard and sensed danger and disaster above him and all around and the only way he could escape was by not for a moment turning to look at it. But suddenly the desire to look overwhelmed him. Just at that moment she said:

'Look, you're being inhuman. I could die.'

'All right,' he thought, 'I'll go to her. But I will do as that holy father who laid one hand on the harlot and put the other in the fire. I have no fire though.' He looked around. The lamp. He put his finger over the flame and knit his brows in readiness to withstand the pain. For some time he seemed not to feel it, but suddenly, before he could decide whether or not it hurt and how much, he winced and pulled away his hand, shaking it. 'No, I can't do it.'

'For God's sake come! I'm dying. Oh!'

Am I then lost? No, I am not.

'I'll come in a moment,' he said. Then he opened the door and without looking at her walked past and went through the door into the porch where he chopped his firewood. There he felt for the chopping-block and for the axe which stood against the wall.

'Just a moment,' he said, and taking the axe in his right hand, he laid his left forefinger on the block and with a swinging blow of the axe struck it below the second joint. More lightly than a piece of wood of its thickness the finger flew off, turned and with a thud dropped first on the edge of the block, then to the floor.

He heard the sound before he was aware of any pain. But before he could be surprised that it did not hurt he felt a fiery pain and the warm flow of blood. He quickly pulled the hem of his cassock round the stump of his finger and pressing it to his thigh went back through the door. He stopped before the woman with eyes lowered.

Quietly he asked: 'What is it you want?'

She saw the pallor of his face and his quivering left cheek, and was suddenly ashamed. She leapt to her feet, snatched up her fur coat and wrapped it round her.

'Oh yes, I felt ill ... It's a chill ... I ... Father Sergius ...
I ...'

He raised his eyes, which shone with tranquil joy, and looked
at her.

'My dear sister,' he said, 'why did you wish to destroy your
immortal soul? Temptations must come into the world, but
woe betide that person by whom temptation comes ... Pray
that God may forgive you.'

She listened, looking at him. Then suddenly she heard a
dripping sound. She looked and saw blood running from his
hand down his cassock.

'What have you done to your hand?' She remembered the
noise she had heard and, seizing the icon-lamp, ran into the
porch. She saw the bloodstained finger on the floor. She came
back, paler than he, and was going to speak, but he quietly
went into the store-room and fastened the door.

'Forgive me,' she said. 'How can I redeem my sin?'

'Go away.'

'Let me bandage your hand.'

'Go away from here.'

Without speaking she hurriedly dressed. When she was ready
with her fur coat on she sat and waited. There was a jingle of
bells outside.

'Father Sergius, forgive me!'

'Go. God will forgive.'

'Father Sergius, I'll lead a different life. Don't abandon me.'

'Go.'

'Forgive me. Give me your blessing.'

'In the name of the Father, Son, and Holy Ghost,' came the
words from behind the partition. 'Go.'

She went sobbing from the cell. The lawyer was coming
towards her.

'Well, I've lost and that's that. Where will you sit?'

'It doesn't matter.'

She got into the sledge and never spoke the whole way home.

A year later she took her first vows as a nun and in the
nunnery lived strictly under the direction of the hermit Arseny,
who wrote to her from time to time.

VI

Father Sergius spent seven more years as a hermit. At first he accepted many of the things people brought him – tea, sugar, white bread, milk, clothing and firewood. But as time went on he regulated his life with increasing strictness and in the end took nothing for himself except some black bread once a week. Everything else that he was brought he distributed to the poor who visited him.

Father Sergius spent all his time in his cell praying or talking to his visitors, who came in ever greater numbers. He only left his cell when he went – two or three times a year – to church and when he needed to fetch water or firewood.

It was after he had lived five years in this way that the Makovkina episode took place – the nocturnal visit, the change which then came over her, her entry into the nunnery, all of which soon became common knowledge. After this Father Sergius's renown began to grow. More and more visitors arrived, monks came and settled round his cell, and a church and a guest-house were built. Father Sergius's fame – with, as always, exaggerated accounts of his achievements – spread further and further afield; people thronged to him from distant parts and brought the sick to him, declaring that he would cure them.

The first cure he worked was towards the end of the seventh year of his life as a hermit. A fourteen-year-old boy had been brought to Father Sergius by his mother, who asked him to lay his hands on him. It had never entered Father Sergius's head that he might be able to cure the sick; such an idea would have seemed to him a great sin of pride. But the boy's mother kept pleading with him; she fell at his feet and asked why, if he healed others, he would not help her son, and she begged him in the name of Christ to do so. Father Sergius told her that only God heals, but she replied that all she asked was that he should lay his hands on the boy and say a prayer. Father Sergius refused and went back to his cell. But the next day (it was autumn and the nights already cold) when he came out of his cell to fetch water, he again saw the mother and her son, a pale, wasted boy of fourteen, and heard the same entreaties. And he recalled the parable of the unjust judge[8] and though before he had had no doubts about the need to refuse he was now less certain. With this doubt in his mind he knelt and prayed until some resolution came to him. The answer that came was that he must do what the woman wanted, that her faith might save her son; if that happened, he, Father Sergius, would be no more than the insignificant instrument chosen by God.

And Father Sergius went out and did as she wished: he laid his hand on the boy's head and prayed.

The mother and son left. A month later the boy recovered and the fame of the sacred healing powers of the *starets* Sergius (as they now called him) spread through the whole district. After this never a week went by without sick people coming on foot or by conveyance to visit Father Sergius. And not having refused some, he could not refuse others and he laid his hand on them and prayed, and many were healed, and Father Sergius's fame spread further and further.

Thus he passed nine years in the monastery and thirteen as a hermit. Father Sergius now looked like a *starets*: his beard was long and white, but his hair, though sparse, was still black and curling.

VII

For some weeks past Father Sergius had been preoccupied with the nagging doubt as to whether he had been right to accept the situation which had not so much arisen as been forced on him by the archimandrite and the abbot. It had started with the recovery of the fourteen-year-old boy. Since then every month, week, and day Sergius had felt that his inner life was being destroyed and supplanted by an outward life. It was like being turned inside out.

Sergius saw that he was a means of attracting visitors and donations to the monastery and that consequently the monastery authorities were ordering the pattern of his life so as to take full advantage of him. For instance, he was no longer allowed any opportunity to work. His every need was provided for and all that was asked of him was that he should not fail to give his blessing to the visitors who came to see him. For his convenience they arranged days when he might receive visitors. They provided a room for receiving men visitors and a place where he could give his blessing to others who came – it was enclosed by a rail to protect him from being knocked over by the rush of his women visitors. If he was told that these people needed him, that it would be contrary to Christ's law of love to deny these people their wish to see him, and that it would be cruel to remove himself from them, he could only agree. But as he surrendered himself to this way of living, so he felt his inner life turn outwards and the fount of living water in him fail, and he felt that what he did was more and more done for people and not for God.

In all he did – exhorting people or simply blessing them, praying for the sick, advising people on the way to live, receiving thanks from those he had aided by healing (as they claimed) or by instruction – he could not help taking pleasure and being concerned about the results of his actions and the influence they had on people. He thought of himself as a burning light, and the more he thought this the more he felt the divine light of truth inside him fade and die. How much is what I do done for God, how much for people? – this was the question which tormented him all the time and which he not so much could not as would not answer to himself. In the depths of his heart he felt that the devil had turned all his service for God into service for people. He felt this because whereas before it had distressed him to be forced from his seclusion, it was now seclusion that he found distressing. His visitors were a burden to him, but in his heart of hearts he was pleased that they came and was pleased to be surrounded by their praises.

There was even a time when he decided to go away and hide. He even worked out how he would do it. He provided himself with peasant clothes – a smock, cloth leggings, a caftan and cap, explaining that he needed them to give to those who came to him for help. And he kept these clothes in his cell, planning one day to put them on, cut his hair and go away. He would first take a train, then after two hundred miles get off and go about the villages. He asked an old pilgrim, a former soldier, how he travelled and how readily people gave alms and shelter. The old soldier explained, telling him the best places to get alms and shelter, and Father Sergius proposed to follow his example. One night he even got dressed, intending to leave, but he did not know which was more right: to stay or to run away. He could not decide, but his indecision passed – he again settled down and succumbed to the devil, and his peasant clothing served merely to remind him of what he had thought and felt.

Every day more and more people came to him, and he was left with less and less time for spiritual fortification and prayer. He had lucid moments when he likened himself to a place where once had been a spring. 'There was a weak spring of living water which poured from me and through me. That was the true life when "she" had tempted him (he always remembered with rapture that night and "she", who was now the Reverend Mother Agniya). She had tasted of that pure water, but since then, before ever any water can gather people come to drink it, jostling and pushing each other. And the spring has been trampled in and nothing is left but mud.' Thus he thought in his rare moments of lucidity, but his usual state was one of weariness and a pleasant sense of self-righteousness for the weariness he felt.

It was spring. On the eve of the Feast of Mid-Pentecost[9] Father Sergius was celebrating the Vigil service in his own church which was built in a cave. There were as many people as the church would hold – about twenty. They were all wealthy people – gentry or merchants. Father Sergius allowed anyone to come, but the choice of congregation was made by the monk appointed to assist him and by the attendant who was sent to his cell each day from the monastery. A throng of people, eighty or so pilgrims (mostly peasant women), crowded outside, waiting for his blessing when he came out. Father Sergius celebrated the office and when he came out to process to the tomb of his predecessor, singing *Glory to God*, he staggered and would have fallen had he not been supported by a merchant standing behind him and by the monk acting as deacon who was behind the merchant.

There was a chorus of women's voices: 'What is it? Master! Father Sergius! Dear soul! Lord almighty! He's gone white as a sheet.'

But Father Sergius at once recovered and, though very pale, pushed aside the merchant and the deacon and went on with the singing. Father Serapion, the deacon, and the sub-deacons, as well as Sofiya Ivanovna (a lady who resided permanently near Father Sergius's cell and tended to his needs), all begged him to bring the service to an end.

'I'm all right. It's nothing,' said Father Sergius with a smile that was barely perceptible through his whiskers. 'Don't interrupt the service.'

'Yes,' he thought, 'this is the way of the saints.' And immediately he heard behind him the voices of Sofiya Ivanovna and the merchant who had supported him: 'He's a saint, an angel of God!' Not heeding their entreaties, he went on with the service.

Everyone crowded back through the narrow passages into the tiny church and there he completed the service, shortening it only slightly.

When the service was over Father Sergius blessed those present and went out to the bench that stood beneath the elm tree by the entrance to the cave. He felt the need of rest and fresh air, but as soon as he went outside a crowd of people rushed forward wanting his blessing and asking his advice and help. Among them were women pilgrims who spent their lives visiting holy places and *startsy* and being moved to ecstasy by every sacred place and *starets* that they saw. Father Sergius knew well this common type of pilgrim, the most irreligious, unfeeling and conventional of all. There were men, too, mostly discharged soldiers, old men who had lost the habit of a settled life; living in poverty, drunkards for the most part, they drifted from monastery to monastery just to keep themselves fed. And there were common peasants, men and women, who came with their selfish requests for cures and for help in deciding some purely practical question – marrying off a daughter, renting a store,

buying land or getting absolution for a child accidentally smoth-
ered or begotten out of wedlock. For Father Sergius it was all
long familiar and of no interest. He knew that he would learn
nothing from these people, that they would stir in him no
religious feeling, but he liked to see them: they were people to
whom he, his blessing and his words were precious and necessary, so although seeing them was irksome, he found it also
gratifying. Father Serapion wanted to tell them that he was tired
and send them away, but Father Sergius, recalling the words of
the Gospel 'Forbid them (the little children) not to come unto
me'[10] and feeling touched at the thought of his own goodness,
said they should be allowed to stay.

He got up, went over to the crowded rail and began to bless
them and answer their questions. Even he was moved by the
faintness of his voice. But, despite his wishes, he could not
receive them all: once again everything went black, he staggered
and grasped the rail. Once again he felt a congestion in his
head. He turned pale, then suddenly flushed.

'We must wait until tomorrow,' he said. 'I cannot go on
today.' He gave them his blessing and moved towards the
bench. Again he was supported by the merchant, who, taking
his arm, helped him to the seat.

There were cries from the crowd: 'Father! Father! Good
master! Don't leave us. We are lost without you.'

The merchant seated Father Sergius on the bench beneath
the elm, then, acting in the role of policeman, took vigorous
steps to get rid of the crowd. True, he spoke quietly so that
Father Sergius could not hear, but his tone was firm and sharp:

'Clear off now, clear off. He's given you his blessing – what
more do you want? Hop it now or you'll catch it from me. Go
on, off! You there, granny, you in the black socks, get away!
Where do you think you're going? You heard – it's all finished.
There's another day tomorrow, but that's it for today.'

'Master, I only want to peep at his dear face,' said the crone.

'I'll give you a peep! Where do you think you're going?'

Father Sergius saw that the merchant was being rather hard
and in his faint voice told the lay brother to stop him driving
the people away. Father Sergius knew he would do so anyway

and he was anxious to be left alone to rest, but he sent the lay brother with the message in order to make a good impression.

'It's all right,' replied the merchant. 'I'm not chasing them, I'm just appealing to them. I mean, they'll cheerfully do a chap to death. They've no pity, these people. They only ever think of themselves. No, you can't come through, I've told you! Go away. Tomorrow.'

And the merchant dispatched them all.

The merchant's zeal stemmed partly from his fondness for order and for chivvying and telling people what to do, but it was mainly prompted by the fact that he had need of Father Sergius. He was a widower with an only daughter, a sickly girl who was still single, and he had brought her a thousand miles to be healed by Father Sergius. In the two years she had been ill he had taken her to various places for treatment. First he took her to the clinic in the provincial capital (which had a university), but to no effect; then he took her to a peasant healer in Samara province, which made her slightly better; after that, at great expense, he took her to a Moscow doctor, but again to no effect. He had been told that Father Sergius performed cures and had now brought her to him. So after getting rid of all the people, the merchant went up to Father Sergius and came straight to the point: falling on his knees he said in a loud voice:

'Holy Father, have mercy on my ailing child. Deliver her from the pain of her infirmity. I make bold to supplicate at thy holy feet.'

And he placed one hand cupped on the other. All this he did and said as if it was something clearly and firmly established by law and custom, as if there was no other right and proper way to ask for his daughter to be cured. He acted with such assurance that Father Sergius also felt it was right that he should act and speak in this particular way. However, he told him to rise and explain what was the matter. The merchant told him that his daughter, a single girl of twenty-two, had fallen ill two years before, following the sudden death of her mother. It came on 'just like that', as he put it, and she had never been the same since. So now he had brought her a thousand miles and she was waiting in the guest-house until Father Sergius sent for her. She did not go anywhere in the daytime because she was afraid of the light and could only come out after sunset.

'Is she very weak?' asked Father Sergius.

'No, she's not especially weak. She's a well-made girl. It's just the neurastheny, like the doctor said. Father Sergius, if you told me I could bring her today, I would have her here straight away. Holy Father, bring life to a father's heart; restore his offspring – by your prayers save his ailing child!'

And the merchant again fell on his knees and remained motionless, his head turned to one side above his two cupped hands. Again Father Sergius told him to rise. He reflected on the hardships of his work and how he nonetheless humbly carried on; he gave a deep sigh, then after a few seconds' pause said:

'Very well. Bring her this evening. I will pray for her, but I am tired now.' He closed his eyes. 'I will send for you later.'

The merchant withdrew, tiptoeing over the sand (which only made his boots squeak louder), and Father Sergius remained alone.

Father Sergius's whole life was taken up with services and visitors, but this had been a particularly trying day. In the morning an important dignitary had called and talked to him for a long time; after that there was a lady and her son. The son was a young university teacher, an atheist; his mother, who was a fervent believer and devoted to Father Sergius, had brought him along and persuaded Father Sergius to have a talk with him. It had been very hard going. The young man, evidently not wishing to argue with a monk, had condescendingly agreed with everything he said, but Father Sergius could tell that the young man did not believe and despite that was perfectly happy, untroubled and at ease. Father Sergius looked back on their conversation with displeasure.

'Will you have something to eat, master?' inquired the lay brother.

'Yes, you can bring me something.'

The lay brother disappeared into the tiny cell, which stood ten yards from the entrance to the cave, and Father Sergius was left on his own.

The time had long passed when Father Sergius lived alone, fending for himself and living on nothing but communion loaves and bread. It had long been demonstrated to him that he had no right to neglect his health, and he was now given lenten food of the more nourishing kinds. He did not eat much, but he ate a great deal more than previously and often took pleasure in his food, unlike earlier when he had eaten with loathing in the consciousness of sin. So it was on this occasion: he ate some millet porridge, and had a cup of tea and half a white loaf.

The lay brother went away and he was left alone on the bench beneath the elm.

It was a glorious May evening. The birches, aspens, elms, cherry trees, and oaks had just come into leaf. The cherry bushes behind the elm were in full blossom, their petals still unshed. Nightingales, one near by and two or three more in the bushes by the river, trilled and warbled. From the river came the distant sound of workmen singing, evidently on their way home from work. The sun had sunk behind the wood and its broken rays burst patchily through the greenery. On this side everything was light green, on the other side, where the elm was, it was dark. There were beetles in the air, flying into things and dropping.

After supper Father Sergius began his mental prayers: 'Lord Jesus Christ, Son of God, have mercy upon us.' He then began reading the psalm, but while he was doing so a sparrow suddenly flew down from one of the bushes on to the ground. It came up to him, chirping and hopping, but then, frightened by something, it flew away. He said the prayer in which he spoke of the renunciation of the world and hastened to finish it so that he could send for the merchant and his sick daughter. She interested him. She interested him because she was a diversion, a new face, and because she and her father regarded him as a holy man, a person whose prayers were answered. He repudiated such ideas, but at the bottom of his heart he too saw himself in that way.

He often wondered how he, Stepan Kasatsky, had come to be such an extraordinary holy man, indeed a miracle-worker;

but that he was these things he never had any doubt: he could not fail to believe in miracles which he himself had witnessed, from the sickly boy up to the old woman who through his prayers had recently had her sight restored.

Strange though it was, it was fact. And so it was that the merchant's daughter interested him – because she was someone new, because she had faith in him, and because she presented him with an opportunity to give further proof of his powers of healing and to bolster his reputation. 'They come from hundreds of miles away,' he thought. 'I am written about in the papers, the emperor knows of me, and so do people in Europe, in unbelieving Europe.' And he felt suddenly ashamed at his vanity and again he prayed to God: 'Lord, heavenly king, comforter, the spirit of truth, come unto us and dwell in us, and cleanse us from all impurity, and save, good Lord, our souls. Cleanse me from the corruption of worldly fame by which I am afflicted,' he repeated. And he remembered, too, how many times he had prayed in this way and how fruitless these prayers had been: his prayers performed miracles for others, but for himself he could not obtain God's release from this trivial passion.

He recalled his prayers when he first lived as a hermit, when he prayed to be given purity, humility and love, and how it had seemed then that God had heeded his prayers; he had been pure and had cut off his finger – and he raised the wrinkled stump and kissed it. It seemed to him that then, when he was always loathing himself for his sinfulness, he had been humble; and as he recalled the tender joy he had felt at that time on meeting a drunken old soldier who came to him and asked for money, and on meeting 'her', it seemed that he had been capable of love too. But now? He asked himself: did he love anyone? Did he care for Sofiya Ivanovna or Father Serapion? Did he have any feeling of love for those people who had visited him today? For the learned youth he had talked to so didactically, concerned only with showing how clever he was and how abreast of the times in education? He liked and needed their love, but for them he felt none. He had now neither love, humility, nor purity.

He had been pleased to discover that the merchant's daughter was twenty-two, and was interested to know if she was good-looking. When he asked if she was weak, he had actually wanted to know whether or not she was attractive as a woman.

'Have I sunk so low?' he thought. 'Lord, help me and raise me up, oh Lord, my God.' He put his hands together and prayed. The nightingales warbled. A beetle flew into him and crawled across the back of his head. He brushed it off. 'But does He exist? I might be knocking at a house locked on the outside . . . The lock is on the door and I might see it. The lock is the nightingales, the beetles, nature. Perhaps that young man is right.' He began praying aloud; he prayed a long time, until these thoughts had vanished and once again he was calm and assured. He rang the bell, and when the lay brother came, told him that the merchant and his daughter might be fetched.

The merchant arrived with his daughter on his arm. He brought her into the cell and left straight away.

The daughter was a fair-haired girl, extremely white and pale and plump, extremely short, with the frightened face of a child and the full rounded body of a woman. Father Sergius remained on the bench at the entrance. The girl stopped as she passed him and he blessed her. He was horrified at the way he studied her body. She went on into the cell and he felt as if he had been stung. He could tell by her face that she was sensuous and feeble-minded. He got up and went inside. She sat on the stool, waiting for him.

When he came in she stood up.

'I want to go to Daddy,' she said.

'Don't be afraid,' he said. 'Where is the pain?'

'It's all over,' she said, and a smile suddenly lit her face.

'You will get well,' he said. 'Pray.'

'What's the point of praying? I have prayed and it doesn't do any good.' She was still smiling. 'But you say a prayer and lay your hands on me. I've dreamt about you.'

'What was your dream?'

'I dreamt that you put your hand on my heart like this.' She took his hand and pressed it to her breast. 'Just here.'

He gave her his right hand.

'What is your name?' he asked, trembling all over and feeling that he was vanquished, incapable now of controlling his lust.

'Mary. Why?'

She took his hand and kissed it, then she put her arm round his waist and hugged him.

'What are you doing?' he said. 'Mary. You are a devil.'

'Well, what does it matter?'

And holding him in her arms she sat down with him on his bed.

At daybreak he went out on to the steps.

'Did all this really happen? Her father will come. She will tell him. She is a devil. And what shall I do? There it is, the axe I used to chop off my finger.' He seized it and turned to go into the cell.

He was met by the lay brother.

'Do you want me to chop some wood? Let me have the axe, then.'

He gave him the axe and went into the cell. She lay there asleep. He looked at her in horror. He went through, got down his peasant's clothes and put them on. He took some scissors and cut his hair, then set off down the path to the river where he had not been for four years.

A road went along the river. He took this road and walked until dinner-time, when he turned off into a rye field and lay down. Towards evening he came to a village by the river. He did not go into the village but kept along the steep bank of the river.

It was early morning, half an hour or so before sunrise. Everything was grey and gloomy and there was a cold dawn wind blowing from the west. 'Yes, I must make an end of it. God does not exist. How shall I do it? Throw myself into the river? I can swim, so I would not drown. Hang myself? Yes, there is my girdle, just put it over a branch.' It seemed so simple and so close that he was horrified. As usual in moments of despair he wanted to pray. But there was no one to pray to. God did not exist. He lay with his head propped on one elbow. Suddenly such a desire to sleep overcame him that his arm could no longer support his head; he straightened his arm, laid his head on it and at once fell asleep. But he slept only for a moment and immediately woke again and lay half-dreaming, half-reminiscing.

He dreamt of himself when he was little more than a child at his mother's house in the country. A carriage drove up and out of it got his uncle Nikolay with his enormous black spade beard. He had with him a little wispy girl – Pasha; she had large, gentle eyes and a pathetic, timid face. They were all boys together and she was being brought to join them. And they had to play with her, and it was boring. She was silly. In the end they teased her and made her show them how she could swim. She lay on the floor and went through the motions and they laughed and made fun of her. She saw them mocking her and blushed in patches. She looked so pathetic that he had been ashamed and he could never forget that crooked, kindly, submissive smile. And Sergius remembered seeing her again. It was long afterwards. She was married to a landowner who had squandered all her money and used to beat her. She had a couple of children, a son and daughter, but the son had died as a boy.

Sergius remembered seeing how unhappy she was. He saw her later in the monastery, by then a widow. She was just the same – not exactly stupid, but insipid, insignificant, pathetic. She came with her daughter and the girl's fiancé. They were poor now. Then he heard that she lived in some district town in real poverty. 'Why am I thinking about her?' he wondered. But he could not get her out of his mind. 'Where is she? How is she getting on? Is she still as unhappy as when she showed us how to swim on the floor? But why am I thinking about her? What am I doing? I have to put an end to myself.'

The thought again struck horror into him and to escape it he again turned his mind to Pashenka.

He lay a long time thus, thinking of the need to end his life and of Pashenka. Pashenka seemed to him a means of salvation. Finally he went to sleep. He dreamt that an angel came to him and said: 'Go to Pashenka and learn from her what you must do, how you have sinned and how you can be saved.'

He woke up and having decided that his dream was a vision sent by God, joyfully resolved to do as he had been told. He knew the town where she lived – it was two hundred miles away – and he set off towards it.

VIII

Pashenka had long since ceased to be 'Pashenka': she was now Praskovya Mikhailovna,[11] old, withered and wrinkled, and mother-in-law to Mavrikiev, a government clerk – who was a failure in life and given to drink. She lived in the district town where her son-in-law's last appointment had been; there she kept the family – her daughter, her sickly, neurasthenic son-in-law and five grandchildren. She provided for them by giving piano lessons to merchants' daughters at fifty copeks an hour. Some days she would have four hours, other days five, and this brought in about sixty rubles a month. That is how they lived for the time being while they waited for some new opening for Mavrikiev. Praskovya Mikhailovna had sent off letters to all her friends and relations asking for help in finding him a situation and she had also written to Father Sergius, but her letter did not arrive in time to reach him.

It was Saturday and Praskovya Mikhailovna was mixing some currant bread which long ago her father's serf cook used to make so well. She intended it as a Sunday treat for her grandchildren.

Masha, her daughter, was fussing with the youngest child; the older children were at school. Her son-in-law had had a wakeful night and was now asleep. Praskovya Mikhailovna had also slept little the night before, trying to mollify her daughter who was angry with her husband. She knew her son-in-law was a weakling incapable of talking or acting in any other way, and she knew it was a waste of time for his wife to reproach him, so she did what she could to appease them, to put a stop to the reproaches and ill feeling. It was almost physically too much for her when people were at odds with each other. She saw so clearly that behaving like this could only make things worse, not better. It was not even something she thought; the sight of malice simply upset her, just as she would be upset by a bad smell, a harsh voice, or someone striking her.

She was just telling Lukerya how to mix the leavened dough and feeling rather pleased with herself, when Misha, her six-year-old grandson, wearing his apron and darned stockings, came running into the kitchen on his little bent legs. He looked frightened.

'Granny, there's a terrible old man looking for you!'

Lukerya glanced outside.

'That's right. It looks like a pilgrim, m'am.'

Praskovya Mikhailovna rubbed her thin arms together to clean them, wiped her hands on her apron and was on the point of going into the living-room to fetch five copeks from her purse when she remembered that ten copeks was the smallest she had. She decided instead to give him some bread and went to the larder, but then suddenly blushed at the thought of grudging him the money. She told Lukerya to cut him a piece of bread while she went for the ten-copek piece. 'It's a punishment to you,' she told herself. 'Now you give twice over.'

She apologetically handed the bread and money to the pilgrim, feeling no pride in her generosity as she did so but rather shame that she was giving so little. The pilgrim had such an impressive look about him.

Sergius had begged his way for two hundred miles. He was now tattered, thin, swarthy in face; his hair was cut short and he wore a peasant cap and boots; yet despite this and despite the humble way he bowed, he retained that impressive look which was so attractive. But Praskovya Mikhailovna did not recognize him. It was impossible that she should, not having seen him for nearly thirty years.

'I'm afraid it's all we can manage,' she said. 'Perhaps you would like a bite to eat.'

He took the bread and money. Praskovya Mikhailovna was surprised that instead of going away he looked at her.

'Pashenka. I have come to you. Please take me in.'

His fine black eyes, glistening with rising tears, looked at her intently, imploringly. His lips quivered piteously beneath his now almost white whiskers.

Praskovya Mikhailovna caught at her shrivelled breast, her jaw dropped and she stared goggle-eyed at the face of the pilgrim.

'It can't be! Why, it's Stepan! Sergius! Father Sergius!'

'Yes, it's him,' said Sergius quietly. 'It's not Sergius, though, nor Father Sergius, but the great sinner Stepan Kasatsky, the great lost sinner. Take me in and help me.'

'It's never possible! But how do you come to be so lowly? Come along in.'

She stretched out her hand, but he did not take it and followed her in.

But where should she take him? It was only a small apartment. At first she had a tiny room, little more than a box-room, for herself, but she had let her daughter have it and she was there now getting the baby to sleep.

'Just sit down here. I'll only be a minute,' she said to Sergius, pointing to the bench in the kitchen.

Sergius at once sat down and with an obviously accustomed movement slid the straps of his knapsack first from one shoulder, then from the other.

'My goodness, how lowly you've become! You were so famous, and now suddenly . . .'

Sergius made no reply and just smiled gently as he put his bag by his side.

'Masha, do you know who this is?'

In a whisper Praskovya Mikhailovna told her daughter who Sergius was, then between them they carried the bed and cradle out of the box-room so that Sergius could use it.

Praskovya Mikhailovna took him into this tiny room.

'Have a rest in here. It's not much, I'm afraid. But now I must be off.'

'Where are you going?'

'I give lessons here. I'm ashamed to admit it – I teach music.'

'Music – that's fine. There's one thing though, Praskovya Mikhailovna. I have come to see you about something. When could we have a talk?'

'Perhaps this evening? It would be a pleasure.'

'Yes, all right. But one more request: tell no one who I am. You are the only one I have confided in. Nobody knows where I have gone. That is how it must be.'

'Oh, but I have told my daughter.'

'Then tell her not to mention it.'

Sergius took off his boots, lay down, and having had no sleep the night before and having walked twenty-five miles, he at once fell asleep.

When Praskovya Mikhailovna came back Sergius was sitting in his room, waiting for her. He had not come out for dinner, but ate some soup and millet porridge that Lukerya brought him in his room.

'You are back sooner than you said?' asked Sergius. 'Can we talk now?'

'That I should be blessed with such a visit! I missed a lesson. I can make it up . . . I always dreamt about going to see you, I wrote to you, and then I am blessed in this way.'

'Pashenka, I want you to take what I am about to say as a confession, as what I would say before God in the hour of my death. Pashenka, I am no saint. I am not even a simple, ordinary person. I am a sinner, a puffed-up, foul, loathsome, lost sinner, whether the worst in the world I do not know, but I am the lowest of the low.'

Pashenka at first looked at him wide-eyed: she believed what he said. Then, when the truth had fully sunk in, she touched his hand and with a smile of compassion said:

'Steve, might you not be making too much of it?'

'No, Pashenka. I am a fornicator, a murderer, a blasphemer and a fraud.'

'Gracious heavens, what are you saying?' said Praskovya Mikhailovna.

'But I have to live. I who thought I knew everything, I who taught others how to live – I know nothing and would like you to teach me.'

'What do you mean, Steve? You are joking. Why do you make fun of me?'

'All right then, I am joking. But you – tell me about yourself. What sort of life have you had?'

'Me? My life has been vile, bad, it couldn't have been worse, and now God is punishing me, and rightly. There is so much wrong in the way I live.'

'What about your marriage? How did that go?'

'It was all wrong. I got married, fell in love – it was sheer depravity. Father was against it, but I took no notice and married him. And after I was married I never helped my husband, but only tormented him with my jealousy, which I could never get the better of.'

'I heard he drank.'

'He did, but it was I who failed to comfort him. I used to reproach him. But it was a sickness really. He couldn't stop himself, and I remember now how I refused him anything to drink. We had terrible scenes.'

And she looked at Kasatsky with suffering in her fine eyes evoked by the memory.

Kasatsky remembered hearing that Pashenka's husband used to beat her. And now, looking at her thin, shrivelled neck with the prominent veins behind her ears and the sparse hair, half-brown, half-grey, gathered into a bun, he seemed to see it happening.

'Then I was left on my own with the two children and nothing to live on.'

'But you had some property?'

'Oh, we sold that when Vasya was alive, and we . . . spent it all. I had to live somehow and like all of us – young ladies – I had no skill of any kind. Though I was worse, more useless than most. So we used up the last of what we had, I taught the children and learnt a little myself too. Then Mitya fell ill – he was in his fourth year at school – and the Lord took him. And Masha fell in love with Vanya – that's my son-in-law. He's really a good fellow, but just unlucky. He's not well.'

She was interrupted by her daughter calling: 'Mother, do take Misha. I can't be everywhere at once.'

Praskovya Mikhailovna started, got up, and with quick steps went through the door in her well-worn shoes and came back at once with a little boy of two who sprawled back in her arms and grasped her kerchief with his little hands.

'Where was I? Oh yes ... he had a good position here, the head of the office was very nice, but Vanya couldn't cope and resigned.'

'What is the trouble with him?'

'Neurasthenia. It's a terrible thing to have. We've seen doctors about it, but they say he would have to go away and we can't afford it. I'm still hoping he will just get over it. He has no special pain, but ...'

'Lukerya!' they heard him call in his cross, feeble voice. 'They keep sending her away just when she's wanted. Mother!'

'I'll just be a minute,' said Praskovya Mikhailovna, breaking off her story again. 'He hasn't had his dinner yet. He can't eat with us.'

She went out, attended to something in the other room and came back wiping her thin hands.

'So that's how it is. We keep complaining and are never satisfied but, thank God, the grandchildren are fine and well, and life is not too bad. But what need is there to talk about me?'

'What do you live on then?'

'There's the little bit I earn. I used to find music so boring, but it really has come in useful now.'

Her small hand rested on the chest of drawers by which she was sitting and she worked her thin fingers as if playing an exercise.

'What do you get paid for your lessons?'

'Some pay a ruble, others fifty or thirty copeks. They are very good to me.'

'And do your pupils make good progress?' asked Kasatsky with a hint of a smile in his eyes.

At first Praskovya Mikhailovna thought he was not being serious and looked inquiringly in his eyes.

'Yes, some get on well. There's one splendid girl, the butcher's daughter. She is a nice, good girl. Of course, if I were a respectable woman I would have been able to use Father's connections to get Vanya a post. But there it was, I could not do a thing, and this is the state I have brought them all to.'

'Yes, of course,' said Kasatsky, bending his head forward. 'And tell me, Pashenka, do you go to church at all?'

'Oh, don't mention it. It's terrible how slack I have got. I keep the fasts with the children and sometimes go to church, but I might not go for months at a time. I send the children.'

'And why don't you go yourself?'

She blushed.

'To tell the truth, I don't feel it fair on my daughter and the grandchildren if I go to church in rags. And I have nothing new to wear. And then I'm just too lazy.'

'And do you pray at home?'

'Yes, I pray. But it is just automatic, not real praying. I know that isn't the way, but I don't have any proper feeling. I have nothing, only the knowledge of how thoroughly bad I am . . .'

'Yes, yes, that's right,' said Kasatsky, as if in approval.

'All right, I'm just coming,' she said in answer to her son-in-law who called, and straightening her thin braid of hair, she went out of the room.

This time she was gone for some time. When she returned, Kasatsky was sitting as before with his elbows on his knees and his head bent forward. But his knapsack was now on his back.

As she came in carrying a small tin lamp without a globe, he raised his fine, weary eyes to look at her and heaved an enormous sigh.

'I didn't tell them who you are,' she began diffidently. 'I just said that you were a pilgrim and came of good family and that I used to know you. Let's go into the dining-room and have some tea.'

'No . . .'

'All right, I'll bring it in here.'

'No, I don't want anything. God save you, Pashenka. I am going. If you pity me, tell no one that you have seen me. By the living God I beg you to tell no one. Thank you. I would bow at your feet, but I know it would upset you. Goodbye, in the name of Christ.'

'Give me your blessing.'

'God will bless you. In Christ's name, goodbye.'

He was about to go, but she made him wait while she brought him bread, cracknels and butter. He took them and went outside.

It was dark and before he was past the second house Praskovya Mikhailovna had lost sight of him and could only tell where he was because the priest's dog barked as he passed.

'So that was the meaning of my dream. Pashenka is all that I should have been and was not. I lived for people, pretending it was for God, while she lives for God and thinks she is living for people. Yes, one good deed, one cup of water given without thought of reward is worth more than all the benefits I ever worked for men. But surely in some part I genuinely wished to serve God?' he thought. And the answer came to him: 'Yes, but that was defiled and choked by human glory. And God does not exist for one such as I, who lived for human glory. I will seek Him now.'

He set off, travelling from village to village as he had done on his way to Pashenka, now in company with other pilgrims, now going on his own, begging for his bread and a lodging overnight. Occasionally he was scolded by a bad-tempered housewife or cursed by a drunken peasant, but in the main people gave him food and drink and now and then something for the journey. The upper-class look about him disposed some people in his favour. But there were others who appeared to take pleasure in seeing one of the gentry also reduced to beggary. All, however, were won over by his gentle manner.

If he found a copy of the Gospels in a house he often read out of it, and wherever it was those who listened were always moved and astonished, as if what he read was something completely new and at the same time long familiar.

If he managed to help anyone – by giving advice, writing a letter, or settling a quarrel – he saw nothing of their gratitude because he would go away. And gradually God began to manifest Himself in him.

Once he was walking along with two old women and an old

soldier when they were stopped by a lady and gentleman in a chaise drawn by a trotter and another couple on horseback. The two on horseback were the husband and daughter of the lady in the chaise, whose companion was evidently a visiting Frenchman.

They stopped them so that the Frenchman could see *les pélerins*,[12] these people who were driven by the superstition characteristic of the Russian common people to do no work and wander from place to place.

They spoke in French, supposing that they would not be understood.

'*Demandez leur*,' said the Frenchman, '*s'ils sont bien sûrs de ce que leur pélerinage est agréable à Dieu*.'[13]

The question was translated and the old women answered:

'As God sees fit. Our feet have found us favour, may our hearts not do the same?'

The soldier was asked and replied that he was all alone and had nowhere to go. They asked Kasatsky who he was.

'I am a servant of God.'

'*Qu'est ce qu'il dit? Il ne répond pas*,' said the Frenchman.

'*Il dit qu'il est un serviteur de Dieu*.'

'*Cela doit être un fils de prêtre. Il a de la race. Avez-vous de la petite monnaie?*'[14]

The Frenchman had some small change and he gave them each twenty copeks.

'*Mais dites leur que ce n'est pas pour les cierges que je leur donne, mais pour qu'ils se régalent de thé*.[15] Tea, tea – for you, old chap,' he said, smiling and patting Kasatsky's shoulder with his gloved hand.

'Christ save you,' answered Kasatsky, not replacing his cap and bowing his bald head.

Kasatsky was specially gladdened by this encounter, for he had scorned worldly opinion and had done a very paltry, easy thing: he had humbly accepted twenty copeks and passed them on to a fellow pilgrim, a blind beggar. The less he cared for the opinion of men, the more he felt the presence of God.

Kasatsky travelled about in this way for eight months. In the ninth month he was detained in one of the provincial capitals, where he was passing the night in a refuge with other pilgrims. Having no papers, he was taken to the police station. When questioned about his identity card he answered that he had no card, that he was a servant of God. He was classed as a vagrant, taken to court, and exiled to Siberia.

In Siberia he settled on the holding of a wealthy peasant. He still lives there, working in the owner's vegetable garden, teaching the children and tending the sick.

Appendix 1

Postface to *The Kreutzer Sonata*

I have received, and continue to receive, a large number of letters from people I do not know, asking me to explain in clear, simple terms what I think of the subject of the story I wrote entitled *The Kreutzer Sonata*. This I shall endeavour to do; that is, I shall attempt briefly to express, within the limits of the possible, the substance of what I was trying to say in that story, and the conclusions which in my view may be drawn from it.

The *first point* I was trying to make was that in our society there has been formed the solid conviction, common to every class and receiving the support of a mendacious science, that sexual intercourse is an activity indispensable to health, and that since marriage is not always a practical possibility, extramarital sexual intercourse, committing a man to nothing except the payment of money, is something perfectly natural and therefore to be encouraged. So firm and widespread has this conviction become that parents, following the advice given by their doctors, make arrangements for the depravation of their children; governments whose sole purpose is to care for the moral welfare of their citizens bring in institutionalized debauchery by regularizing the existence of an entire class of women who are obliged to suffer both physically and emotionally in order to satisfy the imaginary needs of men, so that the unmarried give themselves up to debauchery with a perfectly clear conscience.

And what I was trying to say was that this is not a good state of affairs, for it cannot be right that for the sake of the health of some the bodies and souls of others should be caused to perish, just as it cannot be right that for the sake of the health of some it should be necessary to drink the blood of others.

The conclusion it seems to me natural to draw from this is that one ought not to yield to this delusion, this fraud. And in order not to yield to it, it is necessary, in the first place, not to lend credence to immoral doctrines, whatever the pseudosciences that give them their support and, in the second place, to understand that sexual intercourse in which men either extricate themselves from its possible consequences – children – or else shift the entire burden of those consequences on to the woman, or practise contraception – that such intercourse is an offence against the most elementary requirements of morality, is an infamy, and that therefore unmarried men who do not wish to live a life of infamy must not indulge in it.

In order to be able to abstain from it they must, in addition to leading a natural way of life – not drinking, not eating to excess, not eating meat and not shirking physical toil (not gymnastic exercises, but fatiguing, genuine toil) – exclude from their thoughts the possibility of having intercourse with chance women, just as every man excludes such a possibility between himself and his mother, his sisters, his relations and the wives of his friends.

Abstinence is possible, and is less dangerous and injurious to the health than non-abstinence: every man will find around him a hundred proofs of this.

That is the first point.

The *second point* is that as a result of this view of sexual intercourse as being not only a necessary precondition of health but also a sublime and poetic blessing that life bestows, marital infidelity has become in all the classes of society (especially, thanks to conscription, among the peasantry) a most common occurrence.

The conclusion that follows from this is that men should not act in this way.

In order for men not to act in this way, it is necessary that carnal love be envisaged differently, that men and women be educated by their families and by public opinion in such a way that both before and after marriage they view desire and the carnal love that is associated with it not as a sublime, poetic condition, as they are viewed at present, but as a condition of animality that is degrading to human beings, and that the violation of the promise of fidelity given at the time of marriage be censured by public opinion in at least the same degree as it censures commercial fraud and the non-payment of debts, and that it not be sung to the skies, as is done at present in novels, poems, songs, operas, etc.

That is the second point.

The *third point* is that in our society, as a consequence of the same false significance accorded to carnal love, procreation has lost its meaning: instead of being the goal and the *raison d'être* of marital relations, it has become no more than an obstacle to the agreeable protraction of love relations. Because of this, and as a result of the advice given by the servants of medical science, there has begun either the spread of an employment of means which prevent the woman from conceiving, or else a certain practice has started to become common, one which did not exist formerly and is still unknown in the patriarchal families of peasants: the extension of marital relations into pregnancy and nursing.

And I think this is a bad thing. It is a bad thing for people to use contraceptive devices, in the first place because it frees them from the care and hard work which children bring and which serve as an expiation of carnal love, and in the second place because this is something very close to the act which is more repugnant to the human conscience than any other: the act of murder. Non-abstinence during pregnancy and nursing is likewise undesirable, because it damages the physical, and more importantly, the emotional strength of the woman.

The conclusion that may be drawn from this is that men should not act in this way. And in order not to act in this way, they must understand that abstinence, which forms the essential condition of human dignity outside marriage, is even more necessary in marriage itself.

That is the third point.

The *fourth point* is that in our society, where children are considered either as a hindrance to pleasure, as an unfortunate accident, or as a particular form of pleasure (when born in predetermined quantities), they are brought up not with any view to those tasks of human life that may await them as thinking, loving beings, but solely with a view to the enjoyment they may be able to afford their parents. In consequence of this, the children of men are raised like the young of animals, and the principal concern of their parents is not to prepare them for an active life worthy of human beings but (and here the parents receive the support of that mendacious science that is called medicine) to feed them as well as possible, to make them as tall as possible, to make them clean, white, replete and attractive (if this is not done among the lower classes, it is only because necessity will not permit it – their view on the matter is the same). And in these pampered children, just as in all animals that are overfed, there is an unnaturally early appearance of an unmasterable sensuality which is the cause of horrible torments during their adolescence. Their clothes, their books, their entertainments, the music they play and listen to, their dancing, the sweet food they are given, the whole environment of their lives, from the pretty pictures on their tins of candy to the novels, stories and poems they read, inflame their sensuality even more; in consequence, the most fearful sexual vices and illnesses become a normal condition of growing up for children of both sexes, and often retain their grip even in adulthood.

And I think this is a bad thing. The conclusion that may be drawn from it is that we must stop raising the children of men as if they were the young of animals, and set other goals for the education of the children of men than merely an attractive, well-groomed body.

That is the fourth point.

The *fifth point* is that in our society, where the love between a young man and a young woman, the foundation of which is none the less carnality, is elevated into the loftiest poetic goal of all human aspirations (all the art and poetry of our society are the witness), young people devote the best years of their lives, if they are men, to spying out, hunting down and taking possession of the objects most worthy of their love by means of an affair or of marriage, and if they are women and girls, to enticing and drawing men into an affair or marriage.

Because of this the finest energies of human beings are wasted on work that is not only unproductive but also harmful. This is the source of most of the mindless luxury of our day-to-day lives, and it is also the cause of the idleness of our men and the shamelessness of our women who think nothing of parading, in fashions borrowed from prostitutes, those parts of their bodies that excite men's lust.

And I think this is a bad thing. It is a bad thing, because the achievement of union either in marriage or outside it, with the object of one's love, no matter how poeticized, is not a goal that is worthy of human beings, any more than is the goal, considered by many as the highest good imaginable, of procuring large quantities of delectable food for oneself.

The conclusion that may be drawn from this is that we must give up thinking of carnal love as something particularly exalted, and must understand that a goal worthy of man, whether it be the service of mankind, of one's country, of science or of art (not to mention the service of God) is, as soon as we consider it as such, not attained by means of union with the object of our love either inside marriage or outside it; on the contrary, love and union with the object of that love (no matter how hard people may try to prove the opposite in verse and prose) never make the achievement of a goal worthy of man any easier, but always render it more difficult.

That is the fifth point.

This is the substance of what I was trying to say, and of what I thought I had indeed said, in my story. It seemed to me that while one might argue about the best way of remedying the evil designated in the above propositions, it was impossible for anyone not to agree with them.

It seemed to me impossible that anyone would not agree with these propositions in the first place because they are fully in accord with the progress of humanity, which has always proceeded from libertinage towards an ever greater degree of chastity, and with the moral awareness of society, with our conscience, which always condemns licentiousness and esteems chastity; and in the second place because these propositions are merely the inevitable conclusions to be drawn from the Gospels, which we profess, or at least admit to be the basis of our conception of morality.

Things have turned out differently, however.

No one, it is true, contests outright the propositions that one must not indulge in lust either before marriage or after it, that one must not prevent conception by artificial means, make of one's children an entertainment, and place the love-bond higher than all else – in short, no one will deny that chastity is better than libertinage. But people say: 'If celibacy is better than marriage, then it follows that people must do what is better. But if they do it, the human race will come to an end, and surely the ideal of the human race cannot be its own extinction?'

But quite apart from the fact that the extinction of the human race is not a new idea for mankind, that for the religious it is an article of faith and for the scientifically inclined an inevitable deduction to be drawn from observations concerning the cooling of the sun, there is concealed in this objection a grave, widespread and ancient misunderstanding.

People say: 'If human beings attain the ideal of complete chastity, they will cease to exist, and so this ideal must be a false one.' But those who talk like this are, wittingly or unwittingly, confusing two things that are different in nature: the law – or precept – and the ideal.

Chastity is neither a law nor a precept but an ideal, or rather one of the preconditions of an ideal. An ideal is only genuine, however, when its realization is only possible in idea, in thought, when it is only attainable in the infinite and when, consequently, the possibility of approaching it is an infinite one. If there were an ideal that was not only attainable but could be imagined by us as being attainable it would cease to be an ideal. Such is the ideal of Christ – the establishment of the Kingdom of God upon earth, the ideal, already announced by the prophets, concerning the advent of a time when all men, instructed by God, will beat their swords into ploughshares and their spears into pruning-hooks, the lion will lie down with the lamb and all beings will be united by love. The entire meaning of human existence is contained in the movement towards this ideal, and thus not only does the striving towards the Christian ideal in its totality and towards chastity as one of the preconditions of that ideal not exclude the possibility of life; on the contrary, it is the absence of this Christian ideal that would put an end to that forward movement and consequently to the possibility of life.

The opinion that the human race would cease to exist if people were to devote all their energies to the attainment of chastity is similar to the opinion (still held today) that the human race would perish if people, instead of continuing the struggle for existence, were to devote all their energies to loving their friends, their enemies and the whole of living creation. Such opinions stem from a lack of understanding of the difference between two types of moral guidance.

Just as there are two ways of indicating to the traveller the path he should follow, so there are two methods of moral guidance for the person who is seeking the truth. One of these consists in pointing out to the person the landmarks he must encounter, and in him setting his course by these landmarks. The other method consists simply in giving the person a reading on the compass he carries with him; he keeps this reading steady as he travels, and by means of it he is able to perceive his slightest deviation from the correct path.

The first type of moral guidance makes use of external precepts, or rules: the person is given the clearly defined characteristics of actions he must and must not perform.

'Keep the sabbath, practise circumcision, do not steal, do not drink alcohol, do not kill, give a tenth of what you own to the poor, do not commit adultery, make your ablutions and say your prayers five times a day, be baptized, take communion', and so on. Such are the precepts of the external religious doctrines: the Brahminic, the Buddhist, the Muslim, the Hebraic and the Ecclesiastic, mistakenly referred to as the Christian.

The second type of guidance consists in showing the person a state of perfection impossible for him to attain, the striving for which he acknowledges in himself: he is shown the ideal, and he is forever able to measure the degree of distance that separates him from it.

'Love thy God with all thy heart, and all thy soul, and all thy mind, and love thy neighbour as thyself. Be perfect like your Heavenly Father.'

Such is the doctrine of Christ.

One can only verify the fulfilment of the external religious doctrines by the concordance of men's actions with the requirements of those doctrines; such a concordance is possible.

One may verify the fulfilment of the doctrine of Christ by one's awareness of the degree of distance that separates one from the ideal of perfection. (The degree of approximation is not visible: all that can be seen is the distance that separates a human being from perfection.)

A person who follows the external law is like someone standing in the light of a lantern that is suspended from a post. He stands in the light shed by this lantern, its light is sufficient for him, and he has no need to go any further. A person who follows the teaching of Christ is like someone carrying a lantern before him on the end of a pole of indeterminate length: its light is always in front of him, it constantly prompts him to follow it and at each moment reveals to him a new expanse of terrain that draws him towards it.

The Pharisee thanks God for the fact that he is able to fulfil all his duties.

A rich young man may have fulfilled all his duties ever since his childhood, and yet be unable to see that he is lacking in anything. Such young men cannot think otherwise: there is no goal before them towards which they might continue to strive. They have given away a tenth of what they own, they have kept the sabbath, they have honoured their father and mother, they have not committed adultery, theft or murder. What more is left to them? For the person who follows the teaching of Christ, however, the attainment of any degree of perfection makes it necessary for him to climb to a higher degree, from whence a yet higher degree is revealed to him, and so it continues.

The person who follows the doctrine of Christ is perpetually in the situation of the publican. He always feels imperfect; he cannot see behind him the path he has already travelled; instead, he constantly sees in front of him the path along which he has still to go.

Herein lies the difference between the doctrine of Christ and all the other religious doctrines. It is not a difference in moral demands, but in the way human beings are guided. Christ laid down no rules as to how one should live one's life; he never established any institutions, not even the institution of marriage. But people who do not understand the special nature of the doctrine of Christ, people who are accustomed to external doctrines and who want to feel righteous in the way that the Pharisee feels righteous have, contrary to the entire spirit of the doctrine of Christ, interpreted his teachings according to the letter, and constructed a body of external precepts called ecclesiastical Christian doctrine, and have substituted this for Christ's authentic doctrine of the ideal.

In the place of Christ's doctrine of the ideal the ecclesiastical teaching calling itself Christian has, with regard to every manifestation of life, instituted external rules and precepts which are alien to the spirit of that doctrine. It has done this with regard to the authority of the State, justice, the armed forces, the Church and the holy ritual, and also with regard to marriage: in spite of the fact that not only did Christ never advocate marriage, but, if one looks to the matter of external precepts, took a negative attitude towards it ('leave thy wife and follow me'), the ecclesiastical doctrine which calls itself Christian has established marriage as a Christian institution; in other words, it has determined certain external conditions in which carnal love is supposed not to contain any sin for the Christian, and to be completely lawful.

But since there is no basis in the true Christian doctrine for the institution of marriage, the result has been that the people of our world have fallen between two stools: they do not really believe in the ecclesiastical dispositions concerning marriage, for they sense that this institution has no basis in Christian doctrine, and at the same time they lose sight of Christ's ideal, which is now obscured by the teaching of the Church, they lose sight of the ideal of chastity, and are left without any guidance where marriage is concerned. Hence there arises a phenomenon that seems at first sight strange: among the Jews, the Muslims, the Lamaists and others who profess religious doctrines of a far lower order than the Christian one, but who have precise external rules governing marriage, the family principle and conjugal fidelity are incomparably more deep-rooted than they are among us so-called Christians.

They practise a form of concubinage, a polygamy that is regulated within certain limits. Among us, on the other hand, there exist outright licence and concubinage, polygamy and polyandry, subject to no rules and disguised as monogamy.

Solely because, in exchange for money, the clergy performs a special ceremony, called Christian marriage, over the heads of a certain number of couples, the people of our world imagine, either naively or hypocritically, that they are living in a state of monogamy.

There never has been and there never will be a Christian marriage, just as there never has been nor can there be a Christian ritual (Matthew vi:5–12; John iv:21), Christian teachers and fathers (Matthew xxiii:8–10), Christian property, or a Christian army, justice or State. This was always understood by the true Christians of the earliest times, and by those who lived thereafter.

The Christian's ideal is the love of God and of one's neighbour; it is the renunciation of self for the service of God and of one's neighbour.

Marriage and carnal love are, on the other hand, the service of oneself and are therefore in all cases an obstacle to the service of God and men – from the Christian point of view they represent a fall, a sin.

The contraction of marriage cannot promote the service of God and men even when the partners have as their aim the propagation of the human species. It would make much more sense if such people, instead of entering into marriage in order to produce children, were to sustain and rescue those millions of children who are perishing all round us because of a lack not of spiritual, but of material food.

A Christian could only enter into a marriage without any consciousness of having fallen or sinned if he could be absolutely certain that the lives of all existing children were assured.

It is possible not to accept the doctrine of Christ, that doctrine which impregnates the whole of our lives and on which our entire morality is based; if, however, one does accept it, one cannot but recognize that it points towards the ideal of total chastity.

The Gospels, after all, tell us quite plainly and without any possibility of misinterpretation that a married man must not divorce his wife in order that he may take another, but must live with the one he originally married (Matthew v:31–2; xix:8); second, that it is a sin in general, and thus just as much for the man who is married as for the man who is not, to look upon a woman as an object of pleasure (Matthew v:28–9), and third, that it is better for a man who is single not to marry at all, to remain, that is, completely chaste (Matthew xix:10–12).

To very many people these ideas appear strange and even contradictory. And indeed they are contradictory, but not of one another; they contradict our entire way of life, so that involuntarily a doubt arises: Who is right? These ideas, or the lives of millions of people, our own included? I experienced this very same feeling most acutely when I was in the process of arriving at the convictions I am now setting forth: I never expected that the train of my thoughts would lead me where it did. I was horrified at my conclusions. I tried not to lend them any credence, but that was impossible. However much they might contradict the entire fabric of our lives, however much they might contradict all that I had previously thought and even said aloud, I had no alternative but to accept them.

'But these are all merely general reflections, and they may very well be correct; however, they relate to the doctrine of Christ and are obligatory only for those who profess it; after all, life is life, and one cannot, having pointed to the unattainable ideal of Christ, abandon people at the heart of a problem that is one of the most urgent, universal and productive of catastrophes with nothing but his ideal, yet at the same time fail to provide them with any sort of guidance.'

'A young man, full of enthusiasm, will be carried away by this ideal at first, but he will not persevere, he will break loose and, no longer taking account of any kind of rules, will sink into utter depravity.'

That is how people usually reason.

'The ideal of Christ is unattainable, and so it cannot serve us as a guide in our lives; it can be talked and dreamed about, but it cannot be applied to life, and so it should be left alone. What we need is not an ideal, but rules and guidance that are within our power to follow, that are within the power of the average moral level of society to follow: honest marriage in church, or even marriage that is not completely honest, where one of the partners – in our case, the man – has already had relations with a large number of women, even civil marriage, or even (following the same logic) the Japanese type of marriage, which only lasts for a definite period of time – why not go the whole way, and allow licensed brothels?'

People say that this is better than allowing debauchery in the streets. That is precisely the trouble: once one has permitted oneself to lower an ideal to the level of one's own weakness, one can no longer discern the limits beyond which one should not go.

This line of argument is mistaken right from the outset; above all, it is mistaken to assert that an ideal of absolute perfection cannot be a guiding force in our lives, and that in its presence we must either wave it aside, saying it is of no use to us because we will never be able to attain it, or lower it to the level our weakness desires.

To argue in this way is to be like a navigator who tells himself that since he cannot follow the course indicated by his compass he will throw his compass away or stop paying any attention to it (abandon his ideal, in other words), or else that he will fix the needle of his compass on the point that corresponds to the course of his vessel at any given moment (lower his ideal to the level of his weakness, that is). The ideal of perfection set by Christ is not a dream or a subject for rhetorical sermonizing – it is a most necessary and universally accessible form of guidance for the moral conduct of men's lives, just as the compass is a necessary and accessible instrument for the guidance of the navigator; all that is required in either case is for one to believe that this is so. In whatever situation a person may find himself, the doctrine of the ideal set by Christ will always be sufficient for him to be able to receive the most reliable indication of those actions he must or must not perform. But he must believe in this doctrine completely, and in this doctrine alone, he must give up believing in all the others, just as the navigator must believe his compass, and cease to look at and be guided by what he sees to either side of him. A person must know how to be guided by Christian doctrine as by a compass, and for this he must above all be sure of his own situation, and not be afraid to determine precisely how far he has diverged from the ideal course. At whatever level a person finds himself, it will always be possible for him to approach this ideal, and he can never attain a situation where he can say that he has reached it and is unable to come any closer to it. Such is the nature of man's striving for the Christian ideal in general, and for chastity in particular. If, where the problem of sexuality is concerned, one envisages to oneself all the different situations – from the innocence of childhood up to marriage – in which abstinence is not practised, at each stage of the way between these two situations the doctrine of Christ and the ideal it represents will always serve as a clear and definite guide as to what a person should or should not do.

What should pure, young, adolescent lads or girls do? They should remain free of temptation and, in order to be able to devote all their energies to the service of God and men, strive for an ever greater chastity of thought and intention.

What should pure, young, adolescent lads or girls do, who have fallen prey to temptation, are swallowed up by thoughts of an object-less love or by a love for a specific person, and have thus lost a certain part of their ability to serve God and man? The same thing: not connive at a further fall, in the knowledge that such connivance will not deliver them from temptation but merely reinforce it, and continue to strive towards an ever greater degree of chastity in order to be able to serve God and men more fully.

What are those people to do who have been vanquished in this struggle and have fallen? They should consider their fall not as a legitimate source of enjoyment, as is done at the present time when it is absolved by the rite of marriage, nor as a carnal pleasure in which they can indulge repeatedly with others, nor as a misfortune, when the fall occurs with someone not their equal or without the consecration of marriage, but regard this initial fall as the only one, as the contraction of an indissoluble marriage.

For those who are able to enter upon it, this contraction of marriage, together with its consequences – the birth of children – specifies a new and more limited form of the service of God and men directly, in the most various forms; the contraction of marriage reduces the scope of man's action and obliges him to rear and educate his offspring, which is composed of future servants of God and men.

What are a man and woman to do who are living together in marriage and performing this limited service of God and men through the rearing and education of their children, consequent upon their situation?

The same thing: they should strive together to free themselves from temptation, to make themselves pure, abstain from sin, and replace conjugal relations, which are opposed to the general and the particular service of God and men, replace carnal love with the pure relations that exist between a brother and a sister.

Thus it is not true to say that we cannot be guided by the ideal of Christ, because it is too exalted, too perfect and unattainable. The only reason we can fail to be guided by it is because we lie to ourselves and deceive ourselves.

Indeed, when we tell ourselves that we need rules that are more practicable than the ideal of Christ, that if we fail to attain this ideal we sink into debauchery, what we are saying is not that the ideal of Christ is too exalted for us, but only that we do not believe in it and do not want to make our actions conform to it.

When we say that having once fallen we will sink into debauchery, all we are really saying is that we have already decided beforehand that a fall with someone who is not our equal is not a sin but an amusement, a diversion which we are not obliged to atone for by what we call marriage. On the other hand, if we could only understand that such a fall is a sin which must and can be redeemed only by the indissolubility of marriage and by the whole of the activity involved in the rearing of the children born of that marriage, our fall can never be the cause of our sinking into debauchery.

This is, after all, just the same as if a farmer were not to consider those seeds which failed to germinate as seeds at all, but only the ones that, sown elsewhere, gave a yield. It seems obvious that such a person would waste a great deal of land and seed, and would never learn how to sow. As soon as one makes of chastity an ideal and realizes that every fall, no matter who the partners in it are, is a unique marriage that shall remain indissoluble for the whole of one's life, it becomes clear that the guidance given by Christ is not only sufficient, but is the only guidance that is possible.

'Man is weak, he must be set a task that is within his power,' people say. This is just the same as saying: 'My hands are weak, I cannot draw a line that is straight, the shortest one between two points, that is, and so, in order to make it easier for myself, instead of drawing the straight line I should like to draw, I shall take as my model a crooked or a broken line.'

The weaker my hand is, the greater is my need of a model that is perfect.

It is impossible, once one has understood the Christian doctrine of the ideal, to behave as if one were ignorant of it and to replace it by external precepts. The Christian doctrine of the ideal has been revealed to mankind precisely because it is capable of guiding mankind at the stage it has presently reached. Mankind has outgrown the era of external religious precepts, and no one believes in them any more.

The Christian doctrine of the ideal is the only doctrine that is capable of guiding mankind. One cannot, one must not, replace the ideal of Christ by external rules; on the contrary, one must keep this ideal firmly before one in all its purity and, most important of all, one must believe in it.

One may say, to a man who is navigating close to the shore: 'Steer by that rise, that cape, that tower,' and so on. But there comes a moment when the navigators sail away from the shore and only the unattainable stars and the compass may indicate the direction they should follow, and serve as their guides. We have been given both.

Appendix 2

Alternative Conclusion to *The Devil*

[*From p. 246*] . . . he said to himself and, going over to the desk, took out his revolver. Examining it, he found that one of the cartridges was missing. He stuck the gun in his trouser pocket.

'My God! What am I doing?' he exclaimed suddenly, and putting his hands together began to pray: 'Oh Lord, help me, deliver me. You know that I don't desire any evil, but I can't manage on my own. Help me,' he said, crossing himself before the icon.

'I *can* control myself. I'll go for a walk and think it all over.'

He went out to the hallway, put on a sheepskin coat and galoshes and emerged on to the porch. Without him really being aware of it, his footsteps took him past the garden along the country road towards the farm. The threshing-machine was still droning away there, and the cries of the drover lads could be heard. He went into the threshing-barn. She was there. He caught sight of her at once. She was raking up the ears of grain, and when she saw him she made her eyes laugh and started to trot pertly and skittishly here and there among the scattered grain, skilfully gathering it together. Yevgeny did not want to look at her, but could not prevent himself from doing so. He only recovered his senses again when she had disappeared from view. The estate manager came over to him and told him that they were threshing the flattened corn and that this was taking longer and giving a lower yield. Yevgeny went up to the threshing-drum, which rattled every now and then as the inadequately separated sheaves were fed into it, and asked the manager if there were many of these flattened sheaves still to come.

'There's another five cartloads, sir.'

'Then listen, I tell you what . . .' Yevgeny began, but did not get to the end of his sentence. She had gone right up next to the drum of the threshing-machine to rake the grain from under it, and as she did so she turned on him her incandescent, laughing gaze.

That gaze spoke of the happy, carefree love between them, of her knowledge that he desired her, that he had come to her barn, that she was, as ever, willing to make love with him and have a good time with him, without regard to the consequences. Yevgeny felt that he was in her power, but he did not want to give in.

He remembered his prayer, and tried to say it over again. He started to say it to himself, but felt at once that it was no use.

He was now wholly absorbed by a single thought: how could he make a rendezvous with her without anyone noticing?

'If we get through this stack today, do you want us to start on a new one, or can it wait till tomorrow?' asked the manager.

'Yes, it can wait,' replied Yevgeny, following her mechanically over to the pile of grain she had raked together with another woman.

'Is it really true that I can't control myself?' he wondered. 'Am I really ruined? Oh God! But there is no God, there's only the Devil. And it's her. It's taken possession of me. But I won't let it, I won't! She's the Devil, yes, the Devil.'

He went right up to her, took the revolver out of his pocket and shot her in the back once, twice, a third time. She teetered forwards and fell on to the pile of grain.

'Almighty Lord! Sisters and brothers! What's happened?' cried the women.

'No, it's not an accident. I meant to kill her,' shouted Yevgeny. 'Send for the police.'

He returned home, and without saying a word to his wife went into his study and locked himself in.

'Don't try to get in,' he shouted to his wife through the door. 'You'll find out soon enough.'

An hour later he rang for the manservant, and told him: 'Go and find out if Stepanida's still alive.'

The manservant already knew what had happened, and told him that Stepanida had died an hour ago.

'Very well. Now leave me alone. Tell me when the police arrive.'

The police arrived the following morning. When Yevgeny had said goodbye to his wife and child, he was taken away to prison.

He was put on trial. These were the early days of trial by jury. He was found to have been temporarily insane, and was sentenced only to do ecclesiastical penance.

He spent nine months in prison and a month in a monastery. While he was in prison he began to drink. He continued to drink in the monastery and went home an enfeebled, irresponsible alcoholic.

Varvara Alekseyevna claimed to have seen this coming all along.

She said she had observed it in his eyes on all those occasions when he had argued with her. Neither Liza nor Marya Pavlovna had the slightest notion as to why it should have happened; on the other hand, neither of them believed what the doctors said, that he had been mentally ill. On no account could they agree with this diagnosis, as they knew he had been more sensible and level-headed than hundreds of people of their acquaintance.

And indeed, if Yevgeny was mentally ill when he committed his crime, then everyone is mentally ill, and most of all those who see in others symptoms of the madness they fail to see in themselves.

Notes

FAMILY HAPPINESS

1. *Sonata quasi una Fantasia*: The Sonata in C sharp minor, Op. 27, No. 2 ('Moonlight') by Ludwig van Beethoven (1770–1827).
2. *the Feast of Peter and Paul*: An Orthodox religious festival, falling on 29 June.
3. *Schulhof*: Julius Schulhof (1825–?), Czech composer and pianist.
4. *Lieutenant Strelsky . . . Alfred . . . Eleonora*: Characters from romantic fiction.
5. *Mozart's Sonata Fantasia*: The Fantasia in C minor, K. 475.
6. *the Fast of the Assumption*: i.e. the period from 1 to 14 August, preceding the Feast of the Assumption, or Dormition of Mary.
7. *. . . And he, mad fellow, begs a storm . . .*: The last two lines of Lermontov's well-known poem *Parus* (The Sail), 1832.
8. *'saw boys running'*: The expression refers to an apocryphal story about Boris Godunov (*c*.1551–1605), according to which he 'saw bloodstained boys running'. Boris became virtual ruler of Russia, ostensibly as regent for Ivaniv's young son Fyodor I, who was married to Boris's sister. Boris was popularly believed to have ordered the murder in 1591 of Fyodor's younger brother and heir, Dmitry, in order to secure the succession for himself. The expression is used to suggest a sensation of guilt.

THE KREUTZER SONATA

1. *the Nizhny Novgorod summer fair*: Nizhny Novgorod (now known as Gorky) was a major Volga port, and one of the centres of trade and navigation on the river. Each summer an important trade fair was held there.

2.   *Kunavino*: Suburb of Nizhny Novgorod, place of amusement for visitors to the fair.

3.   *Domostroy*: A medieval Russian treatise on domestic life.

4.   *Rigolboche*: The *nom de théâtre* of the French dancer and cabaret singer Marguerite Badel, who had a great success in Paris during the 1850s and 1860s.

5.   *I let her read my diary*: A recurrent trauma in Tolstoy's own life which haunted him until he died. He refers to it in *Anna Karenina* (IV, 16), and it is a theme that is obsessively present throughout the *Intimate Journal* of 1910.

6.   *Hartmanns*: The reference is to Eduard von Hartmann (1842–1906), pessimistic philosopher, author of *The Philosophy of the Unconscious*. He wrote a refutation of Schopenhauer's *The World as Will and Idea*.

7.   *Shakers*: The members of the religious sect which emerged in England during the mid-eighteenth century. The Shakers preached celibacy, communal ownership of property, obligatory physical labour, conscientious objection to military service, etc. During his work on *The Kreutzer Sonata* Tolstoy received letters and books from Shakers in the United States, and grew interested in their teachings.

8.   *Trubnaya Street, on the Grachevka*: Trubnaya Street, also called the Truba, was the centre of a low-class district of Moscow where the brothels were situated. Tolstoy was in the habit of referring to the Imperial Court as 'the Truba'. The Grachevka was another street in the same district.

9.   *zemstvo*: Elective district council in pre-revolutionary Russia.

10. *versts*: One verst is approximately two miles.

11. *Vanka-Klyuchnik*: The hero of a Russian folk-song that exists in a number of variants. He is the lover of either the wife or the daughter of his master, and he boasts about the relationship. Denounced by a serving-maid, he pays for his bragging with his life, but not before he has taken a last mocking dig at his master, who in most versions is the Prince Volkonsky.

12. *yard-keepers*: The entrances to apartment houses in Russian towns were generally patrolled by a yard-keeper or concierge whose task it was to keep the yard and the street in front of the house clean, and to keep an eye on visitors.

13. *Prostite . . . Proshchayte*: *Proshchayte* is the customary Russian form of farewell. *Proshchat'* (perfective aspect *prostit'*) also means 'to forgive'.

THE DEVIL

1. *desyatinas*: One desyatina is 2.7 acres.

FATHER SERGIUS

1. *cadet school*: The cadet schools (more literally, 'cadet corps') were select schools run on military lines, which prepared boys intending to take up a career in the army.

2. *addressing her affectionately*: Specifically, Kasatsky addresses his fiancée, using the intimate second-person singular form of 'you', the equivalent of *tu* in French, *Du* in German.

3. *Nevsky*: The Nevsky Prospekt, the principal street in St Petersburg.

4. *Feast of the Intercession*: A major Orthodox festival commemorating the Virgin Mary's intervention to protect Constantinople from Saracen invaders in the ninth century.

5. *starets*: The English equivalent is 'elder', but the Russian word is accepted in modern English dictionaries. The *starets* (plural *startsy*), usually, but not always, a monk, was a man with special qualities of spiritual discernment, humility, ascetic living, and, sometimes, healing powers. It was not a rank in the hierarchy, but a title accorded to those who had these qualities. An important function of the *startsy* was to instruct others in their way of life. The tradition of *starchestvo* originated in Athos and from the eighteenth century spread to other Orthodox countries. The *startsy* mentioned were noted bearers of the tradition: Paisy Velichkovsky (1722–94) established it in monasteries in Moldavia (Tolstoy refers to its origins in Wallachia, probably using the word in general for the Romanian lands); Makary Ivanov (1788–1860) and Amvrosy Grenkov (1812–91) were both monks of the Optina Monastery in Russia. Amvrosy is considered to have inspired the character of Father Zosima in Dostoyevsky's *The Brothers Karamazov*.

6. *Vigil service*: The 'All-Night Vigil' is an Orthodox service combining evening and morning prayers, which is held during the night before certain major festivals.

7. '*Lise, regardez . . . tellement beau*': 'Lise, look there to the right, it's him.'

'Where, where? He's not all that good-looking.'

8. *the parable of the unjust judge*: See Luke xviii:1–8.
9. *Mid-Pentecost*: Church festival celebrated on Wednesday of the fourth week after Easter, halfway between Easter and Whitsun.
10. *'Forbid them (the little children) not to come unto me'*: Luke xviii:16.
11. *'Pashenka'* ... *Praskovya Mikhailovna*: 'Pashenka' is a double-diminutive form of the name 'Praskovya' applicable to a young child: the name and patronymic 'Praskovya Mikhailovna' indicates grown-up status.
12. *les pélerins*: the pilgrims.
13. *'Demandez leur ... agréable à Dieu'*: 'Ask them if they really believe that their pilgrimage is pleasing to God.'
14. *'Qu'est ce qu'il dit? ... de la petite monnaie?'*: 'What does he say? H... ... H... ... ... must ... chang...
15. *'Mais ...* candl...